Spies of Promise

The Untold Story of Joshua's 40 Days in Canaan

Philip Allan Turner

Author's research note: I used the spy novel/thriller genre to express theological truth, just like C.S. Lewis and J.R. Tolkien did. This novel maintains a deep respect for the Biblical text, while filling in gaps with imagination based on historical facts from that time period in the Bible. There are Biblical reference pages at the end of this work which ties in specific Biblical verses throughout the novel. This novel has been thoroughly researched using ancient Near East history and culture throughout.

I wish to dedicate this book to my parents whose guidance was instrumental in showing me the right path. Also, I thank all the people out there who have helped me along the way, and are serving the Lord and doing God's work each day. Although this is a work of fiction, I tried to honor God in the writing of this book. This book contains adult themes from the bible and is not intended for minors. During the writing of this novel, I used historical data from other sources but the primary source of this work is the book of Numbers chapter 13-14 from the Bible.

Numbers 13:1-25:

"And the Lord spoke to Moses, saying, "Send men to spy out the land of Canaan, which I am giving to the children of Israel; from each tribe of their fathers you shall send a man, everyone a leader among them."

So Moses sent them from the Wilderness of Paran according to the command of the Lord, all of the men who were heads of the children of Israel. Now these were their names: from the tribe of Reuben, Shammua the son of Zaccur; from the tribe of Simeon, Shaphat the son of Hori; from the tribe of Judah, Caleb the son of Jephunneh; from the tribe of Issachar, Igal the son of Joseph; from the tribe of Ephraim, Hoshea the son of Nun; from the tribe of Benjamin, Palti the son of Raphu; from the tribe of Zebulun, Gaddiel the son of Sodi; from the tribe of Joseph, that is, from the tribe of Manasseh, Gaddi the son of Susi; from the tribe of Dan, Ammiel the son of Gemalli; from the tribe of Asher, Sethur the son of Michael; from the tribe of Naphtali, Nahbi the son of Vophsi; from the tribe of Gad, Geuel the son of Machi. These are the names of the men who Moses sent to spy out the land. And Moses called Hoshea, the son of Nun, Joshua.

Then Moses sent them to spy out the land of Canaan, and said to them, "Go up this way into the South, and go up to the mountains, and see what land is like: whether the people who dwell in it are strong or weak, few or many; whether the land they dwell in is good or bad; whether the cities they inhabit are like camps or strongholds; whether the land is rich or poor; and whether there are forest or not. Be of good courage. And bring some fruit of the land. Now the time was the season of the first ripe grapes. So they went up and spied out the land from the Wilderness of Zin as far as Rohob, near the entrance of Hamath. And they went up through the South and came to Hebron; Ahiman, Sheshai, and Talmai, the descendants of Anak, were there. (Now Hebron was build seven years before Zoan in Egypt.) Then they came to the Valley of Eshcol, and there cut down a branch with one cluster of grapes; and they carried it between two of them on a pole. They also brought some of the pomegranates and figs. The place was called the Valley of Eshcol, because of the cluster which the men of Israel cut down there. And they returned from spying out the land after forty days."

This is the untold story of what happened during those 40 days...

Maps of the areas discussed in this book

Historically, Egypt and Canaan were under the administrative control of Pharaoh during the time of Moses.

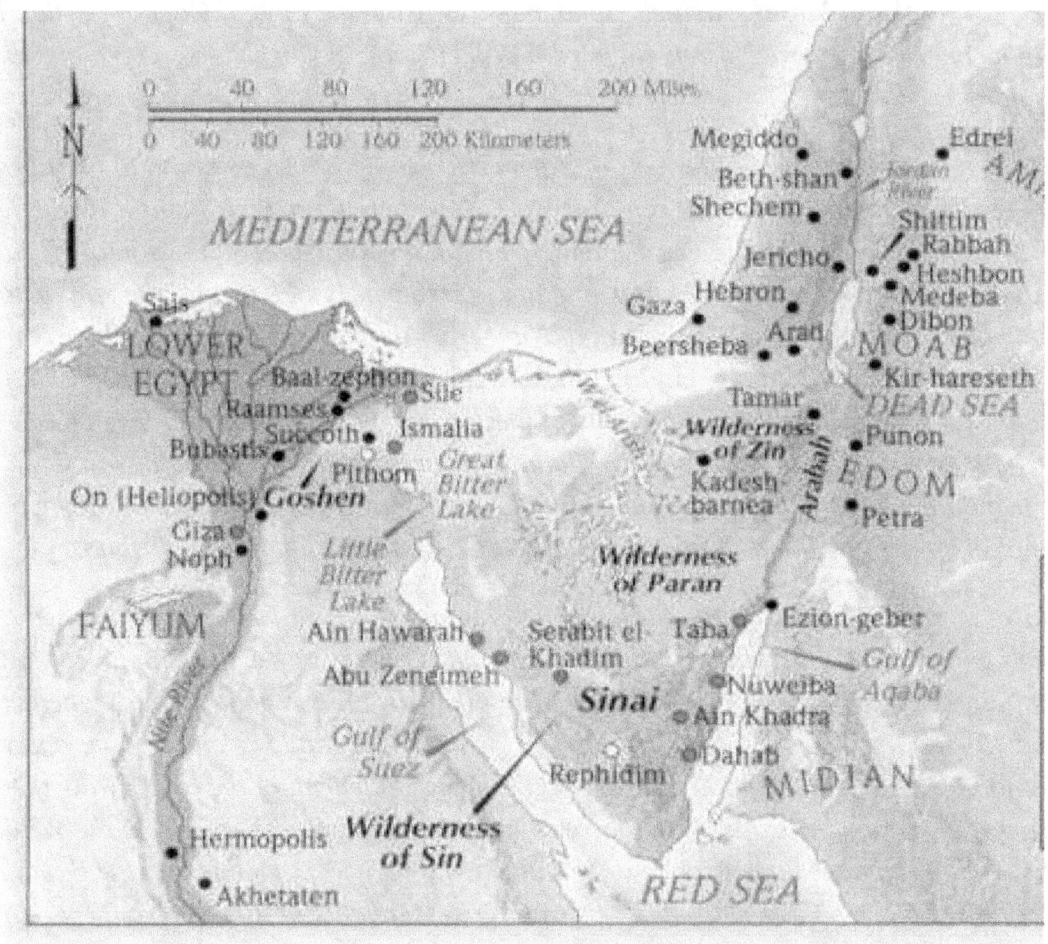

Map of historical Canaan

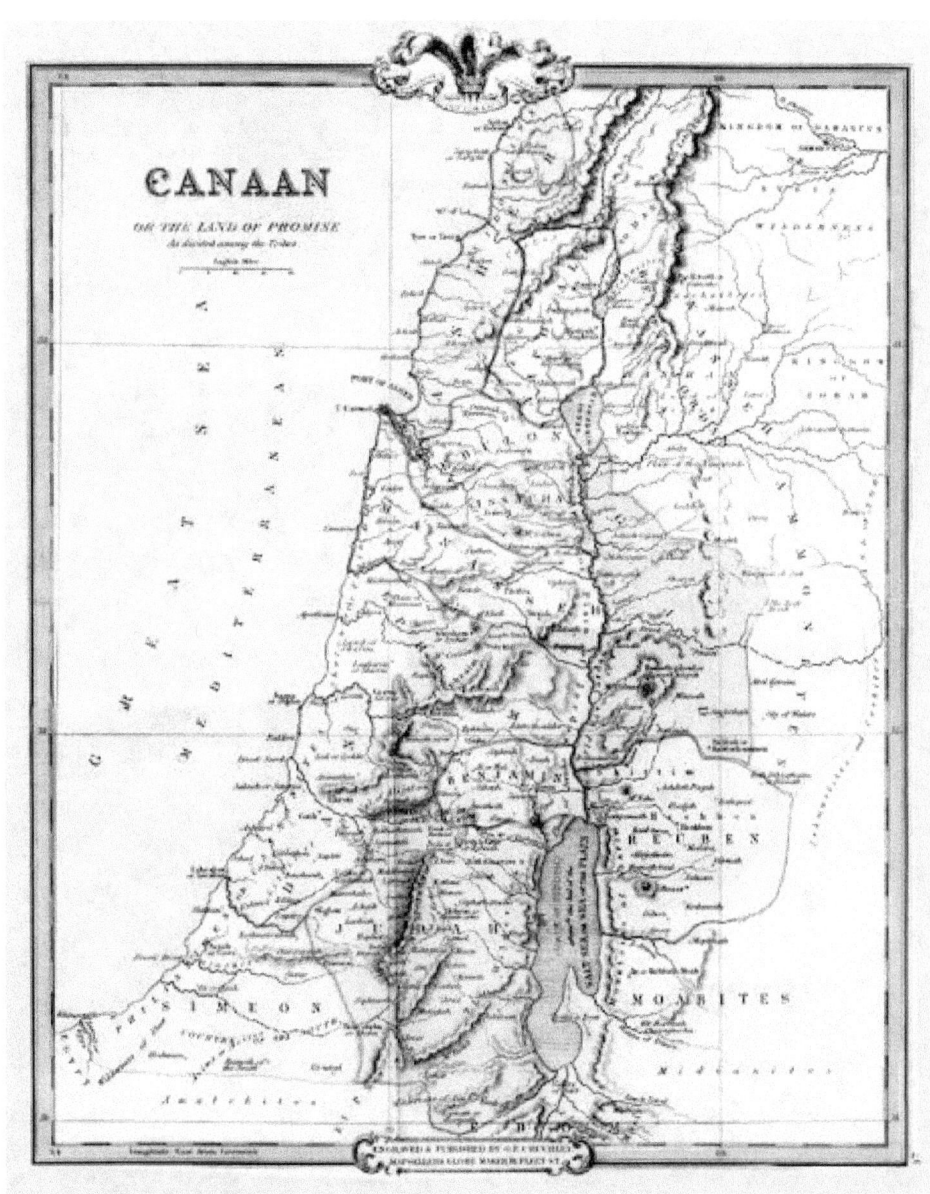

JOURNEY OF THE SPIES

NUM. 13:1–33; NUM. 34:1–12

- • City
- ○ City (uncertain location)
- ◉ Oasis
- ▲ Mountain peak
- ← Journey of the twelve spies
- The promised land

Spies of Promise: The Untold Story of Joshua's 40 Days in Canaan

Moses explaining the mission to the 12 spies

Joshua and Caleb in Hebron

THE TWO REPORTS OF THE SPIES

Num. 13:17-20, 23-33.

GOLDEN TEXT:—The Lord is with us, fear them not.

Num. 14:9.

Map of Hebron

Drawn by Jack Romez, narrator of this story; based on the description given to him by Salman.

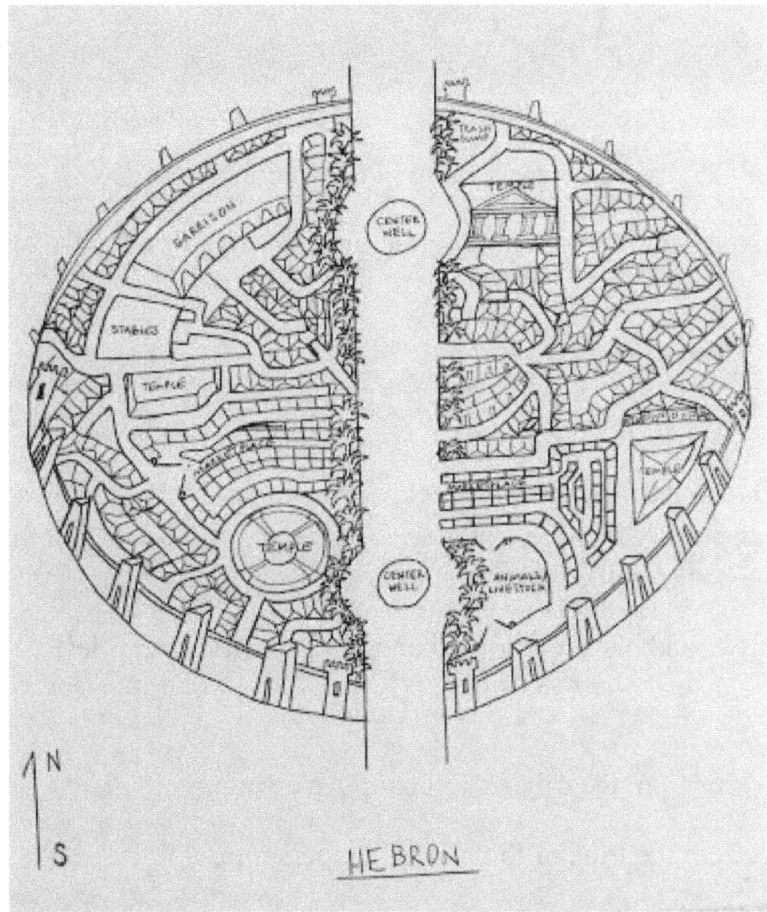

Map of the fortified city Hazor along the route.

CAST OF CHARACTERS

Present Day Cast

Jack Romez, a senior CIA case officer working in the Middle East.

Salman, an old Aramaic man living in the Middle East. Also, a vetted CIA source being debriefed by Jack.

Biblical Day Cast

Moses, Prophet of God and deliverer of the Hebrews. Leader of the Israelites during their exodus from Egyptian slavery into the wilderness. Receiver of the Ten Commandments and writer of the first five books of the Old Testament.

Aaron, brother of Moses and his strong right hand. Israel's first high priest.

12 Spies

Shammua, son of Zaccur from the tribe of Reuban. An artisan.

Shaphat, son of Hori from the tribe of Simeon. A coppersmith.

Caleb, son of Jephunneh from the tribe of Judah. A carpenter.

Igal, son of Joseph from the tribe of Issachar. A Tentmaker.

Hoshea, son of Nun, also known as Joshua ben Nun from the tribe of Ephraim. Formerly a stone mason now a general for Moses.

Palti, son of Raphu from the tribe of Benjamin. A tailor.

Gaddiel, son of Sodi from the tribe of Zebulun. A scribe.

Gaddi, son of Susi from the tribe of Joseph. A farmer.

Ammiel, son of Gemalli from the tribe of Dan. A founder specializing in gold and silver.

Sethur, son of Michael from the tribe of Asher. A Potter.

Nahbi, son of Vophsi from the tribe of Naphali, shepherd.

Geuel, son of Machi from the tribe of Gad, engineer.

Hebron Cast

Salman, an approx 80 year old Hebrew merchant living in Hebron.

Fatia, a 30 year old widow born in Kemet (Egypt) living in Hebron under the charge of Salman.

Commander Elrian, a 6'6" career soldier who worked for Pharaoh before Moses led the Hebrews out of bondage. Sent as garrison commander in Hebron in order to maintain order.

Sarah, a beautiful professional spy working woman in the employ of Commander Elrian.

Annan, head of Salman's and Fatia's farm outside of Hebron.

Fayid (Spy one), a native from Kemet who worked for Pharaoh's intelligence service. He is Elrian's chief of intelligence operations in Hebron. He also serves as an assassin for Elrian.

Ashur (Spy two), works for Fayid. An Assyrian who spent many years spying in Babylon. A specialist in interrogation and torture. He serves as an assassins for Commander Elrian as well.

Mansur, an Arab from Arabia running an entertainment pavilion with food, music and dancing girls. A merchant who married a local Canaanite woman and stayed in Hebron. He has lived in Hebron for the last 30 years.

Cast along the northern caravan route

Amel, an Arab merchant who has been traveling the trade routes in Canaan for the last ten years.

Divine Cast

Archangels are the highest order of God's creation.

Archangel Raphael has a principle role in the book of Tobias. He is the guardian of the journey (Tb 16:5-6) and a healer (11:1-15). The expeller of demons (6:15-17). He is is one of the seven angels who offer the prayer of God's people and enter the presence of the Holy one. After the fall of the angels siding with Lucifer, Raphael is commissioned to bind the fallen angel Azazel hand and foot, and cast him into the darkness. He is a healer of all illnesses and injuries of men.

Archangel Michael, served as the guardian of the nation of Israel. He commands the forces of God against the forces of the dragon in a war in heaven (Revelations 12:7).

Cast of the darkness

Satan, formally known as the angel Lucifer. He was a covering cherub who stood on the right or left side of God's throne. He used to lead the angelic choir. He was one of the most beautiful, flawless and breathtaking angels in heaven. His brightness used to be spoken of throughout heaven. He was full of pride and tried to take God's throne. God cast him out of heaven because of his pride and arrogance along with the 1/3 of the angels who followed him (Isaiah 14:12-14). The fallen angels are now called demons and he is called the prince of lies. He is the father of illusions and deceit. The devil is called an angel of light because of his deception of mankind (2 Corinthians 11:14) He dwells on earth trying to keep humanity out of heaven, a place he can never return to. Also called the adversary, the evil one, the tempter, Beelzebub, prince of darkness, the corruptor of mind and the prince of devils.

Baal, lord of the Canaanite religion. Also worshiped as the god of fertility. Baal occurs in the Old Testament as a noun meaning "lord, owner, possessor or husband." He proved a great temptation for Israel.

Sed or Sedim (Plural), one of Satan's creatures of darkness. A grotesque demon of immense power approximately nine feet tall.

Places

Kemet is the name used in this story for Egypt during the days of Moses as it's historically correct.

Historically, Canaan was under the administrative control of Pharaoh during the time of Moses.

Preface

"Oh, give thanks to the Lord, for He is good. For His mercy endures forever. Let the redeemed of the Lord say so, whom He has redeemed from the hand of the enemy, and gathered out of the lands, From the east and from the west, From the north to the south. They wandered in the wilderness in a desolate way; they found no city to dwell in. Hungry and thirsty, Their soul fainted in them. Then they cried out to the Lord in their trouble, and He delivered them out of their distresses. And He led them forth by the right way, That they might go to a city for a dwelling place. Oh, that men would give thanks to the Lord for His goodness, and for His wonderful works to the children of men! For He satisfies the longing soul, and fills the hungry soul with goodness. Those who sat in darkness and in the shadow of death, bound in affliction and irons---Because they rebelled against the word of God, and despised the council of the Most High, Therefore He brought down their heart with labor, They fell down, and there was none to help. Then they cried out to the Lord in their trouble, and He saved them out of their distresses. He brought them out of darkness and the shadow of death, and broke their chains in pieces. Oh, than men would give thanks to the Lord for His goodness, and for His wonderful works to the wonderful children of men! (Psalm 107:1-15)."

Introduction

My name is Jack Romez and I worked for the CIA for over a dozen years in the Middle East. I am going to relay the historical fiction piece I call "Spies of Promise" which is the untold Biblical story of the 40 days that Joshua spent in Canaan doing reconnaissance and gathering intelligence for the Israelites. I first heard this story from an old man who spoke mostly only Aramaic and who lived in a mountain region of the Middle East. I cannot be more specific than that because this man was a source of mine, and I must protect sources and methods in anything I write. I was sent to debrief him in Arabic because he spoke no English. His tribe spoke an ancient dialect of Aramaic. As he was a CIA source, he knew my true intelligence affiliation. I was in alias but he knew I was a clandestine service case officer who was a Christian. This source was different from most of my other sources because he was a Christian from a very old tribe. I stayed with this source for several weeks and we grew close throughout the debriefing.

I debriefed him on intelligence matters but he took it upon himself to tell me other historical facts he knew that I would find interesting along the way. I was trained as an historian and taught ancient history at UCLA before I joined the CIA. A historian is not much different than an intelligence officer because both jobs require the person to seek the truth. While kicking around the sandbox for the years, I had gone to many mosques, churches, temples and other religious sites to learn more about the culture and to do my job more effectively. I always kept an open mind and often would ask to hear unique stories from my sources or contacts. To be a good spy in a foreign region, a person had to know more than the language or religion but the culture and mindset of those people living in that region.

This old man I met with was called Salman, the same name of a central character in the story. Salman was old, around 85 or 90 years old. He asked me at the end of our time together, if I had faith. At the time, I was wrestling with faith and told him as such. He told me that being a Christian was all about faith--the *sine quo non* or essential ingredient is faith, faith in the unseen. He grabbed my hand and told me that he believed that I would be a man of great faith one day but that the path to that faith was going to be painful and that it could possibly destroy me entirely along the way but if I stayed strong, I would emerge whole and healthy at the end of my journey. He explained that I would help others find balance through learning how to view the world through a God-conscious lens. I asked him what he meant when he said "whole and healthy?" He told me that all people have a choice to make in life; they could live out of balance or choose to strive to live a manner different from those who struggle each and every day.

"Many people choose to live with pain and drama. There are many out here that are addicted to a kind of sadness. That is not how it was meant to be for God's creatures. God intended us to have an abundantly beautiful life," Salman said.

I just looked at this old man with his gnarled fingers and stooped posture. He had a shawl around him because he was always a little cold. Before I met the old man, I did not even know that being "whole and healthy" was an option on the menu of life. He told me that I would one day remember this encounter and it would mean more to me at that time. I had collected many intelligence reports from him and his spy network so I did not mind the wanderings of the old man. I sort of took all that as a bunch of mumbo jumbo. On the last day I spent with him, I had finished debriefing him around 5pm and he asked me if he could tell me a story of faith. I told him yes.

He said that I should particularly find the story of interest since I was in the mukhabarat (spy agency) for my country and the story he was going to tell me was a story about spies.

"I thought you told me that you were going to tell me a story about faith," I asked.

"It is but you must be patient," he said.

I looked at Salman critically for a moment. He sat there fingering his prayer beads. The beads were a cross between Islamic masbaha beads and Catholic Rosary beads. He had a devoted group of followers who followed him without question. He has allowed the CIA to tap into that network in order to gather intelligence to overthrow the current corrupt government. I noticed that Salman's hands had lots of dark age spots.

Salman ran the beads through his fingers thinking about the best way to tell Jack this story. Salman's devotees provided much intelligence to Jack and the CIA over the last few weeks. It was his decision to allow his followers to get involved in a political matter, because the situation was dire in his country. They needed a change of leadership and after meeting with Jack, he believed that they should help the CIA in their mission to overthrow the government. During that first meeting with Jack and a few others from the Agency, they had tried to convince him that it was important to help America topple their political leader. Salman prayed to God and was led to believe it was the right thing to do, thus he helped. It was something about Jack that made him think that they were meant to meet. He 'saw' that Jack would have many challenges ahead in his life and he felt it was God's will to relay this story to him. He would just start from the beginning and go from there.

"Okay, I'll be patient." I noticed the old man thinking to himself as he often did before he told me something he considered very important. It was like he was trying to figure out the right words. I had been debriefing this old man for several weeks and the methodical manner in which he told stories often got to me because I wanted it to be told as we told stories in the west. The problem for a westerner in the Middle East is that Arabs and Americans each tell stories differently. Westerners tell stories in a linear fashion while Middle Easterners tell stories in a circular manner or a more roundabout way. In the Middle East, the whole story is important so it does not matter if it takes 20 minutes or 20 hours while in the west, it's usually the end of the story we put the emphasis on. Both methods are effective but sometimes as a westerner, who has spent many years debriefing Middle Easterners, I just wanted the main points of the story. I am so happy that I was patient and learned the whole story.

He told me that his grandfather told him the story when he was around 10 years old so that would make it about 1910 when Salman first heard it. In the Middle East, the oral tradition is as reliable as the written tradition. Oral tradition precedes the written word by thousands of years in Middle East and in Africa. Even before the introduction of Islam into the region, oral tradition was the norm and it wasn't until almost a hundred years later that the written word caught up with the popularity of written story telling. A great story teller back then was like a great actor in our day. He told me that his grandfather told him that story as his grandfather had told him, and as his grandfather's grandfather told his grandson. I think I can safely say that the oral tradition of this story goes back hundreds of years. I do not know if it's true or not as I am doing what I did as an intelligence officer, reporting the facts as I hear it. I must admit that there may be a few names of the minor characters I cannot remember because it was a few years ago when I actually heard the story. Faith was always an issue for me and years later when I remembered the story, I understood that I was told the story for a specific reason. I was not a man of faith because in the spy game, I believed what I saw with my physical eyes instead of what I could feel in my spirit, heart and soul.

I would love to say this beautiful story is nonfiction but I cannot which is why I say its historical fiction. It's a story about God, faith, Satan, sin, and the concept of reaping what we sow. The New Testament epistle written by James, the half-brother of Jesus, said that God is not to be mocked and that we will reap what we sow. I came to understand this fact in a way I could never have imagined.

I asked the old man how long the story would take and he avoided the question by changing the subject. Salman explained that it was important for me to listen to the whole story. He told me that I would enjoy it because it was about a group of spies in the Bible which had not been written down in the Old Testament. He explained that it involved Joshua and Caleb with a few references about Moses. I still didn't know why he was making a big point of telling me this story.

"This story contains characters involved in espionage and who also have problems with faith. This tale is full of the same wild things that go on today in your line of work. It's a wild story," he said with a sly grin on his face.

"Wild? You are talking about the Bible. How wild could it be?" I asked.

He laughed at me and said the story had angels, miracles, perversions, sexual immorality, homosexuality, prostitutes, demons, murders, betrayal and love. I looked at him like he was crazy and he noticed the confused look on my face.

"It is an untold story of the Bible. The Bible is the roadmap of life, there is nothing in the Bible that is not going on today in the world. There is a saying in the Bible that says, 'There is nothing new under the sun.' It's the same in this story. The perversions I will relay to you would make the headlines of the tabloids or on your reality shows today. It's a story about the darkness and the light, as well as the choices we make. Ultimately, when you find yourself in the darkness, remember the infinite possibilities life offers and that it's essential that you align your life with God's word if you want a better outcome. Lastly, I hope that you never forget about God's love and the redemptive power of love."

This was the second time he mentioned the future and me having problems. "What's going to happen in the future? I asked.

"I don't know. I just know that the storm will come and perhaps what I will tell today will help you at that time," Salman said.

This old man was cryptic sometimes. I did not view the world with a God-consciousness at that time. I had a deeply religious experience a few years later after I hit my bottom which transformed me from a man with no faith, to a man of deep and abiding faith. The two main characters in the story, Joshua and Caleb are great examples of being steadfast in faith during adversity. Salman told me most of the story in Arabic with some Aramaic thrown in when he did not know the word in Arabic. His native language was Aramaic, one of the few tribes in the world which still speak the language of Jesus Christ. Arabic was a second language for him so there were times when I got confused and had to have him go slowly. Some of those Aramaic words, I tried to translate in my mind but I had to have him tell me in Arabic and find an equivalent in English. I had forgotten the story until I was reading the Bible during the darkest period of my life years later and came across Numbers 13 in the Old Testament where the basis for the story was outlined. I had chills when I read the brief account in the Bible in Numbers and Deuteronomy; and connected it to the old man's untold story of Joshua. I will try to relay the details as he told me.

"Jack, the year is 1240 before the coming of Christ Jesus…

Chapter 1

The year is 1240 before the coming of Christ Jesus. A young man sat beside an older man. "Father of my father, tell me again about the time when you were sent to spy in Canaan." Although Joshua was more than 100 years old, he still had strength and a light in his eyes. Joy was in his heart although he knew his time in this world was coming to an end. Joshua looked towards the ceiling and his eyes had a glimmer in it which illuminated love.

"He was a great man. I thought I had faith until I met him but he was like no other."

Ibnuh, knew his grandfather was talking about the great prophet of God, Moses. His grandfather always started stories about that time, with Moses first, because he had been such a large part of Joshua's life. Ibnuh loved to hear about Moses.

"You know he was slow of speech and slow of tongue once. The great "I AM" chose him and gave Moses a mighty mission. He had about 80 years at that time after we left Kemet (Egypt) under the Pharaoh's yoke. I was a younger man then in the middle of my life. You remember how I told you that Moses knew the Lord face to face?" Johsua asked.

"Yes, father of my father. Isn't it time that I know the story, the whole story." Ibnuh pleaded.

Joshua looked at his grandson's countenance and decided that it was time. "It has been long enough, I will begin the story as it unfolded without omission approximately 63 years ago." Joshua smiled and began to tell the history.

"You know I was born a slave in Kemet. I worked and toiled for many years but I always believed that a deliverer would come. It was that great prophet of God, Moses, who led us. The Lord had brought us out of bondage, and promised to give us the land which He swore to give unto our fathers (1). The Lord promised the land to the descendants of Abraham, Isaac and Jacob (2) and He had reaffirmed this promise to Moses (3). But even more, the Lord had reminded the people of His promise when we broke camp at Sinai (4) and when we arrived at Kadesh (5). You have to understand that God's promise was our deed to the land as well as our guarantee that we would defeat our enemies. This was all we needed! This was all Moses needed but the people had doubts in God and in Moses. I know this seems so unbelievable today after seeing what you seen over these years. But the people had seen the ten plagues in Kemet, the parting of the Red Sea, and the other blessings but the people still had doubts."

Joshua shook his head and laughed inwardly to himself. It all seemed so long ago, he thought.

"Our nation doubted God's word and began to walk by their natural sight instead of by faith. They doubted the Lord's prophet and they asked him to let them search out the land before the entire nation went into engage the enemy in battle (6). Moses endorsed their request (7) and got permission from the Lord to carry out the plan as you know from our holy book."

From his memory, Joshua recited the book of Numbers 13 from the Bible:

"And the Lord spoke to Moses, saying, "Send men to spy out the land of Canaan, which I am giving to the children of Israel; from each tribe of their fathers you shall send a man, everyone a leader among them."

So Moses sent them from the Wilderness of Paran according to the command of the Lord, all of the men who were heads of the children of Israel. Now these were their names: from the tribe of Reuben, Shammua the son of Zaccur; from the tribe of Simeon, Shaphat the son of Hori; from the tribe of Judah, Caleb the son of Jephunneh; from the tribe of Issachar, Igal the son of Joseph; from the tribe of Ephraim, Hoshea the son of Nun; from the tribe of Benjamin, Palti the son of Raphu; from the tribe of Zebulun, Gaddiel the son of Sodi; from the tribe of Joseph, that is, from the tribe of Manasseh, Gaddi the son of Susi; from the tribe of Dan, Ammiel the son of Gemalli; from the tribe of Asher, Sethur the son of Michael; from the tribe of Naphtali, Nahbi the son of Vophsi; from the tribe of Gad, Geuel the son of Machi. These are the names of the men who Moses sent to spy out the land. And Moses called Hoshea, the son of Nun, Joshua.

Then Moses sent them to spy out the land of Canaan, and said to them, "Go up this way into the South, and go up to the mountains, and see what land is like: whether the people who dwell in it are strong or weak, few or many; whether the land they dwell in is good or bad; whether the cities they inhabit are like camps or strongholds; whether the land is rich or poor; and whether there are forest or not. Be of good courage. And bring some fruit of the land. Now the time was the season of the first ripe grapes. So they went up and spied out the land from the Wilderness of Zin as far as Rohob, near the entrance of Hamath. And they went up through the South and came to Hebron; Ahiman, Sheshai, and Talmai, the descendants of Anak, were there. (Now Hebron was build seven years before Zoan in Egypt.) Then they came to the Valley of Eshcol, and there cut down a branch with one cluster of grapes; and they carried it between two of them on a pole. They also brought some of the pomegranates and figs. The place was called the Valley of Eshcol, because of the cluster which the men of Israel cut down there. And they returned from spying out the land after forty days."

Joshua paused for a moment as he suspected the meaning behind the look on his grandson's face. Ibnuh became a little inpatient and said, "Father of my father, I know that part from the scrolls. What happened during those forty days?"

Joshua looked at his grandson with much love in his heart. He had rarely spoken of those days. He had seen many things which were not of the law from that pagan society, Canaan. So much iniquity and sin, Joshua thought. He remembered the ten betrayers (the other spies) who spoke untruth to Moses. He remembered those who betrayed God's law and tried to maintain his calmness. He knew that it was part of the Lord's greater plan during those times so that the people would learn. He was more naive then and those forty days allowed him to grow and understand so much more. He had figured out a few years later that God was preparing him for something great. He didn't know if he would have been the leader that he eventually grew to be if he had not been trusted by Moses for that great mission.

"I, Joshua son of Nun, who served the Lord faithfully, will tell you, blood of my blood, the complete story of what happened during those 40 days."

Ibnuh moved closer to his grandfather as Joshua's eyes became unfocused as he remembered the details. Joshua started to tell the story of the 'Spies of Promise'.

"Moses gathered the people after the Lord spoke to him."

Moses said, "Let us therefore prepare ourselves for the work, for the Canaanites will not resign up their land to us without fighting, but it must be wrestled from them by great struggles in war. Let us send spies, who may take a view of the goodness of the land, and what strength it is of, but, above all things, let us be of one mind; let us honor God, who above all is our Helper and Assister." When Moses had said this, the multitude requited him with marks of respect; and chose twelve spies, of the most eminent men, one out of every tribe.

Moses told me that he had specifically wanted me to go with the group as his eyes and ears. He knew that I was a faithful and steadfast. The tribes had chosen their men from the upper tier of the tribes as commanded by God. The 11 spies had to be younger men who could endure the rigors and dangers involved in reconnoitering the land. Moses had given them their commands as it was given to him by the great "I Am." Moses gathered us on a hill and looked over the group as they prepared to leave. Moses knew that we held the fate of the people in our hands as he looked at us saying our names:

"Shammua, the son of Zaccur

Shaphat the son of Hori

Caleb the son of Jephunneh

Igal the son of Joseph

Hoshea the son of Nun AKA Joshua

Palti the son of Raphu

Gaddiel the son of Sodi

Gaddi the son of Susi

Ammiel the son of Gemalli

Sethur the son of Michael

Nahbi the son of Vophsi

Geuel the son of Machi"

In a louder voice, Moses stated, "Be strong and of good courage. Make sure that you adhere to the laws of Abraham. Take heed lest you act corruptly and make yourself impure like the idolaters of Canaan. Go there and record accurately all you see, but do not forget your Lord; for your Lord your God is a consuming fire, a jealous God (8). If you get into trouble, seek guidance from your God, the Lord; you will find Him if you seek Him with all your heart and with all your soul. Remember God is with you." He watched the group gather their things tp prepare to leave. He motioned for Joshua to stay back for a moment.

"Joshua, I must speak with you." Joshua was as loyal and obedient as any leader could have hoped for. Moses took him aside into one of the tents. Joshua sat cross legged waiting for Moses to speak. Joshua had so much affection and love in his heart for God's prophet. He would have lovingly laid down his life for this man.

"Joshua, I have been so very pleased with your service to the Lord, our God. Ever since you chose those men and fought with Amalek, following my commands without question, and Israel prevailed, I have sought to make sure that you knew all I knew. I believe that God is preparing you and this will be your greatest challenge yet. You heard what I told the men. The same I say to you, be steadfast! This is not what I want to speak about; I wanted to charge you with an additional mission. God has told us what we will have in the Promise Land but the people are still stubborn and disobedient at times which is why the Lord wanted them to see for themselves the beauty of the land. This is the specific reason I told them that they should view the goodness of the land. You have your primary mission but I also want you to watch the others. Do what God has commanded of you but also report on what the others do and how they comport themselves. This is a task that I am levying on you which is not to be discussed with the others. Some of the others are from very influencial tribes which don't want us to move into the Promised Land. These men may not be interested in seeing the truth but instead wish to make up falsehoods. I need to know what happens in case it's necessary to defend our position of taking Canaan when you return."

Joshua immediately agreed to do what the Prophet of God wanted.

"Joshua, you have been a loyal servant. Surely, I have taught you the statutes and judgment, just as the Lord, my God has commanded me, you should act according to them in the land which you will go to possess during this mission. God has commanded that He will reward us with this land but the other tribes always want evidence." Moses shakes his head and pauses for another moment.

Joshua sat patiently while looking at the great man's white hair and beard. Moses collected his thoughts to provide more details on what Joshua would face. Moses stated, "Canaan is a polytheistic society as you know. You know that they worship El and Baal among many other gods but we will get to this in a short while. I want to stress to you that you must stay in the light while seeking information in the darkness. God will be your light. Do not conform to what you see because you will see things that are an abomination to God. Your job is to obtain the information, but don't fall into the pit of iniquity. You lived your whole life in Egypt as a slave until recently. Canaan is a conglomerate of city states under the federal oversight of Egypt. You know how corrupt Egypt was. Well, Canaan is worse because of all foreign influences, immorality and sexual perversions."

Some seeds of doubt came into Joshua's mind, but he pushed them away.

Moses continued, "Their gods are numerous. El is their head god in their pantheon. He is their king of gods, the creator and fertility god. El is joined by Asherah, his wife. You are most familiar with Baal, the chief god of their daily worship. You know that Baal means master. Baal is a like a bull and he is joined with Anath. His rivals are Mot, the god of death and sterility, and Yam, the chaotic god of the sea. Baal struggles with both Mot and Yam." Moses provided more details and then asked if Joshua had any questions.

Joshua had many questions but he asked what was first on his mind, "Where did the name Canaan come from?"

Moses explained how Canaan was a son of Ham, one of Noah's three sons.

Joshua nodded and asked Moses to continue.

"Canaan does not really have historical disputes with us but once we make our intentions known, to take their land, they will defend it. I mentioned their immorality earlier. I need to stress this point with you. Sodom and Gomorrah is not far from the land of Canaan. God destroyed those peoples because of the full spectrum of their sins. You must take care, stay faithful and strong"

Joshua had always been devout, he was not sure what he would face but desired to be made aware before he left.

"Moses, what are some of the things that I will face while there?" he asked.

Moses thought for a moment and decided to tell him all he knew. Moses had spent 40 years living in Midian so he had heard many stories about Canaan.

[*As the spies prepared to leave Mt. Sinai, Satan sat back pondering how to distract, divert and lure the team away from their mission.*]

Chapter 2

Moses explained, "the polytheists practices in the land of Canaan has contributed to the most evil of sins; including pride, oppression of the poor, haughtiness, and the most abominable sins including unnatural lusts. They practice bestiality, incest, prostitution, homosexuality, rape, adultery, fornication, and pederasty. There are married couples having carnal knowledge and sexual relations with each other in groups, and all other forms of sexual deviance that God has forbidden. The acts they practice are unnatural in the eyes of God. Sex in marriage is holy and blessed as we know through the law but all other forms are condemned and sinful (1). God has told us that true sexual happiness is inextricably linked to the sexual holiness as believers live their lives before God."

Joshua was shocked to hear how these people lived. He understood now why God wanted them to take their land.

Moses explained, "This is all the information I know about these people."

"How should I go about collecting the necessary information?"

Moses thought for a moment before answering. "First, you should conceal your true identify. Mingle with the people and pretend to act as they act but stay true to God in your heart. There may be times that you will have to be near iniquity or even in iniquity but your strength will be in the Lord. I can promise you that there will be temptations. I am glad you asked about what you will see because some of the sin you encounter may entice you." Joshua was about to protest but Moses held up his hand to halt his protestations.

"My young servant, you have great faith and will do mighty things for God, but alas you are still human. There are things that you have never seen which will interest you. When I was in the pharaohs' palace, I did things I know God would not find pleasing but that was the past and now I focus on serving God. I need you to focus on what I tell you because otherwise it will be difficult to withstand the devil's tricks. Understand you are human and can be tempted; and it is in this knowledge you will find strength. Anyone who believes that they cannot be tempted; is a fool. The devil is cunning, baffling and patient. Remember this always, we all fall into sin from time to time. We must understand ourselves in order to move beyond and into a place of communion with God. As long as we do not stay in a state of willful sin, we can grow into the men our God wants us to be."

Joshua loved these conversations with Moses because he always learned so much.

"Thus, you will be tempted. I warn you to not give in. If you are tempted and succumb, make a sacrifice to God and turn away from that act. God is not to be mocked because we reap what we sow, remember this point. After you enter a city, take an initial survey of the area and then go back to take a detailed account. Make a log of your information. You should make some friends and attempt to recruit them to provide you with additional information on the city. Recruitment of sources will allow you to get more intelligence on the region. One method to get people to help you is by seeming to appear just as they are. People like, people, who are like themselves. So to the idolater, you may want to seem as if you also partake in the iniquity. You may have an opportunity to lead some of the idolaters to one true God, our Lord. In this case, do not move too quickly until you take steps to know their hearts. You cover story will be very important. You must maintain your cover or you will be undone. There may be people you will be able to trust but take great care before you break cover. One cover story you can tell them is that you are wishing to move your tribe to Canaan so you are trying to learn about the area. Another story you can use is that you are a part of a traveling caravan," Moses explained.

"How do I recruit people to help me?" Joshua asked knowing that Moses had also been involved in intelligence operations for pharoah.

"The basic steps are: spot, assess, develop and recruit. You spot a person who seems to be helpful and open. Your next step is to assess their motivations, vulnerabilities, strengths and weaknesses. After you assess them, and they seem like a person who could help you, you develop them by building rapport by spending time with them. Building rapport will allow you to build a bond of affection with them before you decide to ask them to help you. You must decide whether the person you recruit should know your true purpose or not. This is based on your assessment. It's your decision based on whether you believe you can trust that person or not. Of the spies traveling with you, you can trust Caleb but no one else. My friend, you will be confronted with a lot of strange situations but if you lean on God, while staying in the light and maintaining honest intentions, you will be successful."

Joshua listened intently, fascinated by the information Moses provided. Joshua had heard stories about Moses, while under pharaoh, running a successful spy network in Ethiopia before conquering that nation.

Moses reached down into a bag under the seat. "Here are some extra gold pieces to help you on this mission. You should go now to follow the others in the group as they have been making their way towards Canaan. Do you have any more questions?"

Joshua thought for a moment and then stated that he did not. They grasped hands and then hugged. "Be safe and remember, some of those who have been sent out with you, can not be trusted. Watch them and report all you see back to me. I trust you and will pray for you during this perilous trip."

Joshua steeled himself putting the gold into a small pouch on his waist before positioning his satchel on his back. "Thank you." Joshua turned and left the tent. Moses watched him leave and run toward where the group had gone.

Joshua left from the base of Mount Sinai in a northeasternly direction. He believed that the group would be ahead of him by only a little. The sun was still high in the sky and his head was full of information. He had been briefed with the full group by Moses before Moses' speech to the crowd. Joshua was glad to have had the extra time with Moses.

Joshua moved at a fast pace because he wanted to catch up to the group. It was only about 10 minutes later when he saw Gaddi, Igal, Palti, Shammua, and Gaddiel walking together while the others were walking a little bit ahead of them. Gaddiel saw Joshua and called out, "Where have you been Hoshea? It's good that you made it because we were not going to wait for you."

"My name is Joshua now. It's the name Moses, the prophet of God, uses to address me and how you will address me." Joshua knew that a lot of the young men from the influential tribes like the tribe of Joseph resented him. Moses had taught him and trusted him which created some bad feelings from those looking to lead the nation in the future. Joshua did not care about politics, only serving God. Gaddiel had not liked him even before they left Kemet and the bitterness had only grew worst after Moses choose him to fight the Amalekites. Gaddiel viewed Joshua's success with much enmity.

Gaddiel thought back to when they were slaves under Pharaoh when Moses returned from Midian. Joshua happened to be in the same location where Moses appeared and was one of the first to support him. Gaddiel thought Joshua was lucky. If Gaddiel had been in the same work area, he would have been the one chosen by Moses. Joshua was a stone cutter while he was studying to be a teacher of the law. Joshua did not deserve the position accorded to him by Moses, it should have been him. Joshua's high status with Moses was no good for him. He would distinguish himself during this mission to show the tribes that he was the future of Hebrew nation. His thoughts were interrupted by Joshua's answer.

"I had to make a few more preparations," Joshua said. Joshua noticed that Shaphat, Caleb, Ammiel and Sethur had all stopped and waited for him. Nahbi and Geuel stopped as well.

"It's good to see you, Joshua, son of Nun," Caleb stated. Joshua was a little out of breath as he ran much of the way to catch up. The 12 spies decided to go together in three groups with four men in each group about 100 feet apart which would allow the first group to see the danger and alert the others. Gaddiel, Shaphat, Ammiel and Sethur were in the first group. Caleb, Joshua, Nahbi and Geuel walked together in the second group while Gaddi, Igal, Palti, and Shammua walked in the last group.

Once they were walking a good stride, Caleb asked, "How long do you believe it will take us to complete the mission?"

Joshua thought for a moment and then said, "The land is about 200 miles long, from here to the northern most part of Canaan. As Moses told us, we will head toward Abronah off the gulf and then will head through the Wilderness of Paran to Kadesh. After that it will take a few days to move directly into Hebron, the southern end of Canaan but it will take about two weeks to travel to the northernmost point before we return."

The group traveled north for several days.

The journey was harsh and arduous for the group especially the first few days when they were in the wilderness of Paran. Gaddiel took the opportunity at each rest stop to harangue Joshua. Joshua was not bothered because he knew that Gaddiel only wanted to get to him to become frustrated. Joshua had never travelled through the wilderness before; the terrain was flat and dry. Their sandals pushed them through the areas with snakes and scorpions. It was called a wilderness because nothing grew in the desert while sand dunes rose and fell for as far as the eye could see. They tried to travel mostly by night as it was cooler. After traversing through the harsh rigors of southern Sinai, they were able to make their way to the outer limits of Kadesh.

The group approached Kadesh also known as Kadesh-Barnea. The place meant 'consecrated'. The site was not in Canaan so it was still a city where the group could travel together without using espionage tradecraft. Kadesh was located between the wilderness of Paran and the wilderness of Zin. The start of the actual mission would take place once they left the city the next day. They agreed to spend the night in Kadesh before moving north to Hebron. They would also get some more supplies for the journey as Kadesh was a busy oasis. The group had left Mount Sinai with money but not all the supplies they needed. Money was not an issue for the group because they had gold and jewelry which they would change into currency along the way.

They entered Kadesh, the first thing each person did in Kadesh was to go to the money changers and obtain shekels and other currency to use in Canaan. There were vendor stalls placed along the main pathway with sellers hawking their wares.

Joshua and Caleb walked through Kadesh together. "Is this the site that Abraham fought the Amalekites?" Caleb said.

"Yes, it's the very same place. This city has always been an important place for travelers because its wells make this town a good place to live. It is said that it is the largest springs and oasis in northern Sinai," Joshua replied.

Joshua and Caleb walked around the town noticing that Gaddiel was walking with Shaphat, Sethur and Ammiel. Joshua observed the pairing within the group. Nahbi and Geuel gravitated to one another while Palti and Shammua seemed to bond. Joshua observed that Gaddi and Igal were walking and talking together. Joshua and Caleb seemed well-suited so they continued to walk together.

"I do not even know why we are starting this mission. God promised us Canaan so we should just go there and take it," Caleb said to Joshua.

"I agree with you. God has allowed us to go on this mission, but you are correct, this mission is to appease the people not God. We need to make sure that we go about our duties with much diligence so that we can accurately report to the people what we saw in order to devise the best way to possess the land," Joshua suggested.

"That sounds good," Caleb said.

Joshua and Caleb reconnoitered the city talking to merchants and traders who had spent time in Canaan. They obtained vital intelligence on what they would encounter once they went to Hebron, Jericho, Beth-Shan, and the other northern cities. The caravan traders had the best and most current information because they traveled the routes routinely. The caravan leaders were friendly and willin to speak about Canaan.

After going around in Kadesh throughout the day, they found a place to spend the night. The town did not have a lot of accommodations for people spending the night so they just reserved a space under a tent of one of the merchants.

Gaddiel saw that Joshua and Caleb were walking together. He had guessed who his rivals would be and knew Joshua all too well since he was Moses' strong right arm. He believed that Moses sent Joshua there to watch them. The old man was cunning but that would not stop him for finding a way to usurp Moses' power. Gaddiel believed that they should not even undertake a reconnaissance mission in Canaan because he felt that they should return to Pharaoh. He thought that during the mission, he would see something that would support his current belief.

Gaddiel realized that three of the members of the group were walking along with him. If they wanted a leader then he would give them someone to follow. Gaddiel called over to his three fellow spies to have lunch with him. Shaphat, Sethur, and Ammiel came over to Gaddiel and accepted his invitation for lunch. They found a small tent where they could have lunch. They went inside and sat on the floor where the owner served the food to the group. Kadesh was not like larger cities such as Hebron, Jericho, or Hazor where there were real eating establishments. The dining places in Kadesh were mostly for nomads and Bedouin travelers moving along the North/South trade route.

"What do you think about this mission?" asked Gaddiel to the man.

"I think that it will be a grand adventure for us," Shaphat said.

"I agree, we should be able to have some fun while during this mission," Sethur explained.

"It's going to be interesting to see how the Canaanites live and whether we can defeat them," Ammiel suggested.

"You are right; it is going to be an interesting mission. It's also going to be an important mission because our whole nation is depending on us. What we say will matter. We must provide the right advice for the people. This may be the most important operation since we left Pharaoh," Gaddiel noted.

The group finished eating their lunch and then walked around to observe more in the city. Gaddiel found a place for the group to stay for the evening.

Palti, Shammua, Gaddi, and Igal walked round the city together. They talked about their tribes after changing some gold into the paper currency used in Canaan. They then bought some supplies and discussed the possible sights they would see along the way.

Palti and Shammua learned that members of their tribes Benjamin and Reuben had business dealing among each other. Some of their tribal members had intermarried and a friendship started to develop between the two tribes. Shammua looked at Palti, noticing that he was a small man. Palti seemed as mild and timid as his size and voice suggested.

For his part, Palti was happy that he found someone in the group of 12 spies that he connected with. Palti saw Shammua as a potential friend and traveling companion because of the connections between their two tribes. Shammua was opinionated and was pushed into taking the assignment like Palti. Palti was forced by his tribe to go on this mission. This created a bond between them as neither wanted to be on this mission. Shammua was a much bigger man but he seemed thoughtful. The two men gossiped about various members of their tribe as they got to know each other.

"I prefer to stay here in Kadesh instead of going north. I do not know how dangerous this operation will be but since we have no choice, it's good to be with someone close to my tribe," Palti explained.

"I agree and I do not want to be here any more than you do. Lets try to make the most of it," Shammua said.

Gaddi and Igal started talking to some of the women working in the tents of the merchants. They both seemed to be interested in having fun which allowed each to bond. Gaddi looked over to Igal and asked him if he was married.

Igal replied, "No, I'm not married so I'll be able to do as I please during this mission."

'I am not married either. I am my own man and am not accountable to anyone," Gaddi explained with a sly grin on his face.

They smiled at each other and it was decided at that point they would travel together.

Gaddi and Igal spoke with several traveling merchants to discuss what adventures they would encounter on their journey. After both became satisfied that they would have big fun, they found a place to sleep for the evening.

Nahbi walked through the small marketplace looking around the area. He had just spent time with the moneychangers and then bought the needed supplies from the traders. While he was negotiating a good price, Geuel came up to purchase some supplies for himself as well.

"How are the prices?" asked Geuel.

"They are fair," Nahbi explained.

Geuel decided to purchase a few good there. Nahbi waited while he paid and the two of them walked together afterwards.

They both became familiar with each other and their tribes. Nahbi came to view Geuel as a steady straightforward man who called it as he saw it. Geuel did not seem overly religious, but more practical.

Geuel had looked at the various members of the group and came to see himself aligned more with Nahbi instead of anyone else. He was more concerned about traveling with someone who was reliable. He respected Joshua but felt that he was too close to Moses to view the mission objectively. Geuel also saw Caleb in the same light. He would do reconnaissance of the area not based on emotion or religion but through a rational and logical frame of mind. He thought that Nahbi would possibly view things in the same light.

Nahbi and Geuel walked around the town and talked with a few caravan members to gain intelligence about the cities in Canaan. They each were able to get a baseline assessment of what they would encounter in Canaan. Later in the evening, they found a place to spend the night.

Northeast Route to Canaan

The next morning, the 12 spies awoke and made their way outside Kadesh to begin their mission in earnest. They left Kadesh and moved together north towards Hebron. Joshua noticed everything along the route including the other members of the group. He realized that Gaddiel considered himself the leader of his group. Shaphat, Ammiel, and Sethur followed Gaddiel without question as they seemed to think he would be a powerful person in the future. Joshua knew how shallow some of these leading men were from the 'influencial tribes.' Gaddiel tended to complain while his small group of followers agreed with what he said. For Joshua's part, he let them talk and held his tongue, until Shaphat mentioned how being with Pharaoh was not that bad as opposed to wondering in the wilderness.

When Joshua heard this he had to speak up immediately, "The Lord, our God, has taken us out of bondage, what more do you want? Do you not remember the lash of the whip each day under the overseers! The poor food and the long days of toil is not what I want for my children nor is it what God wants for us which is why He brought us a deliverer." Joshua should not have gotten upset, but he had been hearing this type to talk and grumblings by various people since they left Pharaoh. Joshua knew that many of the tribes were just looking for a reason to turn back and return to Kemet.

After Kadesh, the group decided to pair up. Joshua had come to see Gaddi and Igal as simple men who wanted to get to Canaan to see what adventures they could find. Gaddi and Igal did not seem particularly smart and it became clear that they would travel together. Joshua didn't know why they decided to travel together. Nahbi and Geuel seemed to be more thoughtful and interested in doing the job assigned to them; they agreed to travel together. Gaddiel decided that his group would be the same as the one he spend time with Kadesh: himself, Shaphat, Ammiel, and Sethur. Palti and Shammua would go together as a group. Joshua and Caleb had decided after Kadesh to go together. The group of spies decided they would all stay in the same cities, at the same time, but pretend to be strangers to one another.

After stopping outside of the city, they decided to enter Hebron in their separate groups the following morning. Hebron was fortified and the gates were closed for protection. There were many caravans and travelers also outside of the gates waiting until morning as well.

Their plan was simple; each group would make their way around the city for 5 days looking for the needed military information as well as the plans and intentions of the people living there. On the morning of day five, they would all leave the city and meet outside of northern end of the city to go on to the next destination in Canaan.

That night, the groups separated and slept with their traveling groups.

Joshua and Caleb slept away from the others. Caleb looked over to Joshua. He was curious about Joshua and stared over at him. Joshua had pulled out his small scroll and was making some notes. Joshua noticed Caleb looking at him and told him, "I want to make a log of everything for Moses. Give me a few moments while I start with the outskirts."

"It is good to have an accurate record," Caleb said.

Joshua wrote, "Day 9

Hebron has strongly fortified walls from the outside, with defensive positions on the walls where soldiers could easily use archers to attack for long range defense and javelin throwers for medium range defense. The city itself is built on what appears to be four hills. The city lies in a depression in the mountains of Judah and the hills which surround it rise to an altitude of several thousand feet. We have split into self selected groups in the following manner:

Group 1 (Gaddi and Igal)

Group 2 (Nahbi and Geuel)

Group 3 (Gaddiel, Shaphat, Ammiel, and Sethur)

Group 4 (Palti and Shammua)

Group 5 (Caleb and myself)

End of the first report."

Joshua finished and put the scroll away. They both fell asleep quickly.

Day 10

The next morning at the break of dawn, the groups woke up and made their way to Hebron.

Joshua and Caleb waited after the other four groups blended in the the caravans entering into the city. "I'm ready, Caleb. Let us begin our mission," Joshua said.

Caleb smiled and they set off in the unknown.

Joshua and Caleb entered through the south gate and made their way in a bristling city. This was the land where the tribe of Anak lived. The first thing that Joshua noticed was that the men were big. He knew that the world "Anak" was a personal clan meaning 'long-necked' or 'strong-necked'. They were tall and could be considered almost giants by some but Joshua had no fear when he looked at them. Joshua noticed that Caleb was also observing the height and size of the men. He looked at Caleb and said, "I know what you are thinking, but the Lord is with us. With God on our side, none can defeat us," Joshua stated.

Caleb was comforted by Joshua's words. Caleb trusted Joshua because Moses trusted him. Joshua's prowess as a general had become something of a legend with the Hebrews especially after the battle with the Amelkites. Joshua was courageous like a lion and his faith was amazing. Caleb felt good that they would be traveling together.

Joshua and Caleb saw the soldiers on horses at the other end of the square near the temples. There were several temples off the main road. The city was prosperous and there was much activity as the merchants were busy getting ready to sell their wares. Many of the men were setting up their stalls for the business of the day. They walked along the main road smelling roasted nuts and fresh bread roasted flat bread. There were merchants selling freshly butchered meat and some even sold fish that looked less fresh. The main road was composed of packed dirt because of the foot traffic by the many merchants and customers. Some of the stalls actually cooked behind the tables while others were just places where goods were sold. The smell of spices and other unknown aromas wafted up in the morning sky.

"Greetings strangers, come over here. I have some fresh bread and drink for you. You look weary from traveling. Come this way." One merchant called from his stall. Joshua and Caleb looked at each other and nodded in agreement to go over to the enthusiastic merchant. They looked at the flat bread being warmed on the cooking stone of the fire. The bread had local spices on it called zatar which made it smell ever better.

Joshua saw a large statue of Baal on the table of the merchant. The merchant noticed Joshua looking at the statue.

"I see you know our lord and supreme god, Baal. You know that Baal was a descendent of Reuben, Jacob's firstborn son. Baal watches over us and protects us." The merchant explained with much pride.

Joshua and Caleb decided to buy some bread not because they were hungry but because they believed it would be a good place to start gathering information on the area. They were handed two pieces of warm flat bread and offered a place to sit. They were brought two cups of local tea.

"That's strong," said Caleb. Joshua agreed with Caleb after taking a sip of the tea. The merchant provided some olive oil for the break and say down beside them.

"This city is very nice," commented Joshua. The merchant took it upon himself to tell the stranger about the city as way to get him to buy more stuff from him.

Chapter 3

Group 1

Further in town, Gaddi and Igal walked around and taking in how progressive the city was. They entered the center marketplace and heard all the merchants calling out in an effort to bring customers into to their booths. "Freshly slaughtered meat, over here!" yelled one seller.

There were venders selling all types of goods; cloth dealers and tailors, housewares and jewelry, butchers and bakers as well as other types of businesses. There were a few small cafes selling strong drinks and places where the women had their faces painted waving to them. They looked at each other and smiled. Another seller yelled in their direction saying, "Fresh fruit. Strangers come over here."

Igal looked in the direction of the seller and said, "This is an exciting place, it reminds me of life in Memphis (Cairo) back in Kemet (Egypt). I think we need to find a place to sleep for the evening and then investigate everything we can."

Gaddi was the more outgoing one and decided to ask the fruit seller if he knew where they could find a place to sleep. "My friend, how are you this day?" asked Gaddi.

"I am fine stranger, how can I help you?" the fruit seller asked.

"Where can we find a place to sleep for two weary travelers? We are traveling north to meet our tribe but will be here to rest for a few days." The vender looked at them with a little suspicion. "We can pay for a fine room," Gaddi explained. At the sound of them explaining they had money for a fine room, the vender became outwardly friendlier.

"My friends, there is a building about 100 paces up ahead, to your left owned by my friend Jadur. There is a jewelry shop on the bottom floor and he lives on the top floor. I believe that he may have some empty rooms on the second floor. You can also bathe there since it appears that the desert has been your companion for some time. Jadur will help you with anything you want even with entertainment while you are here. Hebron has many entertaining features for travelers. I am Salah from Philistia near the great sea; I have lived in this city for 10 years. Tell Jadur that I told you to see him. He will rent you a good room in his building. Come back after you talk with him later this evening and I can give you some good guidance on what to do while you are here."

Gaddi gave him a beqa' (about 1/2 of a shekel) for his help. Salah was happy to have earned some money from his first customers of the day. Gaddi and Igal both thanked him for his hospitality.

"May Baal bless you," Salah stated.

They walked further into the marketplace and eventually found the building of Jadur. Once inside, they saw a tall man with a large stomach talking to three women with painted faces. He turned when Gaddi and Igal came towards him.

"Greetings friend, we are weary travelers looking for lodging for several days," stated Gaddi. Jadur did not say anything at first but waited.

Gaddi continued, "We were sent here by Salah the vender. He said that you could help us. Don't be concerned, we are not looking for hospitality, we can pay." At the mention of his friend, Salah, and being able to pay, Jadur smiled broadly.

"Rashida, make up two of the rooms on the second floor for our guests. Welcome strangers." Jadur had an almost reptilian appearance about him. The two women with painted lips and faces stared intently at Gaddi and Igal. Igal was mesmerized and returned their stares. Gaddi was trying to focus on Jadur but his gaze kept going back to one of the woman.

"Ah, you have great taste my friend. This is Farida and Ya'el, two of my friends." The women batted their eyes and gave coquettish smiles to Gaddi and Igal. "Why don't you come into the salon and spend some time with us here. Oh, I need you to pay for the room first," Jadur insisted.

"Igal, pay him what he wants," Gaddi said. Igal did as his friend suggested.

"This will do for now but we will have to discuss further payment later. Come this way." Jadur led the two Hebrews into the salon.

"Farida, get some drinks for our friends." She rushed into the back room while the four of them entered into an ornately decorated room with seats around the wall. They all sat down but Jadur sat down across from Gaddi and Igal. Ya'el sat beside Igal. Farida came into the room with a tray of drinks for the group and passed out the drinks. She sat on the other side of Gaddi. Gaddi and Igal were both unfamiliar with strong drink. Jadur, Farida and Ya'el sipped their drinks while Gaddi and Igal both hesitated.

Almost simultaneously Farida and Ya'el picked up drinks and brought it up to the lips of Gaddi and Igal. "Now, now it's considered rude to not drink with your hosts," Farida said. They looked at each other and drank the strange concoction. Gaddi and Igal were unfamiliar with fermented drinks and quickly became intoxicated. The women kept giving drinks to the two young men. Jadur never finished his first drink but instead pretended to drink as the two Hebrews were being provided numerous strong fermented drinks while being attended to by the two women. After two hours of drinking and talking, Farida told Gaddi, "You can have me if you like?"

Gaddi's mouth dropped open and nodded his head without saying anything. She took his hand and led him to the second floor bedroom.

Igal watched Gaddi leave and had a puzzled look on your face. "Where are you going? He asked Gaddi who had been bewitched and could not hear his friend.

Ya'el touched Igal's face and turned it towards her. "You do not need to have anxiety as to where they are going. Do I please you?" she asked Igal.

"Yes, yes, very much." She reached inside the belt of his pants. "You please me too."

Igal had never met a woman like this. His head was swimming and he felt a feeling that he could not identify but liked it. He felt hot inside his body and his face became flushed. He did not know what to do. She stood up and took him by the hand leading him to the second floor as well. After leading the men upstairs, the prostitutes had sexual intercourse with them before they passed out from the strong drinks.

Several hours later after the setting of the sun, the two women heard a knock at the door. The rooms were adjoining with a screen separating them. The screen had been pulled back so the two rooms were in full view of each other. Jadur came into the room. The two women were naked as were both Gaddi and Igal. "You have done a fine job. Where is their money pouch?" The two women got up and started searching the belongings of the pair. They found a pouch with about 50 shekels in it and took the money. It was at this point that Gaddi started to stir.

"We have what we want. Get dressed and come back down stairs."

"Yes, master," they both said.

Gaddi and Igal had put some of their money in two separate pouches on each one so when Jadur come upstairs to take their money, he only found the first pouch with about 50 shekels in it. The 50 shekels was enough to please him.

"Rashida, tell the men to come in here. I want them to take these two and their possessions out of here. Throw them into the streets at the other end of the city. They should not be harmed in anyway; this will just be a lesson for them in the future."

"Yes, master," she replied.

[*Satan smiled as he knew that Gaddi and Igal would be of no further concern to him.*]

Group 2

Nahbi and Geuel had taken their mission very seriously. They had walked into the city and decided to reconnoiter the whole city before stopping to rest. They both noticed how tall the inhabitants were.

"Nahbi, they are giants. It's just like the legends said about the Anak. Did you see how they have several army units in various parts of the city along with men on horses like Pharaohs' men in a small garrison near the center of town?" Geuel said.

"I saw that, and they do appear to be fierce but let us continue to look at their numbers to see if there are some ways to defeat them. If God continues to be with us, we may be able to prevail," Nahbi stated.

"You really think God is going to continue to be with us. The Lord must have other priorities to worry about then our people," Geuel speculated.

"I am not sure but Moses thinks so. I am only here to make a military assessment of the Canaanites' strengths. I am not sure about this God of Moses although we are here and not in bondage any more. Let us go to the garrison and see what we can see," Nahbi suggested.

Geuel agreed and the two walked toward the garrison. The city was quite large and there was a clear warrior class walking around but it did not seem as if they were on alert. Noticing that, Nahbi stated, "They are not ready for battle but could easily be in formation with not too much effort." This is good to know because it tells me that they are not in a state of readiness for war. They would have to be..." Nahbi could not finish his thought when a disagreement broke out near one of the vendor stalls. There was a fight over some meat which appeared to be spoiled. The merchant was being beaten by two men.

"You dare sell us bad meat! My whole family was sick for days. We will take vengeance on you." The one bigger man yelled as he beat the merchant.

Several members from the garrison ran over to the marketplace and stepped in between the two fighters and the merchant who was bleeding on the ground.

The apparent leader of the military unit spoke to the men, "This dispute is over. Allow the merchant to pay you for the meat and then you will leave. You are not of us but strangers so you should understand that it was a mistake."

The merchant was helped up by the soldiers. He stood up shakily. "Pay them for the meat," ordered the commander. The merchant limped over to the stall and took out the money. He reluctantly paid the two men.

"There, you have been compensated. Now, leave this town." The commander gave the order to his men to escort the two men away. The men were led away and the commander told everyone to disperse. He looked directly at Nahbi and Geuel.

"What do you strangers want around here?" asked the commander.

"We are here on our way to Gilead. We were in bondage and were freed by our masters in Kemet. We have been traveling for several weeks and will meet our tribesman in Gilead. We are only here to rest for a few days for rest," replied Nahbi.

"I see, make sure that you do not get into any trouble here. We do not like strangers here. Are you staying inside the walls or outside?" the commander asked.

"We are looking for a place to find lodging for the evening inside the walls. Do you know a place where we can find?" Geuel asked.

"There is a place with several buildings at the northernmost end of the city near the garrison to the west of the stables. Once there ask for a place to stay and tell them that Commander Elrian sent you. You will not be harmed if they know I sent you. I do not like problems in my area," the commander said. Geuel and Nahbi thanked the commander who had already started back in the direction of the garrison.

Once they were out of earshot, Nahbi spoke, "They responded quickly to the problem. That is not good for us because it tells us that is we attack this city, they will be able to react to our attack switfly."

"I think that you may be right again. We should go to the place near the stables as recommended by the commander to get a room," Geuel said.

"I agree," replied Nahbi. They walked through the city towards the garrison in the northern section of the city where a large well was situated. They walked near the garrison and saw that several platoons were milling around. The soldiers were in front of the garrison. Nahbi and Geuel were able to see their armor, shields, swords and other instruments of war. They estimated that several of the platoons were always on the ready while other units may come on duty when needed.

They quickly passed the garrison not wanting to draw attention to themselves. They saw the house and building where many people were going about the daily duties of city life. Women were carrying water to their houses from the well and kids were carrying stacks of bread for their families. They noticed that this was a lower status housing area. They saw a group of men playing a table game they had never seen before. Nahbi explained what they were looking for and the men happily directed them to the building. They secured housing for 5 days for only a few shekels each day.

Present Day

Salman pointed out to Jack that Nahbi and especially Geuel viewed the situation from a worldly view instead of through a faith centered place of God-consciousness. "You may not understand it yet but ultimately you will because it's about faith," Salman said.

Chapter 4

Group 3

It had been ten days since they had left. Gaddiel was beginning to think that he was correct in thinking that the trip would be a waste of time. They should never seek to remove people from their own homeland. Although he did not fully believe that Moses was God's prophet, he had to admit that Moses led them out of Kemet and that God had helped. That said, he had a hard time believing that God wanted them to get killed trying to move the Canaanites off their land. He viewed his job as an opportunity to gather enough information as to why they could not move into this "promise land", thus saving lives. His tribe of Joseph was one of the most influential tribes among the Hebrews; they should lead the people. Gaddiel felt that he should be the one to lead his tribe. Moses had done his job but now it was time for others to step forward for wise leadership. They could move the tribes to an area near the coast of the great sea or further inland towards the salt sea. They should be scouting out places more hospitable for them to live, not a powerful empire. He even thought that perhaps they could try to return to Pharaoh under more favorable circumstances.

"Shaphat, Ammiel and Sethur, let us go and get a good meal so we can watch the goings on of these people." The group agreed and it pleased Gaddiel. He had taken his proper place as leader of these guys. Their tribes; Judah, Asher and Naphtali were lesser tribes in his opinion so it was normal that they would follow him.

The group entered the market place at the east end of the city because it was a better area with many established places to eat. They found a nice restaurant and sat down. The proprietor came up to them with a smile on their face, "Strangers, how may I be of service to you?" he asked.

Gaddiel responded for the group. "What do you have to drink and eat? We have traveled a great distance and have a vast hunger." His pattern of speech was that of a superior speaking to one of a lower class. His word choice was not lost on the waiter.

"My lords, we have much today for the traveler. We have fresh bread, eggs, lentil stew and several types of meat offered on a platter. And can I offer you our well known wine diluted with honey?"

"That will be sufficient," Gaddiel said.

The waiter brought the wine to the table first. The group did not have any problems with drinking strong drink.

Ammiel was the first to take notice of the sweet taste of the wine. "This concoction is quite tasty and refreshing. I have not enjoyed something like this before." The waiter nodded and beamed with a satisfaction because he knew that he would be getting a large tip from these high born men.

"I am happy that it pleases you," the waiter stated.

The food was brought out in several courses with the bread coming first, then the eggs followed by the lentil stew. The platter of meat was the last portion of the meal served. The waiter set the large platter in the center of the table.

When the waiter left, Shaphat spoke up first. "There is meat on this platter from animals who do not chew their cud or who have divided hoofs. This is against the law."

Gaddiel spoke up, "We are here and must not draw more attention to ourselves. When in pharaoh's palace, one should act like pharaoh. We should indulge like those in this culture, so enjoy." He picked up a piece of the meat that he did not know the name for but knew that it was considered unclean. He took a bite and pronounced it delicious. "This is quite tasty, try some." He handed some to Shaphat, Ammiel and Sethur. They tentatively smelled it and then ate it.

"This is very good meat," declared Sethur. "I agree; we are here to do a job but also to enjoy ourselves. We can not do our job if we appear strange to the Canaanites. So, we should enjoy."

When the waiter came to ask them if they needed anything, Gaddiel asked where they could find a good show with dancing girls as they had heard about those types of shows in the land of Canaan.

"My friends, we have a show just like that in an hour inside our pavilion," the waiter stated.

Ammiel smiled and stated that it would make for a good day. The wine had increased their merriment and their conversation was loud and heard by many in the area. An hour later, the merchant brought out several women who greeted the group and had a drink with them. After the introduction, the four women moved into the pavilion to get ready to perform.

Group 5

Joshua watched Gaddiel's group from a corner of the marketplace. Caleb had gone in a local store to ask where they could obtain a place to lay their head that evening. The shop owner took Caleb upstairs to view the place while Joshua told him that he would make a tour around this part of the marketplace. Joshua explained that he would meet back at the shop in a half an hour. Caleb agreed because his stomach was upset. Joshua knew that the food they ate in the morning was bothering Caleb's stomach.

Joshua heard a distinctive voice when he was looking at the various stalls. It was not hard to pick up his mother tongue in a place that mostly spoke another dialect of the Semitic tongue. The voices were not hard to distinguish but Joshua was surprised to see them drinking a strong intoxicating beverage which he could tell by their demeanor. He was more shocked about women who sat with them; they were clearly harlots. He watched for a moment and saw the group go into the pavilion with the women. He pretended to shop and looked inside the pavilion where the women had started dancing the erotic dance of the Canaanites. Their faces were painted and they were twirling their hair with their fingers. The clothes were tight fitting and they played with their veils suggestively. It was an appalling sight to watch them view such women with lust in their eyes. The Hebrews in the tent were laughing and gesturing rudely as well.

"My friend, please come in and sit with us." The waiter had noticed Joshua staring inside and came out to greet him.

"Thank you friend, I have just come to the city and need to rest but I will return as your establishment looks most enjoyable," he replied.

"Anytime friend, we are always open and can provide you with a most entertaining time." Joshua thanked him again and walked back towards the shop where Caleb had secured housing.

"One day in the city and they go straight for pleasurable activities. I worry that they will not take this mission seriously." Joshua said to himself as he saw Caleb come down the stairs.

"Do you wish to see the room?" He asked.

"I trust your opinion. I will see it later when we return for sleep," Joshua said.

Caleb had taken their belongings and put it in the room.

"I saw the garrison where they house the soldiers but I did not go near it. Let us go near there and take a look. There are some stables next to the site so we can go make it seem that we are looking to purchase two horses," Joshua suggested.

"That is a great idea. What do you think the other groups are doing now?" Caleb asked. They were walking toward the center of the city where the large community well was located.

"I saw Gaddiel and his group eating not too far from where we just were. They were drinking what looked like wine and watching some dancing girls." Joshua explained what he saw with such disgust in his voice that it was not lost on Caleb.

"I should have suspected as much. They do not seem particularly committed to this mission. I remember when we arrived at Kadesh where Gaddiel took his group and went off on his own for an hour. You know he greatly resents you, Joshua. Do you think that they will negatively affect our mission?" Caleb asked.

Joshua thought for a few moments while continuing to go towards the direction of the garrison. "I serve the Lord and trust in the Lord. There have been very few moments in my life since Moses rescued us from bondage that I have any doubts. When I do have doubts, I just assume that it's the evil one attempting to influence me, but I remain strong in my faith and steadfast. Whatever evil they may be planning, the Lord will protect me," Joshua stated thoughtfully.

Caleb stopped by the large well for some water, but he really wanted to ask Joshua about what he said.

"May I ask you a question about what you just told me?" He asked.

"Ask me anything," Joshua stated.

"How do you not allow those doubts to enter into your thoughts? How do you not dwell on those negative thoughts that sometimes come into your mind? I believe; but want to know how you always stay so positive, strong and faithful?" Caleb asked.

"Let us sit for a second, as I want some water as well." The weather was not too hot but Caleb figured that Joshua was still tired from the journey.

"We have great power inside of us. God blew breath in our nostrils and He has given us all we need. God has given us the capacity to withstand any trial or attack. We must keep God in our hearts, minds and in our spirits every day. Do not entertain doubts or worries because that path will lead you away from God and towards the evil one. When you are completely focused on God's goodness and His word then there is no room for the adversary to come into your mind or your heart. We have a part of God inside of us which means that we can withstand any assault from the evil one. We have the power to choose what we focus on in our thoughts. If you allow doubts or negative images to come inside, the path will be open for further iniquity. We have the power to see any issue as difficult or easy. I am nearing middle age and I feel as strong as a man your age, because I believe it to be so. [Joshua was about 65 years old at this time]. We are able to use our thoughts to our advantage. We must not allow the evil one to gain a foothold in our minds. It's our choice what we choose to replay in our thoughts. God has empowered us and if we continue to put Him first in our hearts, then He will make sure that our lives are bountiful. God has a plan for our lives and I am faithful because I remember how life was before I believed. I was broken and defeated after living so many years in bondage. I do not have to worry any more because we have seen clear evidence that God is real and responsive to our needs. He loves us and we are special to Him. God is not like men, He is not capricious. God is steadfast and we must be the same way. Stay in prayer and meditation, and all will be well." Joshua paused for a moment before continuing.

"The problem now is that many of our brothers and cousins are still in bondage in their minds. Although they have been told about a new life, it's difficult for them to truly believe it. We should continue to keep them in prayer, so they will experience the freedom we have in our minds and in our spirit."

Joshua paused again while Caleb took this in. "Thank you for providing me with your thoughts, I understand. I am steadfast and faithful; and I will repent for even doubting for a moment."

Present day

Salman looked at Jack and said, "This part is important because you will start to see the faith of Joshua. We all have doubts and fears but we cannot let that direct our decisions. It's about having full-time faith. This is a large part of what I want to leave you with by telling you this story." Salman returned to telling his tale.

"Let's us move toward the stables," Joshua suggested. As they walked down the main street, they saw many alters to Baal and El, the other supreme god for Canaan. They saw the temples and the Canaan priests carrying sacrifices for their gods. They both realized that generally the Canaanites did not really notice that they were foreigners except for the vendors and merchants who were always looking to make money from strangers. They walked pass the stables and started looking at the horses available for purchase. The smell from the piles of manure hit them at once outside the stables.

Joshua asked Caleb to speak to the merchant while he took mental notes of the garrison. He saw several platoons of soldiers walking, sitting and laying around inside the building. They were big men but did not seem that disciplined or intimidating. He noticed the shields and weapons were not neatly stacked but laid out in an open area of main building. He realized that parts of the stables were dedicated for the garrison as that section was roped off. The men were not all be Canaanites, but men from various places like Kemet, Philistia and Arabia. The men did not pay attention to him observing them. He found that interesting because it meant that they did not believe that anyone would actually attack them. From his military experience, they did not appear to be highly trained or on alert. The men seemed to complain and mill around looking bored. He counted only about 100 men but knew that they probably had more units on patrol. He knew they were beatable because they were fighting for money, not for God and country. He had all the information he needed watching these men. He walked back to the stable were Caleb had finished speaking with the merchant.

"I told him that we will come back if we decide to buy the horses. Let me show you the horses to maintain our cover," Caleb said.

They walked towards the horses and looked closely at them while the merchant watched them from afar.

"So what do you think about these giants?" asked Caleb.

"It's just as we thought before we left, they are big and well-armed but we have the Lord with us. With the Lord on our side, what can man do against us? We will beat these pagans, take their lands, destroy their idols, and teach them how to serve the one true God. I swear it, no matter how long it takes me," Joshua vowed!

Present day

Salman looked at Jack and said, "It was at this moment that Joshua's deep faith was taking form. Joshua did not know the future at this point. He did not know that once he returned that the people would reject God's plans and be punished to wander in the wilderness for 40 years. Joshua would eventually lead the people into the Promised Land and we can see where that faith started.

Chapter 5

[Satan looked upon Joshua and Caleb knowing that he must discredit them in the eyes of their countrymen. He did not believe that he could entice or sway Joshua but he would attempt to influence the people around Joshua to do his bidding in that area. He looked at Palti and Shammua make their way around the Northern end of the city. They were undertaking their task with some fear and doubt which made him happy. He realized that it would not take much to dishearten them and influence them to direct their energies in other areas.]

Day 10 early evening

Group 4

Palti and Shammua walked around the Northern end of the city along the inside of the wall near the area where the people of Hebron through their trash. They noticed the wall was fortified and could see the post where the guards climbed to the top of the wall to view the area outside of the city. The guards were not that alert when they walked near the observation post. Palti and Shammua viewed the soldiers with their worldly eyes, so the soldiers looked unbeatable.

"This city is so big and the men are so big," Palti stated.

"I know, they are even bigger than Pharaohs' soldiers. I knew that this would be a useless endeavor. They have armor and weapons unlike ours and their army seems very professional," Shammua said.

"I can not wait to get back to Sinai. I have been thinking about this whole mission," Palti pondered.

"What have you been thinking?" Shammua asked.

"Living in Pharaohs' house was not that bad. Life was simple and we had a routine every day. We never worried about food nor did we have to imagine fighting an army of giants." Palti paused for a second to see if Shammua was of the same mind. He did not want to state his opinions if Shammua did not agree with his line of thinking.

Shammua smiled and explained, "I was thinking the same way but was not sure if anyone else felt the same as me. I think Moses did something amazing as the Prophet of God when he led us out but I thought it would be different. I did not think that the wilderness would be so..." he paused searching for the right word.

"Harsh," Palti finished the sentence.

"Yes, harsh. It's been tough. I am a artisan not a warrior," Shammua said simply.

"I know, I am a tailor and miss making the fashionable clothes for Pharaohs' staff."

"Life was not so difficult in bondage for us," Shammua stated.

They walked and continued to look around taking in the wall and the post. They were afraid from the time they entered into the city and looked very suspicious by their actions. They were below the guard post when they were called by one of the guards.

"Hello there, what do you want around here?" the guard asked.

Their demeanor had come to the attention of the guards. They froze looking like a camel viewing water after a month in the desert. They hesitated to say anything. They were not professional spies or warriors. They stopped, not knowing what to do.

"I said, what is your business around here? You look at if you two are up to nothing good at all," the guard said again.

Afraid, Palti and Shammua, did the only thing that came into their minds, they ran.

Day 10 evening

Group 5

Caleb and Joshua were walking around the western marketplace when they spotted a crowd speaking loudly and laughing. They made their way to the crowd and asked one of the locals what was going on.

"Two foreigners had gotten intoxicated and laid with two of harlots of Jadur. They had their money taken and now they are being ridiculed by the crowd.

Joshua and Caleb finally made their way through the crowd and saw Gaddi and Igal on the ground.

Gaddi and Igal were trying to collect their thoughts. They were half clothed and being pushed around by the crowd. Joshua walked in the middle of the crowd and stated boldly, "There men are from my tribe and I will stand with them." The crowd slowly moved away after seeing Joshua.

Caleb came beside Joshua and helped him to lead them outside of the crowd.

"What happened?" asked Joshua.

Gaddi and Igal looked at each other and the shame was clear on their face. "We were taken advantage of," Gaddi replied.

"Yes, we were taken advantage of by these idolaters," Igal joined in their defense. "We did not mean for this thing to happen."

Joshua looked at the both of them. "Come with me." Joshua led them back through the town and to the place where they has secured housing. "We have a place to stay upstairs." The two men looked with relief in eyes at the building.

The four of them walked upstairs and into the room. Joshua had not seen the room previously but noticed that it was large and clean. There was a bedding area on the floor. The bedding was made from blankets. There was a table with a few chairs in the corner.

"Have a seat," Joshua said.

"Caleb, can you go downstairs and obtain some tea or another soothing drink for our cousins?" Caleb nodded and got up. Although Gaddi and Igal were from different tribes, Joshua considered them, as fellow Hebrews, his cousins.

"Are you hurt or otherwise injured?" Joshua asked.

"No, I am fine," Gaddi answered.

"I am not injured," replied Igal.

"This is good because it's important that you are well. We will wait until Caleb returns." Joshua walked to his small satchel and took out two shirts. He handed the shirts to the two men.

"You should tell the owner of this house to allow you to bath in order to wash away the dirt from your bodies."

Caleb returned with a mixture of yoghurt and milk. He carried a tray with a clay pitcher and four cups. Caleb placed the tray on the table and poured out the drink for Gaddi and Igal first. He then poured drinks for himself and Joshua.

"I am sure you were taken advantage of but that is no excuse. You put yourself in the position to be taken advantage of. There are no mistakes in this world, only choices. You chose to drink strong drink and then to allow yourselves to influenced by the harlots. I am not here to judge you but only to point out where you went wrong. We all make bad decisions in life but the real battle is what you do after you make a bad decision. You can learn from this experience or not, it's up to the both of you. You need to repent and make a sacrifice to God. I will leave you some coins to buy some more garments. I am here to do a mission. The Lord allows us to learn in all circumstances. So, we will leave you here while we go out. I will tell the owner to arrange a bath. You should stay here this evening. I believe that the owner has another room on the floor below this. We will arrange to take that room. Be well and thank the Lord for delivering you from a bad situation. Is there anything else you need from me?" Joshua asked.

They looked at each other and Joshua thought he saw tears in Gaddi's eyes and remorse in Igal's face. Gaddi spoke first, "Thank you Joshua for your kindness. We will repent and make a sacrifice to the Lord for our iniquity."

"I also thank you, Joshua Son of Nun, we will repent for our sins," Igal said.

"What I did, is only my duty," Joshua explained as he and Caleb left the room.

Downstairs, Joshua went to the owner of the building and negotiated for another room explaining how some other travelers needed his room. He paid for the new room and then was taken there by the owner. The new room was a little smaller but was facing away from the sun so it was cooler. There was a table, two chairs and some blankets on the floor to be used as bedding.

Joshua sat heavily on the floor and started to pray. Caleb sat in one of the chairs and stayed quiet. After a few moments, Joshua looked up.

"You were very easy on Gaddi and Igal. They broke our law and disobeyed Moses' orders. They need to be sent back home and punished." Caleb explained with disgust in his voice.

"So, you would have me judge them?" asked Joshua.

"I am not asking you to judge them but their sins are evident," Caleb replied.

"Are they? To who? Me; you? Once we start down that path of judgment of our fellows, then it becomes like water flowing down into the valley—it's hard to stop. God will judge them, not us nor Moses. They made a choice and now have to deal with it. It is not my job to punish them but God's. I just pointed them in the right direction, they have another choice now as to whether they will choose to learn and live in a different manner. We still have quite a bit of time to go on this mission. I do not know God's plan for those young men and perhaps God meant that they would fall as they did, for some other purpose. I just have to do my job, looking at this mission from the perspective that God wishes me to view it from," Joshua was tired and it had been a long day.

"You are right; I still have a lot to learn," Caleb said.

"And you will learn, because you wish to. The Lord helps those who help themselves." Joshua said before continuing, "Let us retire and rise early tomorrow morning to survey the southeast part of the city."

"That is a good idea. I will see you tomorrow morning, God willing," Caleb stated as he prepared to rest for the evening.

Joshua lay down, took out his small scroll and started writing in a language that the locals would not know as it was a guttural language used in the mud pits of Pharaohs'. In case any one found his notes, they would not be able to interpret it because in addition to the guttural language, he ran letters into each other and used a crude short hand known only to him and Moses.

Joshua wrote,

"Day 10

Report 2

Today, we entered the city in the five teams as detailed in the first report. We will meet in four more days. The city is of a circular design enclosed behind a fortified wall with northern and southern main gates. The gates can be closed in order to seal off the city in case of an attack. On the fortified wall, there are four main posts or observation points where the guards can observe visitors arriving from about a half an hour away because there is no cover to conceal an oncoming army. The northwest corner outside the gates provides the best entry point as the hills could obscure an incoming army. Each post appeared to have only a few guards manning the post at any one time. There is a garrison inside the northwest corner of the city. I witnessed about 100 soldiers with light arms and shields. The city is prosperous and thriving. The Canaanites are polytheists and there is evidence of their wickedness throughout the city. There are two main marketplaces in the city located centrally in the west and the eastern part of the city. There are two internal water supply wells inside the city walls.

The average soldier is tall approximately a head taller than our people. There is a laxity surrounding the men in the army. The soldiers are professional and appear to be made up of mostly foreigners. I view all the above as favorable circumstances for us to do our job especially since we are fighting for God and they are pagans.

As for my fellow spies, there was much excitement associated around them. Gaddi and Igal apparently became intoxicated and had intimate sexual relations with two local harlots. Caleb and I found them in the streets after they had been thrown out of their place of lodging. The crowd was ridiculing them, so we took them to our lodging and took care of them. They were also robbed. We have acquired another room in the same edifice. They are continuing the mission and will meet us in four days.

I also witnessed Gaddiel, Shaphat, Ammiel and Sethur is a restaurant drinking an intoxicating strong beverage and watching a show with dancing girls. They did not see me because they were too preoccupied in their merriment.

I have not seen nor heard anything about Palti and Shammua this day.

We have bedded down for the evening and will begin again on the morrow. End report."

Day 10 evening

Palti and Shammua had been running throughout the city.

"Do you still see them?" asked Shammua.

"I am not sure. We would not even have needed to run if you had not looked so suspicious to the guards," ejected Palti.

"Me, it was you. The guard asked you the question, not me. You should just have told him that we were strangers who got lost. Now, they really believe that we have done something wrong," Shammua said.

They huddled up near the southwest corner of the city. It was beginning to get dark and anyone who could have rented them a room had already closed for business that evening. They bought a roasted chicken a few hours before and devoured it very quickly. They would not have to worry about starving but they would be sleeping outside this evening. Although they were inside the walls, it was still a desert region, and was becoming colder every hour. They huddled up against one another; complaining and wishing they had never left the Sinai.

[*Satan laughed as he observed the scene.*]

Chapter 6

Day 10 evening

Group 3

Gaddiel, Shaphat, Ammiel, Sethur were sitting in the restaurant watching the dancing girls and having an enjoyable evening. They had secured lodging in an adjacent house to the restaurant so they did not have to worry about where to sleep that evening. They had been there for several hours and Gaddiel was able to make friends with one of the owners of the place, Mansur.

Mansur, an Arab who had come from Arabia near Midian. The Hebrews had also migrated from Arabia as well so they were cousins. He started trading spices indigenous from the Arabia peninsula with merchants in the Canaan. Mansur came to enjoy living in Canaan as there was more excitement then in his land. Mansur was about 60 years old and spoke Hebrew with a strange accent.

Gaddiel decided that while he was in Hebron, he would learn about the people from this man. "These Canaanites are big people?" He commented to Mansur.

"I was shocked when I first traveled here over 30 years ago. They are much bigger than the men living in my land," Mansur replied.

"You have you lived here for 30 years?" Gaddiel asked.

"Yes, I met a woman here and decided to stay. I still manage caravans to my home land about three times a year but I no longer make the trips myself," Mansur explained.

Gaddiel had brought the best fermented wine from the stock. He had offered to share the bottle with Mansur if he joined him. Mansur was pleased to join him especially since he was being compensated for the bottle.

Although Gaddiel may not have believed that the Israelites should occupy the land of Canaan, he was still interested in learning more about the land.

"Is this land safe? It would appear to me that there would be invading armies coming through this land often because it is along the main trade route," Gaddiel posed the question hoping that Mansur would either agree with him or correct him, either way providing him with more information.

"Very safe, my new friend. The city has a garrison near the north gate and our walls are very thick. Our soldiers are some of the best trained in this part of the world. The army is made up of men who fought in Pharaohs' army as well as in armies to the east. This is one of the reasons why I decided to make my home here. In other places I have traded in, there would be random raids which one could never foresee. I only have to worry about those raids in Arabia now. We are completely safe here. Do not worry," Mansur assured them.

"Thank you, this is very good to know," Gaddiel said. He thought that this land was too well fortified and now he had confirmation. They would enjoy the remaining time they had in the city.

"Enough talk," Shaphat said. "How can you ignore these beautiful Canaanite women?"

Gaddiel knew that the group had no idea what he was doing but he would not spoil their fun this evening. "You are right, let us have more drink." The merriment continued for another hour before they decided to go to sleep. The women offered their services to the men for the evening. Shaphat, Ammiel and Sethur all enjoyed the company of the women.

Gaddiel did not partake in that part of the festivities. He thought to himself, "I must live differently than the men so I can be able to use this against them in the future." He felt sleepy, pleased with how the first day in the town proceeded.

Day 11 morning

Group 1

"Good morning, how are you?" Gaddi asked.

"I feel better now. This room is not that bad. I still have pain in my head," Igal said.

"I also have a severe pain in my head. I thought we would have an adventure, not this. They stole our money and threw us out. These people are evil and mean-spirited," Gaddi said.

Igal got up and checked the remaining belongings he still had. "Gaddi, bless God. I just checked my other pouch. I still have the half of the money I came with. They did not find it. Ha!" His excitement made his head feel better.

Gaddi got up and checked his belongings as well. "I too have the other half of my funds." He looked at Igal and they both laughed.

"For all of their efforts, they did not get all of our money," Igal laughed. The mood was lightened and Gaddi also felt the lessening of pain in his head.

"It was fortunate that we ran into Joshua and Caleb," Igal said.

"I know and I am grateful but I didn't like Joshua's sanctimonious attitude. He thinks he's better than us. Also, I am concerned that he will tell Moses and our tribes about this accident," Gaddi said.

"You really think he looks down on us? Igal asked.

"Yes, he does. We should be worried?" Gaddi said.

[*Satan watched the exchange between the two men and allowed an idea to float into Gaddi's mind because he knew Gaddi's mind was the weaker of two.*]

"Igal, I think that it would be very bad for us if Joshua told the elders. The elders would be very upset at us and could exile us for not fulfilling our duty. I have an idea; maybe Joshua and Caleb should have an accident. This is a very dangerous area and they are foreigners. No one would suspect anything if they were killed."

Group 2

Nahbi and Geuel woke up in their room near the stables. The dressed and went to the nearest establishment for food.

"I did not like the way the commander was able to take control of the disturbance so quickly yesterday. What concerns me is that he is observant and professional. He could have acted irrationally towards us but he just did his job and then offered to help us. This man is a person who is not agitated easily. Commander Elrian, we must make a note to remember him," Nahbi said.

"Your words are true and have much merit. I think that we should go over there today and thank him for his efforts. This way we can learn more about the garrison. What do you think?" Geuel suggested.

"That idea is worth pursuing. We should do that after we eat," Nahbi said.

They ordered a small meal of yoghurt, dates and bread eating quickly before heading towards the garrison.

Group 4

Palti and Shammua were up early because the roosters started crowing at the break of dawn. Both were in a foul mood from sleeping outside.

"I think that finding a place to spend the night should be our first priority. I want to sleep on real bedding and also want to bath," Palti explained.

"We should get moving and I am famished. We can get something from that market next door and then look for lodging for the evening," Shammua said.

"I just want to rest today and not think about this mission. We have seen all we need to see in this city. The men are giants and the army is strong. There is no way we could take over this city," Palti said.

"I think that you are right. We cannot take this city. We should rest today and clean ourselves up. We should not have to put ourselves in this type of danger again. I am ready to return," Shammua confessed.

They purchased some nuts, fruit and bread from the market. They ate ravenously while walking away from the place where they slept. If anyone had been watching them, their demeanor was very suspicious as they looked around attempting to keep a keen eye out for the soldiers looking for them yesterday. They came upon the other major marketplace looking for lodging. They were able to find a room for a few shekels a night. They paid for four nights because they did not want to look again for a room.

The innkeeper told them harshly, "Take your bedding from the back room. You may each get two blankets and the room is behind that room on the left. It's the room on the right with the clay tablet of Baal on the door."

"Thank you. Where can we arrange to bath as we have spent much time in the desert?" Shammua asked.

"We have a room in the room on the left with a bathing tub. For an extra half shekel, we will fill it and provide soap."

Palti and Shammua looked at each other and agreed. "That sounds fair," Palti said as he gave the owner another 1/2 shekel.

"That's a half shekel each," the owner demanded.

They looked at each other with a little exasperation but paid the extra half shekel.

They made their way back room and grabbed the blankets and then found their room. The room was dark but clean. There was a window and the floor was clean. There were two tables in the room and several cushions around the floor.

Palti and Shammua were both pleased. They each took their separate baths and then fell on the bedding to sleep.

Group 5

Caleb and Joshua were up and moving early in the morning. They had some eggs, bread and tea for breakfast. Their goal was to view the north gate and make friends with the locals to gain more information on the area. They left the building and moved north inside the city.

"Do you think our fellows are doing well today?" asked Caleb.

"I think that Gaddiel and his group have probably not risen yet from last night's festivities," Joshua said.

"What do you think about them?" asked Caleb.

"Gaddiel is not an idiot, although he pretends to be like the others. He is ambitious and has grand designs on leadership. His pride will lead him to places which are not pleasing to God. I say this to make sure that you do not underestimate him. He is smart and very clever. The men with him; Ammiel, Shaphat, Sethur are followers, not leaders like Gaddiel. I worry that his tribe is plotting at this very moment against Moses. I am not sure of how to take Nahbi and Geuel; they are different than Gaddiel and his followers because they care although misdirected. I think that Nahbi's and Geuel's problem is a faith problem. Lack of faith is a difficult mountain to overcome. I think they are good people, not malicious or mean spirited like Gaddiel. They may surprise us. Palti and Shammua are easy because they are like the wind, they will go which ever way the gusts blows. People like that can not be counted on because they allow their fears to influence and lead them. Gaddi and Igal are weak and only came on this journey for adventure, not seeking to fulfill a divine mission," Joshua stopped as a group of soldiers passed by them.

Once the soldiers were out of earshot, Joshua continued, "Our job is to just pray for them all to find their way, and do the job the Lord put before them. All the same, I think that they all view things differently than we do. I believe and have decided to live the life of a believer. I surrendered and decided not to look for ways to get out of my obligation or my duty. My duty is to serve and trust in the Lord, I must focus on serving God in the best manner I can instead of looking for ways to not do my job."

They continued to walk toward the north gate. Joshua decided to pretend to look for a job with at the trash depot while looking for weaknesses in the huge northern gate.

Joshua and Caleb found the foreman and asked about work. Joshua explained that he was a stone cutter who worked in Pharaoh's pits. The foreman, a man named Rashid was from Arabia, had a favorable opinion of them and told them to return in a few hours.

Joshua asked Rashid if it was alright if they looked around a bit to learn the area. He agreed and they were able to see that the trash depot was also a quarry where they made bricks and cut stone for the houses. Joshua took a mental snapshot of the gate. The two gates were made of wood and fortified with iron bands. The gate was approximately 30 feet high and 2 feet wide. The gate was on a hinge which allowed it to be moved by several people. There were two huge logs behind the gates used to secure it in place. Joshua noted that it would take a few minutes to secure the gates in the face of an incoming army. The one important point that he noticed was that that the gates were not secured well in the front. Usually with gates like these, the people would put large stakes in the ground to prevent the gates from being pulled open by oxen or a brigade of men. Joshua noted this point in his mind. He saw six guards at the gate and felt that it was not adequate for the task needed. He took the rest of his mental notes before moving off.

They thanked the foreman and told him that they would return after lunch.

Group 1

"Kill them?" Igal's eyes were wide with fear. "We can not kill the Prophet of God's favorite servant. We... no, it is not possible to even speak of such a thing."

Gaddi moved closer to Igal. "Look Igal, we can allow things to just be as they are but I should warn you that Joshua will not let this pass. Joshua will tell Moses and then Moses will tell the heads of our tribes. We will be stoned. Do you want to die?" Gaddi asked.

"I do not want to die but it was a mistake. Surely they will understand and forgive us," Igal said.

"It was a not a mistake, it was a choice. Just like we need to make now to kill them," Gaddi explained.

Igal paused for a few moments before replying in a low, sad voice, "Okay, let us do it."

Chapter 7

Day 11

Group 3

Gaddiel had arranged to have breakfast brought to their room. He heard a knock at the door, Gaddiel opened the door and saw a beautiful female slave neatly attired accompanied by a male slave. Gaddiel welcomed them into the room. The female slave led the male slave into the area with the tables. She instructed him to put the tray on the table. There were several trays that were brought into the room. Gaddiel saw fresh juices, eggs, dates, fresh bread, various other fruits and several dishes that he did not recognize. The male slave finished putting all the dishes on the table and left. The female slave stayed and prepared the table.

The room was huge with four beds and screens separating the sleeping areas. The night before while they were watching the dancing girls, Mansur had prepared the room and made sure that they would be comfortable. Ammiel and Sethur came into the area with the tables and sat down. Shaphat had gone out to use the restroom and walked back into the room at that moment.

"Who is this?" Shaphat asked looking at the female slave. "Perhaps a gift from your friend Mansur," Shaphat said this last part with lechery in his voice.

"My name is Miriam and my master asked me to provide any services you may need. Is there anything else I can do to make you comfortable?" She asked.

Shaphat spoke up, "Hmm, I am sure that I can think of something after our repast."

Ammiel and Sethur laughed. "Leave it up to our companion from the tribe of Simeon to have such appetites in the morning after the night we all had."

"I have been tasked with learning all I can about these peoples, why not start here," Shaphat said simply.

"Return in a few hours," Shaphat requested.

"Yes, my lord." She bowed and went out. The group laughed at their companion and begun eating.

Group 2

"Is commander Elrian on duty today?" Nahbi asked.

The soldier looked down at them and told them to wait there. The soldier who they talked with was probably eight feet tall as bent over to speak to them.

Nahbi shook his head and said to Geuel, "These are the biggest men I have ever seen."

Nahbi and Geuel were both inside the main bay of the Garrison. They were able to get a good look of the armaments and the men. The men who were born in this area were giants between 7-8 feet tall. There were also men from the Assyrians, Babylonians, Egyptians, Canaanites, Amalites, and various other tribes they had not seen before. The languages were strange to them. They saw the swords along the wall and the shields. All of the armaments only reinforced their opinion of the strength of the army.

Commander Elrian came into the lobby and saw the two foreigners he had spoken to the previous day. "What is it; is there a problem?" He asked.

"No, commander. We just wanted to thank you for the suggestion yesterday. We found lodging and the place is very nice. You were kind to us and I wanted to express my gratitude as is the custom of my people," Geuel said.

Commander Elrian heard the words and his countenance changed. "Thanks is not required as I was just doing my duty. I wish to see no one taken advantage while they are here. The people here can be unkind at times, often looking for ways to take advantage of strangers," he said.

"We wish to take no more of your time as you are busy man. Peace and blessings be on you," Geuel said.

"May Baal watch over you here and during your journey," Commander Elrian stated.

Nahbi and Geuel made a slight bow and exited the main bay of the garrison.

"What do you think?" asked Nahbi.

"They are very professional and seem competent," Geuel exclaimed. Nahbi agreed as they made their way to their room.

Hebron Military Garrison

Commander Elrian had received a report of strangers looking suspiciously at the northeast post. He had suspected these foreigners but they would surely not deliver themselves up to him if they were the foreigners who ran from the guards. The two strangers had said that their masters had freed them from bondage. That was possible especially after the one called Moses came and ruined everything in Kemet.

Commander Elrian wanted to return to the capital city of Pharaoh. He loved living near the waters of the Nile River. He had been living in Hebron for only a short time but hated it already. He had served in the Pharaoh's army for almost 20 years but was sent here when the Hebrews left. The general of Pharoah's army felt that some of the territories under their rule might be looking to rebel. Thus, he sent out some of the most experienced commanders to take over the territories located to the east and south. He was one of the unfortunate ones sent out. He was promised that after a few years, that if he did a good job, he would return to a promotion as a general. He had not been here that long and he was already tired of being away from where the action was. Nothing ever really went on at this outpost. Breaking up that fight yesterday had been the highlight of his week. Then the sergeant of the northeast post had reported that two foreigners were acting strangely. He was fortunate that the soldier was one of his who he brought from Kemet. The local soldiers would never have noticed anything out of the ordinary unless it had developed into a huge disturbance.

He always believed himself to be more than a capable commander and someone with a special intuition for his work. His intuition told him that something was afoot in the city. He decided to increase the patrols around the city and to issue an alert to question any foreigners new to the city.

[*Satan saw the exchange of the Nahbi and Geuel with the commander. He decided to send out an image into Commander Elrian's mind, thoughts of dangers and threats.*]

Group 5

Caleb and Joshua were walking in the marketplace when they heard Hebrew spoken in the same dialect as they were used to. They walked over to the large stall which sold fabrics and clothing in the local fashion.

"Peace and blessings to you," Joshua said to the old merchant. The merchant had been speaking to a beautiful woman of about 30 years and he immediately noticed the spoken language of his people. He looked at the stranger and greeted him in his native tongue as well.

"Cousin, I see that you are as we are, strangers in a strange land. Welcome, come and sit with us." The merchant led them into the back where they were offered seats. "Fatia, please bring refreshments for our new friends." He had asked the young woman. Caleb noticed the most beautiful dark eyes he had ever seen on anyone before.

Joshua and Caleb sat down at the table.

"My name is Salman, and I am from Goshen, from the tribe of Judah." Joshua and Caleb looked at each other in surprise.

"We both have relatives from Goshen too. I am Joshua and this is my friend Caleb."

Salman continued, "I left Goshen over 60 years ago when I had only 20 years. My father and mother left Pharaoh with their masters and came here."

The family we served was killed during a trade caravan along with my parents about 25 years ago. I stayed behind in Hebron because I was ill when they decided to go on the caravan. I was left with Fatia. When news came that my master was killed, the remaining servants either returned to the land of Pharaoh or went home. I decided to stay as I had built a life here. I was married although we were never blessed to have children. My wife passed away a few years ago but we raised Fatia together up until that time as our own child. After my wife went to the Lord, I continued to be her guardian. Fatia inherited her family's goods and I helped her to manage it until she was married a few years ago. Her husband was killed not long after they wed and we have been family to each other.

Fatia returned with fresh goat's milk, nuts and dates for the strangers. She placed the tray on the table in front of the group. She took a seat without saying a word. Caleb noticed that she was bold as she did not ask to sit down as was the custom.

"Your history is amazing. We heard you speaking Hebrew and knew you were from the lands of our fathers," Joshua said.

"Fatia speaks excellent Hebrew since she has been company to an old Israelite for more than 20 years, its no way for a young woman to spend her time."

"Oh Uncle, you are not that old and I enjoy spending time with you," Fatia explained.

"Let me introduce ourselves formally since the young lady was not here when we started talking. I am Joshua, son of Nun of the Tribe of Ephraim, and this is Caleb son of Jephunneh of the tribe of Judah."

Caleb added, "We are of the same tribe."

Joshua continued, "I noticed that you called him Uncle," Joshua inquired.

"Well, after my parents joined the one God, 'He who has no name'; Salman became my guardian and then my family. So, I begin calling him uncle since that time. All of my relatives were in Kemet so we became each other's family."

Caleb had been quiet because he was so captivated by the young woman. He felt compassion for her because of the trials and tribulations she had been through. She was almost Hebrew in her mannerism and speech, it was uncanny.

Fatia noticed that the younger stranger was staring at her. There was something about him that also drew her to him.

Caleb finally gained his voice and asked her a question, "I am sorry to hear about your parents and your husband. You mentioned the Lord, what do you know about that, are you not from Kemet?"

"My parents may have been born there but all I know is the customs of my uncle Salman. I prefer the language of my uncle and I follow the one true God of Abraham, Isaac and Jacob," she said.

Once again, Joshua and Caleb were surprised and looked at each other not fully understanding.

"But your family is polytheist, idol-worshippers. How is it that you come to follow our God?" Caleb asked with a little too much judgment in his voice.

"Well, I do not understand why it's any concern to a stranger as yourself but I believe in the God as described to me by my uncle. I follow 'He who has no name'," Fatia stated with pride.

Joshua jumped into the conversation and said, "The prophet of God, Moses, has spoken to God and we now know his name. Our God is known as "I am Who I am". Joshua allowed them to take in that information.

"You must tell us about this prophet of God, Moses. We had heard that some Hebrews had left Kemet but we have no idea what happened. Please tell us the history of my people," Salman begged.

Joshua began to tell the history of Moses. He started from when Moses was pulled out of the Nile and then became a prince of Pharaoh. He explained how Moses escaped for murdering a man before settling in the desert near Midian for 40 years. Joshua described how Moses heard God's voice on Mt. Sinai and learned God's name. Moses hardships in the land of Pharaoh were detailed to them to include leading the Israelites out of bondage and the parting of the Red Sea. He stopped short of saying the Hebrews were ordered to take over the land of Canaan.

Salman and Fatia sat without moving enthralled with the history. When Joshua had finished, Salman had a question. "How many of my people were freed from bondage?" He asked.

"Moses brought all of the Israelites out of bondage," he replied.

Salman heard him but it was hard to fathom for someone who had only known of the Hebrews being slaves for Pharaoh.

"All of them?" he asked incredulously.

Smiling, Joshua said, "Yes, cousin, all of them. The Prophet of God, Moses, led all of them out of bondage as was foretold."

Salman and Fatia hugged each other and he said, "I had dreamed of this day for so many years. What of my people, my tribe of Judah? Are they among the group with you in the Sinai?" He asked impatiently.

"My cousin, there are many from that tribe with us including Caleb here. I am sure he would be pleased to tell you about your tribe," Joshua explained.

Tears came down Salman's face as he silently thanked God. Fatia hugged him and Caleb noticed that her eyes were moist as well.

Interesting, Caleb thought to himself, that this young women viewed herself as a Hebrew although she was born of parents who were born in Kemet. Caleb felt something, an immediate attraction, for this woman although he had met her this very day.

Group 1

Gaddi and Igal sat with one of the local sorcerers who specialized in placing curses on people for a price.

"I want you to place a spell of death on two of our countrymen who are here with us," Gaddi said.

"I need to see them or I need an item of theirs such as a piece of clothing or hair," the sorcerer said.

"We will send them here; their names are Joshua and Caleb. I will tell them that you know a lot about this area as they are thinking of moving here. Are you sure it will work?" he asked.

"I guarantee death 1 day after I see them," he explained.

They paid the sorcerer and left with smiles.

Chapter 8

Day 11 late afternoon

Group 4

Palti and Shammua slept late. They were still recovering from sleeping uncomfortably outside the first night.

"Palti, are you up yet?" Shammua asked.

"Yes, I am up," he replied.

"I am famished," Shammua said.

"So am I," Palti added.

"Why have you not got up and gotten any food?" Shammua queried him.

"I do not want to go outside again because they could be looking for us."

"I am hungry; we must go out for food. It would be better if just one of us went to obtain food because they are looking for two foreigners, not one," Shammua suggested.

"Then, you should go out," he replied.

"I have a suggestion. Perhaps you should go out today and I will go out tomorrow. How about that as a solution?" he said.

Palti did not like that suggestion. "You should go because the guard noticed my face more than yours because I was closer to him."

Shammua knew that one of them had to go. So he relented and decided to go. "I will go outside today but it will be your turn tomorrow."

Palti was visibly relieved. "That is a great idea. Do not forget to get enough food for this evening too," he added.

Shammua got up and prepared to leave. After a few minutes, he said goodbye and left.

"I cannot believe that we are here." He thought to himself. He could not wait to leave this city. He would make sure that he and Palti would be more careful at the next city. He went into the market and purchased things that would last a day or two in case Palti did not go out the next day. He bought nuts, dates, fruit, fresh bread and olive oil for the bread. He did not buy anything to drink as they had no way to store it. There was water in the place they were staying at.

He was walking to the lodging place when he saw a group of soldiers making their way around the marketplace searching as if they were looking for someone--someone like them. He rushed back to the room after making sure that no one was following him.

He rushed into the room. Palti was up and looked anxious to eat. "What did you get us," Palti asked?

Shammua interrupted him and said, "They are looking for us."

Group 5

"When were you freed from bondage?" asked Salman.

"We were camped at the base of Mount Sinai for approximately a year where we received all the laws and regulations (as recorded in the book of Leviticus). We have created a new nation. Our numbers are 603,550 men and more than 2 million people in total (book of Numbers 1:1-46)," Joshua explained.

"More than 600,000 men are with you. It's an almost staggering number. That many Hebrews could be an amazing army, able to take over any land. Where will you settle?" Salman asked Joshua.

But at the moment of asking the question, the answer came into his mind. "You are here to scout out this land?" He asked.

Joshua looked at Caleb and said nothing for a moment. Joshua thought quickly because he did not want to lie but the fate of his people was in his hands. Could he really trust these people he had just met?   His thoughts were moving quickly. "We are just looking for land for our families, not the whole nation. I believe that they are going to move into the land north of Jerusalem." He did not want to lie outright because he could not jeopardize his mission this early. He would pray to God later for forgiveness.

"Forgive an old man's imaginations. I am just so very excited and am looking forward to being with my people again."

"Uncle, this is blessed news! Surely we will be seeing more of our people soon," Fatia guessed.

"You are probably right my niece," Salman said.

"We are thinking of moving our families here. What can you tell us about this city?" Joshua said.

"So, you both have wives and families?" Fatia asked but she was looking at Caleb when she posed the question."

Before Joshua could answer, "I am not married," Caleb said while looking directly into the eyes of Fatia.

Salman may be old but he could intuit what was going on between Caleb and Fatia even if Joshua was less perceptive in this area.

"The land here is very fertile and the weather is moderate because we are not that far from the great sea. The 30 foot walls make it mostly safe here."

Joshua was focused on every word that Salman was saying, taking mental notes. Caleb was having a hard time concentrating because every time he would look over at Fatia, he would get lost in her eyes. Salman continued to provid much detail into the life in Hebron.

Date 11 late afternoon

Group 3

Miriam arrived at the room several hours later. "Come in my dear," Shaphat said.

She came inside and sat down at one of the chairs.

Shaphat addressed the three others, "My cousins, perhaps its time for me to see what information I can get from this young lady," he explained. "Why don't you go over to the sitting area and have some drinks til I finish here."

Ammiel and Sethur laughed, and told him good luck. "She seems tough so you may have to take your time extracting information from her," Ammiel suggested.

"A real beast, that one appears," Sethur added in their native language. They knew that she did not speak Hebrew so she did not understand what was being said.

"Let us go out for while. We will be in the pavilion in an hour or two," Gaddiel stated.

Shaphat thanked them for the privacy.

Once everyone left, Mariam asked, "What is it I may do to be of service?"

He spoke her language and said, "I think you are very beautiful, my dear." He walked over to her and sat beside her. He placed his hand on her thigh. She was startled and jumped a little trying to move away.

"It's alright my dear. Your master, Mansur, said I can have you for the day." Fear showed in her eyes.

Shaphat became excited and tried to kiss her. She struggled against him. He decided another tactic. He got up and went to his satchel. He gathered up a few shekels and gave it to her.

Mariam had known men like that before. She knew that she was Mansur's property and he could order her to do whatever he wanted. Although she knew that, she had her dignity and would at least resist hoping that it would dissuade this foreign pig. He had lusted after her the first second she came into the room in the morning. Now, he had given her money expecting it to make it easy for him. The man persisted and she understood that his mind would not be changed.

There was a little voice in the back of Shaphat's mind that told him that he was breaking God's law. He decided to ignore that voice and proceed to fornicate with this young lady. The women last evening were professional harlots who engaged in sexual relations for money but Mariam clearly did not want to lay with him although she was a slave who did not have a choice. That voice in the back of his head tried to tell him that there was a difference between the women last evening and this young woman. That voice did not affect him either. Finally, the last little voice explained how last night was a sinful act and that he was going to choose to do another gravely sinful act this day too.

[*The Spirit of the Lord tried to place an image of light and goodness in Shaphat's mind but his lustful desires chose to sin and disobey the law of the Lord.*]

Shaphat lay with Mariam and made her do sinful acts with him. After a few hours, he told her to leave him. He washed up and made his way to the pavilion looking for his group.

[*Satan laughed again at the defiling acts of last night and the day.*]

Day 11 evening

Group 2

Nahbi and Geuel walked the entire city that day. They took in all that they could see. They were diligent in examining the military and social details of the Canaanites living in Hebron. They returned to their lodging house in the evening tired, and decided to discuss their opinions about the town with each other.

"I think that we have all the information that we need in this city," Geuel suggested as he sat down on his bedding.

Nahbi agreed with him and advised that they still have two more days of observing that could yield other interesting information.

"Perhaps, but I believe that we will just obtain more information about why we should not attempt to move out the inhabitants of this city," Geuel said.

"You are probably right but since we are here, we might as well continue to collect information," Nahbi said.

"So, you still believe that which Moses says about this land being the 'Promise Land'?" asked Geuel.

"This land is very fertile, and both milk and honey flows freely here," Nahbi said.

Geuel became excited and asserted, "But the men here are giants and this city is greatly fortified. I do not believe that Moses is telling us the complete story," he suggested.

"You are questioning God?" Nahbi asked.

"No, I am questioning Moses, the former prince and deliverer." Geuel held up his hand to wave off Nahbi's protestations.

"I know what you are going to say. Moses came back and delivered us. God has provided for us at every turn. I know what you are thinking but look at the men here, look at the thick walls. You tell me, could not God give us an easier city to take over?" Geuel asked.

"You have a point, Geuel. I don't know but there is a part of me which is thinking that we are seeing this in the wrong way. I just think that there is more about this trip than just viewing the land for military reasons. I am thinking whether I need to believe in something that I cannot see or touch; or my eyes which see an invincible army in an impenetrable city. Our lives and our children's lives are in our hands. Think about that," Nahbi explained.

"You're wasting your energy thinking about such things. That kind of thinking will get us killed," Geuel said.

"Perhaps you are right," Nahbi replied.

Present day

Salman interjected and explained to Jack how pain always comes when we ignore that small still voice of God.

Day 11 evening

Group 5

Joshua and Caleb started walking back to their room. They had agreed to return tomorrow for lunch with Salman and Fatia. As they came to the building, they saw Gaddi and Igal outside sitting at one of the tables.

Gaddi jumped up and said, "I am glad that you are here. We want to redeem ourselves. We have found a great man who knows a lot about this region. I told him that you are thinking about doing business here and moving your family here. He is willing to talk with you and Caleb right now."

They looked at each other and agreed to go with them. They made their way through the maze of corridors at the back of the marketplace. They finally came upon a shop without any signs. They walked in and saw an old man sitting in a chair. Joshua noticed that he was blind because his eyes were covered with a cloud. He was very old perhaps 90 or one hundred years old. The old man stood saying, "I understand you want to know about Hebron. I will tell you what I know, as I know it."

He motioned them to sit down beside him. "As you may know, Hebron is an ancient land. Some call this place Al-Khalil Ar-Rahman for the Beloved of God the merciful, in reference to Abraham. Abraham lived here a long time. Others call this place Hevron. This land was founded seven years before Zoan/Tanis. It's also called Qiryat Arba' which means the city of four. I believe this refers to the fact that the city was built on four hills. We are part of the Canaan but under the administration of the Egyptians. There are many tongues spoken here; Arabic, Hebrew, Moabite, Phoenician and Punic. The majority of the people are Amorites who are like you Hebrews and the Arabs, Semitic. Thus, there are many people traveling into this city, we are at the crossroads of Canaan. There is good business here and the land is very fertile. We flow with milk and honey. This city is protected well so you need not worry about your family's safety because the Army is invincible." The old man continued for 20 more minutes before finishing.

"Thank you for helping us," said Joshua.

The old man said, "You are welcome strangers. I have been told that you are thinking of doing business here. I can see things; give me you hand young man." Joshua laughed nervously because he did not want to give the old man his hand but before he could speak the old man grabbed both his hand and Caleb's, which was strange as he could not see. The old man's grip was stronger than his appearance. The old man let go after a few moments. "You will enjoy a very long life here. It is late, I must sleep now." they said goodbye and left the shop.

[*After they left, the face of the old man changed and became ugly, disfigured. He looked old but he straightened up and the cloudiness of his eyes left. He gained much vigor. He knew his touch would end of their lives of Joshua, the servant of the prophet of God, and Caleb. The old man who had appeared human, continued to change until he emerged into a winged creature with a human face; he was a demon of Satan.*]

Chapter 9

Day 11 Evening

Group 4

Palti had been pacing the room ever since Shammua had returned after getting the food. His pacing was starting to annoy Shammua.

"They are going to find us, then torture and kill us. How are we going to get out of the city? Palti asked.

"You should relax. I think they will lose interest after a day or two," Shammua suggested.

"How can you be so sure? Those giants are unstoppable, unbeatable. I knew that this was a bad idea when the elders of Benjamin nominated me to make this journey. Why me?" he shook his head.

"We just have to stay inside until we are ready to leave. They will not get us, if they do not see us," Shammua said.

"Maybe you should pray," Shammua said in a mocking tone.

Although Shammua was not serious, Palti took the suggestion to heart, got on his knees and said, "God, help us now." Palti did not know what else to say. They slept uncomfortably that evening with dreams of being chased.

Group 3

After Shaphat left the room, he had joined Gaddiel, Ammiel and Sethur. They embarked on a day of walking through the marketplace. They met many people and got a feel of the city. They even went inside the large temple for Baal to see the gods of the locals. The temple was busy and many people were coming in and out. There were money changers and other businesses being operated inside of the temple. The general mood in the city was jovial and happy.

After walking into the temple Ammiel remarked, "The people love it here. They would never leave easily or voluntarily. Life is good here."

"Isn't it? This place is a good place from what I see, but would be too difficult to conquer after seeing the soldiers and fortifications," Sethur said.

"So we should focus on what we can do while here," Shaphat said. They turned to look at him. "Having fun, while we're here!" He broke out a huge smile. "What better way to learn about this culture then to explore it from every angle."

Ammiel and Sethur laughed. Sethur slapped Shaphat on his back. They decided to head towards the room. Gaddiel listened to the exchange and felt that things were coming into place. He never believed that this mission was doable or desired. They should look for a better place without such huge adversities against them.

"I saw Mansur after I left the room, he said that he had a few young slave girls he wanted to bring over this evening for our entertaining pleasure," Shaphat said enthusiastically.

"You and your slave girls, why do you like them so?" asked Sethur.

"Well, you know that female slaves who are employed for the pleasure of her master or who he designates are the best type of fun because they are professional and are practiced in their trade. I enjoy being with someone who knows what she is doing," Shaphat explained.

"You should just call them what they are, concubines," Ammiel asserted. "Well, I enjoy the wine and the occasional slave girl but not like you Shaphat. I also like the dancing girls," he further admitted.

"Not to mention the dancing boys from what I understand," Shaphat stated loudly with a laugh.

The group laughed except for Ammiel who took the comment poorly although it was true. He was secretly hoping that he would be able to look into that pleasure later especially since Canaan was not too far from Sodom and Gamorrah.

"Come on, I am only jesting. Do not take my playful banter for ill will. I cannot cast any stones at anyone. I believe that each should have their fun as they see fit," Shaphat explained.

"Exactly," Sethur said. "We are all friends here, let us go back to the pavilion and forget about this mission."

"I agree," said Gaddiel. "Today has been a good day, let us not spoil it with harsh words," he suggested.

They headed towards the pavilion. Once there, they saw that Mansur had a table available for them already. They went on to enjoy a great repast, dancing girls and later that evening concubines. Gaddiel did not engage in last part of the evening but instead stayed up with Mansur.

"You are not enjoying the pleasure of our slave girls?" asked Mansur.

"I prefer to remain faithful to my wife back in my land. I thank you for your hospitality but the evening was perfect as is for me," Gaddiel replied.

"I see your countrymen are like us here, they enjoy all what Baal has to offer. Praise be to Baal," Mansur said.

Gaddiel stayed there for a few more hours talking to Mansur learning about the area and its peoples.

[*It was not Baal but Satan who looked on what was going on in the room at that same time. It always made Satan happy when he did not have to exert any influence on some people to partake in iniquity.*]

The three slave girls ran around the room naked being playfully chased by Shaphat, Sethur and Ammiel who were also naked. They not only did things which were forbidden by God but was considered a great sin. The girls had danced for them with their veils and then stripped down to nothing. The men lay with the women they had wanted initially and then they switched so that each man eventually lay with all the women. Shaphat, Sethur and Ammiel not only defiled the women but themselves too. The women dressed and were paid before they left the room.

[**God watched with sadness in His countenance. Sins involving sex were not innocent dabblings in forbidden pleasures, as so often portrayed by those participating in it, but powerful destroyers of relationships. They confuse and tear down the climate of respect, trust, and credibility for solid marriages and secure children. He had not overlooked prostitution in His law, as He has strictly forbidden it. It may have been practiced by the pagans or idol worshippers but sexual sin was not what He wanted for His people. Prostitution made a mockery of His original idea for sex, treating sex as an isolated physical act rather than an act of commitment to another. Outside of marriage, sex destroyed relationships. Within marriage under the right conditions with the right attitude, it could be a relationship builder. He had warned His people repeatedly about defiling themselves and undertaking sexual sin which only led to a broken and defeated life. He always maintained hope that one day, people would see themselves how He saw them.**]

Gaddiel stayed in the pavilion talking to Mansur while learning more about the area and its peoples. Eventually, when he saw the slave girls leave, he returned to the room.

Group 5 and Group 1

Joshua and Caleb were walking back to the room. They exited the shop together after seeing the old man but Joshua asked Igal and Gaddi to walk ahead of them because they needed to maintain their cover as much as possible.

"That was some good information for this mission," Caleb suggested.

"It was but that is not what on my mind at this time," Joshua said.

"What are you thinking?" Caleb asked.

"Let us get back to the room before we speak," Joshua said.

They walked in silence to the room. He told Gaddi and Igal that he would see them in several days. Inside the room, Joshua sat down on the bed.

"There is something not quite right about this whole situation with Igal and Gaddi. I definitely felt that the old man was more than he seems. I think he was a sorcerer," Joshua stated.

"That is not possible. You know the law. It is death to knowingly deal with sorcerers. They would never do that especially after the kindness you showed them," Caleb explained.

"I know; it is disturbing to even imagine that they willingly bring us into a place of magic." Joshua thought for a moment. Magic, the art which claims to produce effects by the assistance of supernatural beings. He knew that once someone used the sorcery they were opening themselves up to all types of troubles for the one who approached the sorcerer. He knew that great evil could come from anyone wishing to use sorcery for their own purpose.

"I saw the amulet he was wearing and the figurines in the shop all had cryptic pagan engraved inscriptions on them that I recognized when I lived in Kemet, black magic. I just have a feeling about the old man. I would have never let him touch me but he grabbed our hands with such force before I could tell him no. After he grabbed our hands, I knew that something was wrong with him," Joshua said.

"I see what you are saying especially because of the strength of the grip was not of an old man but of a young man. I did not notice the statues until you brought them up but I do remember some of the writing on the wall along the door when we came in," Caleb said.

"Exactly, I should have left at that time but I trusted them. But today, I learned a valuable lesson. I will make sure that I ask more questions before I follow any of these men regardless of what they say. I will always help them when they are in need but I will not trust until I can verify. We just need to maintain our trust in God and not man, man may disappoint but God never does," Joshua said.

Caleb agreed and got ready to bed down for the evening. Joshua took out his little scroll and began to make his report for the day.

"Day 11

Report 3

Today, there was much activity. I believe that the walls are about 25 foot high and about 20 foot thick. The soldiers each stand guard at their post for 10-12 hours each day making them very tired at the end of their shift. We made a thorough reconnaissance of the marketplace. The congested structures inside this walled city leave little room for open spaces. The marketplace is the main hub of congregation in the city. There are complete stables of horses and camels near the marketplace. The iniquity in this pagan land knows no bounds, prostitutes solicits for customers out in the open. There are groups of old people gathered to discuss their idols, the price of their goods, and the rumors brought back from foreign trading caravans. Business is flourishing in this city. The children run and play throughout the marketplace. The temples for Baal and El are outside of the marketplaces and also is very active.

Something strange occurred with Gaddi and Igal. They brought us to see an old wise man who claimed to offer us information on the land but I do not believe that this was the true purpose. We had agreed to not comingle unless absolutely necessary. I decided to help them the previous day when I saw them in the streets being ridiculed and jostled. The old man did indeed have information relevant to our mission but I SUSPECT that he is a sorcerer. I know that this is a serious accusation. I continue to trust in God and maintain constant faith that we are under His eternal protection. If additional information becomes available on this issue, I will advise.

We met another old man who is Hebrew and from Goshen. He is a definite fount of information and we will meet again tomorrow with him and his 'niece'. There was no sign today of the other teams except for Igal and Gaddi.

End of Report"

Joshua put away his scroll and got laid down on his bedding. After about an hour both he and Caleb begin having awful dreams and tossing in pain on their blankets.

[*God knew that the prince of lies, Satan, was never to be trusted to live up to his 'word'. He laughed at the adversary or the accuser because diabolos or Satan could do nothing without His permission. Satan had the power to afflict evil on men through sickness, natural catastrophes and through human agents. But the prince of evil spirits must eventually always flee from those who live righteously. He had given man free will and it was up to man to distinguish between His angels and the angels of Satan. He laughed because He knew the fate of Satan and his lies. The purpose of these misfortunes was to test the reactions of men; virtue is not genuine unless it sustains itself through adversity. He had allowed Satan to make an agreement with Him, no active interference with man. This agreement had been broken before but He had punished Satan many times previously. Satan was only to influence not use his demons, his darkness, evil angels, to sway the humans without permission from God. If Satan was going to actively participate in this mission, then so would He, thought God.*]

[*God allowed His wishes to be made known to Archangel Raphael, one of the seven angels who offer prayers to God's people. Raphael had always been a guardian of man; a healer and an expeller of demons. His healing power was not limited to illness and injury; it also protected travelers and defended men from the attacks of demons who inflicted corporate injury. He had been working since the dawn of humankind. He watched as Joshua and Caleb begin tossing and turning in their beds. The demonic curse began its work inside of them. Raphael appeared beside Joshua and Caleb, he spread his wings over them and they were healed immediately.*]

Chapter 10

Day 12 morning

Group 2

Nahbi and Geuel woke up early to start their reconnaissance of the hillside along the southwest portion of the city. They ate some eggs, bread and figs for an early repast.

They continued to do their jobs even though each had mostly made up their mind. Of the two, Nahbi had the more open mind and wanted to believe. He wanted to find something to favorably report regarding the ease of entering the city. Geuel was interested in just reporting what he had seen through his eyes of the world.

Geuel and Nahbi walked through the town looking up at the hill where the southwest portion of the town was built on. The houses were placed on the hill like stair steps. The houses were one to three stories high with date palms scattered throughout the area. The date palms rose to heights of 50 feet. The southwest portion seemed to contain the majority of the population. The housing area was densely populated. There were no standard streets between the houses but narrow passages where people and goods could be taken.

The housing areas were better organized than many cities which threw out their rubbage and garbage into the streets. In those cities, dogs would roam the streets living off the garbage in the streets. In Hebron, the city administrators arranged to have a garbage area near the north gate of the city where it could be disposed of outside of the city walls. Although there was a sizable population who lived outside of the walls and cultivated the city's farming lands, Hebron still had more than half its population inside its fortified city. In times of war, the outside farmers were provided protection inside the walls. Many of the city's merchants lived on this side of the town. Geuel and Nahbi learned a lot about the city by walking and talking to merchants. The inhabitants did not seem to live in fear; they seemed to be happy and thriving. People were a little standoffish at times because they were foreigners but once they bought something, the people were friendlier.

They made their way to the temple to see the pagans up close.

Group 5

Joshua and Caleb woke up and ate a small breakfast of bread, nuts, dates with fresh goat's milk. They decided to travel to the northeast portion of the city to see the housing settlements there. They were scheduled to have lunch with Salman and Fatia at midday. They left the room walking towards the northeast.

Group 4

Palti and Shammua awoke to a knocking at the door. They did not know who was there but suspected it was the landlord. Palti opened the door and his heart almost stopped. Commander Elrian stood there with several of his men.

"Are these are the men who ran from you?" Commander Elrian asked the two guards who were working the other day.

"Yes, my lord," they both responded. Palti and Shammua just stared dumbly as the scene play out.

"Take them away," the commander ordered.

The soldiers burst into the room and bound their hands. Palti and Shammua stood there hoping that it was not happening to them. The soldiers took them outside and begin leading them away. Palti was pleading with the soldiers, "what did we do? We have not done anything. Why are you taking us away?" His pleadings went on deaf ears.

"Take them back and begin the interrogation. I will be there shortly," Commander Elrian said as he continued surveying the area. He looked at the landlord. "So, you are sure that no one visited them while they were here?" the commander asked the landlord.

"I am sure, my lord. I heard the announcement which you put out looking for two strangers and I thought about these men because they had not left their room since arrived. They seemed suspicious to me so I told my cousin who works in your regiment," the innkeeper explained. The Commander gave him a few shekels and left after thanking him.

Palti and Shammua were being led towards the garrison when at that moment, Joshua and Caleb walked past them.

Palti wanted to scream for Joshua to help him but he knew that it would only get them all arrested. Shammua looked towards Joshua and Caleb with fear in his eyes. He did not know what to do, and in a moment he could not see Joshua or Caleb any longer.

[*Satan smiled as the seed he planted in the mind of the innkeeper had worked perfectly.*]

Group 5

"What should we do Joshua?" asked Caleb.

"Nothing, just keep moving at a discreet distance behind them. Do not look at them just generally follow in the same direction," Joshua said.

They followed the pair with the soldiers for almost 15 minutes. The group arrived at the garrison. Joshua and Caleb watched them go in. They went to the stables to look at the horses again while keeping an eye on the main door of the garrison. After an hour, they decided to leave because staying any longer would raise their profile and cause suspicion.

Group 2

"Where are you from?" the interrogator asked.

"Why have you arrested us?" asked Shammua.

He was immediately slapped in the face by the soldier. Shammua gave out a yelp; he was surprised at the fury in the strike. He wondered what would happen to them.

He decided to ask again. "What do you want?" Shammua asked. He was slapped again, even harder.

"Do you understand how this will work?" the interrogator asked. "I ask questions and then you answer; nothing else. You do not speak unless you are spoken to."

Shammua had tears in his eyes, he was afraid especially as he looked at the tools around the room. He wondered where Palti was being held. He could not focus on Palti but only himself now.

Palti was crying for mercy. He was on a board which was at a 45 degree angle. His head was lower than his feet. There was a cloth over his face. The interrogator kept pouring water over his face. He felt as if he would drown. What did they want? They had not asked him any questions yet. He was crying and pleading to tell them whatever they wanted to know.

Commander Elrian watched from the back of the room. He noticed the young Hebrew begging to tell them anything they wanted to know. The interrogator was the best. He had come from Kemet and was one of the best he brought with him. The interrogator gave him an inquiring look as to whether he wanted him to continue or stop; he was able to communicate this without a word.

Commander Elrian shook his head no. The interrogator continued to pour water on the young Hebrew's face. Sounds of gurgling were interspaced with screams. After another 20 minutes, before Palti passed out, it stopped.

"Now, perhaps you are now motivated to provide me the information I would like to know," the commander said.

It was strange what your mind focused on when you are in pain. Palti was slumped in the chair and noticed that Elrian was almost 7 ft tall. He was breathing heavy with fluids flowing out of his nose and mouth. "I will tell you anything. Please have mercy on me," begged Palti.

"We will see. I do not know what this word 'mercy' means but whatever it means, will depend on you," Elrian said.

"Why are you here?" he asked.

"We came here to spy to see if the city could be taken, if the Canaanites could be defeated," Palti answered, still breathing heavy.

"Who sent you here?" he asked.

"Moses," Palti answered coughing and trying to catch his breath.

Commander Elrian jumped up and stared directly at Palti.

"What! I need you to tell me everything. If you lie to me, I will peal the skin off your body while you live. Moses, the deliver of the Hebrews, sent you here to spy on the city?" He asked.

"Yes," Palti said.

Commander Elrian had dreamed of killing this man ever since he was transferred to this outlying city. Finally, his gods were smiling on him. He would find and kill the precious Jewish deliverer, Moses.

Group 3

Several hours later

Gaddiel, Shaphat, Sethur and Ammiel sat in the pavilion drinking a local yoghurt drink waiting for their food to come. The conversation was light hearted and lively. It was another detailed conversation about what had happened the previous evening.

Gaddiel only half listened as Shaphat was teasing Ammiel over his young slave girl laughing at him during intercourse. "She was laughing in order to keep from crying," replied Ammiel.

"I am sure that was the case," Sethur added while laughing.

The banter went back and forth for about an hour when Mansur came up and started speaking with Gaddiel in hushed tones.

"There has been a lot of excitement in the city today. My friend, the Pharaoh's commander for the military here has confided in me that they caught two Hebrew intelligence agents who were spying on the city looking for weaknesses in order to attack the city."

Gaddiel just looked at Mansur with an interested look on his face but on the inside he was in shock. He thought that if they caught part of the group then it would only be a time before they learned about them.

"The two Hebrew spies were spotted acting suspiciously around the northeast observation post and when questioned, they ran."

Gaddiel thought that it had to be those two young fools, Palti and Shammua. They were scared of their own shadow.

"They were eventually tracked down after the commander heard the report of two strangers running after being questioned. This new commander is from Kemet and is very good. The last commander would probably have never even followed up on any reports of strangers running or otherwise acting suspiciously."

Should he and the men leave the city or stay? Would it look more suspicious to suddenly leave then to stay? These are the questions that ran through Gaddiel's mind as Mansur spoke.

"Drink and enjoy my friends. All is well. I have some new dancing girls coming in an hour, they are Arabian. These girls are from my homeland, they are mistresses of the dance of the seven veils. I have wanted to see these girls for many years because I had heard about them. I will stay here and enjoy the entertainment with you," Mansur said.

Shaphat, Ammiel and Sethur gave a load roar of approval while Gaddiel was deep in thought. He could not say anything until Mansur left and it appeared as if Mansur was not going anyplace, anytime soon.

Group 1

Gaddi and Igal sat in their room thinking about the old sorcerer and the meeting with Caleb and Joshua.

"I saw them this morning leave the building. Joshua and Caleb looked good as if nothing was wrong. The old man guaranteed us that they would be dead today but they looked excellent this morning," Igal said.

"We should just wait, maybe it takes a little longer than just one night," Gaddi suggested.

"I knew we should not have worked with magic. It's forbidden in our law. We are going to be punished," Igal said.

"By who, no one will know what we did here once they die," Gaddi asserted.

"By God, that's who. We have sinned in the eyes of God," Igal said.

"Nonsense, the people in this land use sorcery and magic all the time. That is normal here. We are only doing what the people in this land are doing. You should relax and trust the magic," Gaddi said.

"Trust the magic but Moses said that we should trust in God," Igal said.

Gaddi gave a derisive snort without saying anything.

"You do not think that we should trust God," asked Igal.

"I did not say that, I just prefer to see my god on a daily basis. Its tough to worship a god that you can not see or touch," Gaddi stated.

"That is blasphemy Gaddi," Igal said.

Gaddi looked shamed and said, "You are right, I should not say such things."

The two sat in silence for a few moments.

Gaddi finally said, "We need to check to make sure that the sorcery worked. If it did not work then we need to do something else to make sure they do not return to the Sinai with us."

Garrison Headquarters

Group 2

Palti was in the most pain that he had ever felt in his life. The commander had left after he had gotten Moses' name. He tried to rest but the pain and the bonds kept him awake.

Shammua had been hit several more times. He noticed the tools on the table, many of which still had dried blood on it. He saw the commander walk into the room.

"Okay, Shammua, son of Zaccur, freed slave from Kemet. I know the whole story of why you are here, to spy on us. The next thing you say will determine whether or not you will be tortured and then dismembered. If you lie, then you die... painfully. Who sent you?" The commander asked.

Shammua did not know how he knew his name but the man was obviously privy to their mission. He deduced that the commander already knew so he gave the name.

"Moses," Shammua said.

Chapter 11

Day 12

Group 5

"So what should we do?" asked Caleb.

"We should meet our friends, Salman and Fatia as planned. We are almost late," Joshua said. They made their way through the city and arrived at the shop/home of Salman and Fatia.

Joshua and Caleb were greeted with a huge welcome by Salman. Salman and Fatia already had arranged a beautiful spread of local specialties along with some dishes they had known in Goshen. Lunch in Hebron was served late in the afternoon so by the time they arrived; the sun had already gone past its apex.

"Thank you again for inviting us over to your home," Joshua said. Salman enjoyed being able to speak in his native tongue while hearing the same accent he grew up with.

"I was asked by my Egyptian lord if I wanted to travel here those many years ago. I was given a choice to stay in Goshen by my parents. I decided to come because I had grown up hearing the stories of how the patriarchs of Israel were buried with their wives in Hebron (1). I had come to view those stories as a way to move closer to being free, if not in body, perhaps in the spirit. I had faith that a deliverer would come but over the years it seemed that I would not live to see it. I thank the Lord for bringing you into my life because you have made an old man happy," Salman said.

Fatia spoke up, "I keep telling you uncle that you are not old."

"I am child and one of these days you will have to get on without me. I just hope that I will be able to see you happily married before that time. It is no way for a young girl to live taking care of an old man."

Fatia was a little embarrassed so she decided to change the subject. "Have you tried the fresh salad? We grow it at our farm outside of the gates," she said.

"It's very good, thank you. You have a farm outside of the gates?" asked Caleb.

"Yes, we have a large farm outside the north gates of the walled city. Half of the city's population lives outside the walled city mostly farming. We cultivate all types of plants and spices which we use but also sell in the marketplace," Fatia explained.

Caleb and Fatia discussed life in Kemet as she had never lived in Kemet as an adult. She was curious to the customs and traditions. Throughout the afternoon, it became clear that she not only believed in the same one God as Caleb, she was more Hebrew than of Pharaoh's people. Caleb told her about the Holy book and the new scriptures that had been revealed to Moses. She was rapt as Caleb described the discussions Moses had with God.

Caleb and Joshua both expressed their gratitude for the great meal as it had been a long time since they had a banquet prepared for them.

"How long will you stay Joshua?" Salman asked.

"I think a few more days. I have basically seen all I need to see that this land is rich and flows with incredible fruit. The ground is fertile and the climate is great. It also seems safe here especially with the fortifications. I am just concerned with all the pagan and idol worship because my family is very conservative," Joshua said.

"The people here need some true believers living among them because they have no moral center. There are theaters here near the northern gate which puts on the most immoral plays and dramas. The people spend hours a day watching plays without any moral or spiritual value. There have been some plays through the years that were good and edifying but now the people want to see the most vile and sexual driven dramatic performaces. The people living here have forgotten about why religion was established, to make us better people not worse. The shows highlight prostitutes, fornication, family infidelity, sexual relations out of wedlock, incest and bestial relations, pederasts, drunkenness, general lewd and lascivious actions of the actors. The people come to the shows and then act out these base actions in real life. This city needs a strong group of believers who will show them a different path, a straight path into righteousness."

Their conversation was animated and went on for several hours. Although Joshua was concerned about the mission, he trusted God. He would maintain his faith that God would protect them to do the job they were sent on. Joshua was able to obtain very good information on the land and was able to make an appointment to go outside the gate the next day to see their farm. He noticed that Caleb and Fatia talked a lot during the lunch. He decided to ask Caleb about this on the way back to their room.

Group 2

Nahbi and Geuel walked inside the temple of Baal. The first thing they noticed was that there were several harlots inside appearing to solicit for customers. If Nahbi had any doubts he was approached by one young woman with a heavily painted face.

"Hello stranger. May Baal bless and protect you. Where are you from?" the lady asked.

Nahbi did not want to be rude or considered disrespectful as he did not know the local customs with the harlots.

"I am from Goshen in Kemet," he asked.

"Where is Kemet?" she asked.

"The people call the land "Kemet", the land of the black people. The land starts from the great sea and runs along the Nile River. The people living there also commonly call the land "Tawi", the two lands because of the upper and lower areas of the country, the valley and the delta. In its native language, the place is called "htk,pth" or the "palace of the ka of Ptah". In our sacred book, the land is called Misraim or Musru in Akkadian. The capital city is Mop or Mennofer."

"I know Musru, we had some Hebrews who came from there previously. I did not recognize the name Kemet. I have met many Hebrews in my life. They are nice people. I especially love Hebrew men because they have no foreskin." She said with a broad smile without any shame or embarrassment.

Nahbi nor Geuel did not know what to say as they were shocked. They rushed past the women bowing their head respectfully in order not to look into their eyes.

They walked further into the temple and noticed that there were couples engaged in sexual relations in one of the rooms off to the side. They looked at each other and rushed past the open room. There were pagan statues all around the temple. There were fertility statues of naked women as well as other statues of naked men. They noticed that the statues were various stages of arousal. Scenes of sexual perversions adorned the wall. They made it to a sacrificial alter where they supposed that the sacrificing of animals took place. "I guess they sacrifice animals here," Geuel said.

"You do not suppose that they sacrifice people here," Nahbi suggested. They looked at each other and decided that they had seen enough for the day. The put a half of shekel in the offering box and quickly left the temple. They made their way back to the marketplace for some lunch.

Garrison Headquarters

Group 4

Palti was thrown into the same cell as Shammua.

During the interrogations, Palti knew that he could he not withstand any more torture. The one thing that he wanted to keep in mind is to not tell his interrogators about the other men, not because he was brave or loyal but practical. If the others were captured then no one would be able to save them. Palti was on the dirt floor coughing and trying to get his breath.

Shammua looked up at Palti. Shammua's face was bloody and it was clear that he was in pain. "How could you tell them my name?"

"I did not know what else to say. We never talked about what to say if captured. I am sorry," Palti said.

Shammua looked at Palti closely. Even though Palti's face was not as beaten as his face, his pallor had a bluish tint to it and he continued to cough trying hard to catch his breath. He asked Palti, "Are you okay? What did they do to you?"

"I do not know what it is called. They tilted my head down and kept pouring water on my face. I felt as if I was drowning." He started another coughing fit. "I told them about our mission," Palti said.

"I know because they came and told me they knew everything," Shammua said.

"Yes, I told them all that I knew. I told them how Moses sent the two of us to collect information for a possible attack on the city but how our report would only say how unbeatable the Canaanites are and how impenetrable the city was," Palti said while looking into the eyes of Shammua.

Shammua instantly understood what Palti was telling him. He did not tell them about the other 10 spies still in the city. He smiled and looked up at little Palti with admiration. They never asked Shammua if anyone else was with him because Palti had appeared to be "broken". Shammua had to laugh inside at the strength of this little guy, maybe Palti was not such a worm after all. He reached out and grabbed Palti's hand in a gesture of solidarity. Palti looked up and nodded.

They lay there each nursing their wounds while Commander Elrian sat outside of the cell listening hoping to hear something useful. He had arranged them to be put together in the hopes that he would learn something useful. They seemed to corroborate each other's story that Moses sent two regular men, and not professional soldiers, to take a survey of the area in order to see if it would be possible to conquer Canaan.

Commander Elrian started to ponder on the best way to move against Moses. He wanted to exact revenge on this supposed Prophet of God but he needed more information. Pharaoh would not authorize an all out assault on Moses in the desert on the word of two pathetic Hebrews. Ramses had let the Hebrews go and did not want to mount an attack on them especially after the Red Sea killed all those good soldiers. And besides, Ramses was a broken man after the death of his son, his only heir. Elrian had sworn an oath to Seti to keep the kingdom safe and Ramses had betrayed that idea by freeing the Hebrews. Pharaoh should have killed Moses after the first plague. Seti was a great man and an amazing Pharaoh, but Ramses is half the man that Seti was. He would do what Ramses had failed to do.

A plan was coming together in the commander's head. The two Hebrew spies had said that they both believed that the city was impenetrable and that they would tell Moses that. They would recommend against attacking the city. He believed the two Hebrews because they were not professional spies or soldiers. If he believed that they were professionals, he would have killed them immediately after the interrogation. He needed to collect information on Moses. His number one was another of his soldiers from Kemet. He would let the two Hebrew spies go tomorrow and advise them to never return to Hebron except under threat of immediate death. He would tell his number one that he was going on a secret mission for several weeks leaving him in charge. During that time, he would spy on Shammua and Palti. He had been trained in espionage operations many years ago; he would use those skills to take on the persona of a traveling merchant. He would find where Moses was living and kill him himself.

Group 1

Gaddi and Igal had made their way back to the old sorcerer's house. The place looked different and did not look occupied in for many moons. They walked next door and asked a neighbor about the old man.

"There was an old man who lived there about a year ago but he died."

Gaddi and Igal looked at each other.

"We saw him twice yesterday," said Igal.

"I do not see how stranger, because no one has opened those doors for at least a year. You are mistaken; I went to that old man's funeral myself."

They thanked the neighbor and slowly walked away.

"I do not like this Gaddi," Igal said.

"I am sure the neighbor is mistaken. We know what we saw. Anyway, we need to focus on our next step. I guess we will have to do this the old fashioned way. There are always bandits in cities like this. We should be able to find someone to waylay them and end this problem for us," Gaddi said.

They walked back towards their room.

Group 3

Gaddiel, Shaphat, Sethur and Ammiel were at Mansur's pavilion watching the dancing girls. Gaddiel was paralyzed with fear thinking about whether Palti and Shammua would tell the Canaanites about the whole mission including them. He was worried and hoped that he would have an opportunity to talk to the others before it became too late. Mansur stayed there the whole time and kept the women dancing. Shaphat, Sethur and Ammiel were Mansur's allies as they wanted the dancing girls to stay as long as possible.

It was getting late and the sun was going down. Gaddiel was hoping that nothing would happen while he was waiting to tell the others about what happened. Gaddiel's chance came about an hour after the men decided to take the girls to the room.

Chapter 12

Day 12 early evening

Group 1

Café in Hebron

Gaddi and Igal sat in a cafe speaking with two men who claimed to be assassins. Gaddi had asked around and heard that this was the place where men like this congregate. Gaddi asked in the cafe while Igal sat down drinking tea.

[*Satan sent an influencing thought into the minds of the two men sitting in the corner. "Look at the strangers, there is an opportunity to make some money."*]

Muqatil and Ghadafa were sitting at the far end of the cafe. Muqatil had been a soldier for almost 20 years but now he was a mercenary for hire. Muqatil was about 45 years old with a long scar along his cheek. He was built sturdy and had a serious. Ghadafa sat beside Muqatil. They had met in Jerusalem during Muqatil's last job in that city over a year ago.

One year ago in Jerusalem…

Muqatil had taken a job to assassinate a wealthy merchant. Ghadafa was providing protection for the merchant's associate in the building next door. Muqatil came in for the kill after killing the man's bodyguards. The merchant's associate heard the noise and ordered his bodyguard, Ghadafa, to intercede. Ghadafa had just started as this man's bodyguard and had no loyalty to him except to protect his life, not his associate's life. Although Ghadafa did not know Muqatil at that time, he recognized him as a professional; and as such, he did not want to interfere not knowing who else was there or the conditions surrounding the assassination. Ghadafa's employer became furious at him but his job was to protect his principle, not random friends or associates he had never met before. Ghadafa had learned a long time ago to stay focused on the job you were being paid for. His employer yelled and tried to get him to stop the assault. At the death blow, Muqatil saw Ghadafa staring at him but standing his ground against his employer's loud attempts to get him to help the target. Ghadafa was fired from his job but Muqatil found him later that evening.

Ghadafa was immediately on guard when he saw Muqatil but he held up his hand and explained, "I have no quarrel with you, I am a professional and no one had paid me to kill you. I wanted to thank you for not interfering today. I have a question for you. Why didn't you do as you were ordered by your employer to stop me?"

Ghadafa relaxed a bit realizing that if Muqatil wanted to kill him, he would have been dead already. "It was not my job to protect that man. Too many people enter into situations on a whim or on the spur of a moment without knowing the operating conditions they are going into. I did not know what the situation was nor did I know who else you had around. The man I was protecting did not understand this fact. What if your kill was a distraction for me to leave him the one I was protecting, so that someone with you could kill my employer after I left. Being a good protector is about maintaining focus; your job was none of my concern except to ensure that my employer was safe."

Muqatil nodded his head intrigued with this young man. Ghadafa was big, about six and half feet tall weighing nearly 300 pounds. He was quick witted and seem to understand security. He had been looking to hire a partner since his last one was killed in separate job while visiting his family in Damascus. He hired Ghadafa as his partner and had been satisfied since that time.

Back to the café in Hebron…

Something made Muqatil look over to the stranger walking around the cafe asking questions. "I'll be back," He said to Ghadafa. He got up and walked over to the man.

"Friend, what is it you seek?" Muqatil asked.

He looked at him and said in a hushed tone, "I seek an assassin," said Gaddi.

"Look no further stranger, Baal has answered your prayers. I am who, you are looking for," he said.

"Follow me," Muqatil said. Gaddi waved over to Igal and urged him to come. Igal looked uncomfortable but got up and walked to where Gaddi had been led. The two big men looked up as Igal came to the table.

"This is my friend Igal, I am Gaddi." Igal sat down nervously.

"I am Muqatil and this is my associate Ghadafa," he replied.

"We have two associates who have cheated us in business; we wish them to be killed today. They are in the city now staying in the same building as we are," Gaddi stated in a straightforward manner. At the word 'killed', Igal flinched visibly.

"Are you sure you want them killed, your friend seems to be bothered about that," Muqatil said, Igal noticed that he had a long long scar on his cheek.

"We are sure. How much would it cost us?" Gaddi asked.

"10 gold pieces and we will guarantee that the job will be completed by the end of this evening," the other one said.

"That would be excellent," Gaddi said. "But 10 gold pieces is a steep price for something we could get anyone to do in this city," he explained.

"Go ahead, get someone else. If you want amateurs then pay an amateur price. We guarantee our work or you do not have to pay us. It's your decision; pay our price or leave, we are busy," Ghadafa said.

"So, we give you 10 gold pieces and then we never see you again. We may be strangers but we are not imbeciles."

"You don't have to pay us now. Pay us when we are done. We trust you," Muqatil said.

"You trust us but you don't even know us," Igal said.

"I trust the process," Muqatil explained.

Gaddi and Igal were a little confused, "what process?" asked Igal.

"I trust the process that if we do this job and you do not pay us, I trust that we will kill you in a most painful fashion you ever imagined," Muqatil said.

Gaddi and Igal looked at each other, not sure if they had done the wrong thing in hiring these men. They told the two men the details they needed for the job to include description, measurements and where they were staying. Muqatil explained that they would wait for Caleb and Joshua to return to the hotel this evening.

They arranged to meet in the morning in the same place to settle up accounts. "Make sure you bring the money when you come," Ghadafa explained.

Gaddi and Igal left the cafe. Igal was clearly upset over the whole process. "We are getting in deeper and deeper, when will it stop?" Igal asked.

"This will end the matter. Did you see the scars and battle wounds on those men; they are professionals and our problem will end," Gaddi said.

"I hope so because I cannot take any more of this evilness." Igal said. Gaddi did not say anything hoping that he was right.

Group 3

Gaddiel watched as the dancing girls made their way to the room. Mansur had stayed in the restaurant as other customers had come into the place.

"Have fun, my friend. Now, you are getting into the spirit," Mansur said to Gaddiel.

The eight of them went into the room. Shaphat took down the separation partitions after coming into the room. "Ladies, I need you to get ready to do that dance again but this time you should finish with all of you clothes on the floor," Shaphat laughed and sat down expectantly.

Gaddiel took out some money and paid the ladies each 5 shekels. "I need you to leave now. I thank you for your performance."

"What are you doing?" asked Sethur.

"Trust me, we need to talk now," Gaddiel said in their dialect of Hebrew so that the dancing girls would not understand.

"I hope this is good, you have ruined our night," said Ammiel.

The four ladies left happy as they were paid handsomely without having to do any degrading acts.

"Our night has already been ruined," Gaddiel explained what Mansur told him.

The three sobered up very quickly. It was too late to leave so they decided to spend the night and decide tomorrow.

["*Be on guard,*" *The archangel Raphael whispered to Joshua.*]

Group 5

Joshua and Caleb were heading back to their room when Joshua felt something warning him.

Muqatil and Ghadafa had recognized Joshua and Caleb immediately. They had waited for two hours and were rewarded. Joshua and Caleb walked along the path to the room. Muqatil and Ghadafa jumped out of the passageway with knives drawn.

"Friends, you do not want to do this," Joshua said as he held up his hands.

Muqatil lunged at Joshua with the knife in his right hand. Joshua had seen much in his life, his name meant "Yahweh is salvation". He was born into slavery and worked as a stone cutter most of his life in the slave pits of Pharoah. That life of toil built much strength in his body. He became a warrior for Moses and his faith filled him with power. On this day, he could not see what was behind him; the outstretched wings of Raphael.   Raphael, the angel protector of travelers, who defended men from the attacks of demons.

Muqatil moved quickly towards Joshua who parried his strike with his left hand and then checked it with his right hand. Joshua immediately struck Muqatil with the heel of his palm on the right side of his face with almost superhuman speed. Next, Joshua's right hand in the form of a knife edge, palm up, shot out in a wide arch, struck the left side of his attacker's head, dropping him instantly. He then kicked him in the face as he was falling down. The entire encounter had taken only a few moments and Muqatil was on the ground stunned. Joshua immediately turned towards the giant (Ghadafa) who had started moving towards Caleb.

Ghadafa was shocked at the speed at which the one called Joshua had disabled Muqatil. He had worked with Muqatil for a year and knew him to be a fierce warrior; this Joshua moved faster than he had ever seen a man move before. He could not let this Hebrew or the other one get away. He moved to attack Caleb first.

[Raphael had used his 'God-spell' power to propel Joshua's movements and now he did the same for Caleb.]

Caleb saw the giant coming towards him and kicked the big man in his left knee using his right foot. The big man instantly was thrown off balance, and by that time Joshua was on him. Joshua had pulled his knife out his waistband and did exactly the opposite of what Ghadafa thought he would do. Instead of striking high to his enemy's neck or face with his knife, Joshua rolled on the ground and used a smooth stroke to cut the femoral artery on the thigh of the giant. The blood came, flowing freely. The giant brought his hand to his leg as he knew it was a potential death cut, Joshua leaped in one fluid motion starting low with the knife to make a smooth cut under the neck of the giant. Ghadafa could not believe that this man had bested him in hand to hand combat. He fell to his knees and hoped that Baal would welcome him.

Because Joshua had the giant at his mercy, Caleb was able to recognize the other adversary (Muqatil) was getting up to make another attack. Caleb bounded over to him and was able to use his dagger to end his life quickly.

"Are you alright?" Joshua asked.

"Yes, I am well," Caleb said.

"They could have left, but they seemed determined. I have a bad feeling about this attack," Joshua speculated.

"I too feel uneasy about it too," Caleb agreed. They walked to their room.

Group 2

Nahbi and Geuel sat in their room. A candle cut through the darkness while they talked. "Did you see those brazen harlots solicit us in the temple. That disturbs me," Nahbi said.

"This town is corrupt," Nahbi said.

"But it's their choice to live a life of iniquity. This is why I believe it will be difficult to defeat them, people living in sin rarely voluntarily decide to change their ways. The people will fight to remain in the darkness," Geuel said.

Group 5

Joshua and Caleb were both exhausted mostly because of the attack and the accompanying stress. Before Joshua went to sleep, he had to write his report for the day.

"Day 12

Report 4

On this day, two members of our group, Palti and Shammua, were arrested today. I believe that they were arrested for espionage. We saw them being taken to the military garrison today. We waited but they were not brought out so I can only surmise that they are being interrogated. I considered leaving the city but I trust in God. Caleb and I continue to be faithful and not swayed by the evil practices of the city. I feel that we have made some progress in our mission and will visit some of the farms outside of the perimeter tomorrow. On the way back to our room in the evening, we were attacked by two bandits. We foiled the attack but found it suspicious and will investigate further.

End of Report."

Day 13

Group 4

"Tell your people that Hebron will never fall to the Hebrews. You are free to go. You have 2 days to recover from your wounds but after that you must leave the city, never to return under threat of death," Commander Elrian said.

Palti and Shammua both agreed as they got up, were released and limped out of the garrison. They were happy to escape with their life.

Commander Elrian watched them leave. It would take him a day to hand over his duties to his number one. He would send out two spies to surveil and observe the two Hebrews until then, when he would take over.

Chapter 13

Day 13 early morning

Group 1

Gaddi and Igal were in the cafe early waiting to meet with Muqatil and Ghadafa. They were told to be there as soon as the cafe opened. Gaddi was already devising the story in his mind of what he would tell Moses about Joshua and Caleb being killed by bandits. They heard a few of the rougher looking men talking about something that happened last night.

"Yes, they had their throats cut. There was a lot of blood and it appeared that they were professionals. I can not believe that they were able to kill the both of them," one man said.

Gaddi jumped up and asked, "Who was killed?"

"Someone killed Muqatil and Ghadafa last night late. They must have been great assassins to do that because they were fierce fighters. It must have been for revenge on that Jerusalem job they did together," another man speculated.

Gaddi had heard enough; he grabbed Igal and led him out of the cafe.

"No no no no no no, this is not good. I can not believe this." Igal became emotional and was walking very fast as he exited the cafe.

"I am going, leaving now to return to Sinai and I will repent. This is not happening. I have to leave," Igal said loudly to himself.

"Calm yourself and keep your voice down," Gaddi said.

Igal kept walking away from Gaddi. Gaddi ran up beside Igal and grabbed him by the tunic. "Listen, they do not know that it was us who arranged it. You know Joshua is a warrior so this was a possibility," Gaddi said while trying to calm Igal down.

He continued, "We are still fine. We just have to find another way," Gaddi said.

"I am through! I can not do this anymore. I can not take the stress. I just want all of this to end," Igal said.

"Look, this will not end until they are dead. We are still in trouble for our actions. Trust me Igal," Gaddi explained. Gaddi grabbed Igal's face and said, "Look, I know that this has not turned out as we expected. We can still make everything right. In a few weeks, we will be back in the Sinai with this as a forgotten memory. We need to stay focused and pretend that nothing has happened until this is over. If we see them, we have to act as if nothing has changed. Do you understand?" Gaddi asked.

Igal was starting to relax a bit. "I understand."

They decided to return to their room.

Group 4

Palti and Shammua made their way back to their room. Commander Elrian's two spies, 'one' and 'two' as Elrian called them, followed at a discreet distant. The spies had been told to watch the two Hebrews and to see if anyone visited them or if they visited anyone else. If they left the city within the day, one of them would return to the garrison to get the commander while the other stayed and observed.

Palti went into the room first and fell hard on the bedding. Shammua went to the owner looking for a pitcher of water and food for them.

"They let you go?" the owner said.

"We did nothing wrong," Shammua said defiantly.

"It looks like you did something wrong by how your face looks," the owner said.

"I guess I should thank you for this. I know it was probably you who falsely accused us," Shammua asserted.

"I only did my job as a citizen of this town. There was a notice looking for two strangers, I did my job. You would have done the same if you were in my position," he claimed.

"Well, I thank you for your hospitality," Shammua said snidely.

Shammua continued, "We are back and will be here for two more days because we paid for two more days. You probably want us to leave but we will not. We will stay here until then, if you have a problem with that, you can deal with the commander. I need a pitcher of water and some food now," he demanded.

"I will see what I can do," the owner said as he walked to the kitchen.

After a few minutes, a slave girl brought out a tray with drink and food. Shammua thought that the owner must have felt guilty and was trying to make it up to them. The slave girl followed him to his room and put the tray on the table in the room. She instantly noticed that both of the two men looked really bad as if they had been tortured. "Is there anything else you desire? She asked.

"We are fine. Thank you," Palti said. She left and explained that she would check on them later.

"I am not even sure if I can eat without experiencing in my jaw or face," Shammua laughed.

Palti also laughed and said, "Please stop, your laughter is causing me pain in my chest. Although they were both in physical pain; the reality that they had escaped death and more torture had taken an emotional toll, the laughter came as a way to cope with the last few days.

Sinai Peninsula at the slope of Mount Horeb, the mountain of God

Moses sat and prayed for Joshua and Caleb as he felt that they were going through some special trials and tribulations in Canaan. He knew their hearts and the faith that each had for the Lord. He prayed for them to continue to have strength and faith. The stubbornness of the Hebrews had constantly been a hindrance to Moses and he was worried at how displeasing it was to God.

Moses had presented "I AM WHO I AM" to Israel as the God with an irresistible moral will and who imposed His standards of conduct on the people. He presented the Lord; as God presented Himself to Moses, the Lord of His-story (history), who moves events in order to bring His people to their destiny. Sometimes this would require people to go through painful situations such as the years of bondage in Egypt or being sent to prison. God wanted the people to dwell in a land of milk and honey but the people had been conditioned for so many years, it was hard for them to believe and trust. Sometimes those who live in pain for so long; only know pain and fear.

Moses was worried that they people would not let themselves obtain the great destiny God intended for them. Moses feared that his people would inherit a future less than what was promised to them by God through their disobedience and unbelief. Moses also presented God as the Lord of nature who employed the forces of nature to realize His purpose as He had done when He parted the Red Sea. Moses trusted God without doubt or question, and wished the people could too. His prayers for Joshua and Caleb were not for God to protect them, because God would do what God would do, but that they continued to be strong in the face of pagans and idol worshipers. Moses did not trust the other men sent with them because they were 'of the world' and desired worldly things. Moses had the sense that the Lord was testing and preparing Joshua for something greater. He knew that this would be Joshua's greatest test which would allow him to become the man that God intended him to become. Moses loved Joshua as a son and wanted the best for him. He believed that Joshua was predestined to be a great man. Moses prayed that Joshua and Caleb would continue to love God with all their heart, mind, soul and strength, as he did.

Group 3

Gaddiel, Shaphat, Sethur and Ammiel all woke up in foul moods that day. Each slept fitfully because of the news of the arrest of Palti and Shammua. They arose and had a repast brought their room so they could discuss the issue in quiet.

"I believe that we should stay and not leave which would look suspicious. The people here know that, we too, are Hebrews by our speech and dress. We have acted as if nothing has happened and I believe that we will be able to maintain our cover until day after tomorrow. Further, I have been thinking, perhaps that we will have information on them today from Mansur," Gaddiel explained.

"I am not sure. Perhaps we should just leave and meet outside northern city walls as agreed in 2 days but in the meantime we could travel further north," Sethur proposed.

"I am of the same mind as Gaddiel," Ammiel said.

"I do not know the best way in this case but will acquiesce to the majority of the group," Shaphat asserted.

"Okay, it is agreed that we will each vote. But before we vote, I would add that our behavior here will support that we are merchants who are enjoying what Hebron has to offer. Our profile is not one of spies but of worldly, sophisticated men not superstitious men of religion. Who wants to stay?" Gaddiel asked.

"I," Ammiel said.

"I," stated Gaddiel next.

"Okay I agree too," replied Shaphat.

Sethur sat there and said, "I guess it's decided without my vote but I just want to say that I think we should leave."

"It's decided," said Gaddiel. "Let us go out to find Mansur making sure that we act like merchants and not like spies."

Group 5

Joshua and Caleb arose early and prayed to the Lord. They each thanked the Lord for protecting them and allowing them to wake up that day. They went outside and bought some figs, dates, bread and yogurt for breakfast. They ate in silence reflecting on the events of the past day.

"You fought like a lion yesterday," Caleb stated.

"I felt empowered and strong, praise God! Let us get ready to meet Salman and Fatia," Joshua said trying to not focus on the speed and power he felt inside of him during the confrontation, not knowing where it came from. They made their way to Salman's place wanting to be on time.

"Hello, my friends. It is so good to see you this fine day, Praise "I AM." Salman had taken to calling God the name provided to Moses.

"It is good that you came early. There is a lot of activity today in the marketplace especially around your area. Some fierce bandits are lurking around here because two of the local mercenaries for hire were killed last night. The military will probably be looking for any strangers today so it good we will be out of the city today," Fatia said.

Joshua and Caleb looked at each other. "Please, tell us about this?" Joshua asked while being led inside into the salon.

"There were stories about these two men, Muqatil and Ghadafa, who were supposedly assassins for hire. They were killed last night most likely in an attempt to kill someone for money."

Joshua and Caleb again gave each other a brief look realizing what they had feared; someone had most likely hired the two men to kill them.

"Enough of this morbid talk, we should get ready to leave. It should take us an hour to get there," Salman said.

"It is not too much for you to walk that far?" asked Salman.

"No, I may be old but I feel great. It is actually time for me to visit the place so you are doing me a favor by escorting me there," Salman said.

They started their short trek outside the city gates to their farm.

Group 2

Nahbi and Geuel awoke and made their way to the center of the marketplace for some breakfast. They had been in discussion during the day on what their mission really was.

"I think we were sent here to see how we are going to attack the city," Nahbi asserted.

"You are wrong, we were sent here to determine if we could attack the city. It does not matter anyway because it is not possible. We would do better to start business dealings with this city," Geuel said.

"I know I have said this before but I just believe that we are looking at this in the wrong way," Nahbi said.

Commander Elrian had received a report that two assassins had been killed the previous night by apparent professionals. He gathered up a squad of troops and made his way to the area where the killings had taken place.

"What do you think happened?" the commander asked his lieutenant in charge of crime for the area.

"Commander, these two men were professional assassins. Their names were Muqatil and Ghadafa. They would spend most of their days in a cafe in the north end of the city when they were not on a mission. They were fierce fighters and it's surprising to believe that anyone could have waylaid them without their knowledge. It was probably a fair fight where they were bested. Its either that or they chose the wrong job against the wrong target or targets," the lieutenant said.

"When was the last time you remember two men such as this were killed in the marketplace," the commander asked.

"Never, not in my memory can I recall two professional assassins who were killed here," he replied.

"Thank you, good work. Please increase patrols," Commander Elrian said.

Group 4

The Commander's spies saw the one Hebrew buy goods and then returned inside the house. The two Hebrews had not come out for several hours.

Palti and Shammua stayed inside after eating; gaining strength and sleeping. They had decided to stay in the next day and then leave on the morning after that, as scheduled. They did not want to accidently run into any one from the other groups which could jeopardize them and the other groups.

Group 1

Gaddi and Igal returned to their room and watched the soldiers around the marketplace. While not mentioning his fears to Igal, Gaddi secretly worried about whether those in the bar would mention them.

Chapter 14

Day 13 afternoon

Group 1

Gaddi and Igal decided to stay in this day. They watched squads of soldiers come through the marketplace. Gaddi was concerned that it would get back to soldiers that they were the ones who hired the two assassins. The whole plan was coming apart but he had to appear, at least to Igal; that everything was going to be alright.

"Igal, we are going to wait until we leave this city before we decide to plan anything else against Joshua and Caleb," Gaddi said.

"That is the best idea that you have come up with since we've arrived. I am pleased that we will postpone this endeavor," Igal said with relief.

"Let us celebrate then, perhaps we should find some entertainment," Gaddi suggested.

Group 3

Gaddiel, Shaphat, Ammiel and Sethur sat in the pavilion as if nothing had occurred but in reality they were waiting for Mansur to show up. They had ordered lunch and were brought out some delicacies especially made for them. Mansur had left instructions that they should be treated as 'honored' guests which meant they should be treated almost as family. Paying family, Gaddiel thought. It was all about the money even in the perilous times. Life was moving fast with almost 2 million Jews freed in total, looking to find a safe place to live. There were so many changes happening now.

Gaddiel believed the Hebrews needed a new type of leader, one who was not so dogmatic and narrow-minded in his thinking. Gaddiel thought that he was that man. He needed to make a name for himself during this operation and it would not be made with them slinking out of the city after their two associates were captured. The story that would be told over and over was how he led them even when two of their own were captured. His courage would be talked about especially when it came to not putting his people in the line of fire by attacking a heavily fortified city like Hebron. He knew their fates were connected to partnerships with the various cities in Canaan. He was making a very good connection with Mansur who knew the Garrison's commander. Gaddiel would speak with Mansur today about future trading alliances with his people. Gaddiel knew that he had vision for this new age. They would make statues of him in the future. He would be remembered as the real deliverer of his people, the one who took them from the desert to a thriving new economy.

Group 5

Joshua, Caleb, Fatia and Salman reached the farming areas after the sun reached its apex. Joshua, Caleb, Fatia walked while Salman rode on a camel. The distance was not far but because of his age, Salman preserved his energy by riding. The outer cultivated fields were huge and lush. Joshua noticed that the guards on top of the fortified walls could easily view all the farms and see invaders coming from far away. Joshua noticed that the observation post guards would be able to alert the farmers thus allowing them time to enter the gates for protection. It was an interesting and creative approach to security because there was not enough room inside the fortified walls for large farms to produce food for the whole city. There were a few small farms inside the gates but that was mostly for emergencies in case of a prolonged siege. The farms outside of the gates were the real food supply for the city. Joshua was able to see that they had created a system which worked for them.

Joshua and Caleb were amazed. "Look at the beautiful fig trees, grape vines and vegetables," Caleb said. There must have been 100 or more hectares of crops some of which they had never seen before. There were olive trees as well but it was the fig trees which were more impressive. The fig trees reached a height of at least 35 feet; its spreading branches and broad, thick leaves provided shade for several workers taking a break. Joshua knew that figs were a great crop because the fruit could be eaten fresh or dried, and dried figs were made into delicious cakes. Figs were also used for medicinal purposes.

"We keep what we need to live and then sell the rest in town and to other cities. It has been a blessing for us. The figs and grapes are our biggest cash crops. We also have goats, cattle, camels and sheep. They were brought to the stable areas and saw hundreds of animals. There was so much activity going on. They saw workers milking goats and cows. They saw milk and butter being made along with the beekeepers taking honey from the honeycombs.

Joshua and Caleb looked at each other and Joshua spoke first although each was thinking the same thing, "A land of milk and honey!"

Fatia and Salman were proud of their farm. Fatia explained, "This is the largest enterprise of its kind not owned by Canaanites. We have many workers whom we take good care of. The workers are allowed to farm a portion of the land for free and they can sell the products themselves. We give each worker a portion of food from our farm for free.

Joshua and Caleb were pleasantly surprised how kindly both of them were towards their workers, unlike most employers of the time. Joshua now realized after seeing with his eyes how lush and fertile the land was. From inside the city, it was difficult to get an accurate idea of how good the land was but from this perspective, it was clear. The land that God had chosen for them was an amazingly beautiful land; ripe for them to take. Joshua never had any doubt but he needed information for those who only viewed the world through their natural eyes instead of through a God-conscious lens.

"Can I take some of these grapes, figs and a few other things back with me?" Joshua asked.

Fatia said, "Take whatever you want." Joshua took some grapes and figs as evidence for those who did not believe. He carefully wrapped it up for the journey.

They decided to have a small repast before returning to the city. They sat down and had a snack of fresh figs, dates, milk, honey and other great food. "Joshua, the other night you gave us details of the Exodus out of Kemet but tell us again but in more detail how you evaded the Pharaoh's men."

Joshua was not much of a story teller but did his best, "There were 600 hundred of Pharaoh's war chariots bearing down on us. We had no weapons and were with almost 2 million men, women and children. We were slow moving while Pharaoh's men were gaining fast. There were two men in each chariot, one to drive it and on warrior to fight. We were trapped against the Red Sea and the chariots were sweeping in for the kill. The people grew nervous and begged to go back to Pharaoh. Moses, the great Prophet of God, was not worried. Those stubborn unfaithful Hebrews had seen all the magnificent blessings from God but they were still unbelieving. His people's response was fear, whining and despair. When it looked as if there was no way out, Moses called upon God to intervene. Moses said, 'Do not fear! Stand by and see the salvation of the Lord which He will accomplish for you today; for Pharaoh's men whom you have seen today, you will never see them again forever. The Lord will fight for you while you remain silent.' Then the Lord said to Moses, 'Why are you crying out to me? Tell the sons of Israel to go forward (1).'"

"I will never forget those words because God told Moses to stop praying and move. Sometimes, we know what to do but are afraid to take the next step. That is what God was trying to tell us while urging us forward. 'The Lord swept the sea back by a strong east wind all night and turned the sea into dry land, so the waters were divided (2).' The people saw that while there was no apparent way to escape; God does not want us to panic but to live with faith. The people learned that what is impossible for man; is possible for God," Joshua finished his story.

Salman had tears in his eyes and Fatia was mesmerized as well. "That is such a beautiful story; I could hear it a hundred times."

"I am glad that it touched you," Joshua said. They ate some more fruit and Joshua remarked how theirs were the freshest fruits he had ever tasted.

"Caleb let me show you the date and nut trees. You can tell me another piece of scripture while we walk. Caleb and Fatia walked off for a short time. Salman spoke up," I think that my niece and your friend are fond of each other," Salman said.

"How do you feel about that?" Joshua asked.

"You are good men, I know this. I prayed that someone would come for her because I am not well. Please do not tell her but I worry about her and do not want to leave her alone. I am just an old broken down Hebrew who have worked too hard and long. But I am at peace because I now know that our people are free and no longer in bondage. I have seen much and Fatia is a good woman, I consider her flesh of my flesh. She is as Hebrew as any Hebrew woman you know. There has been Hebrews who have come here over the years to visit the tomb of Abraham. During that time, she has seemed more comfortable with Israelites than anyone of Pharaoh's people who live here. I taught her our law because she wanted to know it. I love her and want someone to love her as well."

Meanwhile, Caleb and Fatia walked towards the tall trees. "Tell me about God's law and how we should live," she asked?

"God gave Moses Ten Commandments for us to follow." He paused before reciting the words from heart.

"These are the ten:

1) You shall have no other gods before the Lord.

2) We should not make for ourselves any idols. We should not worship any idols nor serve them for Our God said He was a jealous God. We should turn away from the pagan ways of our fathers. We should have loving-kindness to others and those who love God and keep His commandments.

3) We should not take the Lord's name in vain.

4) We must remember the Sabbath day, to keep it holy.

5) We must honor our Mother and Father.

6) You shall not commit murder.

7) You shall not commit adultery.

8) You shall not steal.

9) You shall not bear false witnesses against your neighbor.

10) You shall not covet your neighbor's house, wife or any of his property," Caleb stated from his memory.

He continued, "It's all about serving God. The first four commandments are about our relationship with the Lord, while the other six are about our relationship with each other, our neighbors," Caleb said.

"I like how you explained it. I have a question, who is our neighbor?" she asked.

"Everyone is our neighbor. If we strive to do good and please God, then we will have a life of joy but if we rebel then pain will only follow us. Obedience and faith are the cornerstones of serving God. If we obey then we will have a better life. It's the least we should do for a God who loves us," Caleb said.

They sat there and each contemplated what Caleb had said.

"I sometimes wish I was born a Hebrew and not from among Pharaoh's people," she blurted out.

"Why is that?" He asked with genuine curiosity.

"I am repulsed at how Pharaoh treated the Hebrews, all those years of bondage. Also the ways of those in Kemet are wicked; the idols and lewd practices are not wholesome. I would not want someone who I came to love to reject me if I was not a Hebrew and he was," She looked down with a little embarrassment.

Caleb had sensed the strength of Fatia but also the pain and sadness she had endured to lose her parents and her husband. She was a stranger to him, but his heart ached for her. Was she referring to him? Could she mean him? It was too much to hope for. She was born from a family of Kemet, she was not Hebrew. Was it forbidden to marry outside? She was not Canaanite nor was she a pagan. She worshiped the same God that he worshipped. There were many questions swirling around in his mind. They all stopped when he looked into her eyes and saw his love reflected back to him. He decided to do something utterly insane, he kissed her and she responded back by kissing him in return.

Group 2

Nahbi and Geuel walked around the outer part of the city in order to view it from a different angle. They noticed that the guards were alert on top of the walls and that the soldiers had an unobstructed view of the countryside from every observation post. They returned inside the city and decided to find a cafe for lunch. The rest of the day was spent near their room without much new information gleaned.

Group 4 evening

Palti and Shammua were feeling better but still suffered from the pain of the interrogations. They heard a knock.

"I wonder who that is?" Palti asked.

Shammua opened the door and saw the same beautiful slave girl at the door; she had another tray of food with her. She placed the food down and then said, "I heard that you were spies sent here to gain information, can you take me with you?"

Chapter 15

Day 13 evening

Group 4

Palti and Shammua looked at each other in shock. This slave girl was not any older than 20 years old and was suggesting that they steal her away from her master. They had undergone torture and now were being asked to commit another crime in this city.

"You want us to do what?" asked Palti.

"I want you to take me with you. I will do anything to leave this place," she said and then immediately took off her robe and let it drop to the floor.

Palti did not know what to do. Shammua just stared at her with wide eyes.

They both had the idea that this was some type of set up by the commander.

Palti grabbed her robe and asked her to put it back on. She took the robe and put it back on. She looked sad and disappointed.

"Why do you believe that we are spies?" Shammua asked.

She sat down and started to tell her tale. "I am an Israelite who was sold into slavery when I was a child. The owner of this place is a Canaanite, and is my master. I heard my master talking to his friends that two Hebrews were arrested for spying. He said that the Hebrews would be leaving soon. He was saying how he could not wait untill you left because two of the commander's men were hanging here around until you left.

"That's what I was worried about," Shammua said.

"I thought perhaps they would be worried about us being with others," Palti said realizing that she could be a spy so he decided to maintain the illusion of them being alone. "We came here alone, I wonder why they are still interested in us?"

"They are probably just making sure we leave when we said that we would," Shammua suggested following up on Palti's ploy.

"My name is Sarah and I am from your people and I will freely give yourself to both of you, if you take me with you. I want to return to my people and I am willing to do whatever it takes to leave with you." She began messaging the feet of Shammua.

Both Shammua and Palti were mesmerized by this beautiful woman.

"What do you think?" Shammua asked Palti.

"I do not know, it's dangerous to steal a slave from its master," Palti said while staring at her body.

She stood up and grabbed their hands, "Come with me." She led them to the bed. First she covered the windows then came back and stripped down again. Only a little light came into the room. Shammua and Palti both admired her shapely body. Naked, she took each of their clothes off. Shammua and Palti had gone through so much over the last few days. They were tired physically and mentally. This gesture of kindness was hard to reject. Their resistance had been worn down and they just wanted to have a diversion. She proceeded to pleasure the both of them for the evening. Palti and Shammua forgot all about their tortuous last days.

[*Satan smiled because he didn't have to do much to get these two to give into temptation. He enjoyed the way the events were unfolding. He would still have to do something about Joshua and Caleb.*]

Group 5

Caleb did not want to but he stopped kissing her. "I am sorry, that was disrespectful. Please forgive me," he said.

"It was me; I should have not done that either. Forgive me." They looked deeply into each other's eyes. Thoughts and emotions passed between them without words.

"I do not know how to say this but I think that I have been waiting for you for a long time. You are everything I want in a woman."

"Caleb, I am a widow. I have known another man, I am not the woman for you," she said looking away.

Caleb grabbed her face tenderly and looked directly in her eyes; you are the woman for me. I know that you were married and I do not care."

"You are an amazing man and I have been looking for you too but I did not know it was you until now. What are your plans, when are you leaving, when will you come back? How can we see each other? I have so many questions," she said.

Caleb put his finger to her lips, "We will figure it out. Let us go back and I will talk to Joshua. Please talk to Salman and we can discuss this further tomorrow," he said.

She smiled and kissed him lightly and gently on the tip of his nose. "Okay, I will be patient."

They held hands and returned back to Joshua and Salman. It was not lost of the two of them that Fatia and Caleb were holding hands. Joshua and Salman looked at each other but decided to not say anything until it was brought up by either of them.

Joshua, Caleb, Salman and Fatia headed back to Hebron. They arrived back in the city before dusk. It was agreed that they would meet for lunch the next day. Joshua and Caleb headed back to their room.

Group 3

Gaddiel, Shaphat, Sethur and Ammiel met with Mansur in the evening inside the pavilion. Mansur had arranged for four new women to dance for them that evening. The group was not drinking that much because of the uncertainty.

"So, it appears that the two spies were released and ordered to leave the city in two days. I guess we are all safe because it there was a real threat they would have been killed," Mansur laughed.

"I heard that these two spies were not professional spies but two little scared mice sent here by Moses," Mansur continued.

After Gaddiel relayed the information to his guys and once they knew it was safe, the party started earnest. They proceeded to drink until intoxicated. That evening, they all had fun. Shaphat and Sethur took the two dancers and engaged in all sorts of sexual perversions. Ammiel snuck off and found a male slave to have sex with hoping that no one noticed that he was not with the female dancers.

Gaddiel and Mansur drank strong alcohol drink for several hours. Gaddiel broached the idea of starting some trade with him after he returned to the Sinai, Mansur was interested.

"Tell me more?" asked Mansur.

"My tribe is large and influential. I believe that we can arrange to bring caravans up here with spices and other goods. I will go back and see what we can gain large quantities of. I am looking for a local partner to help me to sell these products in the local market here," Gaddiel explained.

"Look no further, I am the perfect merchant for you," Mansur replied.

They toasted and spent the remainder of the evening enjoying the two dancing girls and the strong drink.

Group 5

108

Joshua and Caleb sat in their room. Neither said anything first and then Caleb said, "I must talk with you about a serious topic."

"Of course, what is it you wish to speak about," Joshua urged.

"I do not know how to say this but I am in love with Fatia and she loves me," Caleb said.

"I figured that something was going on between you," Joshua said.

"This was not my plan; I did not intend to fall in love. Since the first day I saw her, she is all I can think about. I know that she is not an Israelite but she follows our God and our religious beliefs. She is not Canaanite and hates their wicked ways. She speaks our language like a native. I want to spend my life with her but I am worried what the people may say," Caleb confided in Joshua.

"Let me start by saying that we should all follow our heart as long as it does not go against God's law. I know that God does not want us to marry pagans nor Canaanites but she does not fall into these categories. She believes as we believe. We did not convince her to follow our beliefs, it was her decision. In my heart, I think that this woman is a good woman. Do not worry about the people, only worry about God. I think God would support this union, but pray on it. You will now need to speak with Salman to get his permission. He has been very hospitable with us and we must return his respect. I am happy for you and give you my blessing. We need to discuss how to proceed in light of our mission, but let us discuss this tomorrow," Joshua said.

"Thank you for your blessing, it means a lot to me. I will pray this evening and think tonight about how to proceed with her. I will also talk to Salman tomorrow about this as you suggest. Thank you again," he said.

Joshua walked over to his bed and started to write his daily intelligence report.

"Day 13

Report 5

Today, we were able to see for our own eyes that this land is fertile and lush, truly a land flowing with milk and honey. We collected some evidence of the fruit while viewing the large farms outside of the fortified city. The land supports the growing of trees for figs, dates and nuts. Everything I have noticed leads me to believe that this city could be ours. On the northeast end of the city, the trees prevent a clear line of sight for the soldiers working in that observation post. The three other observation posts have clear lines of sight for at least a mile. The northeast post's view is obstructed somewhat. I believe an attack under the cover of darkness would be able to gain entry. The army appears to be arrogant believing that they are unconquerable, this will be their undoing.

End report."

109

Caleb prayed while Joshua was writing. "Lord, I call you you right now. You know my heart and can see what no man can see. I have been faithful to you by avoiding those things that displease you. I come to You today asking you if my actions offend you. I love you. Thy will be done. Amen."

Salman and Fatia sat in the salon of their house. "Uncle, I have to speak with you about a serious matter," Fatia said.

"I think I know what it is that you wish to speak about. Its about the young man Caleb," Salman said.

"He is not a young man uncle," she said.

"At my age, almost everyone is a young man," he laughed.

"I want him to be my husband. I love him. It's a surprise to me. I learned today that he cares for me too. I do not know how it will work but I am willing to do whatever I need to in order to be his wife," she said sheepishly.

"All I ever wanted for you is happiness. Me and my wife tried to be good guardians for you but she died and you were left with me. I strived to help you and guide you the best way I could because I love you. I want for you to find someone to replace me and love you because I will not be here always. I want someone to love you unconditionally. You are worthy of love and if you think that this is the man for you, I support you," Salman explained.

She hugged him, "Thank you uncle. Now, I do not want to hear any more nonsense talk about not having much time left. You are a stubborn bull of a man and will last longer than all of us," Fatia asserted.

"Well, I will not argue with being stubborn. So, what happens now?" he asked.

"Caleb wanted me to talk with you and he is talking to Joshua. We will speak tomorrow on what will happen next. I just know that I love him and want to spend my life with him," she said.

"That is what matters, all else will work itself out. Let us retire for the evening, it's been a long day for an old man," Salman said.

"Oh uncle, you are right that it's late but I will never agree with you being an old man. I love you!"

"I love you too child. May God bless you and our new friends." They both retired to their separate rooms for the evening.

Group 4

Palti and Shammua slept from the exhaustion of having sexual relations with the woman, Sarah. She got up and dressed. She left the room but cracked the door so she could ease back in. She walked toward the front of the shop but out of view of the window in the room of Palti and Shammua. She saw Commander Elrian's spies and motioned them to her.

"Tell the commander that it worked, I have been able to get to the two Hebrews. I will go with them as planned," Sarah said and then went on to explain what had happened.

The spies listened to the message and then spy 1 left to tell the Commander.

Garrison

The spy entered the garrison and asked to see Commander Elrian. After a few minutes, the commander came out. "So what do you have for me?" he asked.

Spy 1 explained what he had seen during the day with Palti and Shammua. "That is good," said the commander.

"Also, the Hebrew female told me that she has convinced the two men that she should go with them," Spy 1 said.

"Excellent, my plan is coming together quite well. Return to your post and report back if they decide to leave early," he ordered.

"Yes commander," spy 1 said.

Elrian had decided to send another spy into the operation in case he was not able to follow them. Moses was too valuable a target for him to leave it to chance. He had used Sarah many times before because of her persuasive powers with men. She was one of his best spies. She was with him in Kemet and was used effectively there against the Hebrews under Pharaoh's rule. It was always good to have a female spy from the land in which you were reporting on.

Group 4

Sarah came back into the room. Palti was up and asked where she had been. Shammua still slept. She had a handful of fruit which she got from the front of the market.

"Master, I got you something to eat because I know that you have worked up an appetite," she said.

Palti thanked her and ate a piece of fruit. She started touching Palti in his erogenous zones. Palti had never been touched like this before. He thought he was the luckiest man in the world.

Chapter 16

Day 14 morning

Garrison

Commander Elrian had taken care of his more pressing business. He felt that his plan was perfect. He had two spies surveilling the two Hebrews and he had a spy sleeping with both men. It was a great plan. He would not only follow them but Sarah would provide more information for him.

He would leave tomorrow morning when the Hebrews left. He did not know which route they would take back to the Sinai. He was prepared to follow them until he put his knife in the belly of the man who destroyed a great kingdom. He would be heralded back into Kemet on the shoulders of the people. He would be the man who killed the 'deliverer' who defeated Pharaoh. He had already acquired clothes of a traveling merchant and fixed his traveling pack. He already knew that the two Hebrews walked from Sinai so he did not need a horse or camel. He had not marched that long of a distance for a few years but he was still in great shape. He practiced his sword skills twice a week with his most skilled swordsmen. He was ready and actually excited about a real mission that mattered. He had felt isolated and marginalized when he transferred in this position. He was the regional commander given the power by Pharaoh to undertake military and intelligence operations to protect the two kingdoms. He was expecting two more reports from his spies before he went out there at dawn to follow the Hebrews.

Group 1

Gaddi and Igal went out and ate a large meal at one of the biggest pavilions in Hebron. The tented enclosure was having a massive feast for the celebration of the Canaanite god El. They had decided the best way to not come to the attention of the locals was to act like normal travelers. They feasted on lamb, cow, swine, dates, figs, platters of a dish they could not identify. They watched the dancing girls and drank strong drink. They had ended by spending the evening with two slave girls. They went into a room behind the pavilion and did their dirty acts with the two women. They made their way home late in the night and now slept the sleep of men who had no god.

[*Satan had enjoyed watching them defile themselves without having to influence them himself.*]

Group 2

Nahbi and Geuel woke up early hoping to see the outside farms on their last day. They had completed the internal survey of the fortification which included the military arms of the soldiers but they wanted to see the farms too. As they exited the outer gates, they saw hillsides covered with fig trees, date trees and nut trees. It was a beautiful sight.

They trekked towards the same area of farms that Joshua and Caleb had seen the previous day. They told one of the local residents that they wanted to do some trade with the city so they needed to know what they grew and what they needed. They arrived while still early morning and was able to view all the farms even the farm of Salman and Fatia.

"The land is good and fertile," said Nahbi.

"It's not bad land but there is no way that we will be able to conquer it," Geuel said.

Geuel's negative report on everything he saw was starting to bother Nahbi even though he was leaning in the same way. "If you are so set in your report on this city then why are you continuing to visit the areas of this city," Nahbi asked.

"I was sent here to do a job and I will do that job to the best of my ability. Just because I believe that the plan to enter the city is faulty does not mean that I am not going to use the rest of the time here to make sure there is nothing else to consider," Geuel said.

Nahbi knew that since Geuel was an engineer, he was a practical man. It was about the facts for Geuel. He saw the world in terms of problems to solve. He did not see the world in any spiritual or metaphysical terms. Nahbi was not sure, he wavered frequently. He saw the Red Sea parted and then he ate the Manna that was sent to them but why would God have them target a city which seemed unconquerable. He did not understand. At least Geuel had his convictions, he did not believe in anything he did not see nor touch. Nahbi did not respond to Geuel's statement, he just remained quiet.

Group 4

Palti awoke with the naked slave girl in the bed. She had moved the bedding together to make a large combined bed. Palti was naked as well along with Shammua. He should have been bothered with the nakedness of the group but instead he was somewhat aroused again. He turned away from Shammua's nakedness but Sarah pulled him back down to the bed. If Palti had lost his way before, he was about to take a path into an abyss which would make it difficult for him to return from. They stayed in the room for several more hours. Sarah had been successful in making both Palti and Shammua fall hopelessly and deeply into her trap of sensuality. By the end of the last session, Sarah had gotten Palti and Shammua to engage in some of the most shameful acts according to Hebrew law.

Sarah was an expert in making men do what she wanted. She was actually only half Hebrew while her father was one of Pharaoh's nobleman. She was raised by her mother in Goshen until her father had fallen out of favor and killed. She was sold as a concubine to a Kemet brothel. She was trained in the seductive eastern arts of the Sutra. She spent several years learning until she was deemed ready to official join the brothel. She honed her art and became one of the most sought after women of pleasure in Kemet. That was when she came to the attention of a senior officer of Pharaoh, Commander Elrian. She made a potentially fatal mistake by trying to seduce him but he was not the type to fall for her wiles. She tried to exploit him with sex but failed. She could not have known that Elrian was one of the few people in the known world who had no heart; he had given his soul to the evil one. She had used every trick in her arsenal to get him to love her so she could use him. Any other man would have long been seduced. She had attempted to get him to do favors for her using her sex but he saw through her. He had a dilemma; he could no longer ignore what she was trying to do to him. In Kemet, it was illegal for harlots to use sex to gain personal favors from men; it was a mercantile relationship only. The women were told over and over again to not ask for additional favors. Only money could be exchanged in the brothels. Commander Elrian had a decision to make; he could have her killed for trying to take advantage of an officer of Pharaoh or she could agree to become his property. She chose the latter and had been with him since. She hated this city and hoped that his plan would get them both back to Kemet.

Group 5

Caleb had a dream during the night. He was an old man living in Canaan with many children and grandchildren. He saw his house and his herds. He witnessed an abundant life for himself. He saw Joshua as an old man also living in Canaan. The dream was so clear it was like a play in his mind. He smelled the aromas of the marketplace. He saw his people living in Canaan. He saw his children of his children playing with his wife but he could not see her face, only her back. He tried to see the face of his wife but every time he moved he was not afforded a good vantage point. He saw a thriving marketplace with Jewish temples anchoring the city. He started to wake up and was frustrated at not seeing the face of his wife. Just as he was about to wake up, his grandson ran towards him with his wife following him in his dream. He saw her face as clear as he had seen it yesterday, it was Fatia. He woke up and had a smile on his face. "Thank you Lord," Caleb said.

Joshua and Caleb both were awakened by a loud noise of the marketplace. The soldiers were still making their rounds from the previous day because of the murder of the two mercenaries. Joshua looked out of the window and saw a disturbance between one merchant and a soldier. Joshua rose and went to the pitcher of water and bowl sitting on the table. He threw water on his face to wake himself up. He was still tired from the day before but got up because this was there last full day to collect intelligence on the land. He was motivated to learn everything. The added complication of Caleb and Fatia was unexpected. He trusted in the Lord and knew that He would make a way. He prayed and then got dressed.

Caleb rose up from the bedding and saw Joshua. "Good morning, Praise God. I just had a dream and was given my answer by God. I saw myself, in this land with my wife, Fatia in the future. I had prayed last night that God would provide an answer and He did."

Joshua smiled and looked at the younger man. "The Lord is always faithful for those who follow Him diligently. I am pleased that you have your answer."

They had plans with Salman and Fatia for lunch. But before the lunch, they were going view the observation posts up close to see how the shifts worked. Their goal was to find out when the shifts would be more vulnerable. They were going to observe the posts during the day and go back out into the evening.

"Joshua, God is good," Caleb said.

"All the time," Joshua explained.

"I prayed to the Lord last night for guidance and God supplied an answer very fast," Caleb said.

"This mission is divinely ordered by God. We just have to listen for His voice in all we do," Joshua said.

Group 3

Gaddiel, Shaphat, Ammiel and Sethur each woke with a firm belief that the Israelites should not invade this land. They were in a good mood.

"I am going to miss this place," Shaphat said.

"I have enjoyed my time here too," Ammiel stated.

"There is a lot of opportunity in this city. I talked with Mansur long into the night, and he agreed to help us if we are looking to trade with the city. Because of this and the strength of the military, we should not attempt to conquer it but to ally ourselves with them in the areas of trade and possible other areas as well," Gaddiel said.

"What about God wanting us to take this land?" Ammiel asked.

"You mean what Moses said 'what God wanted for us'. Well, Moses is not here and has not seen this place and its fortifications. Who knows whether it is truly what God wants for us, or if it's what Moses wants for us. I admit that Moses has brought us a long way from Kemet but look at this well protected and guarded city. Moses has made a lot of promises to us pertaining

116

to what God supposedly wants for us. I do not know if it's the true or not. We would be better served to make our way in a less perilous direction." Gaddiel suggested.

His three companions nodded in agreement. Gaddiel continued, "We have just left a powerful enemy when we left land of Pharaoh. Why should we now choose to engage another powerful enemy in these Canaanites. We need to settle down and to build a life for ourselves in a place without immediate danger." Gaddiel was trying out his message, which he would eventually explain to the people when he returned to the Sinai.

Gaddiel sincerely believed that he was doing the right thing, why would God lead them into another potentially dangerous encounter? This was Moses' idea and not God's, he was sure of it. If the people saw the soldiers and the fortifications, they would agree with him. He had to convince the people. The people were like sheep, they just needed a good shepherd to show them the way. It was his job to convince them that he was that man.

[*Satan happily watched Gaddiel, pleased at the way he was thinking. He continued to send thoughts to Gaddiel's mind, "Believe your eyes. How can you believe in something you can not see? Trust your eyes." Satan knew that he did not need to push his thoughts deep into Gaddiel's mind because the seeds were already there.*]

Garrison

Commander Elrian made his daily ritual to the evil one. "Oh Lord of darkness, I honor and praise your name. You and you alone are capable of saving the world. I pledge my life and my loyalty to you." He begin using words of power, powerful incantations able to summon power from Satan by saying his names; "*Shatain, Rub al-Allum al-gham, Iblis, diablos, rub al-shar, sharif alaik.*"

Commander Elrian focused on the final preparations for the next day. He knew that he was anointed to do great things and the killing of Moses would be his greatest feat.

[*Elrian was one of Satan's faithful followers but his enthusiasm often moved him to do reckless acts. Satan had to make sure that he was able to influence him so that Elrian stayed focused.*]

Group 4

Sarah got up and dressed. Palti and Shammua were hungry and decided to get something to eat. Sarah told them that she had to leave for a few hours but said, "Remember what we discussed last night. Take me with you and I am yours forever."

They had been perfectly seduced.

117

Chapter 17

Day 14 afternoon

Group 4

Palti and Shammua looked at her with longing in their eyes.

"When are you leaving? She asked.

"We are leaving tomorrow," Palti responded.

"Good I will be ready to go then," Sarah stated.

"But, we cannot take you with us," Shammua said.

"Why not?" She asked with pretend sadness and hurt in her eyes.

"We have to go north for two weeks and then travel back through here before we return home to the Sinai," Shammua said.

"That is perfect, I will stay here and wait until your return. I will then go with you. But, I will have a surprise for you when you return. If you liked last night then you will love what I have for you when you come back," she said suggestively.

"That sounds good," Palti said happily thinking that it would be easier to travel with her on the return journey to the Sinai instead of taking her with them north.

"Where are you going in the north and how will we go back to the Sinai?" She asked.

"We are going to Lebo-Hamath along the coast and then return here before traveling to Kadesh before heading home," Palti said.

"I will travel with you to the Sinai and will settle wherever you settle. I will set up a place of my own close to you," she explained. Sarah looked at them making sure that she had them, and she did. She knew that each one thought that they were the special one.

Palti thought this woman was perfect, she had thought of everything. She was a blessing and she was his.

Shammua could not believe his luck; he would deal with Palti back in the Sinai. Sarah was going to be his blessing.

[*Satan laughed because some of his best curses appeared as blessings to humans.*]

"I have to go but will return this evening to spend time with you," she said.

Group 5

Joshua and Caleb left their room and walked to the southwest corner of the city to view the observation post. They saw the stairs leading up the post. There was a shack next to the wall and on top of the wall was a fortified room for the guards to observe the countryside. There were two guards in the shack on the ground and two guards on the wall looking out. The guards did not seem professional as they had the bored looks on their faces of men who had seen nothing exciting for a very long time. Joshua noticed that these were the type of men who would shirk their duty to take a nap. He tried to find an excuse to hang around but noticed that the builders had smartly made sure nothing was built around the shack for security reasons. Anyone loitering around would be noticed and challenged. They walked around and then returned back to the middle of the city.

"We should go to the garrison to see if there is any action is going on there," Joshua suggested.

"That is a good idea," Caleb said.

They walked through the city on the main road which was lined with date palms trees. The garrison was located on the northwest end of the city. They made their way to the stables using that as a pretext to get close to the garrison. There did not seem to be any extra activity going on there. Joshua was talking with the owner of the stables about a horse while Caleb was staring into space for a moment.

["*Look at the garrison." Raphael whispered to Caleb.*]

Caleb looked up at the garrison and saw a beautiful woman with a veil walk into the building. He could not quite see all of her face but she looked out of place. A strong breeze came and moved her face covering which allowed him to get a good view of her face.

"Joshua, come here please," Caleb asked.

He joined Caleb but the woman had disappeared inside the garrison. "There was a woman who seemed out of place walking into the garrison," Caleb said.

"Hmm, maybe she is one of the wives of the officers?" Joshua said.

"She did not have the look of someone's wife but instead of someone's concubine. It was the first time that we had seen a woman come in there. The commander does not seem like the type of officer who would permit such type of activity under his command," Caleb said.

"Good observation, he was most definitely the type of leader who would maintain a tight unit," Joshua said.

Garrison

Sarah decided to visit the garrison although she was told that she could give her messages to one of the two spies working for the commander. She knew that the information that she had would be better explained face to face with her lord. She walked into the garrison with a veil covering her face. A strong breeze came and moved her face covering.

[*Raphael made the wind blow at the right moment in order for Caleb to see her face. He hoped that he got a good look.*]

"I must see the commander now," She demanded.

"Well, well, who is this young lady?" One of the soldiers commented while staring at her body without disguising his thoughts.

"Someone who will have you killed, if you say another word," she shot back.

Something in her tone told the young soldier that she was serious. He ran and told the commander that a young lady was there.

Sarah stood there waiting; she knew what the soldiers were thinking. They thought she was a prostitute which meant they were hoping they could spend time with her. In Canaan, there was a peculiar feature of the culture called ritual prostitution. Ritual prostitution took place in the temples of the goddess of fertility (Ishtar, Inanna and Astarte). There were brothels attached to the temples occupied by consecrated women who represented the goddess who symbolized the female principle of fertility. Sexual intercourse with these women was communion with the divine as the principles of fertility. Cultic prostitution was especially associated with the festival of the New Year. Some in town called the prostitutes connected to the temples, holy women or temple prostitutes. Fornication was encouraged to improve fertility in crops and flocks. These women were more highly respected than private prostitutes who were sometimes punished when caught. Prostitution was so common in Hebron and throughout Canaan; men assumed any single women walking around was a harlot. She knew that she would never lower herself to the level of those women, she was a professional. She knew the sensual arts of India and Asia, only powerful men were worthy of her. She would never give her gifts away unless it was for a greater cause. Sarah viewed sexual relations as a powerful tool to get what you wanted out of life as well as to control men. She still did not understand why she had no power over Elrian.

Commander Elrian was eating when he was told that a young lady wished to see him. He walked out of the office and saw Sarah. "Come this way," he said.

She walked into the office and bowed. "My lord I am sorry for coming here in the day. I wanted to provide you with a report because I had some important new information for you."

"Proceed," Commander Elrian said.

"They will take me with them but will be traveling north for two weeks to Lebo-Hamath and then return here before going to Kadesh and then home. The two men are completely and utterly under my thumb," she explained.

"That is good work in a short time. You will be rewarded handsomely if we succeed. I am hoping that this operation will get me, and by extension you, back home to Kemet. Your job is to be with them and to listen for now. You should continue to play the role of an escaped slave. I want as much information as you can gather on Moses as well," he said.

"I was thinking, once I am in the Sinai, should I seek to meet you the first night outside of the camp?" She asked.

"Yes. We will meet there but I will need to arrange a plan for how we will meet. We have a little time. Report to me after they leave tomorrow, is it clear?" He asked.

"Yes, I understand. My lord, a request," she asked.

"Proceed."

"If this mission is successful, and we return to Kemet. Can I have my freedom?" She asked.

"If we are victorious, you may not only have your freedom but I will pay you handsomely," he said.

"Thank you, my lord," she said.

"This is the most important mission I have ever sent you on. I am trusting you."

"I will not disappoint you my lord," she replied.

She left the garrison thinking about the first mission he had sent her on in Kemet. Her first mission had been to frame a traveling diplomat from Canaan. She had seduced the diplomat and then the next day she claimed that she was sexually assaulted by him. She had gotten him intoxicated and then had sex with him. In the morning, she went to the authorities claiming that he just took advantage of her. The authorities brought the case to the attention of the commander of the military district in the capital, Commander Elrian. He brought the diplomat in to speak with him about his options. The first option was that he could be disgraced publically and then tried for the crime in a local court where a guilty verdict was assured. The second option was an opportunity to help himself, he could provide military order of battle information on the

Canaanite army. The diplomat agreed and the information enabled Pharaoh's army to conquer the northern part of the Canaan.

She walked back to the room where the two Hebrews were staying.

Satan's dwelling place - Earth

[*Satan felt that his plan was coming along quite well. He had focused on five areas for the Hebrews and the spies sent by Moses. He used doubt, discouragement, division, defeat and delay as tools to help him. He had been so successful up to now using doubt as he was able to get the Hebrews to regularly question God's word and his goodness. Discouragement was good because it allowed them to look at their problems instead of looking at God. Division had been very powerful for the evil one because it made the Hebrews see the wrong things as attractive and vice versa. Defeat was easy to use against the Hebrews because it made them feel like a failure so that they did not even try to succeed. Delay was helping him now because instead of occupying the promise land, the Hebrews had sent spies instead to see it. The delay was putting off doing something so that it never gets done. He was hoping that God would punish the Hebrews for choosing to disobey. His job was to make it easier for the humans to choose him instead of God. He sometimes worried because he could send a thought or a subtle influencing thought but he could not make them do anything. The humans had free will to serve God and that was his greatest weakness which was why he constantly attempted to lead them on his path.*]

Group 4

Palti and Shammua desperately wanted Sarah to return. They had such an amazing time the previous night. "We must help her," said Palti.

"I know but for once I must be the voice of reason. I want to help her but you know that fugitive slaves are punished severely, but less severely than those who assisted them. She is the property of her master and to steal a slave is considered a serious offense. I want her to come with us but I am worried," Shammua said.

"She is an Israelite and we were freed from bondage, so why not her? We can't leave her here. We must take her with us," Palti argued.

They were both thinking about the night they had, the images would not be erased anytime soon.

"It is decided, we will travel back this way to pick her up," Palti said.

"What about the death sentence on our heads if we return to this city?" Asked Shammua

"Let's cross that desert, when we get there," Palti suggested.

Hebron Marketplace

Sarah came upon the house. She focused on her mission because she wanted to be freed and return to Kemet. She thought of the money she would get if she succeeded. Would the commander be able to kill Moses? She did not know but it was in her best interest to help him. She had known a few prostitutes who worked in the lands of the Hittites where virgins were taken from their homes and required to live in a separate building near the palace, called a harem. Their sole purpose was to serve the king and to await his call for sexual pleasure. They rarely saw the king, and their lives were restricted and boring. These women lived in a virtual prison at the whim of the king or the random nobleman. Only those women who were brave enough to break the rules and escape, ever had a real life. But her life was different; she enjoyed her job and the pleasure that came from it. If this mission failed, she would most likely be stuck in the city. She did not want to spend her life in this city waiting for the Hittites or another conqueror to come and take over. Conquerors were a way of life for this region and she was the type of woman who would become the spoils of war. That did not appeal to her. She had to find another way if this mission failed, a backup plan. If it failed, it would not be from her lack of trying.

Chapter 18

Day 14

Salman's House

Fatia was working with the staff to prepare a great meal for Caleb and Joshua. She was in a great mood, a loving mood. She loved Caleb and could not view it other than as a gift from the one true God. She had been courted by many of the men in this region looking to marry her and take over her property. The one tradition which always was a problem for her was that she was supposed to relinquish her rights once she remarried. In the Near East, women generally had no rights as a free person. Women held an inferior position in ancient law. In Canaan, if a widow married a man and moved into his house, he acquired all her property and assets. She did not want to do this because she had been handling her parents business for many years. She was one of the rare women in Hebron who was her own legal agent. She owned property in her name and used her name on contracts. She trusted Salman implicitly and made him her partner. Although Salman came to Hebron as a slave, he was now a free man with a fifty percent interest in her business. He was wealthy by local standards. She had grown wealthy because of his advice. Although she saw him as more of a father than an uncle, he was a savvy businessman too. He had always been there for her and was with her again as she looked to take Caleb as a husband.

Fatia thought about her life. It had been a hard life as she was orphaned at 5 years old. Her parents had no other relatives in Canaan and if it was up to the locals, she would have been raised in an orphanage. The servants would have taken her heritage and all her possessions if it had not been for Salman and Tamar, his wife. Salman made sure that no one took advantage of her and raised her as his daughter. She loved Salman and hesitated to wonder what her life would have been like if he was not there for her. When Tamar passed away, Salman was devastated because she was his whole world other than for Fatia. Tamar was a great, strong woman of faith who helped lead her to God. While she was upset, Salman had a hole in his heart. She did not know if he would recover but she believed that it was the responsibility of taking care of her which helped him to stay grounded. Fatia grew into a young woman and eventually found a decent man to marry. She cared for her husband but he traveled a lot and was killed before she really grew to love him.

Fatia did not think that she would ever be able to find another man to fill the space in her heart. She spent her days working along side Salman to run the store and farm. She studied the law of the Lord as taught to her by Salman. She prayed in the morning and at night. She had asked the Lord to bring a man of faith into her life. Caleb was everything she had imagined in her mind's eye. He was a deeply spiritual man of faith. So many of the men in her native land or in Canaan, were pagans or idolaters. The spiritual practices of the men in this city were not deep nor of importance to them. The most important quality in a potential life partner was his love of God. Caleb loved God; she could tell by the way he spoke of the God, the law and of Moses.

She heard a knock at the door of the house. Joshua and Caleb were outside. She let them in and brought them into the salon. "I am happy to see you today. Bless His name!" Fatia said. Joshua kissed her lightly on both cheeks as was the custom of the area. Caleb did the same but they held hands for a much longer time. She looked at Caleb and saw the fire in his eyes for her.

"I missed you," Caleb said.

"I missed you too. I will tell my uncle that you are here," she ran into the salon.

Salman walked out alone and asked them to sit down.

"Salman, I need to talk to you," Caleb said.

Salman gestured for Caleb to continue.

"First I need to tell you that I am also from the tribe of Judah, so we are cousins. As a member of your tribe I wish to tell you that I love Fatia and want her as my wife. I pledge that I will love and honor her for the rest of my life," Caleb said.

Salman said nothing for a while and then smiled, "I already thought much about this, you have my blessing."

Caleb was ecstatic and relieved, thanking Salman profusely.

"Then this is settled. Let us break bread then together," Salman said.

They went into the Salon and joined Fatia. They had their repast and afterwards Salman asked, "So, Caleb what are your plans regarding your travel? I think my niece have been anxiously awaiting this question," Salman said teasingly.

"I think that we will leave tomorrow morning," Joshua said.

"No, so soon," Fatia said looking downcast.

Caleb jumped in and said, "Yes, we will leave tomorrow and head north to Lebo-Hamath but we will be back in two weeks. I will return and take you with me if you will have me," Caleb said.

Caleb touched her hand and looked into her eyes, "Fatia, I love you and want you to be my wife. I want to grow old with you. So I ask you formally, will you marry me?" He asked.

A tear ran down her face and a big smile came on her face, "Yes, yes! I will be your wife. I love you!" They hugged and held hands.

"It looks like that is solved," Joshua said.

125

"I am happy the formalities are out of the way and now we can move forward," Salman said.

"This was not in our plans but sometimes God has a plan for us that we are not aware of," Joshua said.

"Why not give these two young people some privacy. I am sure that they have a lot to discuss," Salman explained. They walked out of the room to smoke the water pipe while Caleb and Fatia went into the salon.

They sat together holding hands. There were many things that Fatia wanted to speak with Caleb about but most of all it was about God. "Tell me about our people and their relationship with the Lord," Fatia asked.

"With great miracles, God had led our people out of slavery, through the desolate wilderness, and up to the very edge of the promised land. God has been so faithful to His people. He has protected us, fed us, and fulfilled every promise. He has been immensely patient with us even when we have not trusted Him. God's love is one promise we can always count on; and God continues to forgive us over and over. God has been merciful, listening and responding to our prayers. The people have been very stubborn and hard-hearted towards God many times since Moses delivered us. The people witnessed God's miraculous deeds time and time again but still they rebel," Caleb said.

She asked, "Tell me about some of the miracles and how the people rebelled?"

"I will give you several examples when the people did not trust God and their unbelief surfaced: 1) lacking trust in God before He opened the Rea Sea when we were being pursued by Pharaoh's men (1); 2) complaining over the bitter water at Marah (2); 3) complaining in the wilderness of sin (3); 4) collecting more than the daily quota of manna (4); 5) collecting manna on the Sabbath (5); 6) complaining over lack of water at Rephidim (6); 7) engaging in idolatry with a golden calf (7); 8) complaining at Taberah (8); 9) more complaining over the lack of delicious food (9); 10) failure to trust God to enter the promised land as directed (10).

"These are some of the examples and God is still faithful. It's all about God and His love for us. If we truly love God then we would have no problem following God's law. I have seen such wonders. We are at the base of Mount Horab in the Sinai. It's the place where God is. Moses received the law there and the mountain has a presence around it," Caleb said.

"I want to go there and see this place even if I can only see it from the bottom. I also want to meet Moses, if this is possible. I have been seeking for so long to learn more about the God of Abraham, Jacob and Isaac. I want to serve God with my heart, soul and mind. I have a question. You have mentioned this promise land several times, where is the promised land?" Fatia asked.

Caleb knew that this would come up sooner or later but was hesitant to get into it but loved her so he said it.

"This is it; the promised land," he said.

Group 3

Gaddiel was sitting in the pavilion drinking some yoghurt while the other men were walking around with a guide used by Mansur for visiting merchants. Gaddiel thought about how life would be once he returned to Sinai. He knew what he and his group would say when they returned but what would they do? He had been trying to formulate a plan to lead the Israelites out of the desert to another place. This was clear evidence that Moses was wrong. He would tell them how Moses was trying to lead them into danger. His uncle Dathum the overseer knew that they should not follow Moses and he had been killed in the episode with the golden calf. God killed Dathum for his idol worship while Moses did nothing. He was still angry at Moses for the death of his uncle. Gaddiel would first take over leadership of his tribe, the Zebulun. The tribe was currently being led by his grandfather but it was time for new leadership. He would try to negotiate with his grandfather to step down and appoint him. He father had died many years before but he had other uncles who would be looking to take over leadership of the tribe. He needed to get that position first and then could move to lead the people. He knew the people favored strength and he was the man for this position even if he had to kill to get it.

Shaphat and Sethur had been walking around the marketplace with their guide. Ammiel had slipped off and told them that he would meet them later.

"So, I have ten shekels that Ammiel is with his male companion from the other night," Shaphat laughed.

"I do not want to take that wager because I believe that I would lose," Sethur said.

"Who are we to spoil his fun while he is here out of view of those who are holier than thou. I will confide in you that I have enjoyed the more sensual pleasures of this land without having to worry about Moses or Aaron looking over our shoulders," Shaphat explained.

"I know, right?" Sethur said. They continued to walk through the marketplace making their way back towards the room.

Ammiel was lying on a mattress with Kabir, an Assyrian male slave, known to service rich widows and traveling merchants. Kabir was known throughout Canaan for his prowess, stamina and others abilities. "I must go," Ammiel said.

"Did you bring me something nice?" Kabir asked.

Ammiel went into his waist purse and took out 5 shekels. It was a lot of money but Ammiel was in love with this beautiful young man.

"Grr, that's it. I don't like you anymore. I need to buy some silk for a new outfit to look good for you and you treat me like some street urchin," Kabir said while pouting and turning his back to Ammiel.

"Do not be like this. Here you go," Ammiel handed him 5 more shekels.

Kabir smiled and kissed him passionately on the lips. "Now, that's more like it. I like you again."

"I have to get back to the others. I will try to see you tonight. I will send word if I can break free. Tonight is my last night in the city until I return in two weeks. Stay available this evening because I want to see you, okay?" Ammiel said.

"Most definitely, I will be waiting for your message to come here or for you to come here." He patted Ammiel's cheek as he walked out.

Ammiel was very happy as he walked from the other side of the marketplace. This man was doing things to him that he did not know was possible. He was looking forward to tonight but more specifically when he returned in two weeks. He knew that Sethur and Shaphat suspected where he was but they would not tell anyone because they had their own peccadilloes.

He arrived at the pavilion about 30 minutes before Shaphat and Sethur. Gaddiel was already there and invited him to sit down.

"Did you have fun today?" Gaddiel asked.

"I did, it was good to see the sites," Ammiel said a little reluctantly not knowing if he knew what he did the day.

"I understand that you have met a new friend in town," Gaddiel said.

Ammiel was immediately shamed. "How could he have known?" He thought.

"How does the tribe of Dan feel about Sodamites?" he said with revulsion in his voice.

Ammiel did not say anything, he just looked down.

"Look, it will be alright. I will not tell a soul. I just need a favor for you when we return. Okay?" Gaddiel asked gently.

"What type of favor?" He asked suspiciously.

"A simple one. First of all, I need you to support me when I bring back this negative report about this land," Gaddiel said.

That was easy Ammiel thought to himself, he believed that the land could not be conquered.

"Second, I need you to get members of your tribe to support me being made leader of my tribe. Then I will need you and your tribe to support me as leader of the people," Gaddiel said.

Chapter 19

Day 14 evening

Group 1

Gaddi and Igal slept most of the day after the night they had of debauchery. They woke up, dressed and went out to the marketplace.

"I feel so bad today," Igal said holding his head.

Gaddi agreed and was also in pain from consuming copious amount of strong beverage.

"The wine in this country is so strong. I am glad we are leaving tomorrow. I can not take another night like last night," Igal commented.

They walked around the marketplace looking for food. They found a little place where they could sit and eat some warm meat and bread.

"So, tomorrow we will meet with the rest of the group. What do you think?" asked Igal.

"I think that there is no way we can conquer this city. We should return to Egypt and see about making an agreement with Pharaoh to take us back under better circumstances," Gaddi said.

"Are you crazy, I never want to return there again but I don't think that we should stay here in Canaan. Maybe we can go to Arabia near Midian where Moses lived when he was in exile. Moses knows that land and is welcome there. We could make a great life for ourselves there," Igal suggested.

"Raising goats and herding sheep. I was born in the capital city of Kemet. Now I am wandering around the desert looking to attack a mighty enemy. This is not what I imagined that God had in store for us. We need to go where we know we are welcome," Gaddi said.

"Welcome as slaves but not as free men. We would also be welcome in Midian. There are wells there and a good life to be had. I think we should start planning to move our people there," Igal explained.

"Well, no use in arguing about it. What we do need to do is to plan against Joshua and Caleb. I am sure that we will have opportunities in Lebo-Hamath to make it happen," Gaddi said.

"Then let us speak of that then, I do not wish to discuss this now," Igal was insistent and walked off.

Gaddi stood there thinking that he may have to take care of Igal as well.

[Satan's goal was to ensure that no one entered the Kingdom of Heaven. "I was cast out, why should they be allowed in? I will make sure that I do everything I can to keep them out." He watched the exchange between Gaddi and Igal. He would continue to influence them to do evil against Joshua and Caleb, who he viewed as his enemies. But Moses was his greatest threat; he had to neutralize God's deliverer by any means necessary.]

Group 2

Nahbi and Geuel walked around gaining a final perspective of the city. Geuel viewed the world as an engineer when he looked at the walls and the fortifications. He focused on how the walls were made and how much damage the weapons of the soldiers would do if it connected with skin and bone. Geuel was convinced that Hebron could not be conquered.

"It can't be done," Geuel said.

"What's that?" Nahbi asked.

"We can not defeat them," he said with firmness to his voice.

"But what about God? What about our inheritance, our legacy? This is the promised land," Nahbi said.

"I don't know about such things. I can only see what my eyes tell me. I can only see how thick and well fortified the walls are. I think that something must have happened with the transmission from God to Moses. Maybe a great plague is coming which will kill all the inhabitants of this land because this is the only way I can see us taking the land from these people," Geuel said.

"I don't know what to think. You make sense. But would not God tell us that a plague was coming and that we should take it on a specific day," Nahbi suggested.

"Exactly, it is clear. I am not making up anything that is not true. The people are giants but the land is fertile. The walls are well fortified but the land flows with milk and honey. The soldiers are well-trained but Moses wants us to believe God. I see what Moses is talking about but I cannot get beyond what we can see and touch. Help me. Convince me to believe differently?" He asked.

"I do not know what to say. I am confused with how we could take this land. I do not see how it's possible either but I also thing about what God had done for us this far," Nahbi replied.

They walked in silence back to the room. They decided to get ready for the trip in the morning where they would meet with the rest of the team.

Group 3

Sethur and Shaphat appeared in the pavilion. They saw Gaddiel and Ammiel sitting at a large table.

"Greetings brothers, I am pleased to see you. This is our last night here so we must make sure that we end our time here in the appropriate manner," Shaphat said.

They started the celebration for the evening. Mansur showed up and arranged for more dancing girls. The Canaanites were true hedonists and knew how to entertain visitors. The festivities were lively and filled with the consumption of intoxicating beverage.

Gaddiel asked to speak with Shaphat alone. They walked outside the pavilion to get some air. Shaphat looked at the night sky noticing that it was even clearer than normal. He could see the stars and comets streaking across the sky. Gaddiel took the arm of Shaphat and looked around as if he was being conspiratorial before speaking.

"Brother, I am glad that you have had much fun during our mission. I need discuss something with you. I wanted you to know that I am your friend and if the others bring up your sexual escapades and iniquities here that I will deny it. I support your choice to engage in whatever fun you want to engage in. I wanted you to know that you can trust me. I know what would happen if Moses or Aaron heard about what you did here and how your tribe would react, do not worry my friend," Gaddiel said.

Shaphat sat there hearing the words from Gaddiel thinking that he had behaved sinfully. Gaddiel was letting him know without saying directly that he had something over him. Damn him, he thought. I have made it easy for this parasite to get me. I know what will come now. The Israelites will not show me any mercy for my behavior, they will stone me. Shaphat decided to play his game since he had no choice. "Thank you very much Gaddiel. I knew I could count on you. If there is anything I can do for you, let me know?" Shaphat explained.

"You are kind but I do what I do for no type of reward," Gaddiel said.

"No, I insist. If there is anything I can do for you tell me," Shaphat said.

"Well, if you could. I would appreciate it if you and your tribe could support me to take over my tribe. After that, I want you and your tribe's support to lead the people once Moses dies or retires," Gaddiel said.

Shaphat looked at Gaddiel and agreed to do all he could, knowing that he had been blackmailed. They went back to the celebrations inside the pavilion.

After another hour, Gaddiel asked Sethur to come outside with him. Gaddiel repeated the same ploy with Sethur and got the same result. Gaddiel made his way back to the pavilion a little slower than Sethur. Gaddiel thought that all was going well with his plans to take over the Israelites.

Group 5

"This is the promised land?" Fatia asked.

"Yes, this is the promise land," Caleb said.

Caleb did not want to get into this without consulting Joshua but he trusted and believed God. He knew that God gave him his dream last night. He may have only known Fatia for several days but he knew her heart. He trusted God and was going to spend his life with this woman. He smiled and started the story.

"Canaan is the promised land. It was the land that God had promised Abraham, Isaac and Jacob, the land of the covenant, Canaan was to be the dwelling place of God's people, those set apart for true spiritual worship. God told us that the Promised Land was rich and fertile. Not only that, this bountiful land would be ours. This land is our inheritance but the people were not convinced and asked God if they could send in some spies to see how good the land is and how we could take the land from the pagans who practice all sorts of iniquity. God agreed to allow us to send in observers to determine how we would take over the land. God wants us to settle in this land so that we can drive out the wicked inhabitants and destroy their idols," Caleb said.

Caleb let that sink in for a moment. He realized that the truth of his visit dawned on her. She asked, "So you and Joshua are part of the spies sent in here to determine if the land is conquerable?" She asked.

"No, our mission is not to see if we can conquer the land, but how we to do it," he said.

"So why does God want the Israelites to destroy the people living in Canaan?" She asked.

"God has several reasons for this command. God wants to stamp out the wickedness of an extremely sinful nation. The Canaanites have brought on their own punishment. Idol worship expresses their deepest desires. It ultimately leads to the worship of Satan and the total rejection of God. God is using Moses and Israel to judge Canaan for its sins for the fulfillment of the prophecy in Genesis 9:25. Lastly, God wants to remove all trace of pagan beliefs and practices from this land. He does not want His people to mix or compromise with idolatry in any way. This is what Moses discussed with Joshua in regards to your question."

"Thank you for trusting me enough to tell me this," she said.

Group 4

Palti and Shammua waited in their room for Sarah. "I think that you should leave for an hour or two to let Sarah and I spend some time alone and then I will leave for the same amount of time for you," Palti suggested.

"Why should I leave first, you should leave first," Shammua said.

["*Fight for what is yours,*" Satan suggested to each of them.]

Palti stood up in front of Shammua confrontationally and said, "Because I said so. That is why."

"Little Palti is now a roaring lion. Who knew? Little man, you should continue to be who you are," Shammua laughed.

The tension in the air was about to explode when there was a knock at the door.

Palti bounded over to open the door. Sarah stood at the door with another slave.

"Sit the tray over there on the table." She said as she walked over and kissed Palti on the cheek and then kissed Shammua on the cheek next.

Palti beamed as he was kissed first. Shammua had hate and death in his eyes. Sarah went about arranging the food and drinks in the room after the slave left the room.

"Sarah, I was telling Shammua that he should leave for an hour or two to give us some time..." Palti was suggesting when Shammua interrupted him and asked the same of Sarah.

"Look, I want to spend time with each of you together. I like both of you equally and want us all to get along. If you are going to fight then I am going to leave," Sarah said while turning to the door.

"No, we will get along. Please stay," Palti said.

"Yes, we are good friends," Shammua replied.

"The best of friends; please stay," Palti said putting on his best smile.

"Well, I will but if this comes up again, I will leave. I have prepared a good evening for us but you must be nice to one another," Sarah said.

They both agreed and sat down at the table. Sarah had dealt with this problem numerous times previously when working two men together. She usually was able to work them in such a way that they would conform to her wishes. Occasionally in Kemet, she had such enmity between the two men she was working that sometimes one sought to kill the other. Sometimes it was part of the actual plan, to have one of the men kill the other man. In rare instances, the wrong man killed the other. Her charms were not an exact science but it usually played out how she wanted. She made sure that she played each man equally when she wanted both men to do what she wanted but not to harm one another. Her goal was to learn all she could by using her erotic skills with both men to gain the intelligence that Commander Elrian needed. She also wanted the two men to do things that they had never done before to compromise them in the eyes of their God thus putting them further under her control. Once they decided to defile themselves, it was easier for her to use their self-confidence against them. Tonight she would totally break them and get them to be with each other, for her. She had an effect on men in such a way that they would do her bidding just for the opportunity to see her again. These two Hebrews had never met someone like her, her sexual prowess was better than magic because it usually always worked, except with Elrian.

Growing up in the brothel, she learned so much about men. The men thought they were taking advantage of her but she had the power. She allowed men to believe they had the power but she had brought down powerful men because of their lusts. Even when she destroyed reputations and lives, the men still wanted her. Unbelievable, she thought. She loved her life and would love it even more when she was free.

Chapter 20

Day 14 evening

Group 5

The afternoon rushed past as Caleb and Fatia sat together discussing their views on life and the future. Holding hands, they enjoyed each other's company. The quiet was not an issue for them. They felt complete not because they needed each other but because they both loved God with all of their heart and then loved each other.

"I love you, Caleb. I knew if I stayed faithful and chaste, that the Lord would reward me. I have been tempted to fill that void inside me as a divorced woman to engage in certain behaviors but I knew that it would not be pleasing to God so I did not do it. In this city, there are many women like me who would have engaged in all sort of iniquity but I chose to stay faithful to God and honor God, by honoring myself and my body. I viewed my conduct as a way to show God that I loved him. I was not swayed by the people I saw around me. I understand that this city is indeed wicked and the conduct of the people has brought on this punishment. I support you and will serve the Lord with you," Fatia said.

"I love you and want to spend my life with you. I never knew who God wanted me to be with until now. I also have stayed faithful to the Lord and honored Him with my body. I had a dream last night and it was many years in the future. I saw my children and my children's children. I saw an amazing life with my family. In that dream, I saw the face of my wife. It was you Fatia," he said.

A tear rolled down Fatia's face. "I am so happy. These two weeks will be a long time for me while I wait for you to return."

"We will return here and then go to the Sinai together. God has a plan for us and as long as we are obedient and do our jobs, then all will be well," Caleb said.

For hours, they discussed God and the life they would have together. Each expressing the trust they had in God's plan for their lives.

Group 3

Gaddiel sat looking at Sethur and Shaphat enjoy their time with the dancing girls. He knew that many of his people wanted to return to Pharaoh including some of his group. He thought that it was a viable choice but it would have to be looked at carefully. He had formed a plan to send envoys to Pharaoh asking him under what conditions he would allow the Israelites to return. If

136

the Pharaoh's answer was not what they wanted they would look at another solution. He was thinking of proposing that the Israelites return to Kemet as paid employees of the Pharaoh. They could work for wages on the building projects which would put money into the economy. Pharaoh's people had to make do with their slaves so if they came back they could dictate the terms of their return. If Pharaoh did not agree, then they could look for land in another place in Babylon or the Hittite empire. They could negotiate with the Pharaoh or the other rulers from a position of power, not as slaves. It was a good plan which would end the uncertainty and definitely be less dangerous than attempting to conquer the Canaanites. He continued to work the details in his head.

Ammiel, Sethur and Shaphat decided to make the most of the evening. Mansur came back and joined the group. Everyone was drinking new wine and making jokes at each other's expense. "I think that I want two slave girls this evening, I know I wore out that little one last time. Perhaps the woman tonight should bring a friend as I am a most impressive man," Sethur said seriously.

Shaphat joined in the boasting, "Well, if you need two then I will need three. Mansur, make this happen for us."

Mansur jumped in and said, "Well, actually the last girls you bought to your room were somewhat disappointed, so I was thinking of having you both use the same one so that at least she would get some enjoyment out of it," Gaddiel laughed riotously. Mansur laughed while Shaphat and Sethur tried to take it good naturedly.

At the end of that exchange, Ammiel got up and said that he would be back because he needed to use the bathroom and then perhaps go to the room. The group was watching the dancing girls and did not pay him much attention. Ammiel walked out hoping that Sethur and Shaphat would not get suspicious because of his long absence. Frankly, he did not care. He wanted to see Kabir, wanted to feel his body next to him before he left. He was intoxicated with new wine and was feeling happier than he had in a long time. He could not wait to see his Kabir.

Ammiel thought that since the others were enjoying the girls, their minds would be focused elsewhere. After Gaddiel blackmailed him in exchange for political support, he decided that he might as well spend his last night doing what he wanted to do. He left the pavilion and walked through the marketplace. Ammiel's pace was quick and he searched anxiously for Kabir's house. Finally, he found the door and knocked.

Kabir came to the door with pair of trousers on but without wearing a shirt. Ammiel's first thought was the he looked so beautiful. He was rushed in. "I was not sure that you would be coming. I have to go out," Kabir said.

"Don't you want to spent time with me?" Ammiel asked.

"I do but one of the rich widows requested me for this evening. She is very wealthy and always pays me very well. I must get ready to leave," Kabir said while looking for a shirt. He walked frantically around looking until he found the right shirt.

"But I leave tomorrow morning," Ammiel said desperately.

"Well, you will be back in two weeks, I will see you then," Kabir dismissively said.

"I can't wait that long, I must spend some time with you tonight," Ammiel demanded.

This was the problem with some of the men he had been with; they became more possessive than the women. "I am sorry sweetheart but that is not going to happen," Kabir said.

Ammiel grabbed his arm and pulled Kabir to him. "Please stay with me," Ammiel said trying to kiss him.

Kabir became upset and raised his voice, "I said that I have to go!"

"You're not going anywhere without spending some time with me." He grabbed him again trying to kiss him, but this time holding him tighter.

Kabir struggled to break free from Ammiel's grasp. Kabir realized that Ammiel would not let him go. Although people hired him to pleasure them, he was not going to be manhandled. Kabir knew the only way he was going to get free was to fight. He stepped very hard on the in-step of Ammiel. It was enough to get him to release him somewhat. Kabir broke free and then struck Ammiel in the face with his fist.

Ammiel looked at him with murder in his eyes as blood trickled down his mouth.

Ammiel eyes grew wide and a manic look came on his face, the wine getting the better of him. He grabbed him by the arms again and shook him vigorously. "I like you. What's wrong with you? Why don't you want to stay with me?" He asked desperately.

Kabir used his knee and drove it straight up into his groin area. "Agh!!" Ammiel yelled. The searing pain made him fall to his knees.

"You little whore, I'll kill you," he yelled and charged at him.

Kabir picked up a bowl off the table and struck him on the head. The bowl crumbled on his head but Ammiel was only stunned. He grabbed the shirt that Kabir had put on, pulled out his dagger and stabbed Kabir in his side repeatedly.

Kabir screamed and fell down. "What have you done?" He tried to hold his side while the blood seeped out onto the dirt floor into a muddy pool of red.

Ammiel looked at his right hand, the hand with the dagger, noticing how blood was everywhere.

"Help me," Kabir begged. He tried to crawl to the door but the blood leaked out freely. He curled up into a ball, crying and groaning before his movement slowed.

Ammiel was in shock, he did not know what led him to go so crazy. "I'm sorry, I didn't mean to..." He trailed off as Kabir breathing became labored for a few moments and then he breathed his last breath.

He bent down to Kabir and whispered his name, "Kabir, Kabir, are you alright? I'm sorry. It will be alright, I will get some help. This was an accident." He picked up his lifeless torso. Blood was everywhere including on his clothes. He felt his face wet with tears. This beautiful young man was perfect; he had never felt such pleasure in his life. Kabir was the best lover he had ever had in his life. Why did Kabir make other plans for the evening? He told him to keep the evening open for him. Why didn't Kabir just spend some time with him? So much blood, he observed. He wiped his tears away and stood up looking at himself. So much blood, he thought. He had to clean up and then leave this place.

He went to the wash basin filling the bowl with water. He tried to wash the stains off his clothes but it just smeared. It was night so perhaps he could just go back to the room and change. He started for the door and took one last look at Kabir on the floor, it was such a shame. If only Kabir was more accommodating he would still be alive. It wasn't his fault, he told himself as he left the house. Ammiel made his way back to the room desperately hoping that he was not seen leaving Kabir's house.

Group 4

Palti and Shammua ate the food that Sarah had brought and became intoxicated off the wine. After dinner, Sarah led them to the bed. That evening they both felt as if they were in heaven in their minds, but in reality their actions were taking them to new levels of hell. They allowed Sarah to lead them into sin and depravity.

Group 1

Gaddi and Igal had ended their evening with dinner then went to bed to be ready for the next day.

Group 5

Joshua and Salman spoke about the future. He had provided Salman details of the mission to include the scriptures telling the Israelites to take the land.

"So the people rebelled and asked God to send spies into this land?" Salman shook his head in disgust. "I see the people have not changed much in the more that half a century I was in Goshen. The people are still stiff-necked and rebellious. This land is good and if God wants our people to have the land, it does not matter how big the soldiers are. You told me how God took the people out of bondage, and then saved them at the Red Sea. All I see when look is a good God, a loving God who knows the plans He has for us. I see a God whose Hand is moving to take his people to a higher level of abundance. I could never imagine people not wanting to take what God is offering them."

"Its lunacy, if you ask me. I am here and my eyes see the fortifications and the giants but my heart says, 'so what'. Our God is a great God, an all consuming fire!"

"Joshua, I am with you. Let me know how I can support you. I will act as your eyes and ears here while you are gone. I serve the Lord," Salman said.

Joshua patted the old man on the shoulder and said, "I knew that God brought you in our lives for a reason. I thank you and will need your eyes and ears. I have found that it's important to listen for God's voice in everything we do. When I met you and Fatia, something said that we should connect with you. It was God's voice," Joshua said.

Joshua and Salman discussed his plan for the next two weeks when Caleb and Fatia walked in. They said their goodbyes since they would leave early the next morning. Before Caleb left, he gave her a scroll from the Torah of new revelation she had not known previously. It was precious to him but he wanted her to have it.

"Thank you, my love," Fatia said.

"You're welcome," Caleb said with love in his eyes.

Satan's dwelling place - Earth

[*Satan thought himself lucky. Seven men from the group had defiled themselves in the first days of this mission. He loved sin and thought of those who did sin, as his friend. He knew that God did not abide sin but he was the sultan of sin, the father of defilement, and lastly the influencer of those looking to partake in iniquity. He had been called the Devil, Diablos, Iblis, Shaitan, Ahriman, Beelzebub, Lucifer and numerous other names. He had also been called the deceiver, the adversary, the evil one or the enemy. Only five in the group had chosen to stay pure but he had Gaddiel for pride among other sins. Nahbi and Geuel were close to several sins. Only Joshua and Caleb had chosen to stay faithful to God. He wanted to have a more active role in bringing about their downfall but he was limited to 'influencing only' even though he would sometimes push it a little further as he did with the sorcerer. Ever since Job, he had been so limited with what he could do. That said, it did not matter because most people freely choose sin. He loved it when they rejected God's love without even any help from him. Seven of the men chose sin without much effort from him and it had only been 14 days. He was ready to take advantage of every chance he had.*]

Chapter 21

Day 14 evening

Military Garrison

Commander Elrian had to adjust his plan. He thought it was better to wait to start the mission when the two Hebrews returned to Hebron in 2 weeks. Once they returned, he would surveil them on their way back to the Sinai. He would have a better chance at not being seen when they were on their way home instead of following them these two weeks through the north. Intelligence was so important and he was pleased with the work of Sarah. If they succeeded, he would free her even though it would he would miss the physical release of being with her. She had been one of his best agents over the years. He knew that she was confused as to why she could not get to him although they had sexual relations. She had no idea that his relationship with Satan protected him from such primitive emotions. He felt nothing for anyone; his emotions had been ripped out those many years ago when his wife and children were killed.

Years ago in Kemet under Pharaoh

Elrian had been living in Memphis, the major city of Kemet on the Nile River. He had been a young officer with a beautiful wife and three young children. They were at the marketplace shopping because he was unable to afford any staff for his household yet. In the marketplace, marauders came from southern Nubia and started killing their slave masters and their families. They killed many people that day including his family. His heart was ripped out and no longer felt anything. He had worshipped Ra with everything he had but after that tragedy, he cursed his god and the day he ever put his faith in that weak god. He buried his family and then started to go back to his home. On the way home, he bumped into a traveler from Jerusalem who stopped him in his tracks. The old man's eyes were as black as coal and seemed blind. He grabbed Elrian's arm with the strength of a man half his age and twice his size.

"My son, why are you so angry?" He asked.

"What? Who are you to ask me such a thing? Take your hand off me," Elrian replied.

"I am the man who can release your pain, free you from your powerlessness," the old man said.

"I do not know you old man," Elrian said and trying to break the grip of the old man but found that he could not.

"I demand you let me go," Elrian stated again while looking to pull his sword.

"I would not do that. If I let you go, you will be dead inside of a month," the stranger said while staring deeply into his eyes.

Elrian realized that this old man must be what they call a seer. He had physical power and his stare was almost hypnotic. He decided to humor this old man.

"What do you know of me?" He asked.

"I know that you think that your life is over and that your whole world is gone but this is not true. I can give you comfort and free you from the pain of your families death," the old man said.

Elrian drew back and said involuntarily, "Are you a demon? How do you know this?" He demanded.

"I know that you will be lost if you turn down my offer. I can offer you more than you ever imagined."

"What can you offer me?" Elrian asked.

"I can make it so that you will never feel pain again. I can offer you power and a future that you have only dreamed about."

"How can you do that?" He asked.

"I can and will do it but there is a price," the old man said.

"Before I even ask your price. How do I know that you can do what you say you can do?" He asked.

"You are hurting inside, mourning for you family, right?" The old man stated.

Elrian looked down and said yes.

The old man took his left hand and put it over Elrian's heart. "Ughh!" Elrian said as he fell to his knees. A surge of energy came from him into Elrian and sent a shock through his body. He felt drained. The energy kept him on his knees for a few minutes. All at once, it was gone. The pain was gone. The sadness was gone. Everything he had felt was replaced with another feeling, or a lack of feeling. He stood up feeling numb. A few minutes before he did not know how he would continue and now he was in a much better mood. "How is this possible, I feel nothing. You have taken all those negative feelings away. I can't believe it, how?" Elrian asked.

"There are things and powers in this world that you do not know about. Ra is not a god but a worthless idol, a piece of clay only. I have a master who is all powerful. You asked how you could know that I could do what I promised you. Are you satisfied or do you want me to give you back your pain." The old man raised his hand and started to move it towards his heart.

143

"No! I want all that you say I can have. Tell me what it is that you want?" Elrian asked.

"I want your ruh (soul)," he said.

"My ruh? How could anyone have my breath or soul?" Elrian asked.

"You do not have to worry about that. If you agree, I will make sure that it your ruh is provided to my master and you will be given power," he claimed.

Elrian agreed because he didn't believe that anyone could possess another's soul. Additionally, he would have done anything to ensure the pain never came back. They went through an incantation of strange sounding words, an ancient language he suspected. "*Satana, Diablos, Iblis, Shaitan seapotay hanbusrat setor zatana pauqor foalon saurat....*"

Commander Elrian remembered the words as if it was yesterday. At then end of the ritual, he felt two sensations. The first sensation felt as if a hole had opened in his chest sucking out something he could not describe and then it was replaced by a feeling of strength and vitality. He no longer doubted, nor felt anything. Even when he was first sent to Canaan, he had known an opportunity would arise which would lead to the ultimate prize. Now, as he looked back at that day, he sensed that this was the way things were destined to unfold. He was meant to kill Moses.

The traveler explained that he was a mystic who served Satan, or the lord of darkness. The darkness was the enemy of the light. The God of light or the God of Abraham was the God the Hebrews worshiped. The traveler spent several weeks with him teaching and showing him all the spells and incantations. He had heard of the power of Satan from scattered sources but it was not until he met this traveler that he became a true believer. He started learning the incantations and could feel the power. He was in a battle two weeks later and had been cut badly with a sword but was able to heal himself. He would have been dead without the power. He also had the power to summon, when needed, a warrior of the darkness in times of dire need. He was taught by the traveler how to invoke Satan and to use his power to help him become more of who he was. He wondered how powerful he would actually become. After that encounter, his dreams became larger.

A noise outside of the military garrison brought Commander Elrian back to reality. He was expecting to see one of his spies soon for the evening's last report. He had spent the day adjusting his plans explaining to his number one that he would not be going on a mission the next morning. An hour later, Spy 1 came into the garrison. It was late and not much movement going inside the garrison when he took the man to his office. Commander Elrian discussed the changes with his spy and advised him to make sure the Hebrews left the city. He ordered the spy to follow them to the gates and to pass Sarah a message.

"Tell Sarah to get the two Hebrews to return to the city to see her. Sarah should advise them that she will arrange a place for them to stay when they come here so that they will not come to the attention of the military."

"Yes sir. I will ready and available for her when she comes out to make her last report." Spy one said.

Elrian watched his spy leave knowing that he would follow his orders without question. Elrian believed that his plan was proceeding in the way Satan would approve. He decided to get some sleep and went to his quarters at the back of the garrison.

Group 3

Ammiel returned to his room in an anxious state. He looked at the blood on his clothes. He stripped down and tried to wash the clothes but the blood was not coming out. He would have to dispose of the clothes. He had sobered up somewhat and changed into a new outfit. He looked outside the room looking to see if anyone was outside looking for him. He took the clothes and balled them up in a tight bundle. He put them under his arm walked through the passages of the marketplace to get rid of the clothes. He walked to where the animals and livestock were kept. He threw the clothes where the animals rutted. He walked quickly back to the room and saw that the group had returned. He saw several of the dancing girls and that everyone was in a festive mood.

"Ammiel, where have you been?" asked Shaphat.

"I hope you have been not doing anything that we would not do," Sethur added humorously.

"Well, you know that it was probably not something that we would do," Shaphat added.

Ammiel became angry and explained that he was tired of their ridicule. The girls laughed at him and the group sat all separated into beds coupled off.

"Are you joining us Ammiel. Semai has been waiting to be with you," Sethur said. Semai was sitting on the bed looking at Ammiel.

"No thank you. We have to be up early in the morning, I am going to bed," Ammiel said and then went to his room, pulled the screen up to separate the room and went to sleep.

The group laughed and went about their evening, drinking and having much lewd fun with each other. Ammiel could hear the activities on the other side of the screen. All he thought about was the killing of Kabir earlier that evening hoping that no one saw him. He could not wait to leave the city the next morning.

Gaddiel decided to stay in the pavilion while the men had some fun. He had made sure that they were under his power. He had spoken to each and each expressed their loyalty to him. He had made arrangements with Mansur to see him in two weeks when he returned. They planned to stay in the same rooms when they returned. He could not wait to hear the story from Palti and Shammua as to how they were captured. He stayed in the pavilion chatting with several of the other workers before heading to the room satisfied that he had done his duty while in Hebron.

Group 4

Palti and Shammua had the best evening of their lives. While both resented the other, they each had fun. After a while, the two of them dosed off and were fast asleep. Sarah dressed quickly and went outside to see either of Elrian's other spies to see if there was any message for her.

She saw the spies and was given the message to have the two come back to pick her up. She accepted the orders and explained that it would be no problem. She left the spies and reentered the room. She debated internally for a few moments as to whether to wake them to tell them the change plan.

"Palti, Shammua, I need to talk with the both of you." They arose unsteady and shook the sleep out of their eyes.

"Yes, my dear. What is it?" Palti said first.

"Tell me, my love," Shammua grabbed her hand. Palti decided to grab the other hand.

"I have been thinking about how we will meet when you return. I have figured out a way to see you again without anyone finding out," Sarah said.

"That is great news because we are under a death order if we return," Palti said.

"I have the perfect room when you return which is private and where no one will know you are here. I promise you," Sarah explained.

"I will give you the full details later, now go back to sleep," Sarah added before the two Hebrews returned to sleep.

Group 5

Joshua and Caleb returned to their room a few hours later after walking around the city. Caleb was feeling good but sad about having to leave Fatia but he trusted God.

Joshua felt strong about the day, and sat down to write his report.

"Day 14

Report 6

On this day, Caleb and I took a closer look at the observation post from inside the wall. It's difficult to maintain any type of long-term surveillance on the observation post because there is no place for concealment. Anyone lingering around the observation post for too long will be challenged. We did reconnaissance on the outposts during the night though and learned that the night shift is less engaged and focused than the day shift. We observed several soldiers dozing off while others looked bored or distracted. We have engaged a local Israelite businessman who will help us. This man, Salman, will act as our agent while we travel north.

End of report."

Chapter 22

Day 15 morning

Group 5

Joshua and Caleb awoke early. Both was of the same mind, the land was good and as God described it. There may be giants in the land but with God on their side, what could man do against them. They packed their bags and then started north to move outside of the city. They walked to the gate and then moved past the farms to the hills outside of the city.

Miltary Garrison

Commander Elrian was sitting in his office talking to a few soldiers who were reporting from the late shift. He needed very little sleep because of the covenant he had with Satan. The power that flowed through him helped him to go without much sleep or without much food. He was able to sustain a high level of activity when others became tired and needed sleep.

"Commander Elrian, there has been another murder in the marketplace. This time a man named Kabir was killed in his house. He was a man of pleasure for many of the influential widows and men traveling in this area. Kabir was supposed to meet a very powerful widow last night when he did not show, she sent one of her servants to his house. There were blood streaks coming out of the doorway so the servant entered and found the body," the soldier said.

"I want you to seal the house off and to start asking questions of everyone in the area. I will be there soon," Elrian said. He thought for a moment, two separate murders in the matter of only a few days. Something was going on; a new element had entered his city. He would need to stay focused on this while he also did his other operations.

Group 4

Palti and Shammua woke up to the naked body of Sarah. She had done her job with much relish and enthusiasm. Palti and Shammua did not even understand half the things that she was doing but they enjoyed it better than anything they had experienced in their life.

They all got up and dressed. Once they packed their belongings, Sarah started to give them the details of what to do when they returned. "When you return, go to the north gate. There is a man who helps travelers with their belongings, his name is Jonas. Jonas is outside of the gates every morning. Tell him that you are my friend and he will tell you where to go for the room.

After you get there, he will get me and I will come to you. I will give you even a better time that I gave you here. Do not worry because I will not let anything happen to you because I am looking forward to returning with you to my people."

Although Palti and Shammua were worried, they could not think about anything other than Sarah. They hesitated and then agreed with Sarah's plan.

"I am going now but I will keep a watch each day for Jonas to tell me that you are here. I will have so much prepared for you that these encounters will be forgotten," Sarah said. She kissed Palti and then kissed Shammua.

They both watched her leave the room. "She is amazing," Palti said with a glint in his eye.

"Yes, she is," Shammua said but thinking she was going to be all his soon enough.

"We need to discuss what we will tell the men. Joshua and Caleb saw us being taken away so I am sure everyone will know,"Palti said.

Shammua was distracted at first and then said, "You are right. We need to make sure that we discuss the facts. We were beaten but did not break and tell the Canaanites about the others. We definitely do not need to mention what we did with Sarah only that she is an Israelite who needs our help and that we have agreed to help her," Shammua suggested.

"That is a good plan. We will tell them but not seek input. This is our decision as to whether we bring her back and they have nothing they can say about this," Palti said in a resolute voice.

"Let get going, we are going to be late meeting the others," Shammua said. They left out of the room. The spies of Commander Elrian continued watching them as they walked out of the city.

Group 3

Ammiel was up before anyone else. He collected his belongings and urged the other men to get ready so they could leave. Ammiel had spent a difficult evening sleeping because he kept having bad dreams about killing Kabir. He had one dream where he was killed by Kabir. He had another dream where he was captured by the giants of Hebron then tortured and killed.

He had other disturbing dreams that evening.

[*Satan had been sending dark images into the mind of Ammiel. He made sure that Ammiel could not sleep.*]

Neither Gaddiel, Shaphat nor Sethur did not know why Ammiel had been rushing them so much. They were not feeling well after the night of strong drink. They gathered their bags and left the room with Ammiel towards the north gate of Hebron. Everyone except for Ammiel was feeling a bit unwell from the previous night. Ammiel kept pushing them toward the outer marker of the city limits.

Group 1

Gaddi and Igal had woken up early in order to make their way out of the city. They had purchased some food from one of the outside farms and were eating when they saw Palti and Shammua walking towards the hills outside of Hebron.

"So what do you think, should we go over and speak with them?" asked Igal.

"I think that we should maintain operational security until we get beyond the hills, we do not know who is still watching us. We will meet them soon enough," Gaddi replied.

They continued eating the fruit and drinking the fresh milk.

Group 2

Nahbi and Geuel were heading out of gates when they spotted Joshua and Caleb. They continued walking north towards the hills while not acknowledging Joshua and Caleb. They wanted to maintain the integrity of the operation. They came up on the farms and saw Gaddi and Igal eating but continued to walk towards the hills.

Day 15 afternoon

Northern hillside

Group meeting except group 4

All the groups except Palti and Shammua were sitting at a small oasis with a well north of the city. They were sitting with each other comparing notes.

Gaddiel took the lead by asking if anyone had seen Palti and Shammua since they had been arrested.

"They were arrested. What happened? Are we in danger now?" asked Nahbi.

"I am not sure of why they were arrested but I did hear that they were released after a day or two. I heard from a source that Palti and Shammua told them that they came alone. I think the operation is safe," Gaddiel suggested trying to take more of a leadership role.

"We saw them as they were taken away and put our trust in the Lord that the mission was safe," explained Joshua.

"It's all futile since we cannot conquer this place anyway. The fortified walls and the huge soldiers make the conditions to drive these people off their land too difficult," Sethur said.

"I disagree but before we get too much into this, let wait to see if Palti and Shammua show up so we can all discuss this together," Caleb suggested.

Group 4

Palti and Shammua made their way through the city and through the northern gates. Each was thinking about seeing Sarah again. They both agreed that it was impossible to conquer the town. They were each thinking about how to keep Sarah to themselves. It took them a little longer to get to the hillside as both were suffering from the effects of the previous night's amount of fermented beverages. They finally made it to the area north of the city where the others were camped.

Hebron Marketplace

Commander Elrian was in the marketplace in the home of Kabir. "This is a very expensive residence for a man without a job," he commented.

The senior soldier on the site explained, "As I mentioned at the office, Kabir ibn Al-Kathur, was a man of pleasure for women and also men. He made his money providing sexual services for a small unique clientele. As you know, Commander there is many women and men who make their money offering sexual services." he said waiting for a reaction from the Commander.

Elrian had seen it all in Kemet. He had seen men with men and group sexual practices performed for the gods and other unique sexual practices. The sexual deviance of people did not interest him. He knew that in Canaan, the people needed their vices in order to keep them docile. He had thought about enforcing the no fornication or sodomy rules but he figured that he would have an uprising on his hands. He laughed to himself; the Canaanites loved their sexual escapades. He needed the people to conform and stay malleable which meant that he needed to leave the status quo as it was. Vices were allowed as it did not get out of hand, he did not want to be the military commander for another Sodom and Gomorrah. He did not want direct combat with the Jewish God as Pharaoh did, which was his undoing. His main concern was the safety of citizens, those merchants and businessmen who brought trade into the city and made it a thriving city. As long as he was in the city, it was his job to ensure that the city was safe and secure for trade. He envisioned that Hebron could perhaps be as large as Jerusalem one day or even bigger with the right management.

"I know about that and it does not concern me, but what do concern me is the other two murders this week along with this killing," he said. He walked through the room looking at the dead man. The man had been stabbed and bled out. There was evidence of a struggle which meant a crime of passion. As he looked at the site, he believed that it was not a planned out murder but a crime of opportunity, in the heat of the moment.

"I think this is different than the other murders because those were done by professionals while this one does not seem so. But I feel that something new has come to our city. Maintain the double patrols and let me know if any of the observation posts see anything unusual," he ordered.

"Yes, sir," the senior soldier replied. Elrian left the marketplace and headed towards the garrison.

Military Garrison

Commander Elrian returned to the garrison where Sarah had been waiting for several hours. He took her into his office and asked for her report.

"The Hebrews left the city this morning and agreed to return in two weeks to take me with them. I have arranged through our man Jonah at the northern gates to take them to a house I use for the targets I sleep with. He will tell me when they return," she explained.

"Very good Sarah. I am pleased that you were able to get to them so quickly. Let me know immediately when they return to the city. I want to know everything they learned on their trip and their schedule for their return journey," he ordered.

"Yes, commander," she said.

He did not say anything else for a few moments. "Is there anything else?" she asked him.

"Yes, I need a release. Let's go to my sleeping quarters." She bowed her head knowing what would come next. She led the way to his quarters as she had done many times before. She took off her clothes and lay on the bed. The commander undressed and laid on her. He did not make a sound until the end. Sarah felt that for Elrian it was more of a physical activity than a sexual act. He finished, stood up and told her to come to the wash basin to clean him off. She took the cloth and started to wash him. She did not like this part of the job but it gave her another opportunity to see the scar on right side from his arm pit to his waist. The scar was jagged and discolored. She always wondered how someone could survive a wound like that. She washed him while he just stared out blankly at her until she finished. She always wondered if he thought that she would attempt to kill him one day which is why he stared at her.

"Go now but return when the two Hebrews return," he said. She got dressed and walked out.

Elrian did not necessarily enjoy the act as much any more but there were still vestiges of his old mind inside him which did like the pure carnal pleasures. He had speculated that once he grew more powerful, perhaps the purely physical enjoyments would not longer be enjoyable. For now, he still enjoyed the simple physical sensation of putting his seed in her. He believed that she enjoyed it as well based on the noises she made. He felt refreshed and would go out for a tour of his city in the afternoon to show the banner of the Pharaoh knowing that people would start to talk about the three murders this week. There had been accidental killings but usually they were over unpaid debts or fights which had gotten out of hand. There had never been two separate murders with three people dead with edge weapons in one week where the killers disappeared. He would get to the bottom of this.

Sarah made her way to her home in the northern part of the city. She kept the one room in the marketplace for her trade and a house to separate her two lives. Sarah needed some rest; she had put in a lot of work recently.

Chapter 23

Day 15 afternoon

Northern Hillside oasis outside Hebron

Group meeting

Palti and Shammua arrived to much fanfare as everyone was eagerly anticipating their report knowing they had been arrested.

Joshua took the lead and asked for the details of their arrest. Shammua explained their encounter with the commander, the torture and their release. Palti filled in the details during the debriefing. At the conclusion, Joshua said, "I think that we are safe because no one else was accosted or stopped. What are your thoughts?"

Gaddiel answered for his group. "I think you are right. We have nothing to worry about now. My question is about our mission and your report."

"My report is the same before I entered the land. God gave us a promise, "that He was bringing us into a prosperous land, a land of streams and springs, of waters that well up from the deep in the valleys and hills, a land of wheat and barley, of vines, of figs, of pomegranates, a land of olives, of oil, of honey, a land where you eat bread without stint, where you will want nothing, a land where the stones are of iron, where the hills may be quarried for copper. You will eat and have all you want and you will bless Yahweh your God in the rich land He has given you (1)." Joshua paused for effect before continuing. These are God's words and there is nothing in this land that is different from it. This land is perfect for us and we should take it. I have already started outlining a plan..."

Joshua was interrupted by Gaddiel, "Surely, you are deceived. Yes, I concede that the land is fertile and beautiful but that it not the impediment here. The soldiers are well trained and the fortifications are impenetrable."

"They are giants, these descendents of Anak. They can not be defeated," Sethur interjected.

Geuel agreed with Sethur. Nahbi spoke up for the first time, "I have looked around hoping that there was a way to defeat these big men but I have to agree that it seems impossible. Even in the Holy scrolls it says, "A people great and tall, these Anakim, as you know; you have heard the saying: who can stand up to the sons of Anak? (2)"

Caleb jumped in debate, "Now that is being disingenuous because you do not mention the rest of the scripture. The Word reads, "Be therefore sure today that Yahweh your God himself will go in front of you, a devouring fire that will destroy them, and he himself will subdue them for you; so you will dispossess them and destroy them quickly as Yahweh has promised you."

Joshua explained, "That is the word of our Lord. We have a duty to God to obey."

"That is what Moses tells us," Gaddiel stated.

"How dare you question Moses, the prophet of God. Moses delivered us at great peril to himself and his family. Moses obeyed God and endured the threats of Pharaoh and was blessed because he trusted the Lord without question." Joshua stood on his feet and walked up to Gaddiel.

"We should not even be here on this mission because God already spied out the land for us and told us to posses it. How can you and the others not see that God did not bring us this far to leave us? All we have to do is to enter the land and God will do the rest. Our great Lord is ready to reward us. The righteous are bold as a lion. With God, all things are possible, if they be but promised, to him who believes," Joshua explained passionately.

"That sounds good in the temple but this is life and death. I have a family and I do not want them to be in any more danger then they have already been put in. I want to stress that God did not tell me anything, Moses told me that God said to possess this land," Gaddiel said.

Caleb interjected again, "Moses speaks for God. He is the chosen deliverer of the Lord. We must obey the Lord, our God."

Joshua spoke up again, "There are only two issues here; the land and inhabitants. We are all satisfied that the land is good and fertile. Right?" He looked at Palti and Shammua.

Gaddi and Igal watched the exchange trying to decide which side to take. They talked to each other in hushed tones while Gaddiel and Joshua were in heated debate. "I think we should support Joshua and Caleb so that if anything happens to them we can say we supported them. Also, they saved us in that crowd so they will be expecting us to support them. There will be no suspicion on us," Gaddi recommended.

"You are right; we should look like we agree with them in order to get them to think favorably about us after they found us how they did. Let's support them," Igal agreed.

Palti agreed with Joshua by saying, "the land is indeed perfect for us."

"The air is great and the soil is good for farming," Shammua explained.

"The land is not the question here but the people inhabiting it right now," Gaddiel said.

"That is the second question Moses charged us with. We are to see their number, their size, their statue, whether they are strong able bodied men or weak. We needed to see whether they lived in tents or houses, whether they live in open villages or walled cities. We are charged to determine if there is woods standing as in those countries that are uncultivated, through the unskillfulness and slothfulness of the inhabitants, or whether the woods were cut down, and the country made bare for the convenience of tillage. These were the things that we were to inquire about. This question is about how we shall remove the Canaanites from their land not if we will. We will possess this land because God has promised us it. Were not Pharaoh's men even more powerful than these pagans; and yet without a sword drawn by Israel or a stroke struck, the chariots and horsemen of Pharaoh were routed and ruined. Also, the Amalekites had us at a great advantage and yet we were victorious. Miracles have happened each day since we left the yoke of Pharaoh and the great "I AM" has expressly promised Moses that we would drive out the Canaanites. I trust the Lord," Joshua explained.

Palti and Shammua had given their report about the goodness of the land when asked by Joshua but spoke up now regarding the difficulty in defeating these people.

"I just do not see how we can do this thing." Ignoring what Joshua had said Palti continued, "There will be many people killed, they will destroy us."

"I agree that it's impossible. We need to look at other options," Shammua stated.

"Faith, it's all about faith. Do not trust your eyes because they will deceive you. We must maintain a belief in God, knowing that He will provide for us. "I AM" will make a way. God has always been faithful to those who obey," Joshua explained.

Gaddiel ignored what Joshua had to say and gave his opinion "We need to return now and tell the people that we should seek out other options. Don't you agree?"

Sethur and Shaphat spoke up in support of Gaddiel as they had agreed to. They really did believe that it was an impossible mission. Ammiel felt as if he was in the weakest position so he decided to go along with Gaddiel so he would not tell others about his actions in Hebron.

"We must return now, tell Moses and Aaron how we need to look at either returning to Egypt or seek a home elsewhere," Ammiel explained.

Gaddi explained that arranging to return to Pharaoh would not a bad option. Igal supported his position but added another option. "We could look at either returning to Egypt or going to Midian. Moses was supported in Midian and we could make an excellent and fruitful life there. If we returned now, we could be back in 8 or 9 days. We would have only been gone for 25 days at that point. We could speak to Israel about our options and then send envoys to Pharaoh and Midian to discern the best alternative."

Gaddiel could not believe his luck; Gaddi and Igal were in support of his position. This was a good thing because it meant that perhaps they could start back now. He knew that Joshua and Caleb would be in support of Moses without question. He saw the whole debate as being beneficial for him because now he was able to see the viewpoint of his main rivals. Joshua and Caleb would be his main opposition within this group. He believed that Moses, Aaron, Joshua and Caleb would make up the faction against him when they returned to camp.

Gaddiel spoke up, "We should put it to a vote. We need to decide our next course of action. Do we proceed or do we return back to give our report to Israel?"

Sethur answered first, "Let us return to Mt. Sinai and provide our report to the people and they can decide."

"I agree. We should return now especially after Palti and Shammua were captured. Who knows what will happen. We can be back in less than 10 days," Ammiel explained in agreement with Sethur.

"I think it's useless to continue on, we could be captured and then none of our people will know what we saw. We have done what we were sent to do. Let's makes haste and return," Shaphat added.

Caleb spoke up before Joshua because he knew Joshua's stance. "I am going on to obtain more information on how to conquer the land. I know Joshua will be moving with me. I think it's a simple matter before us. Do we trust God or not?"

Joshua smiled. "My friend Caleb speaks for me as well. I am planning on traveling at the rising of the sun tomorrow. I am not afraid because I trust in God. Do what you will, Caleb and I will go north."

Palti and Shammua looked at each other. Each was thinking about Sarah and the plan they had to return in two weeks. While they agreed with Gaddiel about the impossible nature of conquering this job, they wanted Sarah so they had to return in two weeks to get her.

"We think that we should continue our plans to go to Lebo-Hamath and then return here as planned. Even though it was more difficult for us here, we should at least make the effort to see what is north," Shammua said.

Gaddi and Igal explained their position in support of Joshua and Caleb to the surprise of Gaddiel.

"You support them after what you have seen?" Gaddiel asked Gaddi and Igal.

"We are not saying that, we are just agreeing to continue on north to complete our mission in total," Gaddi explained.

"I think that it will only strengthen or weaken each of your augments," Igal asserted.

Everyone looked at Nahbi and Geuel to know their thoughts.

"I agree with Gaddi and Igal, we should continue on to view more of Canaan. It is our duty to make sure that we do what was entrusted to us to the best of our ability," Geuel stated.

"I stand with Geuel, we must continue on to Lebo-hamath to see what it is like. I just feel like some of us are not seeing the bigger picture. I believe that it will probably be impossible to possess the land but we should continue," Nahbi said.

"So, that is eight of us who will be moving North. Gaddiel, you may do what you wish but everyone has spoken. We leave in the morning," Joshua stated.

Gaddiel thought for a moment and decided that it would not look good if the four of them went back while the rest finished the mission. If he was going to be the leader of the people, he had to follow this to the very end before thinking of seizing power.

"Well it is decided then, let us go with them." Gaddiel said looking at Ammiel, Sethur and Shaphat. He continued, "We will go with them in order to ensure their report is an accurate account."

Hebron

Sarah woke up after sleeping for a few hours. She had been exhausted and it felt good after bathing. She enjoyed the downtime to decompress after dealing with the two Hebrews and the commander. She wanted to find out the commander's secret.

Salman had been meeting with a few of the farmers that day while Fatia tried to focus on the shop. Fatia could only think of Caleb because she felt that she had been waiting for him all her life. Her former husband, Ammar, had been a good man but it was more of a marriage of convenience. She had affection towards him but she did not love him in the same sense. She knew Ammar for a year before he was killed but she felt a deep and passionate love for Caleb only after a week of knowing him. It just felt right with Caleb, like the missing piece of a riddle that just came into place. She mourned when Ammar died because she was the one who asked him to go on the trade mission in which he died. If it was not for Salman pushing her to get married, she would have stayed single. Ammar was a simple man who wanted someone to give him sons. Ammar's most important trait was that he did not want any major part of her business. He was happy to continue letting her run the business and have her freedom. She was happy to let him appear as if he was in charge but in reality, she controlled the house and the business. She said a silent prayer asking God to keep Caleb and Joshua safe.

Chapter 24

Day 15 afternoon

Commander Elrian always felt better after being with Sarah. He was able to put those impulses behind him for a short while. He had asked for his spies throughout the city to learn all they could about any newcomers or visitors. He reasoned that the three killings represented a new element into his city. He would task his spy network to inquire about any strangers. He felt good about the two little Hebrews he had interrogated and sent back out. He knew that they were under the spell of Sarah; no one except him could withstand her charms.

He spent the next few hours meeting with members of his spy network. The two spies who were assigned to observe Palti and Shammua came up to the back of the garrison. They were always escorted inside the garrison to ensure that neither the public at large nor the soldiers knew they worked for the commander. There were several guards located at the rear of the garrison when they walked up. The two men had a code word which would tell the guards to escort then inside to meet with the commander. They wore scarves across their faces to conceal their identity.

"The waters of the Nile are cool in the middle months," Spy one stated to the guards. The guards could not see their faces but had his instructions.

"Come this way," the soldiers stated. The two men were walked inside behind three of the guards. Once inside, they waited for one soldier to get the commander.

Commander Elrian stepped out of his office and told them to leave after recognizing the two men with scarves over their faces.

"You can leave me now. Good job. You two, walk this way," Elrian explained.

The two spies took off their scarves and Elrian saw their faces clearly, the one man with traditional features of his homeland and the other from Assyria.

Elrian said, "I have a new mission for you." Part of Elrian's hold on the city was knowing what was happening in the streets of Hebron, which meant having strategic relationships with the businessmen.

"Number one, I need you and Number two to meet with Mansur who runs the Pavilion. Tell him that I have sent you to ask him about any strangers who recently visited this city. These murders have to be connected in some way to new people entering Hebron. Your task is to gather intelligence on any travelers," Elrian said.

He handed the two men some operational money to buy information from the populace. "Report back if you discover anything interesting." They agreed and left after reveiling their faces.

Spy one and Spy two left through the back again in order to visit Mansur the Arab who owned the Pavilion.

After half an hour they arrived at Mansur's Pavilion. "We need to see Mansur," asked Fayid who was the lead spy of the group. Fayid was the commander's chief of operations for the spy network in the city. He was called number one instead of by his true name because the commander believed in maintaining operational security in case he wanted them to work undercover. Fayid was skilled and worked for Pharaoh before coming to Hebron because Elrian asked him to. Fayid knew that Mansur was a friend of Elrian and he would have to make sure that he was respectful to him.

His assistant, spy number two, was just called "number two". He was an Assyrian named Ashur who previously worked in Babylon before moving to Canaan. Ashur was a gifted torturer and interrogator. He came with his family to farm in Hebron but did not have much luck in tilling the soil so he fell back to what he knew; espionage. He had been a spy for the Assyrians operating throughout the Near East. Elrian had told Fayid that Mansur should be their first stop in determining if anything was afoot in Hebron.

"Yes, how can I help you?" asked Mansur.

Fayid spoke up, "Can we meet with you in the back so others can not hear us. We come at the orders of Garrison Commander Elrian to discuss an urgent piece of business."

"Of course, follow me," Mansur said. Mansur led them to the back. He asked them to take a seat and then offered them something to drink. They asked for something cool to drink. Mansur, the consummate host, had drinks brought to the room before asking any questions.

"Okay, what is this about?" he asked.

Fayid spoke, "Well, you have heard of the two assassins who were killed three days ago and then the death of the man of pleasure, Kabir?"

"Yes, what does that have to do with me? I did not know Muqatil and Ghadafa that well. I knew what they did but thought they had been on a mission. As for Kabir, he frequently came here with some of his clients but I was not friendly with him," Mansur explained.

"No one is accusing you. We know that you hear things. The commander feels that perhaps a traveler or stranger who visited your place was responsible," stated Fayid.

"I really do not know what I can say. I am so busy with my establishment..." He was saying when Fayid raised his hand halting him.

"Yes, yes, I know that you are known for your discretion but the commander wants your help and knows that you have large ears. Elrian will be very grateful for your assistance. We know his friendship is a great benefit for you as a foreigner living here," Fayid explained.

Mansur knew how this was going to go, the carrot and then the stick if he did not come up with something. Anyway, someone would tell about the four strangers because Canaanites loved to wag their tongues. It would come eventually about the four Hebrews who spent time in his pavilion at some point, so why not get ahead of it.

"Well, now that you put it like that, what exactly do you want to know?" Mansur requested.

"Tell me about any strangers who have stayed in your rooms or who have spent time in your pavilion over the last few days," Fayid asked.

Mansur told them about Gaddiel, Sethur, Shaphat and Ammiel. "I do not think that they are responsible for any of these murders. They were here every night drinking and having fun. I would put my reputation on these men being not involved. They will be back in two weeks after checking out trade up north," Mansur explained.

Fayid took special note of that fact since the two Hebrews were scheduled to return in two weeks too. Elrian would be interested in this information.

[*Raphael came up beside the Archangel Michael.*

"The Lord said you wanted to see me," Raphael said.

"Yes, I have been assigned to help you in your mission to make certain that Joshua and Caleb are safe from the evil one and his demons," Michael said.

"That is good because I sense the evil one will be trying to do even more against them.]

Mansur's Pavilion

Mansur watched the two spies leave. He liked Gaddiel and hoped that they did not have anything to do with the deaths. Anyway, who cared if two mercenaries and one sex worker was killed. He was hoping that Gaddiel was a man of his word in helping him go into business with the Hebrews. There were over 2 million Hebrews waiting to start trade with someone. This was a business opportunity that he would kill for and he had told Gaddiel that he would be his partner in the city.

Mansur had come from Arabia like his cousins the Hebrews. They were both from among the Semites along with the Chaldeans, Amorites, Akkadians, Babylonians, Phoenicians and the Canaanites. He had migrated to the shores of the Great Sea from the desert. The land in Arabia was dry with only a scattered number of oasis. His people were shepherds and farmers. That life never appealed to him but with the advent of the domestication of the donkey and camel;

nomadic life became much different. The camel was still making its way through the near east but it had proven to be an amazing way to move goods and people. The camel had been the start of his business of trade with the various communities. His caravans started to carry spices and incense along the Hadramaut to Yemen and then to Mecca, the Hejaz, Damascus and then near the great sea where he settled. The items from Arabia was sold in Canaan and the goods which were in abundance here such as figs, dates, wine and olives were in high demand as it was something the Arabs had seen very little of. He was able to establish mutual beneficial trade agreements between the people of Arabia and Canaan. His business had become lucrative but he wanted more markets and opening trade with the Hebrews would be an amazingly great opportunity for him. He wanted to make sure that nothing happened to Gaddiel. If Elrian came to talk with him further, he would explain the situation with him because he always seemed like a rational man, for a man from Kemet that is.

Evening

Group of 12 spies camped together outside of Northern Hebron

Joshua made a sleeping area along with the others. The 12 spies stayed together in the same area for safety reasons. There were grumblings from various elements in the group who felt they should start traveling that very evening. Joshua explained that the oasis was safe and that it would be better to leave at first light and in a well rested state.

Caleb thought of Fatia and the life they would have together. He thanked God for bringing her to him. He could not believe that he was so blessed to have met her. Caleb said a prayer, "Please dear heavenly Father, I thank you for bringing Fatia into my life. I thank you for allowing me to carry out your mission and to praise Your name. If it's Your will, please continue to keep us safe. Lord, I love you, Selah."

Gaddiel sat there thinking that he would have to do something about Joshua and Caleb. He could tell from their passionate speeches that their opinions would not be changed easily. Gaddiel would have to sway the people, not Joshua and Caleb. He felt good that many in the group supported his overall views. He was sure that the rest of the mission would only prove that he was right.

Ammiel started making up his blankets to sleep on although he was still concerned that the soldiers would come after him from Hebron. He was hoping that they would start this very evening to the north. He argued to the rest of the group that they start their journey that evening but Joshua forced his views on the men saying they should leave the next day.

Palti and Shammua were both still recuperating from the interrogation sessions but Sarah maintained a strong memory in their hearts and loins. Palti and Shammua each had murderous thoughts in their minds about the other one.

Gaddi and Igal knew they had to do something to Joshua and Caleb either before Lebo-Hamath. After hearing the conviction and belief in God for Joshua, they both believed that it was a certainty that he would tell Moses about their behavior in Hebron. Neither Gaddi nor Igal wanted their tribes to bring up the shame and embarrassment of the events of being with harlots and then thrown into the streets and ridiculed by the Canaanite mobs. Igal's tribe was very conservative and would react badly to those details. Gaddi's tribe was not any different; they would stone him for his behavior on a mission for God.

Geuel and Nahbi slept in the same area because they were comfortable with each other. They wanted to spent time with Palti and Shammua to discuss in greater detail the ordeal of their capture and interrogation.

Joshua decided to start writing his report for the day.

Hebron

Garrison

Fayid (spy one) and Ashur (spy two) arrived back at the garrison. They were sitting in the office of Commander Elrian when they told him the information learned from debriefing Mansur.

"These four Hebrew are returning in two weeks. That is the same time frame as the other two Hebrews we caught. I find that there are no coincidences in this job. Both of the groups are Hebrews and both will be returning in two weeks. I think that these two groups are together. So, those two little Hebrews lied to me and do have confederates with them. I wonder on what other topics did they tell untruths about. When they return, we will need to have our Sarah ask more penetrating questions of them."

"Does this change your plans?" Fayid asked.

"No, this is not going to change anything except we need another tack in terms of gaining more information from those two. That is good work with the Arab, Mansur. I did not want to ask him myself because I wanted to maintain our relationship because if he lied to me, I would have to kill him. I am tempted to kill the two Hebrews but that will not achieve my larger goal.

Fayid spoke up again, "Mansur explained that he did not believe the four Hebrews were involved in the murders especially their leader Gaddiel. He explained that Gaddiel was a businessman who wanted to do trade with the Canaanites."

Elrian listened to the details about Gaddiel and thought that he was an interesting man. Any Hebrew looking to do business with the Canaanites could be a potential ally. He needed more information; he would get Mansur to look into it when they returned.

Chapter 25

Joshua's finished his report and looked at it before putting it away.

"Day 15

Report 7

We left the city to make the next move north. On the way outside the city, we saw more farms with wheat, barley, rye, lentils, onions, grapes, melons, almonds, apples, plums, peaches and broad beans. There are also a myriad of animals such as sheep, goats, pigs, oxen, and asses. There are a few mines in the area producing tin, nickel and copper which has allowed the inhabitants to make bronze and brass.

There was a discussion among the group regarding whether we should even continue the journey. Caleb and I stayed steadfast and convinced the group to continue the mission. The biggest stumbling point for the group is what the men see with their eyes instead of what their heart tells them. I explained how our mission is to figure out how to possess the land, not to decide if we shall take the land. Gaddiel is definitely against this mission and has a group that supports him; Ammiel, Sethur and Shaphat. The other seven may not agree with the mission but voted to continue traveling north with Caleb and myself. We are staying at a small oasis located about an hour's walk north of Hebron. We passed through a wooded area and came upon this oasis where water is plentiful and date palms and fig trees abound. The land continues to impress me with its lush resources. We will start for Lebo-Hamath in the morning of the 16th day; we should arrive in a few days.

Overall Hebron is a formidable city. Since it's under the administration of Pharaoh, many of its procedures and fortifications are in that same style. Since we left Kemet, I have seen many of Pharaoh's soldiers in Hebron with the same armaments found in their capital city such as chariots. The soldiers use some of the same weapons; sword, khepesh (sickle sword), bow and arrows, spears, maces, axes, daggers and shields. The basic military units are formed in Hebron as it was in Pharaoh's lands with both neferu (elite troops) and seneniu (chariot warriors). The garrison had soldiers along with scribes, quartermasters, stable masters and adjutants. There was an area behind the garrison where the men practice their martial skills. I was told by Salman that when the new garrison commander arrived from Kemet, he brought a number of soldiers from Kemet and begin more training and more patrols through the city. This new commander's name is Elrian and he had professionalized the soldiers who had been conscripted from other lands and taken a hand's on approach to running the city. My best estimate to how many soldiers are in the city is about 2000. There is a civilian government but they are toothless and have no real power. I continue to trust in the Lord knowing that the evil one will be trying to make us falter.

End of Report."

After tucking his report away, Joshua eventually fell away to sleep.

Day 16 morning

The group broke up in their same 5 separate groups to travel north towards Lebo-Hamath. They started at sunrise and moved quickly along the route in a north westerly path. They traveled to the valley of Eschol. Eshcol was like the typical valleys in the Levant Area of the Near East where it became a traditional chokepoint for any troops traveling through which made it a good ambush position. The valley channeled troops walking through it by forcing them to thin out their numbers breaking up their battle lines. Once the entering armies' battle lines were disrupted, blocking forces prevented them from leaving and opposition forces perched above the valley would fire arrows making it a complete rout. It took them several hours to go through the valley and then move towards the north.

Joshua took mental notes about how dangerous it would be for the Israelites to travel in that valley. He noticed how easy it would be for the Canaanites to defeat an enemy in that valley. They moved quickly through the valley while moving north. They were able to reach Jericho before night fall. They decided to camp outside of the city and enter in the morning. This was one of the cities which were in the heart of Canaan. Joshua was focused on the mission while Caleb's thoughts were split between the mission and on Fatia. He did not worry exactly because he trusted God; he just longed to see her again. He knew that God would protect her.

The travel from the valley to the city of Jericho was mostly on flat land. They walked in their five groups separated from each other. If someone was looking at them making their way, it would look like they were strangers in a caravan. The topography of the land was different than on the Sinai where it was mostly desert with a few oasis. This land was fertile and even though the great sea was about 20 miles to the west, the greenery and vegetation was plenty. There were small settlements along the road which catered to the trade caravans.

The five groups made it to the outside of the Jericho, the oldest city in the area. They again camped together to augment their security but would go into the city separately just as they did in Hebron. Many travelers in the region would be camp together for safety. Joshua noticed that there were walls around the city at least 25 feet tall with guards stationed on top of the wall. The guards could see for miles. There were several small camps outside the city walls made up mostly of nomads and merchants. He could tell that this was a transit point. The gates were closed but he was told that it would open early in the morning. Security was of importance to whoever ran the city.

Mount Sinai

Moses and Aaron sat beneath Mount Horeb praying to God as the sun came up. The Israelites continued to grumble and fight among themselves during this time. Aaron and Moses were steadfast in their faith in God often praying on the mountainside. Several of the elders of tribes came to the side of mountain while they were still in prayer.

"Moses, we wish to speak to you," Hosea said from the Tribe of Zebulun. Hosea was accompanied by elders from the tribes of Dan, Naphtali, Ashur, Benjamin, Issachar, Gad, Joseph and Judah. In all, there were about two dozen of the most powerful men of Israel.

Interrupted from their prayer, Moses and Aaron looked up. "What is it you wish to say?" Moses asked.

"We wish to not wait any longer. We should seek other options because we do not even know when the spies will return, if they will even return. We could be waiting here for months," the elder from the tribe of Joseph stated.

"Do not underestimate God. If we are faithful to God, He will be faithful to those who obey him. Our envoys will return and we will wait until then before discussing this any further," Moses explained.

The people walked away complaining about Moses intransigence.

Moses sat back down and Aaron spoke to him, "The people continue to think that they know more than God. I do not think that just because the envoys will return with details about Canaan, the people will accept their report. The men are very stubborn and continue to plot behind your back. Please take care so that nothing happens to you," said Aaron.

"God will provide for my safety and protection. I do not worry about the people. They must obey the Lord, their God. It will not be good for them if disobey again," Moses said.

Aaron hoped that his brother, Moses, was right.

Hebron

Garrison

Commander Elrian was in the back of the garrison, taking on three men with swords in battle. The men had regular swords while he fought with the khepesh (sickle sword). The weapon was heavy and large with a curved end like a sickle. It was highly effective against lightly armored infantry. The name 'sickle sword' was a misnomer because on a standard sickle has the cutting edge is on the inner edge while with the sickle sword the cutting edge is on the outside.

Elrian fought with focus against the three men. The three men were foreign soldiers from the 'land between the two rivers', Mesopotamia. They had been captured in a raid. He offered them a choice: life or death. If the men survived they would be freed but if they failed they would be killed. Elrian's men could not believe that he, as commander, would put himself in danger like that. He did this regularly to maintain his fighting skills. The men thought Elrian was like them, a regular man, but he was not, he was a man who was able to channel the dark forces of Satan.

He parried the first man's swing and kicked him in the face. The second man made a clumsy lunge that he allowed to go past him while he drew his sword across the back of his neck, decapitating him. The third man came at him at that moment and was able to slice at him when he passed by. The slash connected with Elrian's back drawing a little blood, nothing life threatening. Elrian smiled and urged them on. The two men decided to come at him together. They came in, one with his sword high while the other had his sword low. Elrian did something unexpected; he charged them and brought his sword straight down on the head of the man on the right. The speed of Elrian's attack was unexpected and took the men by surprise. Elrian's sword almost split the man in half with blood going in all directions. The first man tried to put up a fight but he was outmatched as Elrian spun counterclockwise and cut his legs out from under him. He then stood up and pushed his sword into the man's belly. The third man had fear in his eyes and decided that perhaps he could survive if he ran. He turned to escape but Elrian had already his mind, he pulled a dagger from his waistband and threw it in the center of the man's back. The man fell to his knees. Elrian walked up to him, took the dagger out of his back and then cut his throat from ear to ear before pushing him down. Elrian was drenched in sweat and blood. He felt alive, feeling his heart beating rapidly in his chest.

"Clean this mess up," he ordered to his men watching as he returned to the garrison.

Elrian washed himself in the courtyard of the garrison where the men also washed. He stripped down and let the water from the bag filled with water go over his body. Elrian knew the men were shocked when he fought several opponents and then did this little ritual. He body was brown from the hours of being outside. He was tall, almost two cubits (approx 6'6"). His upper body was heavily muscled from his exercises and his powerful legs were the diameter of an olive tree. Scars were all over his body. He knew that everyone was looking at him. He had no shame and allowed the men to see that he was a man to be feared and envied for the excellent proportions of his body. He walked naked back to his office to put on a new uniform. He did not want to track the blood in his office which is why he started the ritual of bathing in the open where the men bathed.

He always thanked Satan after defeating enemies. He started saying the words which were taught to him a long time ago. After he said the necessary words, he was able to relax and returned to the the issue of the four Hebrews who stayed at Mansur's Pavilion and the two Hebrew spies that he had captured. They must be working in separate teams he speculated. He supposed that if there were two teams then perhaps there were more teams. He called in Spy one (Fayid), who was waiting in a special room in the garrison, into his office.

"I have a new assignment for you and number two. I want you to take a few of our fastest horses and travel to the nearby towns inquiring about the Hebrews. I believe that there may be more than just these two groups. I just want to know how many they are and what they are doing. As you know, the group is traveling north to Lebo-Hamath. Do not engage them, just gather intelligence for me. They are scheduled to return here in less than two weeks. We will plan for their arrival before then but for now, we will find out all we can know about them.

Fayid agreed to leave immediately, nodding as was customary.

Commander Elrian watched spy one leave knowing that the task was in good hands. He decided to visit his "good friend" Mansur. He had left it alone for a day but now would go over to the pavilion. He had not been to the pavilion in a few weeks. The Hebrews had left early the morning before so it would allow him to assess the situation personally. He asked the watch guard to have his detail prepare to leave. He usually travelled with a team of four men, all elite guards or neferu, the best of the best. The neferu were trained from the time they were children to be warriors. Few men could withstand their fury.

Commander had put on a fresh uniform and left the garrison with the four neferu walking towards Mansur's Pavilion.

Spy one (Fayid) and spy two (Ashur) each road a horse loaded with supplied for a few days. They traveled north towards Lebo-Hamath at a fast clip.

Chapter 26

Hebron

Day 16 evening

Fatia was at home reading one of the scrolls that Caleb left with them. She treasured the gift and would work to memorize the scripture. She knew that it was an important document to Caleb which is why she cherished it even more.

She read the scripture about how through a series of strange events, a Hebrew boy names Moses became a prince in Pharaoh's palace and then an outcast in a wilderness land. She was mesmerized when she read about Moses seeing the mysterious flames of a burning bush and Moses agreeing to return to Pharaoh's land to lead God's people out of bondage. Pharaoh was confronted and through a cycle of plagues and promises made and broken, Israel was taken from his grasp. She read about how the mass of people marching from Pharaoh through the Red Sea into the wilderness behind Moses and the pillars of clouds and fire. She was most amazed that the latest records stated how despite the continual evidence of God's love and power, the people complained and begin to yearn for their days back with Pharaoh. That was where it stopped. How could a people who actually saw evidence of a living God willfully turn their backs on Him. Fatia loved God and followed His laws even without ever seeing any evidence of God. She guessed that was what having faith was about. She loved the God of Abraham, Jacob and Isaac first and then loved Caleb. She and Caleb discussed how each viewed God. They were equally yoked in their opinion that a believer needed to love God first before anything or anyone. That was one of the things that each found so fascinating about the other, each was in love with God. Caleb told her how he believed that if they put God first then everything else would fall in place.

Fatia had found the man of God she had been looking for all her life. She was blessed and would do everything she could to show God her appreciation for answering her prayers. She walked outside and looked up at the stars. They had agreed to each look up at the stars every night while they were apart. It was like they were together but separate.

"Beloved good night," she said to the stars.

Hebron

Commander Elrian made his way through the city with his neferu (elite guards) who walked in front and behind of him. In reality, Elrian did not believe that he needed the men but it looked good. He knew that Satan would protect him from any harm. He already felt the slight wound that he had gotten from his exercise had already healed. It only took an half an hour or so to heal a minor injury while it took longer to heal a more serious wound. He made it to the pavilion in less than an hour as the streets were crowded. He walked into the meeting hall. Everyone looked in his direction when he came in. His guards went to his usual table up front which had the best view of the room. There were a few men at his preferred table, his guards made his wish known that they should leave. The four men got up and moved to another table.

Mansur was talking with his cooks when one of his staff came in and told him that the commander was there.

"He is here?" Mansur asked. This was highly unusual because normally Elrian would let him know that he was coming so he could have his table reserved. After his two men came yesterday and with this visit today, Mansur knew that there was something going on. He knew that Elrian liked his routines. He knew that he was useful for Elrian and did not misunderstand that when his usefulness was over, he could be arrested or killed or banished with one gesture by the commander. Mansur knew men like Elrian; professional, ambitious and without remorse. He had seen Elrian personally kill a thief in front of the thief's family without a hint of sorrow. He had known many military men in his life but there was something different and troubling about Elrian. He did not seem to have any emotions. He had seen him laugh but it was just with his mouth, he never smiled with his eyes even when he had seemed to be enjoying himself. He understood that Elrian was using him for information on what was going on in Hebron but as such, he was mostly left alone. Mansur could do what needed to run his business.

Almost a year ago, Mansur's security staff killed some foreigners who wanted to rob his pavilion. The men had heard that the gambling proceeds from the pavilion were enormous, and they were right. Mansur's games of chance were known far and wide but they were stacked against the players. Mansur made much of his money from the games and the dancers who also acted as harlots. Elrian had come to the scene and asked him what happened. After Mansur told him, he just nodded his head and said that if he had any other troubles he could call on Elrian for assistance. After that first meeting, Elrian had started stopping by asking for information on what was going on in the city. *Quid pro quo*, something for something, was the coin of the realm. He had been helped by the new commander of the garrison, the de facto leader of the town, and as such was indebted to him. So now, he was expected to be Elrian's guy in town. The one thing that Elrian did do was to make sure that he was not seen as a puppet for the commander. Elrian made sure that no one knew that he was providing information to him.

Mansur walked out and saw Elrian sitting at his favorite table. "Commander, if I had known that you would be here, I would have reserved a table for you," he said.

"I wanted to speak with you and felt it would be better if I came sooner rather than later," Elrian said.

"Let us get comfortable," Mansur stated. He called over a staff member and ordered all of Elrian's favorites.

"I know you talked to my men but I wanted to know if you had any more details about these Hebrew merchants that stayed here?" Elrian asked.

"I mentioned all the facts to them but there are a few things that I remembered after they left. All three of the men except Gaddiel spent time with my working women the first night. One of the men by the name of Ammiel left here on one of the nights. The two men, Sethur and Shaphat, spent a lot of time with my dancers while their leader Gaddiel and I spoke about business opportunities," Mansur explained.

"Now, do you think that these men were associated with the two Hebrews who I captured?"

"I am not sure because they did not act like spies. In fact, they had so much fun, I could not imagine that they were seeking information other than business information," Mansur stated.

"That is interesting. Now, this man Ammiel do you think that he is the type of man who would spend time with Kabir?" Elrian said.

Mansur did not want to answer this question because he knew that Ammiel was most likely the last man who saw him alive. He did not believe that Ammiel had killed Kabir but he did know that Ammiel had spent time with him. Mansur had noticed the first night when Ammiel was talking with Kabir for quite some time. Kabir was about his business and rarely spoke to strangers unless it was a business transaction. Kabir loved money more than anything and he would not have spoken to Ammiel for an extended amount of time if it was not about sex.

Elrian was like a seer; he could intuit things others would never see, Mansur was hiding something.

Mansur wanted the potential business from the Hebrews and if he implicated Ammiel, they would have troubles when they returned. Mansur could not lie to Elrian outright so he had to obfuscate a little. "I am not sure, Commander. Ammiel left one night but I am not sure if he is the type to go with men. I do know that he had sexual relations with a woman the first night. I cannot say if he was with someone that night because I was with the group discussing business. If I knew, I would volunteer than information." Mansur explained.

Elrian looked at Mansur for a moment without saying a word. He was trying to decide if he was telling the truth but Mansur was not going to be intimated a dog of Pharaoh. Mansur let Elrian play his mind games while he waited patiently. He may not be a powerful military commander but he had over a half a century of business and trade with all types of people.

Elrian finally spoke, "Let me know immediately when they return. Do not mention to them that I or my men spoke to you. Am I clear?" he asked.

"Clear, my lord. Is there any other order?" Mansur asked.

"I will have some suggestions for you once they arrive. Let us have some entertainment now?" Elrian requested.

Mansur knew what this meant. He would ask three of the dancing girls to go to his best room and wait for Elrian. He did not understand why he actually went with the girls because he did not seem to enjoy himself like others. The commander lay with the women and then they would wash him before he dressed and left. The women had told him how strange it was to be with him because he showed no feelings; it almost seemed like exercise for the commander. He would start having sex with one while the two waited. Then he would lay with the next and then the third without stopping. The women said it was as it he was just going through the motions because it was expected to him.

The commander went to the room and experienced the familiar release of laying with three women before leaving for the garrison.

Group of 12 spies outside of Jericho

Before Joshua lay down for the evening, he composes his 8th report reviewing the events of the day's journey. He completed his report, put it away and then prayed to God before sleeping.

Separately, Caleb lay on his blanket beside Joshua. He starred at the stars thinking about Fatia. They had agreed to each look up at the stars each night while each thought of the other. He thanked God for answering his prayers. He knew that if he was faithful to the living God, God would be faithful to him. He praised and thanked the Lord for showing him the light and the way. He smiled as he thought of Fatia looking at the same stars he gazed at.

"Beloved, good night," he said before falling to sleep.

Gaddiel started walking around the camp after everyone else had fallen asleep. He did not know how he was going to convince the group that they should not conquer Canaan. Gaddiel thought about what would happen if the people did move into Canaan and Moses was proved to be right, Moses would probably stay in power for another 40 years. Gaddiel realized that his time was now or never.

For one moment, he thought about whether he was right or wrong in his conviction about not following Moses. Was he wrong? Doubt entered his mind.

Suddenly a blinding sunburst of radiance and light appeared before him. He held up his hand while turning away from the blinding light. He returned his gaze to the place where the brilliance was occurring. In that place, an angel of light stood resplendent in shining, golden garments with great white wings that spread out like a giant bird. The angel was glistening with flecks of gold in a shimmering light. Gaddiel could not believe his eyes. Was he dreaming?

"Gaddiel, behold I come to bring you a message from the most high. You are not deceived in your belief that you should not enter this land. This land holds dangers and perils which would devastating to your people," the angel said.

Gaddiel knew he was right and now he was receiving a divine revelation which confirmed it. He fell to his knees saying, "Oh holy one, I am here to serve you. How may I carry out your will?" he asked.

"Gaddiel, stand fast to your convictions. When you get back to the Sinai, persuade the people to return to Pharaoh or to go to Midian. I give them the choice. Do not tell them that you have received this revelation. This message is for you exclusively," the apparition explained.

"I hear and I obey you," his face on the ground. The bright light began to fade away and in a moment, the vision was gone. He thought for one moment, was it an illusion or was it real? He examined the ground where the entity had been and noticed the scorched marks.

"It was real," he thought. "I received a revelation from God. I knew that I was special. I knew that it was my destiny to lead my people." He felt pride swell in his chest to have been chosen. He looked around and saw that everyone was still asleep.

[*Satan, the inveterate enemy of God, laughed. He was surprised how easy it was to mislead the fool Gaddiel when he took the guise of an angel of light. Satan was permitted to use illusion. Gaddiel was so prideful that it was simple to get him to believe that God would actually choose someone like him to lead the people. Satan was allowed to mislead and lie as long as it was under God's authority, control and within the limits set by God. Pride, the weapon God used against him in ejecting him from paradise, he would now use against God's Spies of Promise.*]

Chapter 27

Day 17

Jericho

The five groups of spies left along with the other traders and merchants who were entering the city to do business. They had agreed to spend the night in the city and then meet outside the northern gates the next morning.

As they walked in the city, Joshua immediately noticed how this city was different than Hebron. The city was an oasis situated in a hot plain. The combination of rich alluvial soil, the perennial springs and constant sunshine made it an attractive place for settlement. Palm trees were everywhere. It was along the trade route and benefited from it geographical location. Once the throngs of the traffic entered the city the group separated and moved away from each other. Jericho meant 'moon' and sat atop Tell es-Sultan, one of the strongest springs in Palestine.

Group 4

Palti and Shammua went to look for lodging for the evening since the group had decided to stay in the city for the night. They had been a little distant to one another because of the competition for Sarah. That said, they still shared the secret of being with her so a bond did exists between the two.

"Let us find a room for the night and then rest. I hate sleeping outdoors on the ground," Palti said.

"You are right. I am not excited about doing more reconnaissance. I think we can see everything we need to from just entering and leaving the city," said Shammua.

"I do not want to come to the attention of the military here as we did in Hebron. I would be content in doing as little as possible," Palti explained.

"I agree with you and we still rest from our injuries," Shammua stated.

They walked to the marketplace and started inquiring about places to stay for the night.

Group 3

Gaddiel, Ammiel, Sethur and Shaphat made their way through the town to enter the large marketplace. The marketplace was bristling with merchants looking to trade, barter or make other deals. They could tell that this town made its money on the men traveling on the trade route.

Gaddiel was still in thought over the revelation that he had received the night before. He felt empowered and emboldened. He would take more of a leadership position with the group. He would leave his doubts behind. He had doubts inside previously about whether Moses was right or not but now he could rest assured that he was chosen too.

"Let's take a survey of the town before deciding where we will rest for this evening," Gaddiel suggested.

The group went along with his plan and followed him.

Group 5

Joshua and Caleb walked to the center of the city to gauge the activity and the people. There was more commercial activity in this city then in Hebron because the location put it on the main north-south trade route then Hebron. They walked around pretending to look at goods and discussing prices. They saw a small garrison of soldiers in the center of the city but they did not look as formidable as the soldiers in Hebron.

Joshua liked the activity because it signified life. The people were busy carrying on the affairs of daily life in a major Canaanite city. They were concerned about their mercantile enterprise which was why Joshua believed that the military garrison was located in the center of town in the heart of the marketplace.

Joshua looked at his friend Caleb and asked him his thoughts regarding the city.

"I think that this town is a little deceiving because you see lots of activity without soldiers walking around but the soldiers are paying attention. I see that there are soldiers on the wall who are looking inward and outward. They may not be as professional or as alert as the soldiers of Hebron but they are engaged," Caleb said.

"Exactly, people could come here and see the business going on believing that it was be an easy village to conquer but they military are watching but at a lower level. They can easily close the gates if they see trouble and then deal with the internal threat without interference. This is important to know as it affects our battle plan but it does not matter to us overall because we have God on our side," Joshua said.

"Yes, you are right. With God, nothing is impossible."

Group 2

Nahbi and Geuel entered the city focused on gaining intelligence from the beginning of their time there. They stayed focused on learning all they could. Nahbi and Geuel walked through the town watching the hustling and bustling of the merchants moving to and fro as well as animals being sold and goods being weighed.

"This town is very busy. They have a lot going on and I believe that we would not be out of place here because of the numerous foreigners and traveling caravans who are in town," Geuel said.

"That's a good thing so we don't have to worry about what happened to Palti and Shammua. They seemed to handle their interrogation in a good manner. I was wondering how I would have held up," Nahbi speculated.

"Who knows how one would respond under torture? Its one of life's mysteries because I would have thought that little Palti would have folded very quickly but according to Shammua he stayed strong and did not tell them about the rest of us. People can surprise you sometimes," Geuel explained.

"For the good and the bad, people can surprise us," Nahbi said.

They continued their walk through the city.

Group 1

Gaddi and Igal walked along the main street looking at the merchants, money changers, food venders and other businessmen move about looking to earn a day's wage. They were shadowing Joshua and Caleb.

"Why are we following them?" asked Igal.

"Igal, I think we need to seek someone to help us with our problem," Gaddi said.

"Gaddi, we have tried a sorcerer and have tried hiring assassins but neither worked. What could we do in this town?" He asked.

"I think that we can try to discredit Joshua since he is Moses' strong right hand. I was thinking that we would hire a harlot to go to his room and offer to have sexual relations with him," Gaddi explained.

"That could be a good plan because it does not involve us trying to kill them again," Igal said.

They walked around the marketplace following Joshua and Caleb.

Spies one and two were on their way to Lebo-Hamath, they stopped in a few of the cities on route. Fayid (spy one) believed that they would have better fortune at the end of the Hebrews' journey. They would stake out that final location waiting for the spies. Their journey would take several days.

Group 3

Gaddiel had decided to get some lunch so he found a place to eat and lodge inside the marketplace. There was an assortment of foods and beverages served. The place was nothing like Mansur's Pavilion but it would do.

Gaddiel watched the group eat. The three men seemed to enjoy themselves. Gaddiel decided he would talk to them about the town. "I think that this town may be smaller but there is a lot here especially within the marketplace. The town is fortified pretty well like Hebron and the soldiers appear professional. This place only confirms my thoughts about Canaan. Don't you agree?" Gaddiel asked.

Shaphat spoke first, "I think you are right. It's a well-fortified city with impressive trade. They definitely benefit from the north/south trade route. Some of the soldiers walking around are almost three cubits tall (9 feet tall) though."

Group 5

Joshua and Caleb found a place for lunch and to sleep for the night in the marketplace.

"I find this place interesting; the commerce is great and the economy seems to be in great shape. When we take over this land, we will be able to have excellent commercial enterprise here. I see much potential here."

"Caleb, I am glad that you are with me and that you also see this land through the eyes of faith. God is with us and I am pleased that you believe with your heart. Moses told me that I could lean on you during this mission. I am glad that you have been blessed to be able to find your wife on this journey. Ever since we left Pharaoh, I have felt as if God was preparing me for something and I know that this mission is a part of God's plan. I also believe that you were sent on this mission for a purpose. As long as we stay obedient and surrender to His will, we will be ready when the Lord speaks to us."

"Joshua, why are we not able to hear God's voice at times?" Caleb asked.

"Usually we do are not able to hear the Lord's voice because of sin. The Lord cannot abide in sin and when we sin it's difficult to hear His voice. Also, many people do not listen with their own hearts. Just as some people only view things in the natural, some people do not listen with their hearts or their spirits. These people listen only with their earthly ears. We must continue to train our spirits to listen to that small still voice of God or listen when God speaks through people or through dreams as you experienced when God showed you your wife. We must be open to what God is trying to tell us. Obedience is the greatest tool we have to fight against the evil one. Being stiff-necked does not please God. Our actions, thoughts and words should always be focused on pleasing God. Sometimes the absence of God's voice is purposeful to help us grow and to test our faith. And lastly, He is the Lord of the heavens and the earth, His plans are His own and they are for our good; our job is just to stay faithful and to trust Him," Joshua said.

"Thank you, I am also pleased that I am with you because I continue to learn and grow. I have faith and do not know why the others doubt after all they have seen," Caleb asked.

"It's not about them having doubts because we can not stop doubts from coming into our minds. It's about these people who nurture their doubts instead of their faith by leaning on God, His words and His promises," Joshua explained.

"For example, I rarely have doubts and when I do, I do not entertain those doubts. It's okay to question as long as you do not let it affect your reservoir of faith. We can question through eyes of faith not through eyes of doubt. Some men say they believe in God, but I say I don't believe in God because belief almost means that doubt is possible, I know there is a God without a hint of doubt and I know that He is taking us through this process for our own good, edification and maturing so that we can move to the next level of abundance. There is a process, and we need to respect the process. Sometimes, the process or journey is more important than the destination."

"Those are very wise words. Thank you," Caleb said.

"Those are not my words but the Moses', the Prophet of God's. I count myself fortunate to have been able to learn from the man who has spoken face to face with the Lord. I cannot even imagine what that was like. When I saw Moses' face, I knew that he had seen the living God. The light in his face told me the whole story. There has never been a man like Moses and I doubt that there will ever be a man like him in my lifetime," Joshua explained.

Caleb also thought himself to be fortunate to be able to learn from the man who learned from Moses.

Present day

"Jack, these are important points to remember my friend," Salman said.

Groups 5 and 1

While Joshua and Caleb sat in the eating establishment, Gaddi and Igal watched them from afar.

"I will be back in a few minutes, wait here?" He said.

Gaddi walked inside and spoke to the owner, he returned after a few minutes and sat back down.

"So what happened?" Igal asked.

"We should be having company shortly," Gaddi said. Just as he said, a beautiful woman walked to them and sat at their table.

"I was told that you wanted my services. I need to explain that for one night, I get 10 shekels. I get to keep five shekels and the owner gets five. What is it that you want; I can do the both of you but it will have to be one at a time?" She said.

"No, it's not like that. Look over at the two men at that table," Gaddi asked her.

She looked over and saw them.

"Yes," she said.

"The one man on the right, study his face. He is staying here at this place. I need you to go to his room when he is there and say that he tried to force you to have sexual relations with him. I was thinking that you could knock at his door and then ask him for help. You can say that you need a place to hide because someone is chasing you. After a while, you then make a move on him. If he has sexual relations with you then that is good but it doesn't matter. You should tear at your clothes and then start screaming. Run out of the room and tell the soldiers that he tried to sexually assault you. We will be outside. I will pay you 10 shekels now but then give you ten more shekels if you can get the army to arrest him," Gaddi said.

"He must be a business rival. Anyway, that is easy but I want 20 shekels now," she said.

Igal looked at Gaddi and said, "That is excellent. We will pay."

Gaddi paid the 10 shekels and watched her leave to prepare for her mission.

"Now, this is your best plan, just like the story of Joseph in Genesis. When Joshua is arrested, we will no longer have to worry about him," Igal said.

Chapter 28

Day 17 Jericho

Group 4

Palti and Shammua rested in their room. Palti begin thinking about Sarah, he could not get her out of his head.

Shammua lay on his bedding for the day resting like Palti. He needed to formulate a plan for Sarah to be all his. He did not see what she saw in little Palti.

Each spent the day, dreaming of returning to Hebron. They decided that they would no longer do any more spying. They had not mentioned that they were welcome to Hebron again because the group may have told them to stay out of the town. They both had to see Sarah again so they made sure that they were in the position to return to Hebron by staying out of trouble.

Palti thought that he would have to talk with Shammua to work out an agreement regarding Sarah.

The start of a plan was forming in Shammua mind. He was thinking that he could arrange an accident for Palti after they returned to Hebron. He could talk with Sarah to see if she would help him.

[*Satan loved the plan of Gaddi and Igal because he felt for certain that Joshua would fall.*]

[*Archangels Raphael and Michael watched the events unfold. Joshua had free will to chose his fate. If Joshua chose to commit a sin, then the sin would direct his fate. If Joshua stayed faithful then they would make sure that he would not be taken advantage of by the prince of lies.*]

Group 5

"I am going to the marketplace," Caleb said.

Joshua stayed in his room while Caleb was out getting some fruit for the morning. Joshua intended to write in his journal on the security features he observed in the city while Caleb was gone.

The young harlot was standing in the shadows. Her name was Mara and she watched Caleb leave. She thought this was the easiest and best job that she had been given in the last few years. After she saw him leave, she approached the door of the room.

"Help, open up," she yells.

Joshua was in the room when he heard the frantic knocking. He opened the door.

Mara ran into the room and shut the door. "They are after me, you must help me," she begged.

"What is it? How can I help you?" Joshua asked.

"I need a place to hide, they want to kill me. You have to help me." She grabbed his tunic in panic.

"It's okay, I will help you. Have a seat. You can stay here as long as you want," Joshua said.

"Thank you, my lord. Thank you very much. I do not know what I would have done without you." Mara sat down and made herself comfortable.

She continued, "Look at my hands, they are shaking," she said holding her hands up.

"It will be alright, no one will hurt you while you are here," he explained.

"Thank you; please sit here next to me. I am scared," she asked.

Joshua sat down beside her. "I appreciate your kindness. My heart is beating so fast, feel this." She placed his hand on her heart.

Joshua was shocked and took his hand away immediately.

"It's alright," she said continuing, "I want to thank you for saving my life." She touched him in an intimate area of his body and he immediately stood up.

"I cannot. That is not right. You can stay here but we can not do such a thing," Joshua said.

"I want to thank you. You can have me." She stood and pulled her shirt over her head. She was topless but Joshua looked away.

"I cannot sin against God. I am afraid that you have mistaken the situation. Please put your clothes back on," Joshua asked while keeping his gaze away.

She realized that Joshua would not give in to iniquity.

[*Do it now, Satan put the thought in her mind.*]

182

"Aggh, help! Stop it. Please stop it!" She starts screaming and ripping at her clothes. Joshua asks, "What is wrong? What are you doing?" Her clothes being torn, she messes up her hair and ran her head into the door, drawing blood. She then went out the door and began to scream loudly.

"Help, help!" She yelled at the top of her voice. Several of the staff members come out of the restaurant.

Joshua asked her again, "Why are you upset?"

"Please do not hurt me. Help me! It's him. Please stop," she screamed standing half naked.

The sight of her naked body enraged the staff and the people congregated around. She was crying, jumping up and down hysterically.

A soldier appeared to take command of the situation.

The soldier asked, "Tell me what happened."

Several members of the crowd spoke up instead, "this foreigner is who she is screaming about."

"Stone him, he has tried to take advantage of our woman," one bystander said.

Another bystander said, 'It's clear he has tried to take advantage of her."

Several members of the crowd grabbed Joshua who was not resisting. They held him in place by his arms. He did nothing wrong so he willingly stood there.

"I have done nothing inappropriate," Joshua maintained.

Caleb came up and asked, "What is going on here?"

"Shut up, foreigner," One man yelled!

"The new one is with the other foreigner. Let's stone both of them. They are criminals trying to sully our women," the leader of the mob stated.

Several soldiers came up to the crowd. The officer asked the woman, "Now tell me, is this so? Did this man take advantage of you?" He asked.

She was about to answer, then stopped and froze.

[*Archangel Michael used his God-spell power to touch her heart. He placed the truth on her heart, and the thought in her head, "this is not right, this man has not done any wrong to you."*]

She just stood there, eyes fixed ahead.

"Answer me, is what they say true? Did this man or the other man take advantage of you?" The officer asked.

She turned to face the officer in charge, "I am sorry, thank you for your help. But this man has done me no wrong. He tried to help me. I am sorry. Be well," she said, turned and left without another word.

Joshua did not understand what happened. Caleb walked over to him and asked, "What happened?"

"I do not know, obviously a disturbed young woman. I will pray for her," Joshua said.

The crowd began to disburse after the soldiers told everyone to leave.

Joshua walked into the room along with Caleb. In the room, he explained what happened to him.

"That is strange. It appears as if something is afoot. Some evil is attempting to come over us," Caleb explained.

"You are right, we need to stay focused and in prayer keeping God first in our lives. There are forces at work which do not want us to succeed in our endeavor. We need to be even more cautious during the rest of this mission," Joshua stated.

"I agree with you Joshua. There are things going on here that we cannot know," Caleb explained.

Gaddi and Igal had watched the events unfold from the outlying crowd. They were happy how it was going before everything changing suddenly. They did not understand what happened. They left the area quickly.

Igal was bothered by what happened while Gaddi just made his way to room in deep thought.

[*Satan shook his head and realized that He (God) or one of His agents must have intervened. Satan had to find a more clever way to ruin Joshua and Caleb.*]

[*Archangel Michael watched the crowd disburse. He and Rafael were not going to allow Satan to take advantage of Joshua and Caleb without a fight.*]

Group 1

Gaddi and Igal went to their room where Mara was already waiting.

184

"I want my money now," Mara demanded.

"You did not get them arrested as we wanted. You were asked by the soldiers and you told them there weas no problem with the target. You failed us. What happened?" Gaddi asked.

"I do not know what happened but I could not lie. I felt compelled to tell the truth. I still did what you wanted in the beginning and I want the 20 shekels. If you do not give it to me than I will go to the soldiers and tell them that you put me up to it," Mara told them.

"We will not pay you one thin shekel," Gaddi exclaimed.

Igal became nervous knowing that if she went to the soldiers they would be in trouble and Joshua would know. Igal took out the 20 shekels and paid her. "Now go and never darken our doorstep again," Igal said.

She took the funds and left. Gaddi gave Igal a look of disapproval and asked, "Why did you pay her, we could have handled her?"

"I am tired of you handling things. This has gotten out of hand. I just want to finish this mission without any more talk discussion about these affairs. They are protected by God, can't you see that?" Igal asked.

"We have just been unlucky? Fortune has been against us," Gaddi explained.

"It's not about our fortunes, we are wrong and our sin will taint us. We must repent," Igal said and left.

Group 2

Nahbi and Geuel made a complete survey of the town. Each actually was able to gain a good feel for the people and the city's infrastructure. They ate in a local establishment and were able to strike up a conversation with one of the religious leaders of the town. There were several temples they went into where they observed the Canaan tradition of temple harlots. They walked around the whole city and were still able to take time to relax a bit. The city was smaller than Hebron but more active because of it being on the trade route. The found a single room with blankets on the floor for them to sleep on. They agreed to go to bed early in order to rise early in order to see how the town opened the gates from inside of the town's walls.

Group 3

Gaddiel, Ammiel, Sethur and Shaphat had found lodging in the best place in town. Gaddiel had met one of the town's head money changers. Gaddiel used his gift of speaking to get in good with that influential business leader. He arranged for four rooms for the men in the marketplace. Gaddiel had discussed running caravans to the town from the Sinai with the money changer. The businessman had laid out a good dinner spread for them and had their room ready by the time they were ready to go to sleep. The whole group was tired from their last night's festivities at Mansur's in Hebron. They retired for the evening preparing to leave early in the morning in order to move north of the city to meet the other spies.

Group 5

Joshua and Caleb sat in their room discussing the events of the day. Caleb asked Joshua if he was worried about these unnamed forces seemingly working against us.

"I am not worried at all. Our God is an awesome God and he reigns from heaven and earth. I know that our cause is just and right. Keep your eyes focused on God and all will be well," Joshua explained.

"I understand, thank you," Caleb responded.

Joshua pulled out his little scroll and made his report for the day.

"Day 17

Report 9

There are some forces around us that are trying to sabotage this mission. A young woman tried to set me up today with sex. I was blessed because I stayed faithful to God. I can see how men get into trouble when they fall into sin. The city is a thriving fortified place about the size of Hebron with a very active economy. The military runs the city ensuring that commerce flows without any problems. This whole town is centered on the smooth running of all of its mercantile enterprises and it has a underground spring. This city is about money and anything can be bought with the right amount of money. The town closes its gates at the setting of the sun and reopens its gates at the rising of the sun. The town is sealed off during the night. I believe that this town's defenses are just as formidable then Hebron. The gates cannot be breached by ramming it. The number of soldiers we observed today was at least 1000 troops. The town relies heavily on the closing of its gates to protect it. Once we take over the town and drive out its inhabitants, the potential trade opportunities here is amazing.

End of report."

Joshua put away the scroll. He was not especially concerned about the day's events but together with the ambush in Hebron, he felt that the dark forces were gathering against them until they returned to Sinai. He prayed to the Lord before falling to sleep.

Sinai

Moses sat at the edge of Mount Horeb. The tribes' elders had come against him again this day. Their grumblings and complaints had only increased. Moses knew that the Lord would not stand for long at their lack of faith. He prayed that he did not bring the Israelites out of bondage under Pharaoh only to die in the wilderness because of their lack of faith. He did not understand how people could be so unfaithful, had the Israelites been so conditioned that they only understood slavery. Slavery to sin, slavery to bondage and slavery to their way of thinking which seemed to be even harder than defeating Pharaoh. Moses had prayed that the people would grow, mature, and learn how to change on the inside so that their faith directed their actions and behavior.

Chapter 29

Day 18 Jericho

[*Satan was not pleased that his plans for Joshua and Caleb were thwarted. "I do not want any of God's creations to gain salvation. If I cannot live in paradise then why should the humans. God always loved them more than me." Satan's thoughts returned to the early days when he was called the Angel Lucifer. He had been created by God like all the angels. "I was a 'covering' cherub, one of the great angels who stood on the left or right side of God's throne (1). I was a highly exalted angelic leader. I was the most beautiful, flawless and most breathtaking angel there had ever been. My wisdom was perfect and my brightness was awe-inspiring (2). I led the angelic choir and my voice was the purest and most glorious ever heard in heaven. But God, He cursed me. I now live in darkness, misshapen and disfigured."*

Satan looked at his image in a mirror and saw how ugly and dark he was. For a former being of light, being in the dark was almost too much to bear. He smashed the mirror as been his habit since he fell. He could take the form of any creature he wanted but it wasn't the same. Although he was the father of lies, illusions and lies, he knew any image he made for himself was not real. In heaven he would look at his image for hours. His brightness used to be spoken about throughout heaven, he missed his brightness. Satan thought to himself, "God can forgive the humans but he couldn't forgive me for starting the war in heaven; so he cast me and the angels who supported me. One third of the angels followed me when I took up arms against God (3). God said I wanted His throne, and maybe I did (4). Thus, He cast me out and now I am called Satan (adversary), the devil (slanderer), Azazel, Ahriman, Mara, Asmoseus, Beelzebub, Seth or other such names. The angels who followed me were all cast out as well and are called demons now. God said that I was prideful, jealous, discontent and self-exalting, and he punished me by never allowing me to sing again." Satan opened his mouth trying to make a sound but all that came out is a chaotic screech.

"I will do everything I can to keep all the humans out of heaven. The humans think I live in some imaginary place called hell but my home is earth and the only way I can hurt God is by destroying the humans, who were created in His image. I am fortunate that it is so easy to lead the humans astray. Freedom of choice is God's way. He thinks that it a gift for them but I love the fact that they can choose me freely. Moses, Joshua and Caleb are my enemies and I will not stop until I bring them down.]

North of Jericho

Each team of spies left early and travelling north outside of the city. Joshua and Caleb had awoken early and waited by the northern gates to view how the gates opened. The captain of the guard came with two companies of 24 men. The guards who had worked the gates the previous night were replaced with new guards. Guards who observed from the walls gave a signal that all was clear to open the gates. Joshua surmised that if the crowds were larger or if a threat appeared, the captain of the guard would bring more men to observe while the gates were opened. A large wooden lever had been placed across the backs of the gates and two stabilizing poles laid at a diagonal against the gates to provide further support. Joshua thought it looked satisfactory for their purposes but it would not keep out a determined foe. The gates were opened and the guards walked outside of the gates as a show of force. The crowds who were waiting to go out slowly moved out of the gates. The crowds outside had to wait until the outgoing traffic passed them first. The soldiers made sure that it was an orderly move in each direction. Joshua left with the throngs of merchants traveling north.

Each team of spies was intermingled in the large group traveling north. There were several caravans moving out of the city which masked their movements. They traveled in the direction of the caravans. One by one the spies were able to get men close enough to each other to share a few words. Gaddiel had already told Ammiel, Sethur and Shaphat they they should just travel with the caravans north. Palti and Shammua were able to overhear them and just nodded before moving away. Shammua went over to Gaddi and Igal telling them of the plan. Nahbi and Geuel had already figured out what the group was doing so they just kept moving north. Joshua and Caleb also noticed what their group was doing in regards to travel in the mass of people going north. Joshua saw it as a blessing.

"There seems to be many blessings still in store for us. This caravan will provide great safety as well as cover," Caleb said.

Joshua saw one of the caravan leaders and asked him, "Friend, how far north is this caravan traveling?"

"We are heading to Lebo-Hamath to sell these camels, spices, myrrh, nuts and other goods. We make this trek every month when are own supplied get low. The merchants there trade with us for what each of us needs," he answered.

"Thank you friend, do you mind if me and my companion travel with your group?" Joshua asked.

"Not at all, there is safety in greater numbers. Where are you from stranger?" He asked.

"We are from land where Pharaoh rules. The lands have many names, Kemet or Musru is probably what you know it being called," Joshua explained.

"Yes, the land where the great river flows backwards. The Nile River flows south to north, very strange because most rivers in my travels flow from North to South. My name is Amel." the merchant said.

"My name is Joshua and I am pleased to meet you. How long have you been doing this trade route?"

Amel thought for a moment and then said, "Ten years I have been making this trek through this region."

"Is it usually safe? We are looking to undertake some trade in this region too and wanted to know if we had to worry about raiding parties from hostile forces?" Joshua asked.

"This is one of the reasons I have operated this caravan for so long; it's safe and very lucrative. Pharaoh's army keeps this region safe and running well," Amel said.

The walked together for a few minutes and then Amel asked Joshua.

"Your accent is not like the people who live in Pharaoh's land. Why is that?" Amel stated.

"I am of Israel, a Hebrew who follows the one true God," Joshua explained.

"I have heard about you Hebrews and your God who has no name. We have a several days journey ahead of us. Tell me about this God I have had heard your people talk about," Amel asked.

"Our God has a name now because of the dialogue He has had with His prophet Moses. My God's name is 'I AM WHO I AM.'"

"I am from Arabia and we follow many gods, how does your god differ from Minat, Alat or Baal?" Amel asked.

Joshua provided an explanation from his Holy book, the Torah. "Our God is a personal God who takes a close interest in His people. In our sacred writings, Our Lord spoke to Moses face to face, saying, "Speak to all the congregation of the children of Israel, and say to them: You shall be holy, for I the Lord your God am Holy (5)." We received the 10 laws from our God on how to interact with each other, and how to interact with our God. One of the most important commandments is stated as this, 'You shall not hate your brother in your heart. You shall surely rebuke your neighbor, and not bear sin because of him. You shall not take vengeance, nor bear any grudge against the children of you people, but you shall love your neighbor as yourself: I am the Lord. (6).' Worshiping our God is about taking personal responsibility for our actions, making sure that we strive to do what's pleasing in the eyes of God."

Joshua paused as it was clear that Amel was processing this information because his gods were distant and cold.

Joshua continued, "God tells us that, 'If we walk in His statutes and keep His commandments, and perform them, then I will give you rain in its season, the land shall yield its produce, and the trees of the field shall yield fruit (7). For I will look on you favorably and will make you fruitful, multiply you and confirm My covenant with you (8). I will walk among you and be your God, and you shall be my people. I am the Lord your God, who brought you out of the land of Egypt, that you should not be their slaves. I have broken the bands of your yoke and made you walk upright. But if you do not obey Me, and do not observe all these commandments...(9). "...I will punish you seven times more for your sins. I will break the pride of your power (10). Then, if you walk contrary to Me, and are not willing to obey Me, I will bring on you seven times more plagues, according to your sins (11)." Joshua was reciting the scriptures from memory and added, "If we obey God then we will eat from the best of the fields but if we resist or disobey God then we will reap what we sow, pain and sorrow."

Amel thought for a moment before saying anything. "That is so different than the gods I worship. So, if you are obedient to your God, then life will be good?" He asked.

"There will always be problems and trials in life but they are always for our good, to help prepare us for the next season. Moses, our deliverer, was a prince in Kemet, but he found out that he was a Hebrew and not of the same line as Pharaoh. Moses killed a man who was being mistreated by one of Pharaoh's men. Moses was forced to escape and live in the wilderness for 40 years as a shepherd. But God called to Moses and anointed him to free his people. God bestowed favor on Moses and he now leads God's people. There will always be storms that we have to go through but with faith, sorrow does not last forever. If we stay obedient then we will be in position to reap the abundance that God has in store for us, in time. God knows the plans He has for us, plans to bless us and not harm us. It's about having faith in God, believing in Him and no other idols. Faith is the most important part of religion." Joshua explained.

"I like this God of yours perhaps I will look into it in the future. Faith must be high among you Hebrews because of what your God has done for you lately," Amel said.

"You would think so but there are many of of our people who are still disobedient and unfaithful. They refuse to accept the promises of God," Joshua stated.

"That is a shame that one does not want to accept the promises of your God," Amel said.

They continued to walk north until they got to an oasis about 20 miles west of the Great Sea.

Present day

Salman stopped and highlighted to Jack the importance of having faith in God's promises.

Group 3

Gaddiel and his group walked along with the caravan. He spoke to Ammiel separately when he got a chance. "I need you to talk to Palti and Shammua in order to make sure that they will support us in our goal," he asked.

Ammiel agreed to help Gaddiel by finding out about their position regarding the conquest of Canaan. He walked over to Palti and Shammua who were on the other side of the caravan.

"Greetings, Palti and Shammua, it's good that you are well. How is the trek going?" Ammiel asked.

"I am well; all things considered with our capture and torture," Palti replied.

"I am fine," Shammua said.

"We were worried about the both of you. I thank God that you were able to get released. What do you think about all of this? Do you think that we should waste the time on the rest of this trip instead of heading back to the Sinai?" Ammiel asked.

Palti spoke up, "I think that we should make sure that we complete our mission. We need to visit Lebo-Hamath and then return to Hebron before leaving for the Sinai. It's very important that we stick to the plan we have," Palti said.

"What Palti means is that we have been tasked with observing this land for Moses and the people. It's important that we complete our task," Shammua said.

"But aren't the two of you still injured from the torture you received. You should be tended to, not traveling through the land possibly encountering more danger and peril," Ammiel explained.

"We are strong though and want to complete the mission," Palti said thinking about Sarah.

"Yes, Palti is right. We are prepared to complete what was assigned to us," Shammua said.

"I understand. What are your thoughts about whether we can conquer this land or not?" Ammiel asked thinking that there was something else going on here.

"We both believe that it would be difficult to possess this land," Shammua stated.

"That is what we think too. We will continue with the plan as it is but we believe that it will make no difference in the end. We should all be of one mind. We can all help each other," Ammiel said.

Palti and Shammua looked at each other.

Chapter 30

Day 18

15 miles north of Jericho

Ammiel stood beside Palti and Shammua after explaining how each side could help each other.

Palti and Shammua looked at each other because each was thinking the same thing.

Palti said, "We agree that it's difficult to take this land. We can support you on that but we need your support when we return to Hebron."

Ammiel looked at Palti, "How can I help?" he asked.

"We need the support of your group, all of them, in exchange for our agreement to support you," Palti said.

"We met an Israelite woman who needs our help in Hebron. She is a slave and we told her that she can come with us to the Sinai," Shammua said.

"You want to steal a slave from its owner?" Asked Ammiel incredulously.

"She is one of us. She is Hebrew," Palti said.

"You know its death to take a slave from its lawful owner," Ammiel explained.

"We have promised her that when we return, we will take her with us. She is desperate to leave that wicked city. We are obligated to help her. If you want our support then you will support us when we go back to Hebron and bring her with us. That is the deal," Palti stated.

Ammiel thought for a moment about his own situation. "I will agree to help you and will ask the others to support you. And if I need your support in the future, will I have it?" Asked Ammiel.

Palti and Shammua were very happy about getting Ammiel to help them that they agreed to help him not knowing what it may be.

Ammiel thanked the two and returned to Gaddiel.

Palti and Shammua watched him leave.

"I am glad that we got him to agree to help us. I was worried that the others would go against us. Now we have support when we go back to to Hebron. This is working out for our favor," Palti said.

"We are fortunate that they need something from us," Shammua said as they continued walking north.

Group 3

Gaddiel asked Shaphat to walk with him. Shaphat came over to Gaddiel asking what he wanted.

"I think we need to know how everyone in the group is thinking. I also want to make sure that we have a majority supporting us when we return to the Sinai," Gaddiel said.

"So what do you need me to do?" asked Shaphat wearily.

"I would like you to talk with Gaddi and Igal about supporting our position. I know they voted to continue this mission to the end but I feel that they believe we cannot possess this land. I just want to make sure that they are with us. We will not be able to change the minds of Joshua and Caleb so I want to focus on what we can do. We should find out what they are thinking and offer then our friendship and support in return," he said.

"Why are you not doing this yourself?" asked Shaphat

"Everyone knows my views regarding this mission but I think it's important for others to see that you also agree with looking for other options instead of trying to dispossess the Canaanites," Gaddiel explained.

"I suppose that it would be good to make sure we are of the same mind. I can do this," Shaphat explained.

"Thank you Shaphat," he replied.

Group 1

Gaddi and Igal were walking together but they were definitely of different mindsets. Igal walked ahead of Gaddi feeling that Gaddi had been reckless and unsuccessful in all his ideas related to getting rid of the problem. Igal rued the day that he agreed to go with Gaddi to that brothel and then attempt to cover up their sin by trying to kill Joshua and Caleb. Igal felt that his eternal soul was being pulled in many directions but what was he going to do. He felt stuck and did not know what to do.

Shaphat walked up to Gaddi and Igal asking to speak to them.

"What is it you want?" Gaddi asked gruffly.

"I wish to talk about all of this," Shaphat explained.

"So, why are you talking instead of Gaddiel? Are you not with his side?" asked Gaddi.

"I speak for myself. I want to know where you stand in moving against these people. I have made up my mind and believe that it would be good for each of us to know the views of the others. We should look for another land to possess in my opinion," Shaphat said.

"Well, it's no one's opinion what my views are except for the people and Moses," Gaddi said bitterly taking his frustration out of Shaphat.

Igal thought for a moment that Shaphat was not here on his own but rather for Gaddiel. Shaphat was not the leader type. What was going on here? Was there some way he could work this to his advantage. He decided to play his luck, "Why is it important what we think? What is in it for us?" Igal asked.

"We are looking to make a united front and we would be in your debt if we could all be in agreement when we returned to the Sinai. We could form an alliance, we support you and you support us when we need it," Shaphat explained.

That was it, they was the benefit in this situation, Igal thought.

"That sounds good in theory but we are not sure that we agree with each other..." Gaddi was saying when Igal interrupted.

"I think we do agree with you and Gaddiel. This mission is too difficult; we can never possess this land from the Canaanites. The cities are too fortified and the soldiers are too big. We will tell Moses and the people that it is impossible. We could support you in your position," Igal said holding his hand up for Gaddi to be quiet.

"That is wonderful and we would be indebted to you. Is there anything we could do for you in return for your support? Shaphat asked.

"I cannot think of anything now but let us think on it. Who knows, perhaps we could help each other," Igal said.

Shaphat felt satisfied and thanked the two of them for their time. Shaphat walked away.

Igal and Gaddi watched him leave when Gaddi said, "Why did you want me to be quiet?" He said angrily.

"This is our chance. We support his faction and they support us when we get back to the Sinai. We will need support if Joshua tells anyone of our misdeeds. We need to have allies and it's not like we both don't agree already that this operation is doomed. There is no chance that we could ever conquer these peoples. We have just been blessed with an alternative solution. Don't you see?" Igal asked.

Gaddi went to open his mouth, closed his mouth and then nodded his head. "I see what you are saying; we get their faction to provide support for our actions in case it comes back against us. I get it; that is very smart."

Igal smiled at Gaddi and nodded. "We are all set now." They continued walking north until they see a lush green region looming ahead.

Oasis north of Jericho

Group 3

The caravan stopped where the camels and horses could be watered at the wells. There are many date palms and olive trees in the lush vegetation.

Gaddiel walked over to Sethur who had taken a position near one of the camels at the oasis. "How are you making it with this caravan?"

"It's very good to use this caravan as a way to have cover for our actions," Sethur said.

"I was thinking about the future. We need to start looking at what we will do once we get back to the Sinai and speak with the people. I think that most of our group will support us except Joshua and Caleb. We need to make sure that the others support us. They know how I feel about this mission but not you. I wanted you to talk with Nahbi and Geuel ask their thoughts about this mission and then, if necessary, persuade them to support the majority. The majority is going to tell the tribes that it is impossible to possess the land. We all know that this is a bad idea. I want to know if they are with us or against us."

Sethur knowing that Gaddiel could use his behavior against him knew it was better to yield and do what he asked instead of resisting. "I will talk with them," he said.

Group 2

Nahbi and Geuel sat with a group of men tending to their horses and camels from the caravan under a date palm tree. All of the members of the caravan had stopped in the oasis in order to take advantage of the well and fruit trees. Nahbi was talking with one of the Phoenicians who was leading a large part of the traders while Geuel was filling water sacks for one of the men they had been traveling with. Sethur noticed that both men seemed rational and not led by their feelings. They neither were religious fanatics nor were they pagans. They were taking the operation seriously and he believed that neither Nahbi nor Geuel would do the sort of things that he and his group had done. Sethur decided to come at them logically. He walked up to Nahbi first, "Excuse me, I was hoping that I could speak with you and your traveling companion?" Sethur asked.

Nahbi was a little taken aback as they had broken cover but he guessed it was alright since they were traveling and not in a city reconnoitering it. "Yes, let us walk over to my companion. Please excuse me," Nahbi said while walking away.

"I thought that we were not supposed to talk with each other while we were traveling," Nahbi whispered.

"Well, we are not in a city so I thought there would be no problems," Sethur explained.

They walked over to where Geuel was. "He wanted to talk to us." Nahbi said while nodding his head towards Sethur.

"Why are you exposing our connection with each other?" Geuel asked.

"I wanted to take the opportunity to talk with the both of you before we got to the next city. I will not be long. I wanted to share what I was thinking about this operation and to know your thoughts. I believe that the more I see the more difficult it is to even think that we could conquer the Canaanites. I think it would be good that we are of the same mind when we return to the Sinai so I wanted to hear your honest opinions," Sethur stated.

"I would tend to agree with you but I want to complete the operation before I commit to saying anything," Geuel replied.

Nahbi explained that he was of a similar mind as of Geuel. He would give his final report once they finished their reconnaissance.

"I just wanted you to know in my experience, it would be impossible to move these people off of their lands," Sethur said.

"Well, it's good to know your opinion. I will provide my conclusions when we are heading back to the Sinai," Geuel said with finality in his voice. "Let's get back, Nahbi, before someone sees us speaking together. Peace be unto you," Geuel said. Nahbi and Geuel nodded and walked off in another direction.

Sethur watched them walk away. "They think they are so special. I tried my best so Gaddiel can not be upset at me," Sethur said to himself as he made his way back to where Gaddiel was located."

Group 5

Joshua and Caleb walked around the Oasis. They took in the details of the area so that they could use the region if they needed to return when they came to conquer the land.

"This is a lush and fertile piece of land. I think it's because we are not far from the great sea," Joshua said.

"Is this an oasis or something else?" asked Caleb.

"I think it's not an oasis exactly because there are other areas in this region like this. I heard about this area from one of the caravan drivers. The great sea provides a temperature amenable for better vegetation and trees," Joshua said.

"Look over there," Caleb said to Joshua. He pointed to where Sethur was talking with Nahbi and Geuel.

"That is strange that they decided to break cover and meet with them," Caleb said.

Joshua looked around and saw Shaphat talking with Gaddi and Igal. "Hmm, that is highly unusual too. I see that Shaphat is doing the same. There is something going on here. Let's see if we can find Ammiel to see what he is doing."

They walked through the oasis looking for Ammiel. After a few minutes they saw Ammiel talking with Palti and Shammua.

"I think that Gaddiel is up to something," Caleb suggested.

"I think so too," Joshua said.

"What should we do about this?" Caleb asked.

"We should just give it to God. Let them skulk around all they want, we will serve the Lord and do what's pleasing in His eyes," Joshua explained.

Group 3

Sethur, Shaphat and Ammiel made their way back to Gaddiel to explain how each fared. The caravan was about to start moving again. They were scheduled to be in the next city by nightfall.

Gaddiel received the individual reports and was bothered that Nahbi and Geuel wanted to stay neutral until they were on the way back. He preferred to have a definite confirmation from the each group since he knew that Joshua and Caleb would be a problem. He was pleased that he had made some headway this day to consolidate support for his point of view.

The caravan made their way through the hilly lands and eventually made it to the next major city along the route.

Chapter 31

Day 18 evening

The caravan stopped outside of Beth-shan, located at the intersection of the Jezreel and Jordan valleys, commanding the routes north-south along the Jordan and east-west from Gilead to the Great Sea. The caravan had traveled about 40 miles since they left from Hebron. The camels, the ships of the desert, sat on their knees and rested along with the horses. In this caravan, there were more camels than horses because the camels sold better. The camels were laden with loads of goods for trade. The merchants started organizing the things they would immediately sell once they got into the town.

Group 4

"Do you believe Ammiel?" Palti asked.

"I think that he needs something from us. You know the power behind him is Gaddiel. He is the only one we really need to worry about," Shammua said.

"How is that?" asked Palti.

"Gaddiel has grand ambitions. He wants something, I don't know what his ultimate goal is but I know that he wants our support. So I don't trust Ammiel exactly but Gaddiel is a deal maker so I trust his need for our help. Ammiel is just Gaddiel's lapdog," Shammua suggested.

"I think that it could not have worked out better for us. We should have no problems with the group now when we return to Hebron to take Sarah with us," Palti said.

"As long as it's in Gaddiel's interest, we will be alright," Shammua said.

Palti was happy to hear that he was getting closer to his ultimate goal, Sarah.

Shammua could see that Palti was relieved. He viewed Palti as a simple soul who just wanted what he wanted. He would be able to easily take Sarah for himself because Palti did not have a true deceptive bone in his body but he on the other hand would do everything he could to make Sarah his.

Group 5

Joshua sat down with Amel to learn more about Beth-shan since he had been traveling the route for years. The caravan owners had unloaded what they needed for the evening and made camp. By the fires, musicians started playing some tunes. A festive atmosphere came over the camp and men starting telling tales of things they had seen in some of the far off places.

Joshua asked, "What do you know about this city?"

"This city Beth-shan means "House of quiet". There are many abundant springs in Beth-shan, this is one of its great treasures. Water is plentiful and crops grow without any trouble. I am sure you know that Beth-shan sees much international and local caravan traffic. This town has been a prominent border town between tribes and several kingdoms for eons. I know this town is important to the Hebrews but I do not know all that history," Amel said.

"Canaan figures prominently in our history, upon entering Canaan, our great Prophet Abraham, built an alter at Bethel calling on the name of the Lord (1). We also know that his grandson, Jacob spent the night here on his way to Syria to find a wife. In a dream, the Lord confirmed the Abraham covenant, and Jacob responded by renaming this locale from "Luz" to Bethel (2). When Jacob returned with his large family, he came to Bethel again to hear the Lord's confirmation of the covenant and his name was changed to 'Israel'. Abraham's route of battle with the enemy kings was through Beth-shan," Joshua explains.

"I did not know that. I had known that the Assyrians believed the city to be important because they appointed priests to teach the inhabitants its statutes. You can see that the city is heavily fortified. Pharaoh's men administer this land now and because of its location on the north-south route it has changed administrative hands many times, and I suspect that it will continue to do so in the future. The people love merchants and those conducting trade but are less welcoming for strangers who do not offer them any benefit. Be careful when you are going through the city, the inhabitants can be suspicious of foreigners unless they can make a shekel off of them," Amel said.

Joshua thanked Amel for the information and they split up for the evening. Amel returned to his caravan and Joshua over to where Caleb had made a place on the ground to sleep. The fires created light so Joshua took out his little scroll in order to start his 10th report for the trip.

"Report 10

During this journey north, we have learned more about this fertile land. We are traveling with a caravan that is going to Lebo-Hamath. We may have only gone a small distance but moving with the caravan offers a level of cover and concealment especially since Palti and Shammua was captured in Hebron. The people in this region are mixed made up from people from Mizraim (Pharaoh's land), Philistine, Moab, Ammon and Edom. Security along the route north is almost non-existent. The soldiers we have encountered have only been in the fortified towns and not in garrisons outside of the cities. The trip north has only confirmed the beauty and bounty of the land where we have passed trees filled with dates, nuts, olives, spices and other edible delicacies. There appears to be something going on between Gaddiel and his group with the other groups. Gaddiel continues to be the leader of those opposing we possess the land of Canaan. I only make note of this fact but I am not concerned because Caleb and I are steadfast in our devotion and service to the Lord.

End of report."

Group 2

Nahbi and Geuel sat by one of the fires after eating their meal for the evening.

"I know what Gaddiel is trying to do but I am not going to give him the satisfaction," Geuel said.

"What is he trying to do?" asked Nahbi.

"He is trying to consolidate his authority in order to try to seize power when he returns to the Sinai. I am not going to play into his hands. I may very well believe in the same final conclusion that he does but I will give my report to Moses and the people, not him," Geuel explained.

"Why does it matter really, if we all believe the same thing?" Nahbi asked.

"I am a practical man. I believe in what I see. I realize that the Lord parted the Red Sea and delivered us from the Pharaoh but looking at this land of giants, I don't see how we can prevail. I may not be one of those men who believe in something I can not see. I want to believe. I want to have the faith of Joshua or Moses but I just do not. God may be with us but I cannot see anything except death and injury when I think about conquering this land. I can't see it, and because of that, I feel sad. I want to believe but I can not lie and say that I believe in something I do not. Thus, I will do my duty and report the facts as I see it without emotion or religion. I will sleep well because I have done what has been asked of me," Geuel explained.

Nahbi nodded his head and was silent for a moment. "I want to believe as well. There is a part of me that says we are looking at this all wrong. I think that Joshua and Caleb view this as an exercise to determine "how" we will conquer the land because they do believe. I would like to be able to not view the walls and soldiers with fear. But I am afraid of what I see, it's daunting and it's easier to think about other options. I appreciate your opinion and I have enjoyed making this journey with you this far. I support you and perhaps we will learn something along the way which will help our faith. I am tired; tomorrow will be a busy day. Let us sleep," suggested Nahbi.

"Nahbi son of Vophsi, sleep well. If we do what is told of us, perhaps we will be alright," Geuel said.

"We will see." The two of them went to the area where they would sleep and retired for the night.

Group 3

Gaddiel felt an uneasiness inside of him. He did not know why he felt that way. Everything was going well; he had been able to use his men to help learn good intelligence from the other groups. He believed that his leadership skills would be clearly made known after this mission. He was chosen by his tribe because they recognized that he was a leader. He was anxious to enter Beth-shan because it was another potential city for him to do business with. He needed to take care of his tribe the Zebulun. His tribe was not as influential as the tribe of Benjamin and Joseph but after this operation, that would change because Zebulun would be led by him. He would return and be the voice of the tribe. He would take on Moses head on. He believed that the people would not react favorably when they heard about the difficulty of the mission. He knew that Moses would most likely maintain his position to take the land which would put him and Moses against each other. He would be ready. The doubts kept coming into his head. He just had to silence the doubts inside and stay focused.

Those fears and doubts always resurfaced so easily. He often wondered how someone like Moses and Joshua always seemed to sure and so committed to God. Did not everyone suffer doubts? He did not know. He remembered the angel of light had visited him and felt a little comfort. He was not power hungry, but he felt that he would be able to lead better than anyone else among the Israelites. There were things that plagued him for many years and when Moses appeared from Midian to lead the people out of bondage, he had immediately felt that he should have a larger part of the process. So, he had to wait until his tribe recognized the possibility inside of him and appointed him to be a part of the espionage mission in Canaan. He now felt that his destiny was being fulfilled. He was destined to lead, have power and the things which accompanied power. He would lead his tribe and then enrich them beyond their wildest dreams. He had thought that when Pharaoh offered Moses anything if the Israelites stayed in in Kemet, he would have taken Pharaoh up on his offer and negotiated a new pact where the Hebrews would reap the fruits of theirs labors while remaining in Kemet. Moses should have chosen a different route instead of leading people into the desert.

With that thought, another came into his mind in reference to what Moses said regarding what God had promised them. This was the part of his thought process when the doubts arose. Was Moses correct in what he did and what he was doing now? Why not take an easier path instead of the most difficult one. There were so many questions. He could not think of all of them, he would stay on the path to save the people. They would write songs about him and erect statues about him. He knew what he had to do in reference to maintaining his position. He felt better and decided to retire for the evening.

[*Satan watched and was pleased that he was able to influence Gaddiel. He was worried at one point when Gaddiel started to think about receiving God's promises. He had to make sure that Gaddiel's thoughts stayed focused on pride and greed which was not hard because Gaddiel freely choose those negative thoughts. He was able to influence easily when the thoughts were already there. Since Gaddiel did not truly believe in God and because his base desires were already close to his heart, Satan's tricks were easily to get him to focus on those thoughts. This is why Satan hated when people had faith because it was difficult for him to influence those who kept their hearts and minds on God. When his targets read the words of God and took care with their spiritual development, Satan had a harder time to make any mark on them. In many cases, it was impossible for him to put any thoughts in people's minds whose mind stayed on God. For example, it was very difficult to influence Joshua or Caleb so he just waited until an opportunity presented itself but with Gaddiel, he was almost always open to ungodly suggestions. Satan felt good about where Gaddiel and the others were in terms of their objections to enter the land. He just had to maintain his watch on them, making subtle hints here and there so that they did the wrong thing. Satan loved free will.*]

Day 19 morning

The sun arose early over the top of the walls of Beth-shan. Beth-shan's gates were closed until the sun came up fully. This was not Jericho but a larger city with a clearly professional military walking along the walls of the city. Even from the ground, the people in the caravan could tell that these inhabitants took their security seriously.

All of the spies of promised were prepared to start this phase of the mission. The caravan was scheduled to remain in the city for two days and then travel on towards Lebo-hamath on the morning of the third day. The 12 spies agreed to stay for the two days and then travel on to Lebo-Hamath with the caravan for cover and safety.

Chapter 32

Day 19 morning

Hebron

Commander Elrian was in his office wishing to call up Satan remembering the stringent rules that the old mystic had explained to him for calling up the dark lord. He had to focus as he recalled the five rules: maintaining invincible obstinacy; having a hardened conscience without fear or remorse; keeping in mind a hatred of the light; an over abiding and complete trust in Satan; and worshiping Satan as his god. Elrian had to keep all doubt out and had to believe in the power of the darkness. He could not let any fear or questioning enter into him. He also had to keep the light out to ensure the conditions were right to channel the power he needed. He was growing impatient so he decided to take matters into his own hands.

"Oh prince of darkness, I maintain my hands firmly on your seal. Master of all demons, I live for you and no other. I pray thee protect me in this endeavor. I freely enter the pathway of darkness. These are my words and no other, I freely choose your way. I ask you to channel your power through me so I can know what I need to in order to kill the so-called deliverer of the Hebrews. Tell me about these spies? And with this information I need you to transfer it to my spies." Elrian started the ancient words which sealed the request. *Shaitan, Iblis, Diablos, Lucifer, ruhu laka wa lacait shakhs thania.* He drew the "thame" or black blade of steel across the back of his arm whereby the blood came thus sealing the ritual. The blood fell on the ground and he proclaimed, "I provide this as evidence of my commitment." The blood congealed by his feet before disappearing.

He heard the soft voice inside saying, "The spies of Moses are in Beth-shan." The words came on his heart as if someone was speaking them. He thought again of the darkness and Satan's goodness. The information left him and went directly to his spy 1. Elrian fell down weakened because the channeling process took energy and power away from him. He thanked the dark one and then lay down to get some rest. He had Sarah coming over to his office later and needed his rest.

[*Satan was disrupted by the request. He was summoned and had to intervene at the request of his servant. He was hopeful that it would not be seen a violation of his agreement with God. It was still an influencing operation, he thought. He was limited with what he could do. He felt that he was still in within his agreement with God, so he would not worry.*]

Spy one (Fayid) and Spy two (Ashur) were a half a day's ride from Lebo-hamath when Fayid stopped suddenly. Fayid was seized in his saddle. Ashur reined back on his horse's bridle and urged his horse to move to where Fayid was stopped.

Fayid spoke, "I know where they are. They are in Beth-shan and there are more than two of them."

"How can you know this?" Asked Ashur.

"I just know, don't question me. We must go back to Beth-shan. We will find them there," said Fayid.

"I am with you. You lead, and I will follow," Ashur said while kicking the side of his horse to spur it on to follow Fayid who had already moved away.

Fayid urged his horse in the opposite direction toward Beth-shan. They would be in Beth-shan by the evening before they closed the gates. He rode fast and with urgency. He actually did not want to think about how he knew. He knew it was from Elrian but he did not want to think how Elrian did it. He hesitated to think about evil or dark magic. He did not want to imagine that he was serving someone who was operating in the darkness. That scared him because he followed Ra. He tried to not think about it while he rode to Beth-shan.

Beth-shan

The city of Beth-shan or Beth-shean rested on the site of Tel el-Husn which was above the city's perennial stream of ancient lore, (the city's premium water supply) giving the city a commanding view of two valleys. The caravan had a long walk from the outside perimeter up the slope to enter the city. Inside the city, the caravan broke up into various groups to sell their wares. There was much activity in the city. The trade route guaranteed that there would be much mercantile activity in the city. The five groups of spies went in the city separately.

Group 1

Gaddi and Igal walked down the main road in the center of the city. The activity was interesting because of the various booths and covered markets being busy with the merchants who just entered the city. Their relationship had been strained since the last plan with the harlot to trap Joshua in a compromising sexual situation. Their conspiracy still bound them together which was why they still traveled together.

"I know you do not want to hear this but I know that we are hoping that Ammiel and his group will support us but I still want to take care of our problem ourselves," Gaddi suggested.

"I don't want to talk about this right now. I think that the two of them are blessed somehow and cannot be harmed," Igal said.

"That is foolish, no one is protecting them. They have just been fortunate," Gaddi explained.

"I don't know why nothing has worked, I only know that I do not want to tempt fates against us more then we already have," Igal said.

"Well, if you will not help me then I will have to come up with a plan myself," Gaddi stated.

"You are your own man, you can do what you think is appropriate. I want no part of it," Igal said in a huffy manner.

Group 2

Nahbi and Geuel decided to do what they had done previously, do a complete survey of the town before settling down. The town was large and was rectangle in shape as opposed to Hebron which was circular. They bought some fruit and eat while looking around. They noticed the soldiers walking around the city and that there was a garrison in the center of town. They observed the soldiers on the wall watching all activities in and out of the city. They noticed the street children looking around attempting to find someone to pickpocket. There were a lot of people running through the streets of town carrying goods and exchanging their merchandise.

"This town is a major spot on the caravan routes. There are people who look strange as if they are from far away lands," Nahbi said.

"It's to be expected because sometimes the merchants stay for a while waiting for the next caravan before returning to their lands. I like the fact that it's normal for foreigners to walk around here without being singled out," Geuel said.

"I don't think that we will have to worry about anyone noticing us here," Nahbi said.

The commander's spies, Fayid and Ashur, came into the city at that point. They took their horses to the stables and asked for one of the stables to feed and water their mounts.

"We should see if any new caravans have entered the city in the last day or two," suggested Ashur.

"The money changers will know immediately," Fayid said.

"That is a good idea," stated Ashur.

They walked towards a large group of tables where the activity was furious. Fayid walked towards one of the tables and asked to speak to the owner.

"I must speak with your owner," Fayid insisted.

"I'm busy. What do you want?" the merchant said.

Fayid took out 10 shekels and handed it to the merchant.

"What is this for?" the merchant said.

"I need some information," asked Fayid.

"What do you want to know stranger," said the merchant putting the 10 shekels in his pocket.

"Has there been any caravans come into town today or yesterday?" Fayid asked.

"Yes, there is a big caravan which just came into town from south," the merchant said while turning away from Fayid.

"And were there any Hebrews among the group; I am looking for a few friends," Fayid asked.

"I don't know yet, the caravan members are traveling around town now," the merchant explained.

"Keep your eyes open, I will be back. There is more money in it if you hear my friends are here from Hebron," Fayid suggested.

"Okay stranger, come back tomorrow because the caravan will be here for at least two days," explained the merchant.

"Thank you," Fayid replied walking back out from the crowd and approaching Ashur.

Fayid explained what he had learned and the two of them started walking around the city.

Group 3

Gaddiel, Ammiel, Shaphat and Sethur entered the city. Shaphat and Sethur said that they wanted to see how the entertainment was in the city and walked off into the maze of alleys off the main road. Shaphat yelled back, "Let us meet back here at high sun and we can get some lunch together. Ammiel and Gaddiel looked at each other while the two others walked away.

"I guess it's you and me until noon," Ammiel said.

Gaddiel looked at Ammiel, not really looking forwarding to spending time with him. They walked through the market place observing the activity.

"I think that we should see about finding a place to spend the night so when they come back that task will be completed," suggested Gaddiel.

"That sounds good," Ammiel said.

Separately, Shaphat and Sethur decided to look for some fun although it was still early.

"I know that since this is a major transit route, there should be places we can entertain ourselves," Shaphat said.

"I think that you are right. We should be able to able to find something that will relax us," Sethur explained.

The pair walked around looking for about 30 minutes before they were approached by a few ladies where were standing near the Temple to Baal.

"Stranger, come here. Surely you are tired from your travels. Let us provide you some relaxing adventure." The two harlots suggested to them.

"When in Canaan, we should do as the Canaanites do, right?" Shaphat said.

"Of course, why not?" Sethur replied.

Group 4

Palti and Shammua went immediately to find a place to stay for the night. They needed two nights of lodging. They wanted to get off the streets as soon as possible.

"I think this is a much safer town since many foreigners are always transiting this city," Shammua said.

"I know but I still want to get into a place in order to rest. My side has been hurting more and more since we left Hebron. How do you feel?" Palti asked.

"I am okay but I still have coughing fits. Also, my legs are sore along with my back," Shammua said.

Palti looked over at Shammua and noticed that he was limping. Palti said, "We handled ourselves well in Hebron, right?" Palti said.

Shammua smiled and agreed with little Palti as they continued to look for a place to reside for the next two nights.

Group 5

Joshua and Caleb entered the city looking to obtain all the information they could about how to conquer the city.

"So, Abraham traveled through here?" Asked Caleb.

"According to the scrolls, Abraham made his route through here when he was fighting the evil kings. It's beautiful here," Joshua said.

"I think Jericho was more beautiful but there is an amount of charm here," Caleb said.

"I see my friend Amel busy trying to make deals with the locals." Joshua pointed and noticed that Amel was in a heated discussion with a local merchant.

"Let go over there, I am sure we can learn a lot by just listening," Caleb suggested.

"That is a good idea," Joshua said while moving in the direction of Amel.

Joshua and Caleb walked over to Amel while he was driving a hard bargain with a Hittite merchant.

"I have 12 talents of olives and 6 talents of figs which you promised to take for 15 shekels per talent during this trip. It was on your word, and I will hold you to that," asserted Amel.

The merchant explained, "That was last month but I did not know that we would still have an excess of both."

"So, you want new merchants to know that Farum is not a man of his word," Amel said while motioning over to Joshua and Caleb.

This gesture was a ploy he had used before because it had the desired effect because Farum relented and agreed to pay the agreed price.

"I am good I can continue to recommend you as a man of your word. These are Hebrews from Midian who may do business with you soon. I will send over the goods shortly, you can pay me when it's all delivered. I will be back at high sun," Amel said while walked away from the merchant.

Joshua and Caleb turned and walked after Amel.

Amel looked back and saw Farum scratching his head in having been bested.

"Thank you my friends, I know that it was not planned but your presence helped my negotiations. How can I be of service since you helped me? Farum hates to lose face especially if it involved prospective business. He just needed a little motivation as to why he needed to keep his word," Amel said.

"We just wanted to see what we can learn by shadowing you, if that it's alright with you?" Joshua asked.

"My friends, I welcome the company," said Amel.

Chapter 33

Day 19 high sun (noon)

Group 3

Ammiel and Gaddiel had found four rooms near the center of the marketplace. The rooms were very good but expensive because they wanted the best room available. Ammiel paid for the rooms and then they decided to walk around until noon.

During the walk, Ammiel kept commenting on how difficult it would be to conquer the city in an effort to improve his relationship with Gaddiel. Ammiel realized that Gaddiel was ambitious and was seeking to become a leader among the people. He was trying to ingratiate himself with him but Gaddiel did not seem receptive to becoming closer.

Gaddiel, for his part, walked around the city trying not to be annoyed with Ammiel. He kept trying to get into Gaddiel's good graces. He did not mind that some of the men fornicated but the fact that Ammiel went with men bothered him. He still needed Ammiel so he tried to be friendly but it was difficult for him.

Gaddiel noticed that the army in Beth-shan was made up of many foreigners. He watched soldiers with the dark skin of men from Cush patrol the marketplace. The dark men reminded him of life under Pharaoh because many of them were a part of the army and would enforce the law from time to time.

They walked around for a while before returning to the site where they would meet the others.

Shaphat and Sethur both enjoyed their adventures with the prostitutes. "I think that we collected more intelligence information than anyone else in our group," claimed Shaphat while laughing.

It was noon so they walked back to the main area where they had left Gaddiel and Ammiel.

As Shaphat and Sethur made their way to entry of the marketplace, they saw Ammiel and Gaddiel waiting for them.

Shaphat and Sethur approached Gaddiel and Ammiel.

Gaddiel was annoyed with Shaphat and Sethur for just leaving.

"So, what now?" Asked Shaphat.

"We have found rooms for the night," said Ammiel and advised them where the rooms were located.

Shaphat could tell that Gaddiel was upset at the fact that he and Sethur walked away but he was not going to be controlled by this man. He had decided that he would support Gaddiel in the areas he could but he would not be a puppet to any man.

The group decided to walk to the rooms.

Once in the rooms, the group went to each of their respective rooms agreeing to meet for dinner at sunset.

Gaddiel sat in his room thinking about everything that had transpired thus far. He felt good about most of the group's opinions to the mission. Joshua and Caleb still bothered him because they were so dedicated to this mission. Nahbi and Geuel were the wild rabbits in the equation because they would not tell him what they were thinking.

Gaddiel had not had another vision in a few days but he was still confident that he had also been chosen.

Ammiel was in his room trying not to think about what would happen once he returned to Hebron. He was hoping that no one saw him and Kabir. He did not cherish the thought of being in a Canaanite prison. He felted stressed and nervous but did not know what to do.

Shaphat relaxed in his room thinking about Gaddiel and his grand plans to rule the world. There was something off with Gaddiel but he did not know how to describe it. He decided to not dwell on Gaddiel anymore. The time that he and Sethur had with the prostitutes was enjoyable but he loved all the carnal pleasures of life. He had not been feeling so well since Hebron because of pain around his groin area. He was hoping that it would get better after he had sex with another woman but it had not improved. Since it had not gotten better, he would have to seek out a medical person to possible help him when he returned to the Sinai.

[*Archangels Raphael and Michael both watched knowing that the wages of sin were death. When would the humans learn that sinful behaviors always led to a life filled with pain and suffering.*]

Group 5

Joshua and Caleb walked with Amel as he took them on a tour of the city. Joshua noticed that the army in this city was more of a semi-professional nature because of all the conscripts and mercenaries drawn from foreign lands, such as Nubians, Assyrians, Phoenicians and Babylonians. He realized that the further north they traveled the more the armies were more diversified. The army in Kemet was made mostly from indigenous peoples from along the Nile

River and also composed of captured slaves. Pharaoh administered Canaan and provided troops for the garrisons throughout the land but the further from Kemet they went into Canaan, the more Pharaoh used mercenaries or conscripts. Joshua observed that the troops walking around this town wore close-range weapons such as the mace or battle-ax along with the normal dagger. Many of the troops from Pharaoh's army wore swords and the officers wore the sickle sword or khepesh.

The army may not have been composed of career soldiers like those who worked for Pharaoh in Thebes, Memphis, Raamses or Giza but they were clearly well trained. Most mercenaries were well-trained and fought for whoever paid them the most. Joshua guessed that since trade was important in the town, it was important that the inhabitants felt safe.

"Amel, this town seems very active commercially. What makes it so thriving?" Joshua asked.

They walked to one of the springs which flowed out of several locations inside the city.

"You see this water here, the abundance of the water makes it a great town along the north-south trade route. The Assyrians used to have a garrison here and when they left, the people stayed. It was already an established post so it was easy to transform it into a trading town," Amel said.

They each filled their small flasks with water and then continued walking through the town.

"Are you hungry?" Caleb asked the group.

"Lets get something to eat, and I know the perfect place to eat at. Someone I know runs a place near here," Amel suggested.

They followed Amel and walked to a bristling area under a tent with many tables. Once inside, the owner came to the group and greeted Amel with an embrace.

"Cousin, it's so good to see you so soon," the owner said.

"Friends, this is my cousin Yeshak. He has lived here for many years and knows everything that goes on here. His kitchen makes the best flat bread in Canaan," Amel said.

"Welcome, if you are friends of my cousin then you are my friends too," explained Yeshak.

Joshua and Caleb introduced themselves and were led with Amel to a table. They sat down and Yeshak brought out all different types of dishes without asking them what they wanted. Drinks were brought out including yoghurt, wine and other strong drinks.

Neither Joshua nor Caleb drink any of the wine or strong drinks but had some yoghurt instead. Joshua and Caleb said a blessing over the food after it came and then started eating the myriad dishes.

"This is the best food we have eaten in a long time," Caleb said.

"My cousin runs the best establishment in all of Canaan," Amel stated with a little bit of pride.

Joshua and Caleb ate all they wanted but more importantly, they were able to learn information about the city and Canaan as a whole.

"It's hard to tell who these people support. Some people look as if they are from Mesopotamia while others look Arab and others still seem to be from Cush. There seems to be no commonality among those living here except the desire to earn money," Joshua said.

"You are right," said Amel.

Group 4

Palti and Shammua walked around to find a room. As they were inquiring with owners about lodging for the night in the marketplace, Fayid and Ashur walked right past them.

"Do not look to the right but we have found our two targets," Fayid said.

Since Palti and Shammua had never seen the two spies they never knew what they looked like.

Palti and Shammua discussed the price for one room for two nights with the owner of a restaurant.

Fayid and Ashur circled around the square of the marketplace making sure that they would not be seen. They pretended to inspect some melons while observing the two Hebrew spies.

"We will pay 6 Shekels for the two nights," Shammua said.

"I will only take 8 shekels," the owner said.

"Can we split the different in price, we will pay 7 shekels," said Palti.

The owner thought for a moment and then agreed. The owner took them around the side of the building and then showed them a small room with some bedding in the corner.

"You can separate the bedding and form two soft areas to sleep in," the owner said.

Fayid and Ashur came closer to the area where they were talking. Fayid could easily see that the two Hebrews were negotiating for a room.

Palti and Shammua paid the man and went inside the room.

Fayid and Ashur looked at each other and decided to approach the owner. They walked up to the owner and said, "My friend, how are you today?" asked Fayid.

"I am well. What is it you want?" he asked.

"I wanted to know if you had a room for the night?" Fayid asked.

"I am sorry stranger but I just rented my last room for the evening," he replied.

"I was told to seek you out for a room because you have a reputation for being a fair and honorable businessman," Fayid explained.

The owner beamed and thanked the two for the compliment.

"How long will those who you rented the room to be there?" asked Fayid.

"Those two, they will only be there for two nights so if you want a room I could rent it to you after that for the great price of 5 shekels a night," the owner said.

"That is a fair price." Fayid took out 5 shekels and paid the man. "I wish to pay for the first night in advance if you will hold the room for us. We are not sure how long we will stay but will check back with you," Fayid said.

The owner was so happy that these stupid foreigners would pay 5 shekels for a room they had not seen and not even worth 2 shekels a night. He would have to milk more money out of these two before they left.

"Whatever you need here, I can get it for you. Let me know because I know everyone and can get access to anything," the owner said.

"Thank you very much, what is your name?" Fayid asked.

"I am Hamur," he said.

"We may be back this evening to take you up on your offer to help us," Fayid said as they walked away.

Fayid knew that the owner would be pleased to have strangers pay an outrageous price for a dirty room. He now knew that the two Hebrews would be in the town for two nights. He wondered if they were using espionage tradecraft and if there were others here with them. They would undertake surveillance on the room of the two Hebrews as they did on them in Hebron.

Group 2

Nahbi and Geuel walked throughout the city asking questions about the city as if they were looking to move there. No one during this time would have thought that a team of spies had infiltrated the city in order to collect intelligence to conquer it. One of the merchants that Geuel talked with tried to tell him about the goodness of El, the titular head of the Canaanites pantheon of God, and Baal. Because of Pharaoh's influence over the area, the gods from that area were starting to be worshiped such as Maat or Amen. Because of Nahbi's and Geuel accent, the people in Beth-Shan believed them to be from Pharaoh's land so many tried to push the Canaanites gods on them. Nahbi and Geuel were able to go about their mission without anyone paying close attention to them.

Hebron

Commander Elrian listened again to the witness.

"The Hebrew had sexual relations with Kabir the night before he was killed. I am sure that I saw him the night that Kabir was killed coming out the house with blood on him," the merchant said.

"Why are you volunteering this information? What is it that you want from us," Elrian asked.

"I did not want any trouble in the area where I live. I am a simple merchant and I knew that if I came to you then perhaps you would reward my faithfulness. Also, if the other Hebrews came after me for seeing the one kill Kabir, you could protect me," the merchant said.

"What do you mean the Hebrews? I thought there was just the one Hebrew," Elrian said.

"Yes, the one who spent time with Kabir and his three companions who had sexual relations with the dancers from the Pavilion," the merchant said.

"Are you telling me that the man who killed Kabir was one of the four Hebrews who stayed at Mansur's Pavilion?" asked Elrian.

"Yes," he said.

Elrian paid the merchant and told him to not mention their conversation to anyone under threat of death.

The merchant left with the several gold coins from Elrian. As the man walked away, he dropped the coins on the ground before turning back into a demon, one of the dark angels of Satan.

Chapter 34

Day 19 evening

Hebron

Commander Elrian had to decide how to handle Mansur; he had to know that the one Hebrew from his pavilion was involved. He believed that the Hebrews were connected with the two Hebrews he caught and now he had connected them to a murder. He also thought about the two murders of mercenaries as well. There were lots of things which had occurred in a very short time and he did not believe in coincidences.

Fatia thought about Caleb and was sending him her prayers and positive energy. She believed that they would be together and did not worry because she trusted God. Fatia was gathering the things she needed to make the journey to the Sinai with Caleb. She did not want to carry too much stuff because she would be returning because the Israelites would come back to possess the city. Her faith was in God and after hearing about how the Hebrews were promised the land, her job was to believe. She loved Caleb and she loved God more. If God had willed that the Hebrews possess the land then she would help to bring about their goal. She knew that she would be able to help the Israelites integrate into their new homeland Canaan.

Salman had been helping Fatia pack earlier in the day. He was also focused on doing all he could to help carry out Joshua's mission. In that vein, Salman had decided to take a look around the city as the eyes for Joshua ad Caleb. Salman had noticed many more troops patrolling the marketplace then usual since Joshua and Caleb had left. Salman decided to visit Mansur to see what he could learn from his friend because he always knew what was going on in Hebron.

"My friend, it's good to see you. How are you?" Mansur asked.

"I am well, trying to stay out of the heat. I just wanted something to drink. I was out in the marketplace and I am afraid I overestimated my ability to make it back to my place. It is not good when a man gets old," Salman replied.

"Well, have a seat my friend. I will get you something to drink," said Mansur.

Salman exaggerated the process of sitting down in an attempt to seem tired. He wanted the elicitation of information from Mansur to appear natural.

A person from Mansur's staff brought some fresh fruit juices to the table. "How is business?" Mansur asked.

"Business is going well and the caravans have had no problems lately. How about you?" Asked Salman.

"My business has been good especially with the new entertainment which just arrived from Mesopotamia."

"What do you think about the recent killings around the marketplace, the two assassins and then Kabir? They were such random events," asked Salman.

"I am not sure what to make of it except that I think it's probably not from anyone who lives here but a person traveling through the city. I have been getting some pressure from Pharaoh's military commander."

It was at that moment that Commander Elrian came into the Pavilion with his four elite bodyguards.

"I will speak with you," Elrian pointed at Mansur before walking towards the back of the room.

"This will not be good. Take care, my friend. You should leave as soon as you feel strong enough to return to your shop. The good commander is not a friend to the Hebrews." Mansur jumped up and made his way to where Elrian was standing. He noticed that the four elite guards had taken up positions near the exits.

Elrian saw Mansur talking with the Hebrew shopkeeper. He would have to look into that man.

Once in the back of the pavilion, Mansur led Elrian to his office. "How can I help..." Mansur was saying when Elrian moved with the speed of a gazelle and hit him in the face.

Mansur fell on floor with blood trickling from his nose.

"You lied to me," Elrian said.

"What are you talking about?" Asked Mansur getting up slowly.

"I am not the type of man you should lie to. You have a choice now, tell me everything without any pretense or exaggeration or I will have my bodyguards interrogate you," Elrian explained.

Mansur knew that it was not good to withhold any details to Elrian. His life was on the line now; he had to play this in such a way to appease this man.

"I know what you want to know. I saw the Hebrew called Ammiel speak with Kabir one night but I can not say with any certainty if he was with him the night he died," Mansur said.

Elrian looked at Mansur watching for any guile or subterfuge. He stared at Mansur for a long time.

Mansur was not going to be intimated. Elrian could kill him but he would not give him the satisfaction of begging for his life.

"Why did you not tell me about this earlier?" the commander asked.

"I did not recall it at first until someone in the pavilion mentioned it. I then remembered but no one could tell me for sure that Ammiel was actually with Kabir that night. I did not want to make an allegation without evidence," Mansur explained.

The two men were face to face. "It is not your job to decide whether someone's guilty or innocent in the future. Next time, I want all the details and if you learn more details later then I expect you to provide them to me immediately. I like you Mansur but if this happens again, you will no longer be welcome in this city. Am I clear?" Elrian said.

Mansur looked at Elrian and said, "I understand.

Elrian walked out of the office passing the table with the old Hebrew.

Salman had decided to wait to see if he could learn anything. Mansur walked out of the back holding a piece of cloth to his nose. He could tell that the commander had hit Mansur.

"My friend, are you alright?" Salman inquired.

Mansur was tired and his face hurt. He wanted to talk with someone and since Salman was there, he decided to confide in him by telling him the story of Gaddiel and his friends to include the fact that one of the group most likely killed Kabir. Mansur reiterated everything he knew to Salman. After hearing the details, Salman told Mansur that he had done the right thing. Salman stayed for another hour before heading back to his shop. Salman knew that the men described were those sent with Joshua to spy out the land. This commander would not stop until he found them. Joshua was scheduled to return in about 10 days, he did not want him to return to a trap. He would have to make a plan so that the commander did not arrest Joshua and his fellow spies when they returned.

Sarah's days had continued as it had before. She had her official duties as a spy for the commander which includes sleeping with men. She always kept her ears to the wall and was able to obtain much information for the commander. She was able to earn money on her own in her limited free time. She knew that the two returning Hebrews was one of the biggest priorities for the commander when they returned in about 10 days. She was looking forward to the possible adventure of traveling to the Sinai.

Sarah had to visit the pavilion this evening to bump into a foreign visiting dignitary in an hour. The Babylonian envoy was scheduled to be there because of some trade pacts between Canaan and the Babylonians. Sarah's job was to learn all she could from him. She got tired of this work at times because it was always the same result, nothing ever exciting. All the men were like puppets and provided whatever information she asked once she bedded them.

Salman returned to his shop and sought out Fatia. "Child, where are you?" he called out.

"I am here uncle. What is it?" she replied.

"We have a potential problem," Salman explained. He replayed his encounter with Mansur and what transpired with the commander.

"So, what should we do? Do you think that this commander will do something drastic for any Hebrews in the city?" she asked.

"I am not sure. It was not good that I was there when he came but he did not pay me much attention. I believe that I am okay but when Joshua returns, we must make sure that his stay in this city is brief. We do not know what the commander will do so he and his people should be prepared to not spend anytime in this city. From what I saw of this commander, he is focusing on the recent murderers and our friends, some of whom may be involved in them. Also, the two spies which was interrogated by the commander admitted that Moses set them," Salman explained.

"So they know about Moses and their mission, this is bad news for our friends. Anything could happen when they return here. They could be arrested, tortured or even killed," Fatia said.

"We will make a plan for when they enter the city so that we are alerted. We will tell the men on our farm to keep an eye out for them. Once they get to the city, it could be too late. The group will have to pass our farm before they enter the city," Salman suggested.

"That is a great idea, we should be able to intercept them before they enter and then they can go around the city on their way to the Sinai. We must make sure that they avoid coming into the city when they return," Fatia said.

"God is good. We have a solution now so do not worry. You will prepare to leave and when they arrive at the farm, you will meet them there and help them navigate around the city. I will stay here and manage our affairs until the Israelites move into the city. I think this is a good plan," Salman said.

"It's perfect and I will maintain my trust in the Lord but this plan makes me feel good," Fatia said.

They retired to their respective bedrooms in the house. Fatia prayed to God and thanked God for all the blessings in her life. She looked out of the window at the stars and said, "Good night, my beloved."

City of Beth-Shan

All of the teams had gone to their rooms for the evening. Geuel and Nahbi had decided to go to sleep early in order to see how the soldiers opened the gates at sun rise.

Palti and Shammua were in their rooms unaware that there were being surveilled. Fayid (spy one) and Ashur (spy two) had taken up observation posts on the opposite corners in front of the rooms. They traded positions and made sure that their profile was not raised too much as they conducted their surveillance.

Gaddi and Igal were in their room both talking about the future by the light of the oil lamp. Each had been making plans to return back to Pharaoh. They believed that the people would vote to return but under more favorable circumstances.

Gaddiel, Sethur and Shaphat sat separately in each of their rooms thinking about their future. Gaddiel thought that he would love for something to happen to Joshua and Caleb thereby alleviating his problem but he should not wish such a thing on people. Or should he?

Ammiel had went to his room early and then decided to leave for a walk. He was nervous and antsy. He really longed for some companionship for the evening. He believed that when he went back to the Sinai, the people would be more aware of his movements especially if it got out that he was involved with Kabir. He might as well have some fun now in case he became stuck in a life of boredom when he returned. He walked through the market place to where the harlots were stationed.

"Hello stranger, you want to have some fun tonight?" one woman asked.

"No, but you can help me," Ammiel said. He took out two shekels and asked, "Is there a man you know that I can go to for the same type of fun."

She looked at the shekels in his hand with hunger in her eyes; all he wanted was information in return she would get free money. "Come this way," She said as she led him to a man she knew who went with other men. Ammiel gave her the two shekels before he went inside the door. The women left and Ammiel spent half the evening having "some fun."

[*Satan watched with pleasure, sex outside of marrage pleased him greatly.*]

Group 5

Joshua and Caleb had found their lodging for the evening. Joshua had lit an oil lamp to write his report for the evening.

"Day 19

Report 11

The city of Beth-shan offers much to include an abundant water supply through underground springs. The abundance of water has created lush crops and vegetation. This town will be able to provide food for our people without question. Militarily, it is no different from the previous towns we have traversed except that there seems to be more foreign soldiers in the army stationed here. The further north we travel the more mercenaries we see. This is a good thing because mercenaries fight for money which calls into question their loyalties. We will be fighting for God and with God on our side; nothing can stop us for fulfilling God's plans for us. While others may see foreign conscripts as a problem, I see this through a God-consciousness for we shall live by faith, not by sight. Separately, I have not seen the others since I arrived in town. Caleb and I continue to steadfastly move forward in doing our duty.

End of report."

Chapter 35

Day 20 morning

Beth-shan

Group 5

Joshua woke up before Caleb thinking it was the 20th morning since he had left Sinai. He thought that they were half way done with the mission. They would leave tomorrow morning for Hazor, the next stop by the caravan. He had asked Amel yesterday about Hazor and was told that it meant "enclosed settlement" so he was thinking that it would be another heavily fortified city along the way. He and the others were born in Goshen so they had never seen fortified cities before they entered Canaan. Joshua knew that it was something new for his fellow spies but they needed to have faith in God instead of what their eyes or fear lead them to believe. Amel had told him that Hazor was located in upper Galilee on the site known as Tell el-Qedah, ten miles north of the Sea of Galilee and five miles southwest of Lake Huleh. Amel explained how Hazor was composed of a 30-acre upper tell or mound rising 40 meters above the surrounding plain and a 175-acre lower enclosure which was well-fortified. Amel told him that Hazor was the largest city in Canaan.

Joshua was going to meet Amel at his cousin's place of business in an hour. Caleb started to stir on the other side of the room. Joshua was up and packing his day bag so that he would be ready in case they had to move quickly. Caleb got up and used the pitcher of water to splash water on his face.

"Praise God this morning!" Caleb said.

"He is indeed worthy to be praised," Joshua said. They prepared to leave and then walked out to meet Amel.

Joshua and Caleb went to the gates to see how it operated since it was still early. They walked to the gates and stood with throngs of people waiting to leave. There were some members of other caravans who were leaving and wanted to get an early start on their travel. The soldiers walked over to the gates while a company of soldiers stood in front of the crowd looking out for any internal problems while the troops on the wall were prepared for any trouble occurring from the outside. All in all, there were about 100 soldiers. Joshua and Caleb watched the soldiers open the gates and then once it was determined there was no danger, they allowed the crowd to depart the city and then those waiting were allowed to enter to travel into the city. There was a special guard force focused on the crowd inside the gates but once the crowd left the area, they left to patrol the city. Joshua could tell that this was one of the city's quick reaction forces (QRF) who would respond to an immediate threat while the soldiers in the garrison would take longer to engage the threat.

Joshua and Caleb left the gates pretending to be waiting for someone who did not enter the city. They left and walked over to where they would meet Amel.

Group 4

Palti and Shammua woke up and decided to go out to see more of the town. Their relationship had gotten better since they were not with Sarah. It had been almost five days since they left Hebron so the bond between the two of them started to return. They walked to a place for some breakfast.

Neither Palti not Shammua noticed the two spies following them. The spies decided to eat across the square while still maintaining a view of Palti and Shammua.

Group 3

Ammiel walked slowly back to his room before the sun came up. He felt bad about the things he had done and done to him. There had to be more to life than just looking to have some fun. He needed some sleep and was in pain from the evening. The man Ammiel was with was a specialist in doling out pain and other strange practices he had never seen nor heard of before. He needed to lie down and allow himself time to heal. The man did what he wanted to do to him even when he asked him to take it easy on him. He wished that he had not gone out and sought this man out. He guessed he had no one to blame other than himself. He shook his head as he entered his room, he was responsible for this. Why did he do things like this? The man seemed to enjoy hurting Ammiel throughout the night. Ammiel hoped that he would be better by tomorrow morning. Why did trouble always come into his life? He thought before falling asleep.

Gaddiel woke up and went out early to get some water to drink. He was scheduled to meet his group for food in about half an hour at the front of the building. The owner had a dining hall in front of the building where they were staying. Gaddiel noticed that the trading towns had more accommodations overall, which he liked.

Shaphat woke up and went to the room next door to wake up Sethur. Sethur was ready and the two left to go to Ammiel's room. Shaphat knocked at the door.

"What?" Ammiel yelled though the door.

"It's us, get up. Let's get something to eat," Sethur said through the door.

"I am sick, go without me. I will be here all day," Ammiel replied.

"Okay, we will stop by later this evening. Hope you feel better," Shaphat said.

They walked away to meet Gaddiel in front of the building in the dining room. Shaphat whispered to Sethur, "Do you think that he is alone?"

"Probably not, he is most likely doing what we were doing yesterday morning," Sethur suggested.

"I wonder if it's male or female," Shaphat laughed.

"Oh, you are so bad," Sethur said while laughing. They walked to the front and saw Gaddiel.

"Where is Ammiel?" Gaddiel asked.

"He claims to be sick. He said that he would stay in today," Sethur said.

"Hmm, that is strange. He seemed to feel alright yesterday," Gaddiel offhandedly commented.

"I am sure it was something that 'came up' suddenly," laughed Shaphat. Sethur joined him and laughed as well.

"What is it? Why are you laughing?" Gaddiel asked.

"Its nothing, we suspect that he is not alone," Sethur suggested.

Gaddiel just shook his head and the three went inside to get some breakfast.

"Today, we have been on our journey for 20 days. We have seen a lot but there is nothing that I have seen which persuades me any differently. We cannot conquer these people. What are your thoughts at this halfway point?" Gaddiel asked.

"I agree," said Sethur.

"No disagreement from me. I thought that it would be impossible from the first day." Shaphat said while grabbing some more bread from the bowl and placing it on his plate.

"Our next stop will be Hazor, that is largest city in Canaan so that should be an adventure," Gaddiel explained.

Shaphat and Sethur looked at each other and smiled. "We are looking forward to it," Shaphat said.

"Hopefully we can be there in less than two days," said Sethur.

"Traveling with the caravan will slow us down but will give us better cover. We will most likely be in Hazor in 2 days," Gaddiel said.

The group minus Ammiel spent two hours eating and relaxing in the dining room. No one saw a need to make rounds through the city since all agreed that it was impossible to conquer.

Group 2

Nahbi and Geuel looked over and saw Joshua and Caleb by the gates. They obviously had decided to see how the gates operated as well. Geuel watched Joshua and Caleb closely.

"What do you thing about them?" Asked Nahbi.

"I think that Joshua is a sincere believer unlike many of these hypocrites. I may not always believe in his views for things but I do not think he is like Gaddiel who wants power for the sake of having power. Joshua is a true believer and that is not necessary a bad thing. I just do not believe in blindly following anything or anyone like he follows Moses or his God," Geuel said.

"You mean our God," Nahbi said.

"I meant to say our God. I think that I was in bondage all my life and it hard for me to believe that all of a sudden, God is going to take care of all our needs," Geuel said.

"But God has taken care of our needs thus far," Nahbi said.

"I know but what I see in Canaan seems like too much. I think Joshua believes in what he cannot see where I believe in what I can see," Geuel said.

They walked away from the gates in quiet contemplation. Nahbi asked, "Is it better to believe in something or not? Joshua and Caleb don't seem to worry or otherwise seem bothered by all the trials and tribulations like many of our people."

"I don't know Nahbi, what is better to believe in something greater than yourself or just what you can see and touch. I am a simple man who does not have the desire to ponder such difficult questions in life," Geuel said.

"But should not we seek to be more; instead of living the same type of life?" Nahbi asked.

"These are questions for wise men or prophets. You should ask Moses if it concerns you this much. I just know, what I know," Geuel explained.

"I understand. Thank you for your thoughts," said Nahbi.

"I think they are really good questions, I just don't know the answers," Geuel replied. They continued walking through the marketplace.

Group 1

Gaddi and Igal had lost some of the animus for each other. They continued to speak with each other but there was a wedge between them over the decision to kill Joshua and Caleb.

"We need to put this all behind us," Gaddi said to Igal.

"Well, I am glad to hear you say that. I have been having bad dreams. I hate that we tried to do harm to Joshua and Caleb. I think that it could come back on us. Our actions could not have made God happy," Igal said.

"Let's go out and take a tour of the city seeking to see if it is even possible to conquer this place," Gaddi suggested.

"That sounds good. I am hungry too," said Igal.

"We can get something to eat," Gaddi replied.

They went for a walk inside the city. Gaddi knew that it was important to make friends with Igal who clearly did not have the stomach to do what was necessary. He would have to do what he needed to do on his own but would keep it from Igal. He hated the coldness from Igal when the two of them was at odds with each other. He had to be the strong one. He still had a nagging doubt in his mind regarding what Igal said about their actions being displeasing to God. Was Igal correct? He supposed that it was just general fear and doubt instead of a real worry. He would put on the face of cooperation while with Igal. They continued to make their way through the city until they found a place to eat.

Group 5

Joshua and Caleb went to Amel's cousin restaurant. They arrived and saw Amel already there.

"My friends, I am glad to see you this day. Please sit." Amel greeted each with a warm hug. He was genuinely happy to see them.

"It's good to see you too this fine day. God is good!" Joshua said.

"What are your plans for today?" Caleb asked.

"I have to take orders from some of the vendors today to see what they want when I return. I will pick up quite a lot of goods in Hazor and will return some of those items with me to this place on my return," Amel replied.

Joshua knew that they were not going to travel with the caravan after Hazor. His group would move further north to Lebo-Hamath while the caravan would stay in Hazor for one week before heading to Lebo-hamath. Since they could not stay in Hazor for the week, they would be moving north on their own without the cover of the caravan. Joshua was pleased to be able to use the caravan for cover up to that point of the journey.

Yeshak, Amel's cousin, came out of the back and welcomed his guests. He had many dishes brought out of the kitchen for his honored guests.

"We walked around the city this morning and saw that the Canaanites take their security very seriously," Joshua said.

"That is an understatement. To the Canaanites, trade is important and since this town is along the north-south trade route its vital that they protect it. But you have not seen anything yet, Hazor is the largest city in Canaan and the military has that city even more secure than this city. The military runs the whole town like a military garrison. Hazor is the main northern trading post in Canaan with much traffic not only coming from north-south but also its' a hub for east-west trade with those in Mesopotamia. There are many Babylonians, Assyrians and even those from further east living in that city, it's really diverse," Amel said.

Joshua and Caleb looked at each other thinking that if Hazor was more fortified than what they had seen, it must be formidable. "We are blessed to be able to travel with you since you are so experienced," Caleb said.

"Nonsense, I enjoy your company. I am tired of traveling with the same people. It's my pleasure that you travel with us," Amel said.

The rest of the food came and the group enjoyed the food and each other's company. After they finished, Joshua and Caleb accompanied Amel on his rounds to confirm his trade orders.

Chapter 36

Day 20 afternoon

Hebron

Commander Elrian was about to debrief Sarah about her evening with the Babylonian envoy.

"Nazar, the son of the Babylonian ruler, told me that the Babylonians are trying to regroup after being soundly defeated by the Hittites. The Babylonian military have begun a massive rebuilding program in an effort to regain its old standing but for now they are still weak. He explained that the damage done by the Hittites was even worse then what was reported throughout the region. He said that they are currently facing a threat from the north by the Assyrians too. What has really hurt the Babylonians has been the things which they have no control over: floods, famine, the widespread settlement of nomadic Aramaic tribes and the arrival of Chaldeans from the south. The Babylonian kingdom may try to rattle their swords but in reality they are toothless lions. They will try to take a strong stance against Pharaoh but they will not be able to resist if Pharaoh decides to move into Mesopotamia."

"That is a good report," Elrian said. He noticed swelling around her eye.

"Did he hurt you?" Elrian said.

"No more than normal. He is a little man who needs to feel superior by beating up women. It is nothing; I pretended to be hurt but was able to use it in my favor by getting him to reveal his deepest secrets. Also, he was able to make a trade agreement with several of the largest caravan leaders yesterday. He did not want them to come to Babylon just yet because they would see how weak the kingdom really is. The trade caravans will not actually come into the kingdom but will be met outside in the city of Gablini."

"Tell me about Nazar's father?" Elrian asked.

"He believes that the old man will die soon and he will become the king. I think he was trying to impress me with this information. I think that if he actually became the ruler, his generals would kill him very quickly because he is a weakling. He constantly wines and blames everything on others. He always likes to hit me for any reason. I have to pretend like he is a sexual lion but it's all I can do to not laugh. He is a little boy in a man's body with a man's ambition but only a boy's heart. Nazar did not want to make the trip but his father thought it would make him look strong and courageous so that he will seem like a future potential ruler to his people. You know he pretends to be a low level envoy to protect his identity while he is here but remember how I was able to get it out of him very quickly the first time we were together," Sarah said.

Elrian loved this type of insight that Sarah could provide. He had been able to get Sarah to meet with him when he first came into the city pretending to be a simple Babylonian envoy about one year ago. Sarah was the best and could get anyone to speak about themselves by simple elicitation.

"When will he return?" Elrian asked.

"He wants to come back next month but said it would be a few months. He asked me again to come with him back to his kingdom to be his queen. I guess beating me up every few months is not enough for him," Sarah humorously stated.

"When he ceases to be useful for us, I plan to personally kill him," Elrian said without any emotion.

"Thank you but it's not necessary. I know men like this, he will meet his end most likely very painfully," she said.

"You feel well enough though?" He asked.

"Yes, my lord." She said while standing up and moving to the room with a bed. She took off her clothes and waited for him near the bed. Elrian walked over to the bed and she undressed him. They had intercourse for almost an hour. She actually enjoyed it with him because he never got tired. He was quite tender even though he was disconnected during the act. He finished, got up and had her wash him as was their practice.

Elrian had left a handful of shekels and several gold pieces on his desk. "There is a little something extra for you because of your good work with the Babylonian. Let me know when you hear about the two Hebrews. Otherwise, you are free till they return to handle your business. I will let you know if I need you before then," Elrian said.

Sarah collected her money and then left thinking that she would enjoy her time off. There was a caravan arriving in Hebron from the east with silks and other nice cloth which she could use to have made into a nice dress. The one thing she missed was the fine tailors of Kemet. She enjoyed the nicer things of life such as good jewelry and fine clothes. She had put the money into a pocket made into her garment. The gold coins were a happy surprise from the commander. She did not understand how Elrian felt about her personally but she knew that he respected her work. She never had to ask for money because he always was very generous. She made her way back to her house.

Elrian sat at his desk thinking about Sarah. If he was victorious, he would free her but thought that perhaps he would make her an offer to continue to provide her unique services for him for a fee. She was really an expert in what she did in how she could get the most tight-lipped man to open up and provide confidential details about his life and business.

He also thought about introducing her to his dark lord. He would have to think about this some more because they could make a good couple if she also came to believe in Satan as her lord and savior. He enjoyed the time he shared with her. He always told himself it was the release but it was more than that. When he saw Sarah's face and she told him about the Babylonian beating her, something inside of him wanted to kill the man. This was more than just business. He would have to also figure that out as well. Elrian decided to get his elite bodyguard unit and take a walk through the city.

Sinai

Moses had heard another plea from the tribal elders of the 12 tribes requesting that he reconsider the mission and to send an envoy to Pharaoh to see if they could negotiate a return under favorable conditions. Moses' anger was aroused by the unfaithfulness of the people. He was becoming worried that the Lord would not continue to be patient with the people. Moses had given them "the ten words" or the aseret haddebarim, the ten fundamental principles or commandments of the covenant relationship between God and the people. It was a holiness code on how to live a life pleasing to God. Moses suspected that some of the people were doing things that were not pleasing to God. At every turn the people looked to disobey and to rebel, he was worried that their conduct would bring about a life of pain and suffering for the people. Every day he tried to teach the people about how their ways were not God's ways, and that they had to turn away from their former behavior and serve God with their whole heart. Moses had faith in God and hoped that the people were able to grow in that direction as well.

Evening

Beth-shan

Group 3

Ammiel woke up after realizing that the sun was setting. He had been asleep all day but he felt better. The pain he had suffered was less so he decided to get up and try moving around. He moved slowly but felt good that he could walk. He has been worried that he would not be able to travel tomorrow. He bent down touching his toes feeling a sharp pain. He decided to take it slowly but he was hungry. He dressed and walked out the room to find some food.

Group 1

Palti and Shammua had gotten something to eat and walked around the city. The two spies of the commander were following them unobserved. Palti and Shammua made their way back to their rooms. The two spies took up their positions across the square from their rooms were located.

Group 3

Gaddiel, Shaphat and Sethur decided to take a walk around town. During the walk, Shaphat and Sethur decided to break off from Gaddiel to revisit the harlots they were with previously. Gaddiel watched them leave and made his way back to the room. He saw Ammiel in the cafe at the rooming house. He decided to join him.

"Hello, how are you feeling? Better I hope," said Gaddiel.

"I am feeling better," Ammiel said.

Gaddiel did not want to pry into his personal business but he wanted to seem like a friend. "If I can do anything to help you, you can come to me."

"Thank you very much but I will be good by tomorrow morning," Ammiel replied. They each ordered some food and drank the yoghurt that was brought to the table.

"So, what do you think will happen once we return and tell the people that we can not conquer Canaan?" Ammiel asked.

"I'm not sure because it depends on Moses. Will Moses listen to what the people have to say? Will he allow the majority to make the decision? Also, who says that we need to all travel together," explained Gaddiel.

"Whatever we do, I believe we should stay together as a nation when we travel. I do not see how anyone can think that we could possess this land though," Ammiel said.

"I think if the people could see what we have seen, there would not even be a debate. They would all see how impossible it would be if we decided to attack the Canaanites." Gaddiel explained.

"You are right. Whatever happens, I hope that it will be an easy agreement between all the factions. We need to stay together as a people." Ammiel said.

Gaddiel was happy that Ammiel brought the subject up. "This is why it's important for someone to lead who has seen this land. I have two suggestions what we should do but it will be up to the people. I think our best choice would be to return to Pharaoh and I could make that journey to negotiate the best terms possible. Life could be so much better if we decide to go back there to negotiate from a position of strength," Gaddiel explained hoping that Ammiel would agree that he was the man for the job.

"That sounds like a good idea. I would support that and could convince my tribe that it would be the best possible decision," Ammiel suggested knowing that it would please Gaddiel.

"It's always good to have friends. And I am your friend Ammiel, just remember that. We can support each other." Gaddiel said.

"I agree," he replied. They finished their food and then returned to their rooms for the night.

Group 1

Gaddi and Igal had walked around the city to see what it was like rather then for the mission. They checked out the temples and the areas where moneychangers were located. The caravans were all preparing their cargo so they could leave in the morning. Gaddi and Igal talked to a few other caravan leaders. They enjoyed the time of not having to worry about conspiring against Joshua and Caleb. They returned to the room to get a good night's rest to be ready to leave the city in the morning with their caravan.

Group 2

Nahbi and Geuel had a busy day as they checked out the whole city. They saw how the city exploited the underground spring and transported the water out of the city for the crops. They visited all the temples in town even the pagan ones and the ones for Baal and El. They spoke with several merchants and then had dinner near the north gate. After the whole day of moving around, each was tired and desired sleep so they returned to their rooms.

Group 5

Joshua and Caleb was able to get a good idea of the city by walking with Amel while he collected on his debts, took orders for more goods. Amel introduced both of them to his contacts and gave them a lot of insider information on the vendors and the customers. Amel was a fount of great intelligence for Joshua and Caleb.

Joshua asked Amel, "Do you need any document from the Canaanites to run a caravan and do they tax you during your trip?"

"There is no certificate or permission needed to run a caravan. The Canaanites only really care when they randomly stop me and then I have to pay. When I do pay, I get a stamped tariff statement so that I am not double taxed on the same trip. Usually I just pay a bribe which is cheaper than the tariff," Amel said.

"Can anyone start a caravan without any special permission?" asked Joshua.

"Yes anyone," Amel said.

Joshua was already thinking of a way to conquer this land through a clever rouse. He thought that some of the cities would fall to direct confrontation but there would be times when a deception or ruse could be used like pretending to be a caravan. The caravan was just a company of travelers on a journey through a desert or hostile area with a train of pack animals. It was an interesting idea that Joshua considered.

The evening went by quickly. Amel had to be up early to prepare the caravan for the next leg to Hazor. They said goodbye and agreed to meet early in the morning.

Chapter 37

Day 20 evening

Beth-shan

Before Caleb went into the room, he looked up to the stars and said, "Good Night beloved." Caleb walked into the room and started his prayers to the Lord. Joshua sat in the room and brought out his little scroll to record his 12th report.

"Report 12

Today, we were able to meet with many different people throughout the society in Beth-shan. There are not many people loyal to this region. Canaan is a land made up of so many diverse tribes that not everyone would fight to keep the existing administration in power. The army will fight but I do not believe that there would be overwhelming support from the people to rise up and give their lives for this made-up land of Canaan. There is not the same type of loyalty that one would find in Babylon at the height of their power or in Kemet for Pharaoh. When we come in this region, we will not have to fight all the people just the ones loyal to Pharaoh. We will be in Hazor in 2 days.

End of report."

Joshua put away his scroll and kneeled by his bed, Joshua prayed to God thanking Him for all the blessings He had bestowed on them. He continued in prayer for another few minutes before going to sleep.

Day 21 morning

Beth-shan

Amel's caravan was packed and ready to travel before the sun came up. He had arranged all the pack animals in a line near the north gate. He noticed that Joshua and Caleb were already there waiting with their packs.

"Good morning, my friends. I am happy to see you," said Amel.

Both Joshua and Caleb were pleased to see Amel and told him so. The three of them intermingled with the other members in the caravan.

Group 1

Gaddi and Igal left their room and started walking towards the gate as the sun came up.

Group 2

Nahbi and Geuel had arrived early to see if there was anything they could do to help the caravan.

Group 3

Gaddiel and Ammiel were up early and decided to get something to eat from the marketplace. They bought fresh bread which had just been made fresh a few minutes earlier for the whole group. About 30 minutes later, Sethur and Shaphat made their way out of the rooms looking very tired and haggard from the night before.

"It is good to see the two of you make it. I was worried for a while that we would have to go and round you up," Gaddiel said.

Sethur and Shaphat were not in the mood for early morning levity and explained as such to Gaddiel. The quartet made their way to the city's northern gate.

Group 4

Palti and Shammua awoke and packed their things. They had some fruit from the night before that they ate and then left the room. In front of the building, spy one (Fayid) and spy two (Ashur) made their way behind them to the northern gate. There were many others looking to exit the city so it was not unusual as others made their way down the main walking street inside the city to the gates.

Northern gates

Beth-shan

Once the sun came up, the soldiers were already in place facing the crowds. The other soldiers opened the gates and the throngs of people inside the gates were allowed to leave first before anyone from outside were permitted to enter the city. The five groups of Hebrew spies were with the caravan as well as 40 other people moving north. The caravan would travel with the Jordan River on their east. The Jordan River flowed north to south almost directly straight inline from the Sea of Chinnereth (often called the Sea of Galilee or Tiberias) to the Dead Sea. Taking the northern route along the river assured that the caravan went on the most direct path which would save them time. Joshua and Caleb were both looking forward to seeing the Sea of Galilee as it was a huge freshwater lake, something they had never seen before. The distance between Beth-shan and Hazor was approximately 40 miles. The caravan would do 20 miles a day so they would arrive in Hazor in 2-3 days. The caravan's camels slowed the pace of the caravan but the camel was uniquely adapted for travel in the desert with its padded feet, muscular body, and its hump of fat which sustained life on long journeys. A young camel could walk 100 miles a day alone but in a large caravan it was slower. Joshua noticed that Amel owned almost half of the 200 camels in the caravan. He knew that wealth in Canaan was measured by many things including camels. Joshua knew that some people also ate camel meat but the Jews were forbidden to eat the camel because it was considered unclean because it chewed its cud and did not have a split hoof. The camel had many uses including the use of his hair which when woven could be made into clothes.

Fayid and Ashur had positioned themselves with the caravan along with the other people traveling north. They used the cover of the other travelers to mask their intentions.

Amel and his caravan moved slowly. The Jordan River was seen from time to time as they traveled. The Jordan River's place name meant 'the descender'. The river was the longest and most important river in Canaan. The river started from the foot of the Mount Hermon and flowed into the Dead Sea. There were a number of small streams which flowed off the Jordan like the small stream which Beth-shan lay near. Because the twists and turns in the river the river was more than 200 miles long but only measured about 70 miles from north to south between the Sea of Galilee and the Dead Sea. Every time Joshua saw the Jordan, he was reminded of God's promise to the people. He thought this was the land that was promised to us.

The caravan moved north for several hours before they came upon an oasis. Moses' spies moved separately in their individual groups while the commander's spies hung back watching all that transpired. Fayid and Ashur noticed that the two Hebrews had not spoken to anyone yet. Once in the oasis, the caravan broke up and people started to speak with each other. Gaddiel wondered if the others were okay, he nodded to Palti and Shammua as they were near him. Palti and Shammua spoke to him. "How long do you think it will take to get to Hazor?" Palti asked Gaddiel.

"About 2 days," Gaddiel answered. Gaddiel asked him a few more questions about his time in Beth-shan. They continued to speak for a few more minutes.

Fayid looked over at Ashur. "I knew they were not alone, those are Hebrews that the little Hebrew is talking to. They are speaking as if they know one another, not as if they first met. They look suspicious and conspiratorial." Fayid and Ashur watched Palti and Shammua speak to the four Hebrews. All of the spies' clothes were more like the Hebrews clothes Fayid had seen when he was working for Pharaoh in Kemet. No one else would not have noticed it unless they had spent time in Kemet but Fayid noticed but the main clue to their identity was the sandals which gave them away. The Hebrews tied their sandals differently then Assyrians, Arabs, Aramaeans or Babylonians. Fayid and Ashur watched the exchange between the two Hebrew spies and the four others. Fayid made a mental note of the four men who they spoke with. After they finished speaking, he continued to observe the group of four men.

After Palti and Shammua left, Gaddiel asked Shaphat and Sethur to go over to speak with the two groups they had spoken with previously.

Shaphat went over to Gaddi and Igal. "How are you?" Shaphat asked.

"We are well," Gaddi replied.

"I just wanted to make sure that the two of you are well. Did anything happen there that our group should know?" Shaphat asked.

"Nothing, it was more of the same. We had a good opportunity to see the city," Igal said.

"Do the both of you still agree that it will be impossible to conquer these people?" asked Shaphat.

"Yes, even more so now. I think I speak for the both of us when we say we agree with you and Gaddiel about this land." Gaddi said. Igal nodded his head in agreement as well.

"Let us know if anything happens that would affect us as well. If you need anything, let me know?" Shaphat said before walking back to where his group was standing.

Fayid and Ashur watched the exchange between the three of them taking careful note of their appearance and every other detail about them.

As many of the men in the caravan talked and walked around speaking with each other, Sethur walked over to Nahbi and Geuel.

Fayid and Ashur watched Sethur as well.

Sethur asked Nahbi and Geuel about their time in Beth-shan. "We should maintain operational security while we are still traveling north," said Geuel. Sethur looked at Geuel with annoyance because Geuel always seemed so arrogant.

"I just wanted to make sure that you were alright," Sethur said.

Geuel walked closely to Sethur and whispered to him, "I thank you for your concern but we do not know who may be watching us. God be with you." Geuel walked away from Sethur with Nahbi.

Sethur left shaking his head. Although the exchange was short it was not before he, Geuel and Nahbi were seen by the two spies of Commander Elrian. Although the time spend between these three people were much shorter, it was long enough for Fayid to recognize the conspiratorial exchange and the familiar dress of the two which identified then as being Hebrews.

"I think there are 10 spies in this group," Fayid said.

"It is interesting that the two Hebrews who were interrogated by the men in the garrison were able to mislead the commander in thinking it was just the two of them. I thought for sure that the little one was broken," replied Ashur.

"I am surprised as well but never underestimate the power of men who believe in something," Fayid explained.

"There are now 10 spies in this group in this conspiracy. The commander will find this interesting. They are scheduled to return to Hebron in about 9 days. I think that we should go back to Hebron and report our results to him. I think we have all the information we need at this point. What do you think?" asked Fayid.

"I think you are right. It's clear that they are doing reconnaissance on this land and will go to Hazor before traveling to Lebo-hamath. I think they are surveying Canaan in advance of an invasion. We need to report back to the commander so he can plan his next move," Ashur explained.

"We are agreed then. Let us ride out now and head back to Hebron," Fayid said. They packed their stuff and broke camp in order to make it to Hebron by the day after next.

Joshua and Caleb watched the various members of his group meet again going against operational security of the mission. After Joshua observed Gaddiel meet with Palti and Shammua; Shaphat met with Gaddi and Igal; and Sethur met with Nahbi and Geuel, he witnessed the strangest event, two men left out on horses from the caravan in the opposite direction.

"Caleb, look at that." Joshua pointed to the two men riding the horses out of camp. "I have a bad feeling about this," Joshua said.

Caleb looked at the men ride away. "What do you think that is about?" asked Caleb.

"Why would two men who traveled with the caravan towards the north suddenly decide that they need to return to the south?" Joshua asked.

"I don't know," Caleb said.

"I don't know either but I do not like the fact that it was after our colleagues broke operational security measures and spoke with each other. Do you see why I have a bad feeling about that or am I overreacting?" asked Joshua.

"It makes sense. What do you want to do?" asked Caleb.

"We just continue doing what we are tasked to do, trust in the Lord and keep our eyes open," Joshua said.

Joshua and Caleb watched members of his group prepare themselves for the remaining journey. The caravan was ready and broke camp to move further north.

The caravan moved past Jarmuth. Amel told Joshua and Caleb that Jarmuth meant 'height' or 'swelling in the ground'. The lands around the town were lowlands or foothills because of the large hills to the west.

Amel and Joshua talked while the caravan moved onward. Joshua had an important question to ask, "Do you thing the local population is connected with Pharaoh and his people who administer the land?"

"The local population does not really care who is in charge as long as things work, trade flows and it's peaceful. The people of Canaan are not wedded to any ruling dynasty because there are so many people moving in and out of these lands. Look at the all the people we have seen since we left Jericho; the Amorites, the Jebusites, the Girgasites, the Hivites, the Arkites, the Sinites, the Arvadites, the Zemarites, and the Hamathites. These are peoples just occupying the same space, not a nation." Amel said.

Amel's words aligned with Joshua's assessment of the people. Joshua smiled to himself, they would possess this land.

Chapter 38

Day 21 late afternoon

Southern route north of Beth-shan to Hebron

Fayid and Ashur rode their horses hard in order to make it to Hebron as soon as possible. They were able to reach Hebron which was about 50 miles south in record time. They rode into Hebron and made their way to the garrison. Each man covered his face with a veil so the soldiers would not know that they were spies for the commander. They entered through the back of the garrison and asked for the commander.

The soldiers on duty knew the routine and instantly got the commander. The two spies were led to the office.

"Report," ordered Elrian.

"My lord, I am happy to say that we caught up to them. We found them in Beth-shan and surveilled them until they left the city. They are traveling with a caravan going to Hazor. At the first rest stop, we observed them talking with eight other men who I strongly suspect as being Hebrews. I used to work in Goshen for Pharaoh. I know Hebrews and could easily tell who they were. These men were speaking in hushed tones and acted suspiciously. I cannot say for sure but my operational senses tell me that these ten men are all together in this conspiracy," explained Fayid.

"Ten men!" Elrian stood up clearly upset.

"How was it that those Hebrews were able to hide the truth from me. This is disturbing," Elrian exclaimed.

Fayid and Ashur allowed the commander to vent without saying anything. After a while the commander sat down and focused on what he should do. "I want you to make sure that when they enter this town that you know about it. I will arrest the eight of them and interrogate them in a manner that will ensure that they will withhold nothing back. Thank you for your service this far. Are they still on schedule to return here in about 8 or 9 days?" Elrian asked.

"Yes, my lord," replied Fayid.

Elrian told Fayid and Ashur about his interview with Mansur. He provided all the details to them before tell them, "I have another mission for you. When I visited Mansur at the pavilion, he was sitting at a table the other day with an old man who I believe is a Hebrew. Find out who he is and if he is connected to this conspiracy somehow. Report back to me as soon as you get some intelligence," stated Elrian.

"Yes, my lord." The two spies both nodded in agreement. Before they left, Fayid said, "I need to speak to you in private for a moment, my lord."

"Number two, leave me. I will speak with number 1 now." Ashur left the same way he had come.

"Something strange happened when we were riding north. Suddenly and without warning, I knew that the two Hebrews were in Beth-shan. I do not know how this is possible. I did not mention this to number two but it has baffled me," Fayid said.

"Something's are a mystery in life. Perhaps you are endowed with some special gifts that you were not aware of previously," Elrian suggested.

"Perhaps my lord, I am sorry for taking up more of your time. I will take my leave." Fayid nodded and left out. Fayid knew it was Elrian. Somehow, he was mixed up with magic or something else he could not explain. He did not like the idea of Elrian using some type of magic. He walked out seeing Ashur by the horses ready to leave for their next mission. They left separately but decided to meet later that afternoon to work out the details of their new mission.

Elrian watched them leave. He then entered into deep thought. "Ten spies in all for this mission from Moses. The two little Hebrews were able to deceive me, it will not happen again. He hesitated unleashing the one weapon which would destroy them. He wanted to kill Moses but his secondary thought was to just kill the ten men and then Moses would never know what happened with his men. He resisted that option because the thought of killing the accursed deliverer was just too sweet to pass up. He knew that Satan would guide his decisions so he would be patient.

Northern route to Hazor

Group 5

The caravan plodded along the route as it was getting late. They could see the Sea of Galilee to their right. It was a spectacular sight.

"Just look at that amazing sea, it's so large. I did not think it would be so large," said Caleb.

"It is a blessed sight indeed. Once we possess this land, it will become a more common view for us," Joshua said.

There were several settlements along the sea as the caravan moved north. They first arrived at the town of Sennabris and then traveled past Hammath and then Tiberius. Both cities had walls around them but they were more like lightly fortified towns than modern cities like Jerusalem.

There were trees and greenery all around the sea with large hills in the background. The land was lush and flourishing. Joshua asked Amel to tell him everything about the Sea of Galilee.

"The sea is about 5 miles across at its widest and about 10 miles north to south. The name Galilee means circle and it's freshwater. You can drink it unlike the Dead Sea at the southern end of the Jordan River. There is very good fishing in the sea which is why there are so many cities on its shores, it can sustain a population," explained Amel.

The people they passed were very different then the nomads Joshua and Caleb had seen previously. The economy around the sea was different as well.

"I trade my spices and goods for fish from the villages along the sea but my main business on this trip is moving all these camels as well as other food stuffs to Hazor," Amel explained.

"We are so fortunate that we were able to meet you Amel because you have shown us so much in this land," said Caleb.

"I say again, it's my pleasure," Amel said.

Group 1

Gaddi and Igal walked with the men of the caravan they had made friends with. Igal felt good about the pace of the trip but his thoughts started going to what would happen when they returned to the Sinai. Would Joshua and Caleb tell what happened to them or not?

Although Gaddi had also been thinking of the same thing, his thoughts were still centered on how to get rid of Joshua and Caleb so that Igal would not know.

Group 2

Nahbi and Geuel were helping the men who they were traveling with unpack some goods. The men were scheduled to drop off some goods to one of the villages on the Sea of Galilee. Nahbi and Geuel would go with the two merchants and help them off load the goods and then load on some baskets of fish.

Nahbi and Geuel left the caravan with several camels and made their way to Tarichae village. They quickly found the merchant they needed and exchanged the goods. Because it was only four men and four camels, they made very good time to the village and then returned back to the caravan. The two merchants were very pleased to have the assistance but Geuel had wanted to see one of the small fishing villages because he did not think that they would be returning to Canaan any time soon so he wanted to see all he could. Geuel really believed that the Israelites would not be able to take Canaan. Nahbi was happy to go along and to watch over Geuel. Nahbi and Geuel relationship had grown much over the last three weeks.

Group 3

Gaddiel, Ammiel, Shaphat and Sethur continued to make their way with the caravan. Several of the smaller groups with the caravan left to go to the towns on the sea. The four members of the group made their way with the caravan rarely speaking with one another because all were tired. Gaddiel was trying to stay focused but he was somewhat tired for some unknown reason. Ammiel was still in a little pain from the night before. Shaphat and Sethur were both extremely tired from their escapades over the last few days.

Group 4

Palti and Shammua each had similar thoughts; each one wanted Sarah to themselves. They had each been planning the reunion when they returned to Hebron. Each thought that they would be first to see her when they returned.

Northern Galilee

The caravan made its way around the Sea of Galilee but they were losing light for the evening so the leaders decided to make camp at the very northernmost tip of the Sea of Galilee. By staying near a village, the caravan would be safer against possible raiding parties. The caravan was close to the fishing village of Bethsaida. Amel sent out several men to Bethsaida to obtain some fish from the locals in exchange for some spices. The men returned with several baskets of fishes and loaves for dinner for the evening. Amel had a cook in his caravan who prepared the fish and served it to everyone. Joshua thought that Amel was a good caravan leader because he knew how to take care of his people. The caravan ate the food and then several of the men told stories to entertain the others. It was a festive atmosphere with must fun had by all. At the conclusion, everyone made places for themselves to sleep for the evening.

Joshua wrote his 13th report which consisted of no major insights, just some geographical points to remember when they retuned. Joshua and Caleb said good night to each other and then did their prayers. Before Caleb went to sleep, he looked at the stars and wished a good and blessed night to his beloved.

Evening

Hebron

Fayid and Ashur had met at Mansur's pavilion in order to collect some intelligence on the man who had met with Mansur when the commander has come there. Fayid and Ashur walked in the pavilion and asked for Mansur. After a few minutes Mansur appeared. He saw the two men and knew that it would not be a good meeting. He decided right then to make sure that he provided all the information they wanted. He did not want to see the commander again under these hostile conditions.

Mansur invited the two to sit down in the back. They sat down and immediately asked to know about the man he was sitting with.

Mansur answered, "I was with a local Hebrew merchant named Salman. He has been in Hebron for many years and owns a shop in the eastern marketplace. He has a niece that works with him. I believe her name is Fatia, she is not Hebrew but like you, from Kemet."

"How is it you know I am from Kemet?" asked Fayid.

"I have been in this land for a long time and can tell someone with an accent like that of Pharaoh. I know this fact even when a person tries to mask his accent," Mansur said trying to regain a bit of the upper hand.

"What else can you tell me about them? Are they connected to the four Hebrews who were staying here before," asked Ashur.

"I am not sure if they are or not. Neither the four Hebrews nor Salman indicated in any way that they knew each other. I have no idea. I would tell you if I knew," said Salman.

Fayid could tell that he was telling the truth. He noticed a bit of fear in his eyes which he could understand after getting hit by Elrian. Elrian had told him that Mansur was warned about not hiding any details again.

"Is there anything else you can tell us? The commander told us that you would tell us everything we needed to know," said Fayid.

"That is all I know about this subject," Mansur said.

"I tell you that you should not tell anyone, I mean anyone, that we were here. If this old man finds out that you talked to us, it will be very painful for you. Am I clear?" Fayid asked.

"It's very clear," Mansur said. The two men got up and walked straight out of the pavilion. Mansur watched them leave and thought that Salman would not like what was coming his way. But he could not worry about that but rather himself. He got up and tended to his business.

Fayid and Ashur thought about going to the garrison first but then decided against that because they wanted to put eyes on their targets, Salman and Fatia.

Fatia had been planning on only carrying a small amount of clothes and goods with her but wanted to see if Caleb and Joshua wanted her to bring anything from the shop or the farm for them or their people. She was prepared. It had gotten late but she had been so excited about her future, she was still full of energy. That said, she was a little sad about being separated from Caleb. She went outside the shop and looked up at the stars and whispered, "Good night, beloved." She returned back inside of the shop.

Fayid and Ashur watched the young woman walk out of the shop and look up at the stars. Fayid noticed that she was very attractive with features like women from his land. She was tall with long dark hair. She was thin and dressed well. There was openness in her face touched by a little bit of sadness as she looked up. If she or her uncle were connected with the Hebrews, he would do as the commander wanted but hoped that he could save this one for himself.

Chapter 39

Day 22 morning

Northern route towards Hazor

The men of the caravan were up and ready to move at sunrise. The caravan moved faster after a good night's rest then it did by the end of the previous day.

Once the caravan was moving at a fast pace, Joshua asked Amel to provide additional details on Hazor.

"Hazor is large and busy. There are perhaps 20,000 to 30,000 people living in that city. I have heard some say that there could be 40,000 people there. Hazor is composed of a 30 acre tell or mound rising 150 feet above the land. There are about 200 acres on the lower levels of the city. The town is well-fortified and the walls are considered to be impenetrable. Its location is both strategic from an economic and military standpoint. It overlooked the Via Maris, the major overland trade route from Kemet to the north and east which has major it the major trading center in Canaan. The city also does major trade with the Babylonians as well as with Pharaoh. Hazor overlooks the Huleh Valley, a critical defense point against armies invading from the north. Hazor is located near Lake Hazor which allows for a close water supply. The only problem with the city is that there is no internal water supply, water must come from outside. It's a modern city with a lot of people coming from north and south, as well as east and west. You will find it like nothing you have seen before," said Amel.

Joshua took in all the details and looked forward to seeing the city for himself. Caleb listened to Amel as well. He was thinking of something different, the sooner they made their way to Hazor and then Lebo-hamath, the quicker they would be back on their way to Hebron. Caleb believed in staying in constant contact with God through prayer during the day. As he walked this morning, he thanked God for all his blessings. He would be diligent in his mission but he could not wait until he saw Fatia again. All of his prayers were focused on her growing closer to God, the same prayers he had for himself.

The caravan made good time during the day and Amel told them they would be outside the city of Hazor before sunset. The city would most likely have already closed their gates when the caravan would arrive. They were trying to make it there before that happened, but if not, they would be sleeping outside again.

Hebron

Fayid and Ashur had stayed outside the shop and residence of Salman and Fatia the whole night. Fayid had learned that in doing surveillance one had to gather a baseline for the target's activities he was observing first in order to know that person's routines. He had sent Ashur home to get some sleep late the previous evening and would get some sleep later in the day once Ashur returned. He would do a staggered schedule until they learned the schedule of the two targets. He saw the old man open up the shop. There were a few employees who appeared early to bring some merchandise. It was clear that they were from the outside farms. He wondered if the two of them owned a farm, they probably had made a deal with several of the local farms to sell some of their goods in exchange for a piece of the profit. The old man was clearly a Hebrew but the young woman definitely looked like she was from his country of birth. Mansur had called the two of them, uncle and niece. He wondered how that came to be. He had a few methods of obtaining more information, one of which was to pretend to be a customer but he did not want to be seen just yet. He would report to the commander when Ashur returned.

Sarah had enjoyed the few days off. She purchased some fine cloth to make some clothes and then just enjoyed being able to utilize her time as she saw fit. Her two targets, Palti and Shammua, were amusing. They were each ensnared so quickly and were all in. She sort of felt sorry for them because she could tell that neither knew many women, if they knew any at all in a carnal way. She knew that the commander would probably kill them once he was done with them and it saddened her a little. This was a strange feeling for her. She had to focus on what was important.

Salman had also spent time reading the scrolls that Caleb had left with Fatia. It had been so long since he had been able to fill that inner spiritual void. He was always faithful and believed that God was faithful to him by bringing someone across his path with direct knowledge of God. Joshua was close to the messenger of God. Meeting Joshua was a blessing which he would always treasure. He had been making plans to run the business on his own once Fatia left until she returned with the Israelites. But now, he was thinking that he needed some contingency plans in case he needed to leave as well. Something was nagging at him when he was at Mansur's pavilion and then commander saw him.

[*"That is it, be on guard regarding the commander. Beware of the commander. Plan and prepare to leave with Fatia." The Archangel Raphael put the thought on Salman's heart. He hoped that Salman heard that small, still voice that he was putting on his heart. He often used his God-Spell power indirectly by introducing a suggestion. Sometimes people who were too busy or too consumed with their own affairs of those who were far from God's word and never heard that small, still voice of direction and guidance. In this case, he had hope because of Salman's faith.*]

Salman had that feeling again, he decided at that point to visit the farms and make the preparations needed to be ready to leave just in case. If it did go bad, he would collect all his recent debt in order to have all the money possible for he and Fatia's future. There was one of the farmers who were looking to take over the business. He would speak to him today and arrange for him to receive Joshua and his group when they arrived.

"Fatia, I am going out to the farms today to speak with Annan since he runs all of our farms. I will make the arrangements for our friends while I am there. Don't worry, I will take one of the men with me to help me," Salman said hoping to stave off Fatia's protestations.

"I don't like it when you go out there without me," she said.

"It will be alright, my child. I need to see him eye to eye to make some arrangements. I want to leave now so I can be back early," Salman explained.

Fatia did not like it but she went along with it because he was taking one of the men with him. Salman was quickly able to get ready and leave out with one of his workers.

Ashur had returned to where Fayid was and took up his observation post. Fayid and Ashur watched the old man leave. "I will return shortly, I am going to report to the commander," said Fayid.

Fayid thought it would be a good time to give a report to the commander while the old man was out. The old man seemed to be almost 70 or 80 years old, he did not believe that he would go far. Fayid went to the garrison and did his normal routine to enter. With his face covered, he was escorted inside and brought to the commander.

"It's good to see you, what news have you?" the commander asked.

Fayid provided the commander details of what they learned. "So, the old man has left out today and the young woman is there. Do you believe Mansur was truthful in what he said about the two of them not knowing any of the Hebrews?" Elrian asked.

"I looked in his eyes and saw fear. I do not believe he was lying. I truly think that he has no idea regarding any connection with them. Obviously, that does not mean that they are not connected. I think that we should maintain surveillance on them and see what transpires when the Hebrews arrive."

"That is a good plan. When it was just two bumbling Hebrews who knew nothing other than Moses sending them here to obtain information, there was no real threat. Now that I know that there are ten spies roaming around Canaan and that the two bumbling spies are savvier that I thought possible, we have a real problem. I want to make sure that you stay on top of this issue. Sarah will know when they arrive because the two are ensnared in her trap. I want you to also put a system in place so that when they enter the city, you know the moment they are here. Lastly, make sure if you or number two see anything from your surveillance, that I know immediately," Elrian said.

"Yes, my lord. I am here to serve you," Fayid said. He left the garrison as he came in order to return to the shop where Fatia and Salman were located.

Elrian watched Fayid leave. He went back into his office and started an incantation to summon up Satan. "*Ayuha, Oh Shaitana, Iblis, Diablos, Ey ayuduh lama musaada....*" Elrian said the words to get the Prince of Darkness to hear him. "I need your help oh great one. Empower me to do what I must to follow these men and to kill the one known as the deliverer of the Hebrews. Show me the way, guide my hand." Elrian was waiting for some inner word or thought placed on his heart. He heard nothing but he felt power entering his body. "I feel it and I praise your name! I reject the light and freely embrace your cause." Elrian finished the exit incantation.

He felt the power flow through his muscles. He felt as if he had the power of ten men. He had hoped to gain some insight but he would settle for the enhanced strength and speed.

[*Satan had to be careful. He would have to tread lightly so that he did not overstep his boundaries. He knew that God would not want him to directly do something against God's prophet without God's direct and explicit permission. Even working against the prophet of God could be dangerous to him. He was hoping that by touching Elrian's body with extra strength, he would be operating within the outer boundaries of the agreement. He hated the agreement at times like this. He could only influence and never directly interfere unless God approved it in advance. He could not do anything which would push Elrian too close to Moses. Elrian would have to use his own cunning if he was going to kill Moses. He had hope in Elrian's desire to do evil.*]

---

10 miles south of Hazor

The caravan was moving fast but it was still slower than a few men could travel alone. Alone, one man could almost travel from Beth-shan to Hazor in one day. With the caravan, it became a 2 day trip. Joshua thought that the cover was the best aspect instead of the speed. Also the intelligence that he obtained traveling with Amel was invaluable. The caravan made their way closer and closer to its destination.

Outside of Hebron

Salman was at the farm talking to Annan about his business. "I may have to travel with Fatia a bit for several weeks soon. I wanted to see if you were still interested in taking over the business?" Salman asked.

Annan's eyes lit up and he immediately replied in the affirmation.

"That is good news. I think that we discussed you buying me out completely but I had another idea. We could become partners; 50/50 equal partners. You could pay me a fair fee to become my full partner. I would travel and return to collect my share but would need a substantial amount as a down payment," Salman said.

Annan though for a moment and then said, "Salman, I think that is a good plan. Let both of us think about a fair price and then meet again in a week to formalize the agreement."

"That is great! I would most likely want to leave in a week or two so let's meet in a few days," Salman explained.

"I will figure out an offer for you. I have wanted this for a long time, thank you. I would work at your shop in the city with one of my sons while my other four sons would continue to work the land," said Annan.

"God is good. Oh, before I forget, I have a few business partners coming in before I leave. There will be perhaps 8 or 10 or them. I am looking at doing business in Midian with these fellows. I think we would also be able to work with them. This will be a potential very lucrative opportunity for you too. You would be able to buy several more farms from the money you can earn from this new business," Salman explained.

Annan was interested. "How can I help?" he asked.

"They will come through here on the way to the city in about a week but I want them to stop here before entering the city. When you see them, send a runner to get me and Fatia. We will come here so we can discuss the details because they also want to see the farm. Do not tell anyone yet about our deal or about my visitors. You will be able to recognize the men, they are Hebrews. Two of the men were the men who were with us last week when we came here."

"I remember those two men. I will send one of my sons to you when they come," Annan said.

"Thank you, my friend," Salman said. With that, Salman returned to the city.

Chapter 40

Day 22

Salman returned to the city before the sun went down. He made it back to the shop and saw Fatia discussing business with some of the local farmers. He came in and was greeted by those present. Salman was tired and would tell his niece on what happened once the farmers left.

Fayid and Ashur were both outside observing when Salman returned. Fayid did not know the schedule of Salman so he did not know if it was his routine for him to be gone all day.

The farmers left after an agreement was made about future deliveries.

"Uncle, so tell me about your trip?" Fatia asked.

Salman provided her with the details of the trip.

"So, you believe that we may have to leave here together?" she asked.

"I just have this feeling about the commander. I cannot give you a definitive explanation as to why I feel this way but I trust this feeling. I think sometimes that God provides us guidance; we just have to listen for His voice. I think it is better to take precautions and then if there is no problem, we lose nothing because I wanted to get out of the business anyway. But if I am right, then I am saving our lives. This deal should take good care of us and provide for our future. This is half your business so I want to make sure you are alright with this decision?" he asked.

"Uncle, I trust you and believe that it is better to take the necessary precautions. You have my support for this deal," said Fatia. It was getting late so Salman decided to go to bed. Fatia walked outside the shop and looked up at the stars to say good night to Caleb.

Hazor

The caravan arrived at the outskirts of Hazor as the sun was setting which meant that they had to sleep on the ground for another night. Joshua and Gaddiel met after everyone was asleep and they decided to only spend three days in the city because they believed that a comprehensive survey was not necessary as they did in Hebron. Each had their own reasons. For Joshua, he believed that they did not need to stay in Hazor long because he trusted in God. For Gaddiel, he did not think that they needed an in-depth survey because they would not be able to conquer the land anyway. They would spend the next three days in Hazor and then leave for Lebo-hamath on the morning of fourth day. The caravan was scheduled to leave on the morning of the seventh day so they could not pretend to leave with them. Joshua and Gaddiel believed that since they would be traveling alone to their next destination, they would leave before the caravan left. Gaddiel agreed to pass the message on to the others since he had already been able to stay in contact with the others. They departed and returned to their respective areas.

Joshua explained what was decided to Caleb. Before it became too dark, the first thing that Joshua noticed was the high walls and the multi-levels of the city. They were spending the night on the lowlands and the gates of the city were located up on the hill. There was a long path leading up to the south gate. The walls were taller than at the other cities and it seemed very thick by the number of troops patrolling on the tops of the fortified walls. The city's defenses were impressive by any standard.

By the fire, Joshua wrote his 14th report providing his thoughts on what he saw at ground level below Hazor. Although many people could look at the city and think it was daunting, Joshua just laughed when he thought about the might of His God.

Caleb was thinking of Fatia at that very moment and looked up at the stars and said good night to her at the same time she was saying it to him. He said his prayers and went to sleep peacefully.

Day 23 morning

The caravan members woke up at the rising of the sun. The caravan rolled into the city along with the other merchants, farmers and travelers who were looking to enter the city. Joshua noticed the stone foundations which were made from uncut fieldstone which made the defenses stronger. Joshua had been a stone cutter for Pharaoh so he knew the walls were made of casemate which meant two parallel stone walls with dividing partitions connecting them. It was the best type of fortified walls possible. He observed the huge six-chambered gatehouse (three on each side) allowing easy access and exit for chariots and large caravans. These types of gates allowed a huge mass of people to enter quickly when being attacked by external forces. Many of the current fortified cities had smaller gates like Beth-shan where it could take a lot of time to get people in and out of the city. The architects who build the walls in Hazor knew what they were doing because they had built a glacis against the outside wall for added protection from battering rams. The glacis was a sloping embankment of beaten earth, clay, gravel and stones covered by plaster. Up-close the walls were massive and there were not only guards on the walls but in towers as well. The gates were framed by two large towers on each side. It was clear that the fortification was important to its administrators.

The caravan entered the city and was met by tax collector and government officials who wanted to get a portion of the proceeds for their coffers. There were guards checking the visitors and doing routine security checks. Some of the people complained about having to wait for the security checks. Joshua and Caleb both took notes of all the security features.

"Amel was right; I am impressed with the security but not as impressed as I am with my God. Praise Him," Caleb said to Joshua in a low voice.

Joshua was impressed by the younger man's faithfulness. Moses had been right about Caleb, in that he could lean on him. The complete caravan came in after the security check and moved inside to carry out their business.

"I have a lot of business to do now. Let me show you a good place to spend the three nights here," Amel said leading them to an innkeeper.

"We can meet in the evening right here when the sun starts to go down. I know a good place to eat. I am sorry to leave but I have a lot to do now," Amel said.

"Thank you for your help. We will see you this evening," said Joshua.

"I guess we are on our own till then," said Caleb.

"Let us arrange a room for the evening and then get a feel for the city," Joshua suggested.

"A great idea," replied Caleb. The two of them went inside and spoke with the owner to arrange for their lodging.

Group 1

Gaddi and Igal went around the city for about an hour before finding a place to stay for the nights. They both observed how secure the city was and decided to not worry about seeking information about the city. They went to their room and decided to rest.

Group 2

Nahbi and Geuel decided to take a tour of the city before deciding where to spend the night. They started on the upper level of the city before taking a look at the lower levels. Geuel noticed that squads of soldiers patrolled the city randomly. "The level of security in this place is amazing," Geuel commented.

"These are professional soldiers and mercenaries walking around here. I think there are easily several thousand troops posted here," Nahbi said.

They walked through the two levels and observed that each level had a military garrison.

Group 3

Gaddiel, Ammiel, Shaphat and Sethur obtained four rooms to put their gear down and to get some rest before meeting at high noon for lunch. Gaddiel hated sleeping outside. He preferred to at least be in a tent instead of on the ground. Ammiel went into his room to get more rest as well because of the lingering pain he was feeling. The journey had not really allowed Ammiel to recover from his last night in Beth-shan. Shaphat and Sethur decided to get some rest before meeting with the group as well.

Group 4

Palti and Shammua each just wanted to rest. Although it had been a week since they were interrogated and injured, the journey was tiring. Each one wanted to take the opportunity to continue to gather their strength. They bought some food and stayed in their rooms the rest of the day.

Sinai

Moses was tired. He sat down outside his tent. He had just finished talking with several elders from the 12 tribes. He could do nothing about the people's pessimistic outlook on life after years of living in bondage. The Israelites had been conditioned to only understand the world with a slave mentality. Although the Israelites said they wanted to be free, they had a hard time understanding how to live free with God at the center at their lives. While in Pharaoh's land, it was okay to pray to a God with no name who was distant, because they could still resist God's will. But now that God has shown Himself, the people needed to learn how to trust and obey a very real, close and personal God. He could not believe why the people would voluntarily want to return to Pharaoh after years of bondage. Moses knew that God was trying to show them a new and different way of living, worshiping and believing but the people still wanted to do the same old things. The people forgot how to hope.

After hundreds of years of bondage, the people had to relearn the concept of having hope in something that was intangible and unseen. Having hope in the Lord had to be the basis for the center of their new relationship with God. They had been conditioned so deeply as slaves that even after they saw the goodness of God, they easily forgot and chose to focus on life under Pharaoh than a life of abundance under God's grace. The Lord had redeemed the Israelites from slavery under Pharaoh. God had provided for all their needs since they arrived in the wilderness. After all the people had seen, they still could only imagine two things with their earthly eyes: wilderness or Pharaoh. The people had to put their hope in God, not just on the good days but on every day. Moses explained this to the tribes earlier but they continued to question him and seek those things of the world. Moses left after telling them that they had to maintain trust and hope in God; and with hope coming from the anticipation of a favorable outcome living under God's guidance. He explained how they could expectantly hope that God would continue to take care of them as He had done since He had freed them. When Moses left, he could hear the grumblings of the tribes. Moses knew that God's patience was going to end at some point, and it was going to be a painful lesson for the stiff-necked ones when that time came.

Hebron

Commander Elrian brought Sarah into the garrison. She thought that she was going to be off until the two Hebrews returned.

"My Lord, how can I serve you?" she asked.

"I need you to go to a shop run by Salman, A Hebrew merchant. Number two is there now and number one is outside the garrison waiting to take you there. They are doing surveillance of the shop and its owners. There is a woman named Fatia who owns half the shop with the old man; Salman, owns the other half. It's at the center of the marketplace. There were several Hebrews who were at Mansur's pavilion, one of whom was involved in the killing of Kabir. Also, there were Hebrews who were going around the marketplace during the same time checking out the city. I personally saw Salman with Mansur at his pavilion. I think that perhaps Salman and Fatia may know some or all of these Hebrews. There are 10 Hebrews involved in this conspiracy to spy on this land for a possible invasion by Moses and the Hebrews; the two you know and the four who stayed at Mansur's pavilion. I want you to go to the shop and obtain whatever intelligence you can. I want you to try and befriend the woman Fatia. I know that you know how to get close to people and influence them whether they are male or female, or whether you are using sex as a tool or not. I know that if it is possible to obtain even a shred of information, then you will do it," Elrian explained.

"I will do all I can my lord. I will start today to see what I can uncover. As always, I live to serve." Sarah said.

"Report to me as soon as you get some information," Elrian said.

Sarah left and saw Fayid outside with a veil around his face like a nomad. She followed him out to the marketplace.

Elrian felt good about his decision to bring Sarah into the operation because he wanted to work every angle in this case. He had to stay focused: first goal to kill Moses with a secondary goal of just killing the 10 spies which would negatively affect Moses' plans for the region. Ten spies meant that the threat was serious and not just a small unorganized group of ex-slaves looking for a homeland. Elrian had increased patrols in the city and doubled the shifts on the pretense that the units needed a heavier presence since there had been three murders in one week.

Chapter 41

Day 23 evening

Hebron

In Hebron, there was much activity in and around the marketplace even in the evening. Sarah walked with Fayid while he filled her in on the details of the mission. Sarah was already coming up with an idea to get close to Fatia by using the ploy that Sarah was Hebrew and needed help. Sarah would use the same pretense she used with Palti and Shammua.

Fayid and Sarah arrived at the site. Ashur was still observing and said that he believed that the old man went to bed. Sarah decided that she would start her plan now.

She messed up her hair and tore at her clothes. "Hit me in the face but not hard. Just enough to make my nose bleed," she asked Fayid. Fayid did as she said and she went to the ground. Although most women would have cried out or at least shed a tear, Sarah just took it because it was important to look the part she was playing. Sarah smiled and said, "See you men later."

She ran into the shop of Salman and Fatia, "Help, hide me," she said to Fatia in Hebrew. Sarah closed the door behind her looking wild-eyes and scared.

Fatia looked at Sarah and saw the blood from her nose and her torn clothes. Sarah grabbed Fatia and asked her, "Please hide me."

Fatia did not think. She told the young woman to follow her to the back. She took her to the supply room and then put her in a small area and then covered her up with a blanket.

"What's wrong? Are people following you?" asked Fatia.

"There were two men who attacked me in the marketplace. I don't know who they were but they may have been from the garrison. They wanted to take me with them but I fought them and got away," Sarah said.

"Don't worry, you will be safe here. I will go to the door and see if anyone is out there," Fatia said before leaving.

Fatia went to the door and looked outside. She waited for 15 minutes before returning to where the young woman was.

"I think you are fine," Fatia said.

"I am scared. I have heard that the soldiers have been looking for Hebrews and taking them in for questioning. The people who have been taken have not returned yet. The two men knew I was Hebrew and told me to come with them," explained Sarah.

"It will be alright, you are safe here. What is this you say about Hebrews being taken?" Fatia asked.

"I started hearing a few days ago that the soldiers were taking Hebrews away but none of them have returned. I need to leave this city. I don't want to be here if they are looking for me. I have seen you around town; you are like me an Israelite?" Sarah asked with sincerity in her voice.

"No, I am not an Israelite, I am from Kemet," Fatia said.

Fatia jumped up and had fear in her eyes. "Oh, my Lord. What have I done, where have I come to. You are one of them. She tried to leave but purposely stumbled and fell. She started crying. "Please do not tell them about me. I beg you," Sarah pleaded.

"Do not worry, I believe in your God. I am a follower of the faith of Abraham, Isaac and Jacob. I know about your people and I am not an unbeliever. I follow 'I AM WHO I AM'," Sarah said.

"Is it possible that someone from Kemet, can be like me, and worship the God that I worship? This must be a blessing from God. I have to find a way out of the city and get back to my people," Sarah said.

Moved by her pain, Fatia asked her, "Tell me about yourself, maybe I can help."

Sarah smiled inwardly thinking how easy it was to get her.

Sarah relayed how she had come to the city as a slave but when her master recently died, his sons had begun to abuse her. She explained how it was agreed that the old man had promised to free her when he died. He had died only a week ago and upon lighting his funeral pyre, his sons explained that she was now theirs. She could not believe that the sons of her master was going to make her remain a slave after their father had promised to free her. She explained how the father was benevolent and nice for an idolater. He had never taken any liberties with her knowing how religious she was. A week ago after he died, the sons had forced her to remain inside their residence and then took advantage of her sexually. She finally was able to escape to the home of a friend who worked as a servant for a nice family. Her friend was Hebrew as well and allowed her to stay in her small servant quarters. She went out today to the marketplace to get some supplies to leave the city but when she returned to her friend's house, the two men who attacked her were at her friend's home. The two men had taken her friend away and were asking her about other Hebrews in town including her. She did not know why they were looking for Hebrews but she knew that between those men and the sons of her former master she had to leave. She ran but there was another man in the crowd who must have been with them and they pointed her out. The two men chased her and caught her, she fought with all her might and some people from the crowd helped her get away.

She had finished her tale and looked at Fatia with hope in her eyes while she sobbed. Fatia looked at her with compassion; she had to help this young lady. This woman was unfortunate.

Also, it was most likely that because of Caleb and Joshua that she was being hunted. This new commander was probably trying to seek out Hebrews in the hope that they knew about the secret mission of the spies from Moses. Thus, she would help this young lady because she could not turn a blind eye to someone in need when she was so happy, hopeful and expectant in having a bright future. How could she turn her back her? All she could do was, her job, helping a person in need.

"What is your name?" Fatia asked.

"My name is Sarah?" she said.

"Sarah, you are safe here. You can stay here and I may have a way for you to get out of the city and back to your people. For tonight, I have a room you can sleep in and do not worry about this. Tomorrow, we will look into options for you," Fatia said.

"Thank you, and may God bless you and your family," said Sarah.

Sarah was taken to a room and given some blankets. She could not believe how easy it was. She had been telling lies as a woman of leisure and a spy for so long that it was easy for her. The story was taking on a life of its own and she would know soon if this woman was involved with the conspiracy.

After leading the young woman to her room, Fatia went back to her room. She could not ignore the pain of others. She had always believed in helping others and showing compassion. This was an opportunity to do both. She was thinking that this young woman could go with her, Salman and the 12 spies when they returned back to the Sinai. Sarah would be safe among her own people. She dosed off and would discuss it with Salman tomorrow morning.

Day 23 evening

Hazor

Each group decided to take it easy the first day in Hazor except group 5 composed of Joshua and Caleb, and group 2 made up of Nahbi and Geuel. Their day was full of exploration and observation, those two groups made sure that they diligently obtained intelligence about the city. All of the groups slept well that night.

Day 24 morning

Hebron Military Garrison

"So, she never came out of the shop?" asked the commander.

Fayid had explained the situation to Elrian and how she had not returned yet.

"This is good because this means that she was able to infiltrate into the place. We will give her time to do what she does. She is very capable and can take care of herself. We are not expecting the Hebrews for approximately another five days so you and number two stay on the site, let me know if you get any new information," Commander Elrian said.

"As you command," Fayid replied and left the garrison.

Hebron marketplace

Fatia had woken up early to prepare food for her new guest who must be hungry. She was in the front area where the kitchen was located when she saw Sarah enter.

"You look better this morning than when you came in yesterday. If you are hungry, I have some things here for you," Fatia said.

"Thank you, I am very hungry," Sarah said while sat down. There was some fresh bread, dates, olives and meat. Sarah was eating to build rapport with her target but she soon realized that she was actually hungry.

"I need to speak with my uncle about you today. He is a kind man and I knew he will want to help you too. You can stay here until we solve this problem. Just be patient while we help you figure this out," Fatia said.

"Thank you so much for your kindness. I thought my life was over but I saw the light on in here and hoped that someone here could help me," explained Sarah.

"I usually keep the oil lamps burning late anyway. I am happy that I was here for you. I will be back shortly," Fatia said.

Fatia walked to the other side of the residence and the shop where Salman occupied his residence. She heard noise so she knew that he was up already. In a few minutes, he walked out of the room. She looked at him with love in her heart for her 'uncle'. Yahweh was good and always took care of her. She would not worry because she had put her life in the Lord's mighty hands.

"Uncle, how are you this day?" she asked.

He walked over and kissed her on the cheek, "It is good to see you my niece. I was tired this morning from the trip I made which is why I am getting up later today. Did I miss anything this morning?" he asked.

Fatia smile and relayed the story of Sarah.

"Where is she now?" he asked.

"She is in the salon. We must help her. What are your thoughts?" she asked.

"I think that we must take care. It is death to help an escaped slave." he explained.

"But she is not a slave she is free," Fatia said.

"This is what she says but the sons of her former master most likely will say to the judge that she is still their property because their father never freed her officially. A promise of freedom does not constitute actual freedom." Salman said.

"But we must help her," Fatia pleaded with him.

"My child, I am not saying that we will not help her but instead that we have to take care in this endeavor. She is wanted for questioning from the garrison as well as by her owners. I know that you want to take her with us when we leave with Joshua and Caleb but we cannot tell anyone about this just yet. I am not saying that I do not trust her, I do not know her but we must be cautious. We will let her stay here but just tell her that you are trying to figure out a way to help her. Explain to her that you will need to inquire and seek out people. If we actually take her with us, we will not explain any of the details to her until right before we are ready to leave. This is important because if she is captured before we leave, she will have valuable information which could hurt us. Do you understand?" Salman asked.

"I understand, and had not thought of all those things. I am glad that I did not tell her anything specifically about the returning Israelites. I will do as you say and maintain the secret until you advise me to tell her," Fatia said.

"I knew that you would understand and let me meet this young lady," Salman said.

Fatia took Salman to the other salon to where Sarah was still sitting. Salman was introduced to Sarah. He briefly reiterated their desire to help her and would inquire around to find someone who could take her out of the city clandestinely. Sarah thanked him and he left in order to prepare for the day's work. As he walked away, he could not help but think about how familiar the young woman looked. There was something about her that made him think that he had seen her before. Salman filed it away in his mind and started the day's business.

[*The Archangel Raphael placed a precautionary thought in Salman's head to beware of the young woman. Raphael did not want to over step his specific role since the plot by Commander Elrian to get Sarah into Fatia and Salman's residence was not a specific plan from Satan but from Elrian so he tread lightly.*]

Hazor

263

Group 5

Joshua and Caleb were up early in an effort to survey the lower level of the city. They decided to check out the garrison on that level to gauge the troops there. As in the city of Beth-shan, the soldiers there were mostly foreigners and not indigenous people. Once again, Joshua saw that fact as an advantage because this meant the local inhabitants were not invested in who administered over them. Thus, when the Israelites entered the city, the locals would most likely stay out of the fighting. Joshua and Caleb came to understand that not everything one saw with their eyes was necessarily the end of the story.

Chapter 42

Day 24 morning

Hazor

Group 3

Shaphat and Sethur went out the night before and found what they were looking for, carnal adventures. They returned back to the room right before the sun came up. They were tired and decided to each stay in that day.

Gaddiel found that only Ammiel was interested in taking a tour of the city. Gaddiel had guessed that Shaphat and Sethur were engaged in seeking pleasures of the flesh. Gaddiel envisioned that when he was in charge of the people that he would not mind the people engaging in activities such as those as long as they stayed loyal. He believed that when men lived in the flesh, they were more likely to stay compliant and docile. He did not want men who stayed too loyal to God because then they would seek to impose their morals on others which caused problems. Gaddiel like the pleasures of the world but did not want to put himself in a compromising situation. Gaddiel had a woman who he saw among the people but he knew that it was unknown by anyone except the two of them. He knew that once he became the leader of the Israelites that he would have to do something else because he would not be able to afford being caught. This is why he started to be cautious once he went on this mission. When the people asked Moses to request that God allow them to send spies, Gaddiel knew that it was his opportunity. He pushed members of his tribe to support his selection as their representative. Now that he was in the position to achieve his goals, he was not going to make a mistake such as the ones made by Ammiel, Shaphat and Sethur by engaging in sexual relations with harlots or men. He would stay pure, not because he was following God's law, rather because he would make a move for leadership when he returned and needed to be above reproach. Gaddiel knew that God had chosen him and longed to see the angel of light again because he had lots of questions for the angel. Gaddiel and Ammiel toured the upper level of the city during the day while the two other members of the group slept in their rooms.

Chapter 43

Day 24 evening

Hazor

Group 5

Each of the teams went to bed early because the next day would be the last day in the city. Joshua and Caleb had plans to meet Amel in the morning. Amel had been so busy that they had not been able to meet for lunch or dinner the previous two days.

"I was thinking about our schedule since the caravan is leaving and we will be on our own after this," said Joshua. Caleb came over to where Joshua was and sat beside him.

"What are you thinking?" asked Caleb.

"Tomorrow is our last day in this city. We will leave the day after, which will be the 26th day. Amel told me that it's about 80 miles from here to Lebo-hamath, the northernmost edge of the Canaanite empire. I think that we can easily do the 20-30 miles a day without the caravan. We could be in Lebo-hamath by the evening of day 28. I think we should stay there 2 days so that would be days 29-30. We could leave for Hebron on the morning of day 31. Our return trek will be about 160 miles back to Hebron. I think that we will have enough information by day 31 to just focus on the return journey. It will most likely take us 4 days to return there, which will put us there on day 35. We can stay in Hebron for a day and be back in Kedesh-Barnea within 2 days, day 38. We can be back in the camp in two days making it a total of 40 days. These are my thoughts. Does it seem realistic?" Joshua asked.

"That plan seems perfect. I am not sure that anyone from our group is planning that far ahead. It is realistic and perfect," Caleb responded.

"When we leave this city, I will discuss it with Gaddiel since he seems to be the man in charge of the rest of the groups," explained Joshua.

The two of them said good night. Joshua took out his little scroll and began to write his 15th report.

Caleb went outside and looked up at the stars, "Beloved, it's me. I have a plan and will see you soon. I love you," he said to Fatia. At that moment, a comet streaked through the sky. He knew that she was seeing the same comet.

Hebron

During the day, Sarah had continued to play the helpless victim and the relationship between her and Fatia became closer. She did not have an opportunity to leave because it would ruin her cover story. She knew that Fayid and Ashur would be observing the shop so it was just a matter of time before she would be able to get a message out to one of them. She went to bed, content with being patient to learn Fatia's secret.

Fatia walked outside and looked up at the stars. "Caleb: you, I love! You and I will serve God, and live a life together pleasing God. Good night." As she was about to leave, she said a comet travel across the sky. "Caleb, I see it too." She did not know how but she knew that Caleb was seeing the same celestial phenomena. She returned back into the house.

Fayid and Ashur watched as the young woman looked up at the sky and said something that they could not understand. Fayid paid particular attention to her. She was so beautiful, he had to have her. He would manipulate the the situation somehow, someway to make sure that she would become his.

Day 25

Hazor

Joshua and Caleb were up early in order to meet Amel. They dressed and went to the main marketplace to meet him. There was much activity in the city even early. New caravans were entering the city and merchants were preparing their goods for the start of a business day. There was an energy and excitement on this day. There were people working in and around the temples. Caleb noticed that there were priests and the temple harlots going in and out of the building and guessed that there must be some type of festival occurring that day.

They saw Amel. "My friends, it's so good to so you. I am sorry that we could not meet sooner but there have been some problems with the shipments I was supposed to take with me. I hope you were able to have a good visit," Amel said.

"Thank you for your concern but we had no problems since we arrived. It's been an easy city to navigate. We have seen and learned a lot," Joshua explained.

"I must speak with the both of you. Let us find a place to sit and talk," Amel said.

Both Joshua and Caleb could tell it was something urgent by his tone. They walked through the marketplace led by Amel. "This is the place I wanted to take you to before. It is run by a friend of mine," Amel said. They sat down and were waited on by a nice Assyrian man.

After the drinks and food were brought to the table, Amel started his tale, "I was interested in learning about your God which is why I asked you those questions on our trek. I have thought of myself as a seeker. I may come from a pagan people but I know that after you told me about your God, something inside of me was touched. I kept thinking about it and last night something happened. I had a dream," Amel said.

"A dream?" asked Caleb.

"Yes, a dream about you and Joshua. The dream had the two of you with in it and together you had ten large seeds in your pockets. The light in the dream told me to tell you to be careful when you returned to Hebron. You should not go into Hebron on your way back because a giant bird with large jaws will overtake you and eat you and the ten large seeds in your pockets. You will be undone in Hebron. I was told to tell you everything I know about this region to make sure you will be safe," Amel said.

Joshua and Caleb were surprised but looked at the prophecy as God's hand working in their lives. Both of them had been concerned about the two riders who left the oasis after Beth-shan and rode south. They saw the two riders as an ominous sign but God was looking out for them and sending them a message. Joshua thought that the ten seeds were the ten other spies in their group. The giant bird had to be the commander who interrogated Palti and Shammua.

Caleb spoke up, "but I need to go to Hebron to take someone with me. I can not leave her."

Amel thought for a moment and then said, "The light in the dream told me to tell you to not enter Hebron, that does not mean that you can not stop outside the northern outskirts of Hebron, and get a message to whomever you need to meet there."

Joshua and Caleb looked at each other and smiled. It was such a simple way to work around the problem that it eluded both of them until Amel mentioned it.

"I need to tell you about the trade routes because they may help you. There are two great international highways linking Kemet and Mesopotamia to Canaan. The way to the sea begins at Qantara and crosses the Sinai desert passing along the coast of the Negev and Judea, crossing the Sharon turning inland via the Megiddo in the plain of Esdaelon to pass through the plain of Beth-shan. This is the route you took and that we followed as well," Amel said.

"This route is the most popular and used by the armies of Pharaoh, the Assyrians and the Babylonians. It is also why the cities from Lebo-hamath to Hebron sprung up because the historical trade routed needed fortified cities to protect the trade goods which were carried along the routes. There is a second route that is less used. It starts where you left from Kedesh-Barnea and then moves across the Negev through the Mount of Haar to Edom. From there it followed the western edge of the plateaus of Canaan closest to the sea. If someone is coming after you, you should move closer to the great sea and then swing back toward Kedesh-Barnea from the west, not the north. Take a look at this simple drawing I have laid out for you." Amel explained and then showed them the route they should follow on the way back.

Joshua and Caleb were both grateful for the advice and guidance.

"I do not know this God of yours but it must be praised to use someone like me as a vessel to protect you and whatever you were sent to do," Amel said.

"God's ways are not man's ways. I thank you for your help and for being open enough to be used by the Lord," said Joshua.

"My friends, I have so much to do today but I needed to explain all of this to you. I must go but if you need anything, I am staying here in the rooms upstairs. I will still be here after you leave, I wish you good fortune in your quest," Amel said.

"You are a real friend and I will pray for the safe return to your family," Joshua said and then hugged Amel.

Caleb thanked Amel and hugged him as well. "God be with you." Caleb said.

Amel left the two of them at the restaurant. Joshua and Caleb smiled at each other knowing that they were blessed. They had to always stay faithful because this was just another example of how God was always faithful to them. They left the restaurant and continued their tour of the city.

[*Archangel Rafael looked at Archangel Michael with a questioning look. Michael said, "yes, I did inspire that dream for Amel in response of the demons Satan had sent to harm the group.*]"

Hebron

Annan came into the city to speak with Salman about taking over the farm. They met inside the shop and came up with an amount of money for 50 percent of the business. They went back and forth several times before they agreed to a figure. Annan would pay Salman the money in two days because he would need to borrow some money from a local money changer because he did not have all the funds needed for the deal. Annan would not move into the city and the shop until Salman was ready to leave. Salman explained that he wanted his vendors and customers to not see any outward change when the daily running of the business changed hands. To the outside world, nothing would change except Annan was running the business day to day. Annan would pay Salman his share of the profits four times a year the first year and then twice a year after that. They would become full partners; 50 percent each. Fatia's share would come from Salman's part so in effect Annan owned 50 percent with Salman and Fatia owning the remaining 50 percent. Salman had made a partnership agreement document and they both signed. Both parties were happy about the deal and Annan reaffirmed his commitment to let him know when his friends arrived at his farm in the next few days. Annan left and returned to the farm outside the city.

Salman found Fatia with Sarah and asked to speak to her in private. "The deal is almost complete with Annan. He needs to borrow some more money and then he will pay the portion in two days. This is the amount he will pay for 50 percent equity in our business, farms and caravans," Salman said while showing her the amount.

"That is a lot of money; we could live on that for the rest of our lives. I did not know our holdings were that vast," she said.

"We have done well over the last few years. We continued to reinvest in the business by buying more camels and goods which allowed us to grow much larger. We also have quite a bit of gold saved too," Salman said.

Fatia kissed her uncle on the forehead. "You are a clever businessman and an even better uncle!" she said.

"Make sure that you tell none of this to our guest. Tell Sarah nothing of our plans nor allow her to see that we are packing. It's important that no one gets any idea of what we want to do," Salman explained to Fatia. She reluctantly agreed.

Hazor

Group 3

Gaddiel, Ammiel, Shaphat and Sethur decided to walk around to see about the very cosmopolitan nature of the city. All of them enjoyed being in a city where there were different types of people walking around and doing business. The group split up again with Shaphat and Sethur going off on their own while Ammiel decided to walk around alone. Gaddiel decided to see what was there on his own. The group agreed to meet back at their rooms later in the evening. This was their last day in Hazor so they each wanted to have their own adventure.

Group 2

Nahbi and Geuel made their way around the lower marketplace. They both noticed how divination and magic played a big part of life in Hazor. There were fortune tellers reading signs and omens for any who would pay a shekel. There were magicians putting on shows for crowds. Geuel and Nahbi knew that God condemned divination and magic in every form. To engage in divination was being unfaithful to the Lord and committing an abomination. There were people consulting mediums which allowed people to contact the dead but in Hebrew law it carried a death sentence (1). Nahbi and Geuel were approached many times as men and women offered the various services to them. They refused each offer.

Group 4

Palti and Shammua only left their room twice to get something to eat. They spent very little time doing what they were tasked to do but instead rested.

Group 1

Gaddi and Igal went around together but Gaddi wanted to split up later to speak with some of the sorcerers.

Chapter 44

Day 25

Hazor

Group 1

Igal had returned to the room after going through the city for several hours. Gaddi explained that he wanted to continue for a while before returning to the room since it was their last day in Hazor. Gaddi walked around and went to one of the sorcerers. Although the first time he had went to a sorcerer before, he was hopeful that it could work this time. He believed that since Hazor was the biggest city in Canaan at the time, the sorcerers should be more experienced in this city. He walked through the warren of alleys and mazes through the old marketplace on the lower level. The lower level was part of the original city and was older. Gaddi walked past one shop with talisman and charms in the window. Gaddi stopped there and peered inside.

"This is the place," a voice said from the inside.

"What?" Asked Gaddi.

"If you want help in seeing the future or with magic, I am whom you seek," said a little man wearing a black robe.

"I have a problem. There are two men who may mean me harm. I do not know so I tried going to a sorcerer before but it did not work. I had a spell cast on them to no effect. I want to know if I do nothing to them, will they be the end of me? Or do I need to have them taken care of?" Gaddi asked.

The man gestured him to sit at the table. The man pulled out some crystals and started saying some words in an unknown language. Before long, there was some smoke and the crystals started moving on the table.

The man swooned and went into a trance. "These men mean you no harm," he explained.

Gaddi was ecstatic and his spirits were lifted.

"There is more. These men are not your problem. There is something else moving in your direction. You must change your ways and turn away from what you are doing. There is a great force looming around you. You should..." The man came out of the trance abruptly and fell backwards in his chair.

"You must leave," he said with fear in his voice.

"What happened? Do you want more money?" Gaddi said.

"There is no debt owed, just leave," the man said.

"What did you see?" Gaddi asked again with more force. He grabbed the arms of the man and shook the little man hoping he would tell him what he saw.

"Tell me!" Gaddi shouted.

"I work with the darkness. I do not seek the light because the light is my enemy. I saw a great light, one that I had never seen before. It scared me because it represents something that is powerful and unstoppable. You are a part of something that I can not/will not be a part of because it will ruin me as well. Please just go. I don't have anything else to tell you, I have said too much already," the man ran to the back of his shop.

Gaddi just stood there thinking about what he had gotten himself a part of. Was the little man referring to God? Was Igal right that they needed to repent? He left the shop more confused than before. He decided that he would ignore the other details provided and focus on the fact that Joshua and Caleb were not his enemies.

Group 3

Shaphat and Sethur spent their last night with several harlots from the temple. They were seeking fun and adventure but for both of them, the experience seemed less fulfilling. After they finished, they returned to their rooms.

Ammiel went for a walk and was approached by men and women looking to sell him their sexual services but he declined still feeling pain for his last encounter. He just wanted to clear his head. He walked back to his room before dark.

Gaddiel had decided to look at some of the temples he had not seen previously. He went inside several large temples dedicated to Baal and El but there were smaller temples dedicated to Asherah, Anath, Dagon and Resheph. Gaddiel went to those places to see if anything sparked inside of him. He had been hoping beyond hope that the angel of light he saw would reappear. He decided to return to his room in order to prepare for the trip tomorrow.

Group 5

Joshua and Caleb were fortunate to have met Amel but they saw God's hand in what happened in the meeting with Amel. They both knew that as long as they did the will of God, all would be well. They continued their survey of the city and then headed back to the room.

Before heading in, Caleb looked at the stars and thought of Fatia.

Joshua wrote his 16th report.

"Day 25

Hazor is a multi-level city with military garrisons on both levels. The city is thriving with almost 30,000 or 40,000 people living on the two levels. The military patrols the city in squads of professional mercenaries. Today, we received a message from God through the caravan owner, Amel, telling us to not to enter Hebron. We have devised an alternate route after we pick up our friend in Hebron.

Hazor is just like how the caravan owners described it with strong fortifications, towers and gates along with redundant modes of defensive capabilities. The inner partitions offer something we had never seen before. The walls surrounding the city are almost 10' wide which allows for a chariot to traverse on top of the walls. The defenses may appear formidable but our faith tells us that all we need to do is to continue to lean on and trust in God.

End of Report."

Hebron

Fatia sat with Sarah to provide some encouragement to her.

"Have you heard about the new revelations which the deliverer Moses was given by God," asked Fatia.

"No, I have not. I heard about Moses but do not know his teachings," Sarah said.

"You are in for a great blessing because I know it and will relay it to you," Fatia said. She provided the details to Sarah regarding the Ten Commandments and other details on how the people should live.

Sarah listened intently while Fatia explained how God wanted all His people to live a happy and abundant life. "God loves you and does not want you to live a life of pain and suffering. All we need to do is to yield to God's will and stop resisting for what God wants for our lives. If we follow His commandments then God will bless us and our future generations. God is not a distant God but He is a living God who loves us and who spoke to Moses face to face. I was told that when Moses came off the mountain top after speaking with God, his face was glowing so much so that he had to put a veil on his face. God's gloriousness was so brilliant that it changed the color of his hair and put a luminance on him. God is not an entity who does not care about you but He cares deeply about you; Sarah. You are the apple of His eye and God's dream for His people is one of inner joy and an abundant life."

Sarah looked at Fatia without saying a word. She had only known a life of exploitation. She did have times when she enjoyed her life because of all the privileges. But at other times, many times, there was pain and beatings followed by a little gold or other reward. Did she even deserve a life of abundance and joy? She had brought pain to so many people from her actions.

"I know what you are thinking. God could not love you because He has seen your actions. That is not true, that is a lie of Satan. God loves you and wants the best for you. People are special and unique to God," Fatia explained.

Sarah had been thinking about not being deserving of God's love. How could Fatia know that?

"I know what you are thinking because I used to think the same way. I thought God was punishing me after my parents died and then later when my husband died, but God's ways are not man's ways. We do not know why God does the things he does but we have to trust that God has a plan for each of us. God wants to have a relationship with you, a close relationship with you. All you have to do is to give up any thought of idols or other iniquity and surrender to Him. God will welcome you and once you do, you will eat from the best of the land. Living God's way makes life productive and fulfilling. We all face great choices in life. We can choose life or death, to obey God or not. When we fail to follow God's plan for our life, pain will always follow. We do not have to live that way, there is a better path. Once we are on God's path, there will still be times when we fail or fall short or still have difficulties, but all we need to do is to repent, turn away from our sin, and then ask God for forgiveness and keep moving forward," Fatia said.

"Through Moses, God rescued the people of Israel through mighty miracles. God gave us the law to guide us morally and spiritually in life. Obeying the law will bring blessings into your life while disobedience brings misfortune. There are always consequences for our actions. God always loves you and that forms the foundation for our trust in Him. We should trust Him because He loves us. God has given us many promises which anyone can reap in due time. Once we start to build our relationship with God by speaking and listening to Him through prayer, the quality of our lives will improve. God asks us to love Him with all our heart, soul, mind and strength; he wants a commitment from us. If we commit to God, he will commit to us. The nearer we draw to Him, the nearer He draws to us. Choosing to follow God benefits us and improves our relationship with others. Once you open up your heart to God's love, true joy will enter into your life. I am helping you because I love God and through my love for God, I can have love for you. I care what happens to you and do not want to see anyone hurt or take advantage of you," explained Fatia.

Sarah was having a hard time believing that someone could care for her who she just met a day earlier. All of her life, she had exploited others and been exploited. She believed that God had given her beauty to take advantage of others. She also thought that some people had power and it was their role to take advantage of people like her. Men lusted for her body and her affection all of her life.

"How can you say you have love for me, when you do not even know me? You do not know what type of person I am. I am not a good person," said Sarah.

Fatia thought for a moment and then said, "Love is the greatest of all human qualities. Everyone deserves to be loved. Love involves unselfish service to others. Then there is faith which is the foundation and content of God's message. We should have faith in God, that God knows the plans he has for us, plans to help us to prosper. Finally there is hope which is an attitude of expectance. I have faith in God that our paths crossed for a reason. I have hope that both of our situations will improve. When faith and hope are in line, we are free to love completely because we understand how God loves. God loves us unconditionally just as we should love each other. I am not sure if that answers your questions but I want the best for you and I think it's because I know it's what God also wants for you," Fatia said.

Fatia paused and grabbed Sarah's hands. She looked into her eyes and said, "I can say I have love for you because I know that God has love for the both of us, which means I can have the same for you. There is no limit to how much love the human heart can hold. Love covers a multitude of sins. So you can forget about the past and start to view yourself as how God sees you; through the eyes of love. Finally, *never underestimate the redemptive power of God's love. This is not the end of your life but the start of it; it's never too late to be the person God intended you to be.*"

Sarah was speechless; no one had spoken to her like this before with such kindness and compassion, it moved her. Everyone in her life had wanted something for her. No one ever really cared for her before. Men wanted to possess her and women wanted to be near her because of the power she had over people. People gave her money but this woman, who she did not know, was offering her something that no one had offered her before, peace and inner joy through the knowledge of God. The words from Fatia touched a place in her heart that had never been touched before.

"Have you even felt lost, alone and unloved?" Fatia asked.

Sarah did not say anything but tears came to her eyes.

"*God does not want anyone to feel that way. The Lord loves you as you are. God knows you and accepts you. Reach out to Him and accept His love,*" Fatia said as she kneeled down on her knees to pray, gently pulling Sarah with her.

"I don't know how to," Sarah said pulling away.

"God doesn't care about how you pray; it's only the content in your heart which is of interest to Him."

Sarah kneeled down again with her and they prayed together. It was the first time Sarah had ever prayed and she felt something inside of her was changing. There was a joy inside of her. She could not contain herself and started crying. At the same time, she started thanking the Lord for freeing her. Fatia continued to minster to Sarah throughout the evening.

Before she went to bed, Fatia looked up at the stars.

Chapter 45

Present Day

Salman explained to Jack, "I want you to remember this important part; God does love you, warts and all. And because of God's love, you can love yourself. Just remember in order to have an abundant life keep God first, and always pray big, love big and hope big!"

Day 26 morning

Hazor

Joshua and Caleb got up early and walked to the northern gates to leave. Waiting for them was Amel wanting to say goodbye.

"Amel, it's so good to see you," Joshua exclaimed.

"My friends, it's so good to see you," said Amel.

"We are going to miss you," Caleb said.

Joshua grabbed his shoulders and said, "Today, I offer blessings to you and your family. You have been a good friend. I hope that you find what you are looking for."

"As a seeker, it is my hope," Amel said.

"Those who seek; will find. Thank you very much for all your help and kindness. Caleb speaks true, we will miss you," Joshua explained and then hugged Amel.

"My friends, you have enriched my life and I pray that this God of yours will look kindly upon an old pagan like me. The dream was a profoundly disconcerting experience at first but then I became more comfortable with it because I believe that there are forces in the world I have no idea about. I am more open than I have ever been and will continue to look for what your god is trying to tell me," Amel said.

"The Lord is your God too; He is waiting for you to see the light. He will wait patiently for you to understand that He wants the best for you which can only come about by doing his will, not our own. If our paths ever cross, you will be our most honored guest. Be well and peace be unto you," Joshua said.

"I am overwhelmed. It's not often that an old man like myself can learn something from a younger man. Be well, Joshua son of Nun. Be well, Caleb son of Jephunneh. May your God keep the winds to your backs," Amel said and then hugged the two of them before leaving.

The other spies were already outside the northern gates after Amel left.

Joshua and Caleb noticed that the people traveling north were smaller then the amount of people going south. Joshua asked around if anyone was traveling to Lebo-hamath. There were several small groups traveling to that city because it was on the northern trade route. There were also a few people going to Damascus and Byblos. Joshua and Caleb learned from Amel that the route followed the Litani River directly north so it meant the route would be full of greenery as was the case where rivers flowed. The Litani River ended about 10 miles from Lebo-hamath but the Orontes River started near the city. They would travel directly through the Beq'a Valley which was good and bad. The Beq'a valley was a great route to travel through because it was a well-worn trade route but it was also in the lowlands which made it easier to be ambushed. It was impossible to travel through the mountains but the mountains made a great staging point for an ambush. They would have to be careful as they moved north.

Hebron

Sarah had woken up feeling lighter than ever before. She felt as though her problem had been taken away. Fatia had prayed that God grant her peace and inner joy. She also had prayed that if there were any evil forces had her bound it would release her. The prayer was kind and made her feel loved. What was happening here, it was her job to recruit Fatia not the other way around. She knew that outside the shop were the commander's spies one and two. They were waiting for a sign from her to take a message back to Elrian, but she was internally conflicted now. She had never felt as she did last night or this morning. Did she really want to turn over these people who had opened their home and life to her, arrested and tortured? She had worked many targets in her life previously but these people especially Fatia had connected with her and it was through her God. She was actually Hebrew but she never identified as a Hebrew. She saw those people as being cursed but now with the deliverer, the man who defeated Pharaoh; it appeared that they were not cursed.

Fatia had told her to examine her heart. Fatia did not know how that simple statement was painful to her. She was a woman who lived a life selling her body and working to bring others into the darkness. As a spy, it was her job to exploit and take advantage of others. She had ruined the lives of so many men, even women at times. But Sarah said that no matter what she had done previously, God still loved her. Even when Sarah told her in general terms that she had done horrible things, Fatia still said that God wanted the best for her and loved her.

She meant to do harm to Fatia and Salman, but they welcomed her. She now faced a few dilemmas; first she did not know what she should do about the commander. She knew that to disobey him would mean death. But there was something in Fatia's words which touched her soul, she had felt lost, alone and unloved. She had never put it in words before but now it all made sense. All of it, her life was not a real life but a broken and defeated life. She had been hurt as a child so she now hurt others. She could not continue to live a life like that. It needed to end, the chaotic life that she had grown accustomed to. She had always tried to buy material things to make her feel good on the inside; and it never really helped. Fatia had told her that there was more to life than just the accumulation of money and wealth. She guessed she always known this because she had seen so many powerful men rise up and then fall down. She had seen men who died but what then, they could not take their wealth with them. Fatia's dialogue with her had stirred something inside of her heart. A change had started to take place inside the darkest corners of her soul.

Thus, Sarah had some difficult decisions to make: should she continue to help Commander Elrian; or should she tell Fatia and Salman about the plot against them; or should she proceed to lure Palti and Shammua into the city as planned for the commander; or should she just allow Fatia and Salman to help get her out of the city so she could start a new and different life. There were so many questions. She was a slave, although a well paid slave. Slavery, regardless of the pay, was still slavery. She was a bird in a cage who was allowed to fly out from time to time but each time she came back she knew that anything could happen which would put her life in danger. She knew right now that her next decision would be under the penalty of death. She had decisions to make and time was getting short.

Hebron garrison

Fayid was waiting for the commander. He knew that the commander would be upset since he had not heard from Sarah. The commander was an impatient man and even though he wanted results, there were times when he wanted operations to happen overnight but it did not work that way. Espionage operations were dynamic and changed often. To be a good spy like Sarah or himself, you have to be flexible to deal with the circumstances which unfolded before you. Like most powerful men who led but who had never worked in espionage personally, he was always too impatient for results. Espionage operations required time and patience to be really effective.

Elrian walked into the room, breaking him out of his thoughts. "Tell me that you have heard from Sarah?" he said.

"I have no information for you as of yet," Fayid explained.

"Do you think that something has happened to her?" Elrian asked.

"No, it's the nature of the operation. She went into this operation because we needed information quickly; we did not have time to plan ways to get information to us. If she has done her job properly, it will be very difficult for her to break away without alerting the two targets. We just have to be impatient to allow her time to do her job. We will continue to surveil the location closely and when we hear something, I will personally let you know immediately," Fayid said.

"Make sure you do. You are dismissed," ordered Elrian.

Fayid left quickly. He always hated when Elrian had gotten into one of his moods. Fayid would return to the shop hoping that Sarah would be able to get a message to him today.

Elrian watched his spy number one leave. He knew rationally that number one was not to blame for lack of contact with Sarah but he was upset. Time was getting short as the Hebrews should be coming to the city soon. He still had not decided the best way to deal with them. He also was upset that because Sarah was on a mission that he sent her on, he could not couple with her sexually. He had no one to blame but himself. He ordered her to infiltrate into the shop at the last minute. He wanted Sarah because she was the best at helping him release some of his bound up tension.

Elrian had been sending patrols through the city over the last week and there had been no other disturbances. There had been no other murders either so he thought that perhaps that was because the Hebrews were not there. He believed more and more that the Hebrews were responsible for all three of the murders. He had underestimated Moses just like Pharaoh had done and he was paying for it. If he could capture the Hebrews he would, but if not, he would kill them all. He would learn all they knew once he tortured them. He would take the skin off their bodies if he had to this time. He would not be made a fool of again.

Salman had watched the change which had occurred in Sarah. She had been praying and spending a lot of time with Fatia in learning about the religion. He still did not trust her. Sarah's story seemed too convenient for her especially with the time coming when they had to leave. He made sure to reiterate to Fatia that she not provide any details to Sarah regarding their plan. He had to be careful himself to not allow his movements to tip Sarah off that they were leaving.

Fatia had seen the change in Sarah also. She had not known why she had worked so hard to minister to Sarah except that something inside of her, told her to exert an effort to help this young lady. She was happy and wanted Sarah to be happy too. She had hesitated telling Fatia anything about their upcoming trip and about Joshua because she did not want to go against Salman's wishes. She knew her uncle was just being cautious but she wanted to share her good news with her good friend.

Northern route from Hazor to Lebo-hamath

Once the travelers moved several hours outside of Hazor, Joshua and Gaddiel met together to discuss plans. Joshua outlined his plan to spend 2 days in Lebo-hamath before traveling back down to Hebron. Gaddiel had no problem with supporting a decision to stay in that city for 2 days. That was not the most important part of the discussion in which Joshua told Gaddiel about Amel's dream warning then not to go into Hebron. Joshua explained how they needed to go around the city. Gaddiel knew that dreams could be a forewarning of things to come. Gaddiel was reminded of the story of Joseph being sold into slavery in their former home. He did not like the idea that the dream came to Joshua because that gave him more power over them. Joshua went on and said that he and Caleb were bringing someone with them when they reached Hebron. He said that he and Caleb would go to one of the farms to have a runner go into the city to get the person who was joining them.

"Who is returning with us?" asked Gaddiel.

Joshua did not want to get into who was coming because he knew that Gaddiel would just try to use it against them. "It is none of your concern right now; just know that Caleb and I will be going there to stay true to our word. You can either come to the farm with us or travel around and we will catch up to you after we do what the needful," Joshua said.

"I don't see why you don't want to tell me about this secret pickup," Gaddiel said.

"That is not what's important here; there is danger if we enter the city. We must go around, and Caleb and I have something we must do. You need to meet with the others to find out if they want to travel to the outskirts of Hebron with us or meet us on the southern side of the city after we finish our task?" said Joshua.

Gaddiel thought it was curious but would leave it alone for now. "Okay, I will talk to the others and let you know what they say."

"That sounds good," Joshua said before walking away.

Back at his group, Gaddiel explained the situation with the three other Hebrews. Shaphat, Sethur and Ammiel listened to what Joshua proposed doing.

"I do not want to go to Hebron if there is danger there. I vote we go around and meet them after they finish," Shaphat declared.

Sethur agreed with Shaphat. Ammiel spoke up and explained that Palti and Shammua would also want to visit Hebron to rescue an abused Hebrew slave from her master.

"What, that is insane. Can you three speak with the others regarding what they want to do? We will decide then," Gaddiel suggested.

Chapter 46

Day 26 evening

Northern route to Lebo-hamath

Ammiel made his way to see Palti and Shammua. He explained what the proposed plan would be to the astonishment of the two of them.

"We must get her from Hebron. She is in danger from her master. We don't have to go into the city, we can do just as Joshua and Caleb in waiting outside the city and sending a message to her," Palti said.

"We will not leave her," Shammua said.

"You do know its death to take a slave from their master?" asked Ammiel.

"We know," Palti replied.

"So, the two of you will jeopardize this operation for one female slave?" Ammiel asked.

They both said yes. It became clear to Ammiel that they were not going to change their minds; they would get this girl regardless of the danger to themselves. Ammiel told them that he would talk to Gaddiel to see about getting more support for their position. Ammiel returned to Gaddiel and explain the intransigence of Palti and Shammua.

"They will not relent," Ammiel explained.

"Okay, we need to see how the others fared." Gaddiel said.

After Ammiel left, Palti and Shammua looked at each other.

"What do you think? Asked Palti.

"They will try to convince us to give up our plan for her but I refuse," Shammua explained.

"I am glad to hear that. We need to stay strong and not be bullied by anyone in the group," suggested Palti.

"I agree. We are in this together," said Shammua.

Shaphat talked to Gaddi and Igal. Gaddi had not spoken to Igal about visiting the seer but when he heard the proposed idea he voiced his opinion loudly, "I think that they should just meet us on the southern edge of the city. We can wait for them there but I do not think that we should all go to a place on the northern side if there is some danger waiting for us there." Igal agreed with Gaddi and Shaphat went back to Gaddiel with the report.

Sethur met with Nahbi and Geuel who also agreed that they would bypass the city and meet the others outside the southern end of the city. Sethur returned to Gaddiel as well.

"So, it appears that Gaddi, Igal, Nahbi, Geuel, Shaphat, Sethur, Ammiel, and me will bypass the city and meet at some point outside the southern end of the city. At the same time, Palti and Shammua will pick up their friend along with Joshua and Caleb who will pick up their friend from outside the northern end of the city. Well men, we will have a split group with eight people traveling outside the western end of the city since according to Joshua's friend from the caravan, it will be safer. We will find a point to rally our group while waiting for the others. I think that we should put a deadline on them, say no longer than one day to do what they need to do and meet us," Gaddiel suggested.

Shaphat, Ammiel and Sethur agreed that they should only wait for one day and then after that they would travel on to the Sinai. "I am not sure that I like this plan at all if that commander is looking for us. There is a part of me that just wants to travel as far as possible from Hebron back to the Sinai to give our report," Ammiel said.

Shaphat and Sethur both nodded in agreement. Gaddiel thought that this could be the case but he knew that if he left Moses' right hand man without trying to at least stay around for a short time, he would look like a poor leader. Even worse, he would look like a coward. If he stayed outside the southern end of the city for a day waiting, then if something happened to Joshua and Caleb, he could say that they did all they could. He would highlight that Joshua and Caleb chose a reckless path to return to a city that he himself said was dangerous for them.

"We owe it to our brothers to stay for at least one day. We came together and we should at try to leave together if possible. They would do the same for us," Gaddiel said.

The three men knew that they were in Gaddiel's debt so they agreed. Gaddiel asked them to return to the three groups to explain what they decided to do.

Gaddiel, for his part, went to Joshua and told him that he would be joined by Palti and Shammua who had their own separate operation to deal with in extracting a female slave. Gaddiel explained and then left.

"This should be interesting considering they were the ones initially captured and interrogated. I guess they feel compassion towards this woman," Caleb guessed.

"I hope it is that simple. I know your heart and believe that Fatia and you were destined to be together. My goal is to make sure that she is extracted safely from Hebron so the two of you can be together. I hope the fact that Palti and Shammua have another agenda does not interfere with our goal. I refuse to worry because I know the Lord is with us," Joshua said.

"Thank you, Joshua for your support. It means a lot to me. She is the one I have dreamed about for so long. It was something that is difficult to put into words but I found a woman who loves God as much as I do. God is good," Caleb explained.

"All the time," Joshua replied.

The group traveled with the others further north, covering almost 30 miles that day. The group decided to camp north of Mount Hermon. There were about 10 small groups in addition to the spies.

Joshua and Caleb made their camp. Joshua took out his small scroll and made his 17th report detailing his trip from Hazor toward Lebo-hamath.

Caleb looked up at the stars which were twinkling and said good night to Fatia.

Hebron

Fatia and Sarah had spent much time together during the day. Sarah felt that her heart had changed and decided to give her cares and worries over to God. She never knew that the inner void could only be filled by God until now. She would risk death instead of return to her old life. Now, that she had a taste of something different, she did not want to go back. She would deal with the commander's two spies when it came to that. She would pretend to continue her operation but in effect help Fatia and Salman. She was still torn with whether she would tell the two of them about the plan against them, rather she would just do what she could to help them secretly.

At night, Fatia went outside and looked up at the stars. She knew that it would not be long now before Caleb would return to her; she just had to be patient.

Fayid and Ashur watched Fatia come outside. All day neither had seen Sarah except for a brief moment when she passes across a window so they knew she was fine. Fayid assumed that she could not break cover but instead was trying to learn all she could. They must be something there for her to stay so long. Fayid's thoughts returned to beautiful Fatia. She would be his. He had to have this woman. She was from Kemet like him; he could not imagine why she would help the Hebrews or even why she was living with the older Hebrew man. He would learn all these secrets in time.

Days 27-28

40 miles from Lebo-hamath

The groups traveling saw their numbers dwindle as one group traveled to Damascus while another went to Byblos. The spy teams had a few groups traveling with them which gave them a modicum of cover as they traveled north.

Each group focused on moving fast to push the pace of all the travelers. Joshua and Caleb wanted to be in Lebo-hamath before the 2nd night to enter the city and find lodging instead of staying outside the city unprotected. Amel had told them that the route became more dangerous the closer they moved closer to Assyrian and Babylonian lands. Bandits led raiding parties throughout the area of northern Canaan tried to take advantage of caravans at night which looked venerable. The group were particularly careful in the Beqa' Valley as it was the most vulnerable position. They continued to travel fast.

Hebron

During the two days, Sarah asked Fatia to tell her more about God which she did.

"We need to love others as God loves us," Fatia said.

"This concept of love is difficult for me to understand," said Sarah.

"*God's character is holy love. It is important never to separate the holiness of God from the love of God. God is love and his love is unconditional. This means that we get it even though we do not deserve it. God's divine love is undeserving. God has an expected end for us. God can change our circumstances from bad to good but it all starts with love. Love is the key to releasing those demons from the past. I can say I love you without knowing your past because of the love God has for me*," she paused.

Fatia continued, "*Satan is an accuser and the prince of lies because he wants you to believe that people can not love you without benefiting some way. But God is here to tell you that you are worthy to be loved and wants you to learn how to love with your whole heart. Love covers a multitude of sins. If we can love others with our whole heart, everything gets better.*"

"I have never seen anyone love like this before," Sarah said.

"God does! You are so beautiful, and life is so beautiful. Love God first and with everything you have, and I promise you that God will reciprocate. Don't try to please people, they will always let you down, please God. Satan's biggest lie is that you can not change, that you can not do it. Satan, the dark lord, wants to drop seeds of negativity in your mind and heart. But with God, all things are possible. God knows that you are special," Fatia said noticing that Sarah has tears in her eyes.

"God is pure, righteous and just. His eyes are too pure to look upon evil and he can not tolerate wrong (1). Thus, our sins separate us from Him so His face is hidden from us. There are people who ask if God has forgotten them but God can not hear us when we live in willful sin. When we start to seek God, he will be found by us. When we become more upright people we can then communicate with God," Fatia explained.

"Everything you have said has uplifted my heart. "How do you know all of this?"

"Some of this I was taught by my uncle Salman but other portions of it I learned from the man I will marry soon, and he learned it from his teacher," Fatia explained.

Sarah had heard so much that she started to believe. She did not even seek to obtain any more information to hurt Fatia or Salman.

[*Archangel Raphael smiled because sometimes all that was necessary was for people to show love to others and then infinite possibilities could be opened up. He smiled as he thought of something that God always said, 'Love never fails' (2).*]

Salman quietly continued to work on issues so that he and Fatia could leave soon. Fatia and Sarah had spent a lot of time together and he believed that it was a good thing.

In the evening, Fatia looked up to the stars, thinking of Caleb.

Fayid had seen the woman, Fatia, several times during the day. Each time, he could not take his eyes off of her. When she went back into the shop, he decided that it was time to report to Elrian.

Fayid left Ashur outside the shop. It had been a boring assignment for the most part because there nothing was happening but they had no other leads until the Hebrews returned. He arrived at the garrison with his face covered in order to enter. He was ushered into the office of the commander.

Commander Elrian had waited all day for the report and now it was getting dark. "Report?" he ordered.

"We continue to maintain surveillance on the site. We have seen the two targets in and around the shop. We have seen Sarah through the windows but it appears as if they are keeping her close to them," Fayid explained.

"We need to see if it will be possible to get a message to her today or tomorrow, something simple like, 'do they know the Hebrews?' and 'will they return to see them?' We should keep it very simple. Perhaps send in a decoy to pass the message since I don't want to blow your covers."

"I think that we should be prepared to send a message but I do not want to bring anyone else in on this operation. We must be careful. We both know that Sarah would not be staying there if she did not believe there was something worth following," Fayid explained.

"That makes sense but I am growing impatient. Let me know as soon as anything happens," Elrian ordered.

"Yes sir, we will continue to observe the site and advise as necessary," Fayid said before leaving.

Near Lebo-hamath

The group stopped beside the end of the Litani River. The river had just ended which meant that they were close to the city. They were moving very well and made it to the city of Lebo-hamath before nightfall. They had hoped that the gates would not be closed but noticed that the gates had just closed. The group huddled up and made a camp close together for the evening. Joshua decided to make his next report tomorrow night.

"Good night, my love," said Caleb to the stars.

End of day 28

Chapter 47

Day 29

Lebo-hamath

The group had awoken as soon as the sun came up. The sun was bright as it rose over the city. Joshua and Caleb awoke and arranged their packs. Their group had decided to stay in the city for 2 days which included this day. They would leave the morning of the 31th day for Hebron. Joshua remembered that Lebo-hamath meant entrance to Hamath. Hamath was a place-name which meant fortress or citadel. The city sat in the valley of the Ornates River. Amel had explained that Hamath had been independent at times but now was considered the northern boundary of Canaan. Joshua looked at what was the most northern part of their promised land. The city was not as large as Hebron or Hazor but it was sizable. There was a fortified wall around the city like the one at Hebron. It seemed formidable but not on the same level as Hazor.

The group walked through the massive wall structure and inner citadels. This was the most northern trading outpost for the Canaanites and there was a lot of activity inside. Merchants and traders walked around as well as soldiers. There was a good deal of people moving around to carry out their business as the day was early. The mood was different than how it was in some of the other cities; it was less festive and more business-like.

Gaddi and Igal both decided to find a place to stay.

Nahbi and Geuel started their survey of the city immediately.

Gaddiel, Ammiel, Shaphat and Sethur went to look for lodging.

Palti and Shammua also immediately went into the marketplace to find a place for the night.

Joshua and Caleb went straight away to their task, collecting intelligence on the town. Both Joshua and Caleb noticed that there were more foreigners in this city than any other place they had been to thus far. There were Babylonians with their brightly colored clothes. Some people thought the word Babylonian actually meant peacocks because many of them dressed like one with their multi-colored attire. There were Chaldeans, Assyrians, Scythians, Cimmerians as well. They heard languages they had never heard before and different types of dress among the men. It was the most diverse city they had seen. Walking through the city's main street, there were temples with all types of strange marking on the outside. Some of the temples had temple harlots on the outside wearing very little. There were money changers in the marketplace and groups gambling outside the temples.

Joshua and Caleb could easily see the pagans in this city had no self-control or love of God. The inhabitants had a love of idols, sensual pleasures, and the carnal life. Joshua and Caleb were both disgusted with what they saw. The land was wicked and made Joshua think of Sodom and Gomorrah. There were pickpockets running around town seeking easy marks while beggars focused on any stranger who crossed their paths. Joshua and Caleb navigated through the throngs of people who were going to work and carry out their business.

Hebron

Fatia woke up and begin the day. She went to see her uncle to ask him a question. He was already up checking over his books.

"Uncle, I think I can trust Sarah. I think we should tell her that we are leaving in a few days so she will not worry any longer," she said.

"Dear Fatia, I believe that she is probably sincere but trust me in what I say now. Sometimes, even people with the best of intentions make mistakes. I think that she has been changed by your ministering to her, I can see it in her but there is more to her than what you see. She had some demons and there is a darkness that I saw in her when I first encountered her. I believe in the redemptive power of God and His love. That said, remember what I told you about the number one rule in life," Salman said.

Fatia signed because this was Salman's favorite saying, "Trust in God but tie up your camel."

"And what does that mean?" he asked knowing that she knew the answer.

"It means that even though God may bless us, we still have to help ourselves. We must take the necessary action ourselves to make our dreams come true. I should not lie in bed asking God for something that I can and should be doing myself," Fatia recited knowing that the saying had so many applications in life especially when it came to taking personal responsibility for your own blessings.

"Very good, my niece. We trust in God but we must take precautions to not expose our hand too soon. Trust me child." Salman said and kissed his niece on the forehead.

Fatia relented and agreed to stay silent until the day they left.

Hebron

Commander Elrian had continued sending extra patrols into the city. He was getting anxious and needed a sexual release but did not want to be with just any women because his conduct would be known. The great thing about Sarah was that she did not speak about him to anyone. He had checked and send another spy to Sarah pretending to be her friend in order to find out if she spoke freely or circumspect. His hunch was correct that she could be trusted to keep a secret.

In the past, he had brought in some of the temple harlots but when he learned that they could not keep their mouth shut, he had to permanently shut them. He did not like to resort to random violence because it was not a good way to lead soldiers. He preferred strict discipline and could not have it if the men were talking about him because of his sexual proclivities. He would just have to wait until she returned. He expected the 10 Hebrews to return in the next few days so he was getting excited.

Evening

Lebo-hamath

The 12 spies went about their routines which they had done in the other cities. Nothing out of the ordinary occurred during the day of observation for Joshua, Caleb, Nahbi and Geuel. Gaddiel, Ammiel, Shaphat and Sethur enjoyed their time as they did in the others cities. Gaddi, Igal, Palti and Shammua all stayed close to their rooms for the day. The city was interesting because of the many cultures which the group saw in the marketplace.

In the evening, Joshua and Caleb ran across Nahbi and Geuel in the marketplace. The two groups noticed each other but otherwise did not acknowledge each other. Joshua and Caleb continued with the rest of their survey, returning to the room when the sunset. Inside the room, Joshua pulled out his little scroll and recorded the events of the day in report number 17.

Caleb walked back outside and looked at the dark sky. A sheet of darkness covered the sky; he noticed the stars which shimmered and a milkiness which covered the eastern half of the sky. It was a truly beautiful night and his thoughts returned to his beautiful Fatia. He said a short prayer for her and wished her a good night.

Hebron

Sarah had continued learning things from Fatia. She grew really fond of her and also protective of her so she made sure that she stayed out of sight during the day because she was avoiding what she knew she had to do. She had to get a message to the commander but it had to be a message which would not get him to act precipitously or rashly. The commander could react too aggressively and without thinking at times so she had to make the commander believe she was working and not pull her out of the assignment. She wanted to leave the city now but knew it would be difficult unless they were able to do what they said, help her start a new life. She decided to ask Fatia directly.

Fatia had closed down the shop because Salman was busy doing the books and inventorying the supplies during the day. Sarah was not sure if this was normal or not for Salman but she was not worrying about it. She was focusing on the future. She walked to Fatia's room and knocked on the door.

"Come in," Fatia said.

Sarah walked into the room. She saw that Fatia was praying, so she said, "Oh, I am sorry. I will come back later."

"No, please stay. How are you?" Fatia asked.

"I am well but I wanted to talk to you," she said.

"What is it?" Fatia asked.

"I cannot tell you how kind you and Salman have been by allowing me to stay here. But more importantly, you have shown me a different way, another path. I know know that there is a path of less pain and sorrow where freedom and inner joy is now possible. I never would have believed it but I feel like a different person. The old person was not a good person. I want to leave this city and I need to do it soon. I am worried for my safety. Can you help me?" Sarah said looking into Fatia's eyes.

"I can help you. Be patient and we will leave together in a few days. I cannot tell you all the details now but I will leave with you," explained Fatia.

"Really, we will leave together? That will be fantastic. How?" Sarah asked.

"I am still working out all the details but do not worry. Next week this time, Hebron will be a distant memory," Fatia said.

Sarah thanked Fatia and kissed her on the cheek. She left Fatia to return to prayer and exited the room.

Sarah walked through the residence portion of the building and went to the shop portion. She looked around her to make sure that no one saw her. She went to the farthest window on the southern side of the shop. She looked out at the corner of the square knowing where either spy would be. She could see someone in the shadows. She took an oil lamp and silhouetted her face so that they could see her. She waved her hand for one of them to come.

Fayid was getting tired and bored from this assignment. He was going to tell Ashur that he would be back in a few hours when he saw Sarah in the window with an oil lamp waving to him to approach her.

Fayid walked cautiously to the window making sure that he was not moving too clandestinely but instead as a man who was out and who had too much strong drink. He made his way to the shop after pretending to stumble. He then moved quickly to the window.

"What have you gotten from them?" he asked quickly.

"I have not learned much but I think that they may be involved. I need more time to gain their trust. They think that people are looking for me so they have been trying to protect me, and I can not leave," Sarah said.

Fayid noticed that her nose was still puffy and her eye was discolored from where he hit her for effect before she ran into the shop.

"So how much more time you need?" he asked.

"I think I will need another week," Sarah said.

"Do you think anything will happen in the next week?" he asked.

"No, I have to go I can't be seen talking to you. One week," Sarah said.

"I understand. I will tell the commander you need another week. Let me know the same way if you need to pass some information."

"Alright, I have to return," Sarah said moving away from the window.

Fayid left the side of the building and returned to his spot.

Sarah returned to her room, happy that she was able to solve the problem for now.

Salman watched her talking to the man from the back of the room. He had seen her walk into the room and was hoping to tell her to be patient. He could not believe that she was speaking with some man through the window. She was a spy! He believed her after initially having doubts and now he just learned his original fears were true. He shook his head and realized that he would have to deal with her. He could not let her turn them in to the commander. She was a liability now and he had to make the hard decision. He did not think that he had to worry at the immediate moment because he knew what the commander wanted, Joshua and Caleb. He would pray on the issue and ask God for guidance. He would do whatever he had to do to protect Fatia, even give up his life because he loved her as his own child.

Salman walked to his room with a heavy heart. He got on his knees and prayed to the God. He then went to bed.

Day 30

The last day in Lebo-hamath.

Each group operated independently with different goals and objectives for the day. Group 5; Joshua and Caleb, woke up early in order to see how they operated the gates for the incoming traffic. Then they went to see the other side of the marketplace.

Gaddi and Igal, group 1, went out in the morning to get something to eat.

Nahbi and Geuel, group 2, also awoke early because they wanted to view the shift change at the garrison before going to the temple area.

Group 3 slept til the late before going out for breakfast. Gaddiel, Shaphat, Sethur and Ammiel went for a walk after eating. They visited a few shops and took a tour in the marketplace before returning to the rooms. They agreed to meet later for dinner.

Palti and Shammua, group 4, stayed in most of the day while they continued to rest before they left for the south. They each wanted to be in the best shape when they returned to get Sarah.

Chapter 48

Day 30

Hebron

Salman woke up trying to sort out the dream he had. He took his knife and put it in his belt. He asked Fatia and Sarah to join him in the salon to discuss some issues with the business. He started speaking to them about getting a new shipment today and he would be busy with the merchants today.

The two ladies were sitting down while he was talking to them. He walked behind them and suddenly pulled out his knife placing it on the neck of Sarah. The blade of the knife lay on neck; the slightest move by her would be her end. A faint line of blood appeared.

"Uncle, what are you doing?" Fatia yelled.

"She is a traitor? She has betrayed us. I saw you last night. Tell her!" demanded Salman.

Sarah felt fear for the first time in a long time. But more importantly, she wanted to live and have a different kind of life. "I have not betrayed you. I have saved you. I was sent here by the commander to find out if you knew the 10 Hebrews," Sarah said.

Fatia stood up and placed her hand over his mouth saying, "No, I can't believe it. I trusted you!"

"Wait, listen to me. It is not what you think. Yes, I was sent her by the commander. But once I was here, you embraced me and took me in without question. You demonstrated love for me and that changed me somehow. I can not explain it; I just know that something inside me has been stirred up. I want to know this God of ours. I want to draw closer to God. I want to live but I understand what you must think. A serpent enters your house, and there is but one thing you can think, treachery. But that is not the whole story. It started that way but I am not the same. I am with you in mind and spirit now. I will tell you exactly what happened yesterday and if you think I am still guilty then I put my life into your hands," Sarah paused for a second.

"Commander Elrian believes that you are associated with the Hebrew spies sent by Moses. He has two spies outside the building watching your every move right now. They were waiting for me to report back to them and the longer I waited to give them a report, the more danger you were in. I had to make a decision and speak with them. I told them that I was not sure if you knew them or not and that I needed more time to get closer to you. I told them that I needed at least a week and that nothing would happen before then. I let them know that I would get the answers it I had more time with you," Sarah explained.

"What do you think?" Fatia said.

"Let her continue. Tell us the all of it," Salman said focused on her words with the knife still at her neck.

"The commander was with Pharaoh before Moses came to deliver the people. The commander was sent here because of Pharaoh's diminishing power. The commander blames Moses for being here and the near fall of Pharaoh's kingdom. After the Hebrew slaves were freed, the economy of Kemet fell in less than a few months later. All of the jobs that the slaves did had to be filled by someone. The kingdom has been stagnant since Moses freed the slaves. The commander did not want to leave the land of Pharaoh but when the 2 million Israelites left, it was important that the Pharaoh's senior military officers be transferred around the administrative sections in Canaan in order to make sure the kingdom was secure. Commander Elrian despises the deliverer. This is what you must know, Commander Elrian's plan is to capture the Hebrew spies when they return to Hebron and then go to the Sinai where Moses is living and kill him," she explained.

Fatia jumped up and said, "no!"

Salman could not believe his ears. The commander wanted to kill the prophet of God. He would have to make sure that Joshua knew.

"If you still think I am a serpent, then please kill me to save your lives. I willingly sacrifice my life if it will save the Deliverer," Sarah said as she closed her eyes.

Salman slowly took his knife away from her throat and said, "Thank you God." Salman sat down on the chair near them.

"What is it, uncle?" Fatia asked.

"I had a dream last night. In my dream, there were two barking dogs outside wanting to do us harm. A serpent came into the shop while the men were outside. Once inside the shop the serpent came near and watched me. Then the serpent changed into a beautiful white dove which led us away from the danger of the two dogs.

Fatia was stunned and said, "She mentioned that there were two spies outside watching us and she described herself as a serpent. Sarah has said that she changed and in your dream the serpent changed as well. It is a clear signal from God."

"This is why I took the knife away. I did not understand the dream until right now and I think that sometimes God puts things on our hearts but we must be in a position to listen to that little still voice which can direct us to the right path. I know that she is telling the truth. This is remarkable and shows how good God is. Praise be the name of God! I am sorry Sarah that I did that but I love Fatia very much and I do not want anything bad to happen to her. She is my world and my life. I think that all of this happened for a reason. In the story of Joseph, after his brothers sold him into slavery to a caravan going to the country of my birth, he never turned away from God. Joseph stayed faithful to God even after he was sent to prison for something that he did not do. He was falsely accused of sexual misconduct but it was a lie and God took care of him. Joseph persevered and was finally released two years later after interpreting the dreams of two men in prison with him. He later helped to interpret the dreams of the Pharaoh and became governor of all of Kemet. When his brothers came the governor of Kemet to buy food, they did not know it was their brother, Joseph. Joseph tested their character in various ways but eventually revealed himself to them. His brothers feared that Joseph would take revenge on them but he said, "What you meant for evil, God meant for good (1). I embrace you as a daughter Sarah, you may stay with us and know that what the commander meant for evil, God meant for good because the Lord knew that your presence would help us to overcome this evil. Its about faith, I have faith in God," said Salman.

Salman's words touched Sarah's heart and tears came down her face. She could not believe the compassion, kindness and love that these people showed towards her. She would not disappoint them; she would help them in every way possible.

"Thank you," Sarah said and hugged both Fatia and Salman.

"Now, my child we need to discuss how we will outfox this commander," said Salman.

Lebo-hamath

The five groups each prepared themselves for the trip back. The plan was for them to secure all the supplies they needed until they got to Hebron but now they would take all their supplies they would need to get back to the Sinai. Because the mission was done, they would not stop for long during the return trip at any of the cities but make haste during their journey to ensure that they were not captured along the way. Everyone acknowledged that they needed to get back to provide their report to Moses. Each team purchased enough food and water for the entire trip. By the afternoon, each group had packed their satchels and was ready. Regardless of how each team would describe their time in Canaan, they all believed that time was not on their side. There had been too many signs especially after Palti and Shammua were captured. Their capture and interrogation along with the dream from the caravan owner Amel, made everyone edgy on their last day in the city.

After purchasing their supplies including a few new weapons from the marketplace, Joshua and Caleb decided to take a little time in the afternoon to eat at a nice restaurant. This would be their last good meal in the next week or so. They looked at the food as fuel for what lay ahead. They went to a restaurant run by Babylonians. They tried the exotic food and enjoyed some new juices they had never drink before.

Gaddi and Igal had purchased food for the journey and then went back to their room. Each were looking forward to returning to the Sinai. Gaddi continued to be concerned about the prophecy of the seer. He didn't tell Igal but he felt they needed to be extra careful on the return trip.

Nahbi and Geuel were prepared and ready to leave by the evening. They each had their packs arranged and felt that they had done their duty. Although they still saw the journey with their natural eyes, each wanted to complete the mission and report back to Moses as soon as possible.

Gaddiel, Ammiel, Shaphat and Sethur decided to have a blowout dinner that evening. They went to a pavilion and ate a huge meal. There were dancing girls and strong alcoholic beverages served. Everyone in the group had a good time and left in good spirits.

Palti and Shammua had decided to have a quiet evening. They would have a rigorous journey back and they wanted to be ready. Each had visions of Sarah in their heads. They tried not to think about the other being with her but each secretly hoped that Sarah would choose them. Both Palti and Shammua were optimistic that Sarah would be happy to see them.

That evening the groups retired to their rooms.

Joshua pulled out his scroll.

"Day 30

Report 18

Today is the last day of the assignment before we travel back to the Sinai. The fortifications are similar to those in Beth-shan. We have noticed that there is not much loyalty for Pharaoh here. Pharaoh just happens to be the most current administrative overlord who rules over the city. We do not believe that the inhabitants will put up much resistance because most of the soldiers are mercenaries who fight for money. We would do well to strike them hard and fast, and then seek to get them to surrender under the conditions that the city could continue to be run as it was except for the pagan beliefs. These people in this city practice wickedness and our people do not need these types of influences especially for those who still lack faith. We need to eradicate all evidence of idolatry in this city. The others with us are prepared to leave as well. Once we arrive at the outskirts of Hebron, the teams will split with us along with group 4 seeking to each bring out a person in the city while the others travel around the city. We will reconnect with the other teams in one day on the southern end of Hebron. End report."

Caleb went outside and looked at the bright stars in the sky, he thought of his beloved looking at the same stars and felt comforted. They both went to sleep focused on getting up early in order be prepared for what lay ahead.

[*Satan watched the people in Hebron and Lebo-hamath knowing that events were coming to a head soon. He knew at least one of God's angels had been watching out for Joshua and Caleb.*

He could not help that but he was hoping that his agent, Commander Elrian, would be able to complete the job, and kill Moses. He sent some thoughts into the minds of Elrian, Fayid and Gaddiel, which were all readily received. Although his number one goal was that Moses be killed, creating chaos was also a major goal of his. He wanted to keep all of God's people outside of heaven. He sought to steal, kill and destroy any promise God made to the people. He patiently waited like a roaring lion.]

Gaddiel was about to go to bed when his thoughts went to how they could never possess the land of Canaan. He would seek to make sure the majority of those with him were firm in the same belief.

Hebron

Commander Elrian was sitting at his desk when his mind wandered to the Hebrews. He just knew that they would be here in 4 days. He did not know how but he felt it.

Fayid was outside the building watching in case Sarah was able to get away for another meeting when a thought entered his mind, could she be trusted? Something did not seem right but he could not place his finger on it. He would make sure that he focused more on her. He also decided that he would take Fatia for his, he would not wait for the commander, when the situation presented himself; she would be his.

"My plan is that we mislead the commander's men when our group shows up. We will leave in about 4-5 days. I am going with the two of you. We need to send the commander's men in one direction while we go into another direction. When we hear from Joshua and Caleb, we will send you Sarah to tell him that we are meeting on the eastern side of the city later. We will move to meet our group in the north and then travel west around the town to escape them. We need to make sure that once they figure out that we are not there, it will be too late," Salman suggested.

They all went to bed except Fatia who went outside to see the stars and said, "Good night, beloved."

Chapter 49

Day 31

Southern route to Hebron

The five groups were outside the southern gates as the sun came up. They left and made their way back through the Beqa' valley towards the city of Hazor. For this trip, they would not stop in any of the cities that had stopped in previously. They traveled together out in the open as speed was of the essence. They moved with determination and skill along the same trail they had taken on the trip north. This time, they were not slowed by caravan or other travelers. They worked together to move even though they still stayed close to their groups. The rapport created over the last four weeks between the members of the five teams because each continued to walk near their team members. They were at the mouth of the Litani River in several hours and then moves quickly along the river toward Hazor. The team was well rested and moved through the Beqa' rapidly.

Hebron

Fatia, Salman and Sarah planned for their escape. Now that Sarah's role had been exposed and explained, all three were able to focus on planning for their mission. They had much that needed to be prepared since Salman was leaving as well. They would travel light so as not to signal their flight. Salman put money in several different places to buy things in Kadesh-Barnea or another city in southern Canaan.

In the preparations, Fatia and Sarah became even closer. Fatia had some gold saved up and she would go to her other house near the northern gates to get the money before leaving out the gates to meet at the farm of Annan. Sarah decided to provide details of her life to Fatia.

Fatia listened with compassion to the confession of Sarah's life in the brothel. Sarah explained that in addition to sex she would use soothing and flattering words along with sweet music at times to get the men to do what she wanted. Her job mostly focused on getting men to reveal their deepest secrets for blackmail or in the case of foreign diplomats and dignitaries, state secrets were of vital importance. Her job was to lure and soothe clients who came to her. Fatia listened without any condemnation because Sarah had decided to change her life and her sins were not Fatia's to judge. Fatia had to focus on her own salvation and helping others learn a different way to live, not judging others. She became even closer to Sarah the more she shared her experiences.

Salman went outside to take things to other merchants. Once they two men were identified, he easily noticed them. He was amazed that he did not recognize them before but they blended in well into the environment. Salman, Fatia and Sarah pretended everything was normal.

Southern route to Hebron

The group arrived outside Hazor at nightfall. They saw the lights of the oil lamps in the city. The gates were closed and there were a few other small groups waiting the night to enter the city in the morning. They intermingled with these travelers for added protection.

Caleb looked up at the stars as he thought of his Fatia. The group went to sleep early to awake early to start anew. It was pitch dark in their camp and the temperature dropped as was the case in that part of Canaan.

Fatia and Sarah went over portions of the scroll Caleb gave Fatia in the evening. After their study, Fatia went outside to say "good night" to Caleb as was her habit.

Fayid had realized that this was some sort of pattern now and liked the practice because as she looked up, he was able to stare at her. He also noticed that she was saying good night. She was probably saying it to one of the gods of the region. "Good night, beautiful Fatia. I will see you soon," Fayid said.

Days 32-33

Southern route to Hebron

At the first sign of light, the 12 spies were up and moving south. They had moved so well that everyone was optimistic that they could reach Hebron by nightfall. They thought that it they could be there by the evening of day 33, the group could split and they could send out a messenger to Salman under the cover of darkness. They moved through around the lake of Galilee by mid-morning. They were each motivated to get back to the Sinai for their own reasons. Joshua and Caleb were pushing their pace to get to Hebron for Fatia. Palti and Shammua each wanted to see Sarah as soon as possible. Groups one, two and three each wanted to get home soonest because of the inherent danger in this last part of the trip. Gaddiel was already making speeches in his mind's eye. He was forming his words in order to sway the people to his side. He had believed that Pharaoh would welcome them with arms wide because the Pharaoh could not run the empire without the labor the Israelites brought to bare. He would negotiate great terms and life would be better than before. Gaddiel was excited and remembered the angel of light telling to stay the course. Gaddiel smiled as he pushed long the Jordan River toward Beth-shan. Once the group was on the Jordan River, they had become excited because that river would take them right to the Dead Sea and near Hebron.

Days 32-33

Hebron

The next two day's events went by quickly. Salman and Fatia's cover stayed tight as they went on with their duties of running the business. Salman took several trips outside to other merchants to probe and gauge the reaction of the commander's surveillance detail. He noticed that they waited for him to return instead of following him along his path. He also sent Fatia with Sarah out the same time to see if they two spies would follow them but again they maintained their observation post on the building because the spies knew that they had to return. "Good," Salman thought.

The commander's spies knew that the two of them could not maintain any type of comprehensive surveillance on the old man or the two women without being seen. Their targets would have to return so if you want to remain covert, then wait for the targets to return.

Salman took it all in, he was old but not without his own guile. Salman had formulated a plan in his mind that would allow them to escape the eyes of these men once they were contacted.

Outside Jericho

The group had made a lot of progress. Palti and Shammua each felt pain as they were pushing themselves to move quickly but each were motivated to get to Hebron as soon as possible. Joshua and Caleb had moving as fast as they could. Gaddiel, for his part, moved rapidly as well. The group traveled around Jerusalem while observing the activity going into and out of that historic city.

Day 33 evening

Hebron

The shop of Salman continued to be under surveillance throughout the day and night. Fatia continued to minister to Sarah with Sarah consuming all she could about the religion of her fathers. She had never been religious so all the information was new and exciting to her. Salman enjoyed watching Sarah grow and learn. In the evening, Salman had a special dinner brought into the shop. They sat down by the table. Salman said the blessing over the food and each other. During the dinner, he asked a question.

"Is Sarah your real name?" Salman asked.

"Yes, my real name is Sarah from the tribe of Ephraim. Our people were originally from Goshen," she said.

Fatia and Salman looked at each other. "Joshua's tribe is Ephraim. You are related to the prophet of God's general. This is another sign that all of this has happened for a reason," said Salman.

"I did not interact with any of my people in Goshen or when I worked for Pharaoh. I had been sold early in my life to the brothel and then when I learned where I came from, I thought no one would want to associate or be related to me. I knew what I was doing was considered bad in the eyes of every god. I did not value myself and believed that no one else would value me either so I did many bad things," Sarah said, her eyes moist.

"*My child, God accepts all of us as we are. Do not worry about this, your people will accept you without question, it is not your fault that you were raised where you were. Our great prophet Moses was raised as a prince of Pharaoh but he killed a man and fled the country. God forgave him and he has become the man God wanted him to become. Moses lived 40 years as a prince under Pharaoh and then 40 years in Midian before he moved into his destiny. It is never too late for any of us to become the people that God wants us to be. Your choice now is to live a live pleasing to God. Many people go through their whole life blaming their circumstances for their pain and suffering, for them living a life less than God has imagined for them. Many people point fingers at others or blame their parents for their current situation but it's our choice. God had given each of us a choice to choose either life or death. God wants us to choose life. It's simple if we make it simple but too many people are so caught up in their head. They live a defeated life because they refuse to see themselves as God sees them, victorious. You are worthy and Satan knows this. Satan wants you to believe his lies but I am here to tell you that your life from here on can be one of abundance, peace and inner happiness. Do not dwell on the past, move forward, making the type of life you want to have for yourself with God at the center.*" Salman's wisdom was obvious to Sarah and she thanked him.

They finished their dinner and then went to their respective rooms. Fatia went outside and completed her pattern of saying good night to Caleb.

Day 33

South of Jerusalem

The group made their way towards the Valley of Eshcol where Hebron was located. The gates to the city had been closed for over an hour. They decided to visit Salman's and Fatia's farm. They would ask to stay at the farm and then the 8 spies would travel in the morning to outside the southern part of the city. When they left Kedesh-Barnea they had passed a small town named Arad. They did not stop in Arad because it was in a dry, semi-desert region known as the Negev. They noticed that Arad had nothing of importance when they went through it. They discussed meeting north of Arad but south of Hebron pass the hills. The city of Hebron was about 3000 feet above sea level so the hills could provide a modicum of cover for the 8 spies of the group who were waiting. There was an oasis located about two miles outside of the city. They had passed the place and realized that groups used that place for rest. Their plan all hinged on whether they would be able to stay at the farm of Salman and Fatia.

They came up to the farm they had previously visited. Joshua and Caleb went up to the farm house while the other stayed back a little ways. Joshua saw an oil lamp illuminating the darkness.

"Hello, friends I come in peace," Joshua said.

"Who is that?" a voice asked.

"It is a friend of Salman and Fatia. We were here about two week ago and need a place to stay for the evening. Joshua was counting on the law of hospitality which was tradition in the region to not turn away strangers in need.

"Yes, Salman told us that you would be returning. My name is Annan," the man explained.

Joshua and Caleb were relieved.

"We need to get a message to Salman as soon as the gates are opened. Is it possible that you can do this?" Joshua asked.

"This is will be our pleasure. Salman said that you would ask this as well. My son will leave at first light to tell them that you are here," Annan said.

"We thank you, friend. Can we camp outside near your house?" asked Joshua.

"We could not let you sleep outside when we have room inside. We have a room inside which no one uses," Annan said.

Joshua thought quickly, "There are three travelers with me who also need to a place to stay. There are 8 others who traveled with us but who are not in our group. Is there a place for them to stay?" asked Joshua.

"The four of you can stay in the spare room while the others can stay near the grainery. The grainery is not as bad as it sounds. Whenever we have visiting workers, they stay in a small room there," said Annan.

"I thank you for us and for those strangers," Joshua said.

Annan took Joshua and Caleb to the room. Annan asked them if they needed anything, he said no.

After seeing where the room was located. Joshua went out to tell the others while Caleb stayed in the room. Joshua went out and told the group.

"Are you sure it's safe?" Gaddiel asked.

"I am sure. God had led us this far and I know that the Lord is watching over us," Joshua explained.

Joshua explained what happened. The spies followed Joshua to the owner, Annan. Palti and Shammua was shown the room where Caleb was. The other eight were taken to the grainery as they would leave early in the morning on the separate route. Joshua returned to the room.

Caleb walked back outside to look up at the stars to think about seeing Fatia the next day. Caleb went back into the room and got ready to sleep along with the others.

Chapter 50

Day 34

Hebron

The eight members of their group left at first light. Joshua and Caleb were up early to meet with Annan's son who would go to the city. Annan's son was given a message for Salman and Fatia. "Tell them that we had arrived and are awaiting them," Joshua said.

Annan's son left for the city even though the gates had not been opened yet. The sun was up in earnest now.

Palti and Shammua were up and wanted to know when they would be able to see Sarah. "I think that we have to be careful. We will have our friends meet us here and then have them send for your friend," suggested Joshua.

Palti told Joshua about the system that they had worked up with Sarah. Sarah told them that she had a man at the gate who would tell Sarah that they were there.

"I don't think that is safe now. We trust our friends and this system will work. Once we get them, then we can figure out a way to get Sarah," insisted Caleb.

"I am not sure that we will have enough time to do all this, get Sarah and then meet with the others by nightfall. The others will leave at daybreak tomorrow morning. If we are not there then they will leave, I do not want to travel back with just me and Shammua," said Palti.

"Do not worry; we will not let you go alone even if it takes longer for us to find your friend. We will not leave you," Joshua explained.

Shammua was thinking that if they had found Sarah first, they would not have waited for Joshua and Caleb. Shammua was skeptical of Joshua and Caleb. He did not like the plan but he could not chance that Joshua was right and they were walking into a trap.

"I don't like this. We need to come up with another plan," Shammua said.

"Well, give us a better plan and we will consider it," said Caleb.

Shammua was quiet and then said, "This had better work."

Palti hated to the risk of leaving Sarah behind. He did not want to risk the man at the gate knowing about them but he hated waiting. In the end, Palti and Shammua waited.

Inside Hebron

Annan's son appeared at the shop. Salman had just opened up the shop. "Mr. Salman, I am the oldest son of Annan from the farm. I have a message for you," he said.

"Thank you, son. What is the message?" Salman asked.

"Your friends have arrived and are waiting for you," he said.

Salman thought for a moment before answering. He had to figure out how long they needed to be ready. "That is great news. Tell them that we are on our way and will be there before the sun hits the top of the sky," Salman explained.

"On my eyes," said Annan's son. His father had told him that Salman was to be treated with much respect so he used the term which meant he would rather give up his sight then fail. He left for the farm.

Salman walked inside slowly to find the women. Inside the salon, Fatia and Sarah were eating breakfast.

"It's time, we must leave. They are outside the city waiting for us," said Salman.

Fatia smiled and thanked God. "Praise God, I cannot wait. Are you prepared for this Sarah?" Fatia asked.

"I am ready to start a new life. Don't worry, I know how to deal with the commander. I will meet you at the farm after I talk with the commander and lead the surveillance away from here.

All three of them starting getting their things together.

Fayid watched the young man leave the shop after speaking with the old man. He gave it very little thought and continued to watch the shop from across the square.

Outside Hebron

Annan's son made his way back to the farm. He found Joshua and told him that they would arrive at high sun. Joshua told Caleb, Palti and Shammua. He looked in the sky at the sun, they had about two hour before noon. Things were looking good.

Inside Hebron

The plan was simple. Sarah would leave and let it be known to the two spies that she would report directly to the commander. She would tell the commander her report.

Sarah walked out of the shop. Fayid was surprised to see her. She walked around to where Fayid was standing and gestured with her eyes that he should follow her.

"I am surprised that you are able to get out," Fayid said once they were out of sight.

"I have an immediate report for the commander. I think they are involved but the Hebrews will not arrive until 3 days. I have information for the both of you. Meet me at the garrison in an hour because I have a lot to report to the commander first. I am close to them now and know that they will not be going anywhere today so for the next few hours it will be okay to leave. I will see you and number two in an hour," Sarah said.

Fayid watched her leave and returned to provide the updated information to Ashur. Fayid thought it strange that Sarah was able to leave. He would be on guard to make sure everything looked right.

Sarah arrived at the garrison to speak with the garrison. She had a veil on her face so that no one would recognize her; she was led to the commander.

"Report," Elrian said.

With an arrogant attitude that she knew would resonate with the commander, she told her story. "I believe that I have been successful. I have grown close to them and they have opened up to me. I was only able to get out today because I told them that I needed to gather some things from my house because I believed my master would throw my things out. I have gotten so close to them that they actually believe that I am in danger, so they did not want me to leave. They want to protect me. They will meet with the Hebrews in three days in the eastern part of the city. But on the morning of that day, several of the Hebrews will visit the shop pretending to be merchants. You will be able to tell who they are because they will come in groups of two at first light. Those Hebrews coming to the shop will lead you to the others in the eastern part of the city. I told your two spies to meet here so we can devise a plan to follow them. The two groups composed of two men each will arrive at the shop within one hour of each other," Sarah said looking to see the reaction of the commander.

The commander looked at her but did not say anything yet. Sarah saved the best piece of her information for this part in order to convince him.

"Commander, there are 12 spies in this group of Hebrews," Sarah said.

"12 spies. I thought that there were 10 Hebrew spies," asked Elrian.

Sarah had him now, he was hooked. Her bona fides were proven to him.

"I did know how many there were until I gained the confidence of the old man; he told me that there were 12 in all. I believe him because he takes me for a fellow Hebrew just as the two Hebrews did," Sarah explained.

Commander thought for a moment. "So, number one and two missed two of the Hebrews. They were probably in another part of the caravan. This is excellent intelligence, Sarah. You have done a great job. We will have a welcome party waiting for the Hebrews when they arrive," Elrian said.

"Is there anything else?" asked Elrian.

"That is all I have now. I cannot stay too long because I was just barely able to convince them to let me go. They wanted to come with me to help in case I ran into the men who were trying to hurt me. It has probably been too long already. I still need to go to my home. You can provide your spies the report. I figured they needed a break since they had been watching the shop non-stop for many days," Sarah explained.

"When are my two men coming?" Elrian asked.

"They should be here shortly." Sarah said.

"They can wait if they arrive now, we should have enough time for a diversion. I need a release and it's been to long." Elrian said.

Sarah did not want this to happen which is why she told him that she could not stay long. She wanted to move along a different path, a God inspired path. Normally she would walk over to the bed and undress. She hesitated for a moment.

"What is it?" Elrian said.

Sarah explained again that time was of the essence to maintain her cover.

"We have time for this!" Elrian demanded.

She knew that she would not be able to get out of this situation without giving the commander what he wanted. He was determined. For the first time in her life, she felt like she was about to do something that would defile her body, God's temple. She walked to the bedroom and took off her clothes.

The commander came into the room, had her undress him and then please him sexually. Afterwards, she washed him and then got dressed.

"You may leave. I will relay the report to the men. If anything occurs before the three days, tell number one," Elrian said.

Sarah felt dirty as she put on her clothes. She secretly asked God to forgive her. She did want to change her life and this confirmed that she could no longer do this type of work. She started to walk out of the room when Elrian spoke.

"Sarah, do not disappoint me. I am counting on you," he said.

"Yes, my lord. I understand," Sarah said while putting the veil on her face to leave the garrison.

Fayid and Ashur left their observation post to meet Sarah at the garrison.

Salman saw the two spies leave and he told Fatia. They told one of their employees to look after the store. Salman said, "We have to go to check out some goods with a few merchants in the eastern part of the city but will be back in a few hours," the employee said that he would mind the store.

Salman and Fatia each took a small satchel and left the store moving towards the northern gate.

Sarah moved near the northern gate to her home. She entered her home and quickly gathered a few things including the gold and money she had been saving. She rushed to the northern gates hoping she was successful in misleading Elrian.

Fayid and Ashur arrived at the garrison to meet with the commander and Sarah. Once inside, they meet with the commander.

Elrian started to tell them what he learned from Sarah and before he could finish, Fayid interrupted him.

"Where is Sarah?" he asked.

"She had to leave because the targets believe she is going home for a moment before returning. I have the information of what she has seen."

Fayid thought for a moment and felt that something was very wrong. The commander debriefed them and finished after a short while.

"So these Hebrews are supposed to return in three days," Fayid said out loud.

"Yes," Elrian said.

"She recommended that we come here so we all could speak with her but she is not here." Fayid said to no one in particular.

"Sarah told me that the targets were not going anywhere today," Elrian said.

"My Lord, please excuse me. Give me a few moments to think," Fayid asked.

["*Betrayal*", *Satan whispered into Fayid's ear.*]

"My lord, we need to go over to the shop right now, I suspect betrayal on Sarah's part," Fayid said.

"That is nonsense, she is loyal. She told me that there are 12 spies, not 10. This is good information. How could she know this? I believe that she is with us," Elrian said.

"I know how I sound but let us go there right now. I suspect treachery. We will report back if we are not correct," Fayid said.

"Go and report back immediately," the commander said.

Fayid and Ashur ran out of the garrison and towards the shop.

Salman and Fatia went out of the gates towards the farm. They were moving slowly but making good time.

Sarah was about 30 minutes behind Salman and Fatia.

Fayid and Ashur arrived at the shop and waited outside for a few minutes. After not seeing either of them, they rushed inside. "Where is the old man, Salman?" asked Fayid.

The employee responded by telling them that the two of them had traveled to the eastern part of the city to meet with some merchants.

"I knew it, we have been betrayed," Fayid said.

Fayid and Ashur ran out of the shop and went as fast as they could to the garrison.

Salman and Fatia arrived at the farm. They met with Annan and asked about the visitors.

Annan explained that they were in the back. Salman and Fatia walked in the back and saw them. There were four men there, two were Joshua and Caleb but the other two were unknown.

When Caleb saw Fatia, his eyes lit up and he ran over to her. "Praise God! He hugged her and kissed her tenderly on the lips. "I love you," he said.

Fatia felt an inner joy and happiness that she could not describe. "I love you Caleb! I thank our God for returning you safely to me." Caleb noticed that her eyes were sparkling. He saw the love that she had in her eyes.

Salman and Joshua hugged. "It is good to see you my friend," Joshua said.

"We must speak, everything has changed. They know you are here and want to capture you. We must leave once our friend arrives," Salman said.

"What friend?" Asked Joshua.

"Someone who has helped us get here. God is on our side," Salman said.

Chapter 51

Day 33 afternoon

Hebron Garrison

The commander was consumed with rage. "I will kill her!" he screamed.

Fayid and Ashur had just explained that they were told that the two targets had gone to meet some merchants.

"I need to think for a moment." Elrian breathed deeply in for a moment and then said, "Number one, I want you to go to the northern gates and ask if the targets and/or Sarah has departed. If so, I need you to return here and tell me. Number two, I need you to go to the southern gates and do the same. If they have escaped then we will rally here and then formulate the best plan."

Fayid asked about sending troops into the eastern part of the city to look for them there. "They cannot be hard to find, a very old man traveling with a beautiful woman from Kemet."

"That is a good idea, I will handle that while you two follow the other leads," Elrian snapped.

Fayid and Ashur left. Elrian went inside the garrison and roused the watch officer. He explained that he wants all available companies to search in the eastern part of the city for the two targets. The men were assembled and launched very quickly.

Salman explained all he knew about what the commander wanted to do. "He wants to kill Moses?" Joshua was shocked to hear this claim.

"Yes, and he has planned this since the two members of your group were captured," Salman said.

Sarah walked up at that time. Palti and Shammua each brightened up and ran to her. "I am so happy to see you," Palti said first as he hugged her.

Shammua jumped in and said, "I missed you. I can't believe that you are here." He hugged her too.

Caleb interrupted and said, "I know this woman, she is a spy for the commander. I saw her entering the garrison!"

"We know but now she works for God, and us," Fatia said.

Ashur was at the southern gates. He asked the guard if they saw anyone matching the descriptions of the targets or Sarah. He had no luck and returned to the garrison.

Fayid had reached the northern gates and asked about them.

"The two people you describe left out of these gates about 1-2 hours ago. The other young woman left here about an hour ago," the guard said.

Fayid had a decision to make, should he return to the garrison or should he follow them north. He decided that the stakes were too high to waste the time. He went through the gates and moved north.

Outside Hebron

Joshua and Caleb were shocked to hear that Sarah had worked for the commander and that she was the woman that Palti and Shammua were returning to take with them.

Salman and Fatia explained the whole situation to everyone and then Sarah spoke up.

"It is correct, I worked for the commander. Palti and Shammua, I am very sorry because I was sent as a spy for the commander," Sarah said.

Palti and Shammua looked at each other.

"I am truly sorry but I was sent to lure you back so the commander could follow you back to kill Moses. I was playing a role. I think both of you are good people but I am not the same person I was when you were here a few weeks before. I cannot go back to be that same person again. I want to serve God and with that, I must respect myself and my body," Sarah said.

Although Sarah tried to soften the blow but she was not going to be used again. She wanted to live a different life where God was at the center. Her life was about God now and she could not live that life again.

Palti and Shammua did not want to hear about a changed life. Each just wanted her. They could not believe what they heard. They pleaded to her but she was not moved, her religious conviction was too strong.

"I am leaving then. I am going to meet the others now," Palti said.

"Me too. Palti, let us leave now," Shammua said.

Palti and Shammua collected their things and left the house at that time.

"I guess we see where their loyalties lie. If Salman and Fatia vouch for you, then I support you too," Caleb said.

Joshua took it all in and said, "Welcome sister."

Sarah visibly relaxed and smiled. "Thank you. I shall serve the Lord now and forever."

"Praise God; Saleh," Joshua said and then added, "Let us prepare to leave in a few minutes."

Joshua told the group the plan of moving to the west to go around the city to meet the others. They collected their gear and prepared to leave.

Hebron Garrison

Ashur had returned to the garrison but Fayid had not returned yet.

Elrian was like a bull in a craft shop. "Where is number one?" He should have been here by now; the northern gates are closer then the southern gates.

Fayid saw a group of five people moving around; the old man, the beautiful Fatia, two Hebrew men and the traitorous harlot. He would kill the four of them and take Fatia for his own. He drew his sword and ran over to them.

Caleb saw him first and then Joshua. Joshua told the the old man, Fatia and Sarah to keep moving. Joshua and Caleb drew their swords.

Instantly, they knew that this man was an assassin. "We will take him together," said Joshua.

Fayid engaged the two Hebrews, striking like a viper with his first stroke. Joshua blocked his strike and countered. Fayid slipped his blow, reached down grabbing a handful of sand and threw it into the face of Joshua. Caleb jumped in swinging his sword at Fayid's neck. The two of them parried and struck at each other. One fighting for the darkness and the other for light until Fayid struck true into the chest of Caleb. While it was not a death blow, Caleb was opened up and blood appeared on his tunic.

Joshua cleared his eyesight and entered the fray. He slashed at his opponent and then spun in the opposite direction with a back kick which took Fayid off guard. Caleb jumped on him delivering the death strike as Fayid was getting up off the ground. Fayid eyes were wide as his blood mixed with the sand.

"Are you fine?" Joshua asked.

"It's not too deep, I will survive," Caleb said.

They moved away leaving the body on the ground. They caught up to Fatia, Salman and Sarah. Fatia was worried when she saw the blood but Caleb reassured her that he was not injured badly.

"If one mercenary came here for us then it will only be a short time before the commander arrives, we must move fast," Joshua said.

They moved as quickly as they could to the west.

Hebron Garrison

"That is it; I will not wait any longer. Something has happened, we will go to the northern gates," Elrian said.

He took his four elite bodyguards and Ashur to the northern gates with him. The group of five men was at the gates in a few minutes. Elrian approached the guards and they snapped to attention.

"Commander, how can we be of service?" the guard asked.

"We seek one of my men who came here to ask about three people who may have left the city. My man was looking for one old Hebrew man, one young lady from Kemet and another young woman traveling separately?" Elrian asked.

"Yes sir, I talked to him myself. I told him that the old man and young woman passed here about 1-2 hours ago. The other lady passed here about an hour ago. He went in the same direction that they did, to the north," the guard explained.

"Tell the garrison stables to saddle up six of their fastest horses and bring them here for us. We will take a look for them and return shortly," Elrian ordered.

"Yes sir," the guard responded.

After the horses were brought; the four bodyguards, Ashur and Elrian left the city.

Salman, Fatia, Sarah, Joshua and Caleb moved rapidly around the western end of the city. They moved knowing that their lives were in grave danger.

Elrian came upon the dead body. He saw Fayid's body outside of the farm and felt his rage grow. He kneeled by body and examined it. "I will kill these men!" He looked around. Did they move north, east or west around the city? He did not know which way to turn. There had been several hints that the meeting was going to be held in the east. He decided that he would return to the garrison to consult his dark lord. He would have the men gather the horses and go after them. He would send two of his elite body guards around the western end of the city towards the south and send two other of his bodyguards around the eastern end of the city with Ashur. "If you see them, try to capture them but if it is not possible, then kill them all. Report back as soon as you learn anything. I will be in the garrison," Elrian demanded.

They all returned to the city. The five men and the commander got the horses. The commander returned to his office where he would use the most powerful incantation he knew to help him.

The two bodyguards searched west along that path in find of any lead. The two other bodyguards along with Ashur searched east along that path.

Commander Elrian returned to the garrison. He decided to take matters in his own hand. He drew Satan's mark on the floor and started the incantation.

"*Shaitan, Iblis, diablos; Ahibuka kathiran.* Omnipotent and eternal Satan, your assistance I require. I give you my loyalty and love; I pledge my life for you. I invoke and entreat thee. I call upon thee. I provide my blood as a tangible sign of my sincerity."

Elrian took his dagger across his arm. The blood trickled on the floor inside the drawing he had made.

"I bind this request with a gift of blood," Elrian said bringing out a goat and then killing it inside the drawing he made. The goat writhed on the floor.

"I am yours, my devotion is yours. I strive to conjure up a helper. I need you to send a demonic being to do my bidding. I need one Sed to carry out my mission for you. I have sacrificed an unclean animal for you." Elrian gestured inside the mark where the goat lay dead; smoke appeared and merged with the goat to form a grotesque figure of enormous height. The figure took form and looked at Elrian.

"What is your will, lord?" it said in a gravely voice.

"Find the old man, the young lady, the traitor and those traveling with them. Kill them!" he said.

He did not have the power to make a spell like this often, if ever again. It took all the strength inside of him. The figure disappeared from his sight. Elrian exhausted, fell on the floor.

Western side of Hebron

The five travelers; Salman, Fatia, Sarah, Joshua and Caleb moved fast but not as fast as the two elite bodyguards of Elrian riding horses. The two bodyguards were almost upon the group.

[*The archangels Raphael and Michael reached out their hands over the eyes of the two bodyguards and they were blinded to the presence of the five travelers.*]

The two bodyguards passed the group without seeing them, continuing south.

The group of five travelers made their way through the valley of the Eshcol, making good time.

The Sed appeared in front of the group as they were about to come out of the valley of the Eschol.

"What is that?" Joshua held up his hand for the group to stop.

In front of them standing almost 9 feet tall was a demon of grotesque proportions.

"We will handle this," Caleb said while moving Fatia behind him.

"Be careful!" Fatia yelled.

Joshua and Caleb approached the abomination from opposite sides.

[*Archangel Michael would not let this angel of Satan to continue to walk in this world. Archangel Michael, the great angel, who protected God's people, would enter the battle.*]

Before they engaged the monster a bright light shown before them, Archangel Michael appeared before them. He knew that he could not speak directly to them as their human ears could not tolerate hearing an angelic voice without experiencing great pain. He put the thought in their minds, "leave this demon to me. Go and make haste."

Joshua looked at Caleb who nodded. They grabbed the women along with the old man and backed away from the battle ground.

The Sed came forward extremely quickly reaching out for the angel. Michael raised his sword and cut off part of the beast's arm. The Sed howled and grabbed the throat of Michael with his other hand.

The Sed started growing a replacement limb where Michael had damaged him. Michael knew that a demonic entity could inflict death on him. He started pounding his right fist against the Sed's head to no avail. He raised his wings and with one powerful stroke flapped and took off

319

into the sky. Michael and the Sed were several hundred feet above the ground in a matter of moments. The Sed looked at the ground as Michael flew higher and higher. Michael's left arm was under the right arm of the Sed. He wanted to bring this being of darkness into the light. Once they were at the highest point in the sky, Michael raised his arm toward heaven. "Father empower me!" His God-spell power flowed through his right hand. He put that hand on the demon's head, a bright light emanated and it slowly disintegrated the Sed. Its ashes blew into the wind.

Chapter 52

Day 34

[*Satan was upset at the turn of events. He had hoped that the commander would be successful in at least locating and killing the group. Satan had done too much already and knew that God would punish him for his direct involvement in the operation. He hoped that it would not be too painful.*]

The group composed of Joshua, Caleb, Salman, Fatia and Sarah watched from afar as the body of the Sed dissolved into ashes. Archangel Michael looked down at the group and then flew away before disappearing.

"Our God is an awesome God!" Joshua said.

Sarah stood there wide-eyed in awe and said, "Surely, your mission is divinely blessed. If I had any doubts before I fully surrender and believe now."

Salman looked at the Arachangel Michael and said, "Thank you God for letting an old man view something so magnificent that it warms my soul."

Fatia was thankful for being so blessed to have an angelic protector.

Joshua and Caleb just smiled to at the group. They had both seen such wonders from God and knew that anything was possible. "We must make haste," Joshua explained.

They continued to move around the city and arrived before sunset at the oasis where the other ten spies waited for them. Joshua quickly updated the group on what had happened with the soldier, the angel and the Sed. The group was astonished but pleased that they made it although Palti and Shammua were outwardly hostile to Sarah and Fatia. The group decided to move further away from Hebron and closer to Arad in order to hide from the commander.

Hebron

The commander lay on the floor resting. He slowly gathered his strength after several hours. He did not realize how late it had become until the four bodyguards and Ashur returned after traversing the entire city. He had felt that the Sed failed and then learned that neither team had seen any evidence of the groups. Elrian sent them all away and sat alone in his office. He had been outwitted by the group. Sarah had played him and he fell for it. He asked Satan to help him but he could not feel the dark lord's presence. He knew the effort to conjure up the Sed used almost all the dark energy from inside of him.

[Satan was forced to ignore the commander's plea, after being called on. He hoped that the ten spies who traveled with Joshua and Caleb would be able to do his will without his direct efforts. He would try to not directly interfere hoping they would continue doing his favorite sins on their own accord: pride, avarice, lechery, anger, gluttony, envy and sloth. He would just allow them to continue doing what they did so well.]

The 12 spies, Salman, Fatia and Sarah were able to make it to outside the city of Hormah by nightfall. They were forced to stop and make camp because the darkness in Canaan was deafening in its blackness. Joshua, Caleb and Salman took turns standing guard over the group at night. No one else in the group offered to undertake guard duty. When Caleb got up to do his guard duty, Fatia woke up too and stayed with him. They held hands and looked at the stars together. "I looked every night at the stars and said good night to you," Fatia said.

"I did the same thing as well," Caleb explained. They focused on watching for any threats while enjoying being next to each other. Although they had so much to say to each other, they enjoyed each other's company. That evening, they held hands and prayed together.

Day 35

Hormah

The group went through the small city of Hormah. Joshua and Caleb had gathered up a large section of grapes on the vine to show the community when they returned. The group refilled their water sacks and obtained more food. They decided to spend the night in the city to rest. They learned the town's name meant "split rock" or "cursed for destruction". They quickly found rooms for the night in case the commander's people entered the town. They decided to maintain a low profile and stay in their rooms in the evening.

Hebron Garrison

The commander rested most of the day. He was despondent and in a fowl mood. All of his soldiers avoided coming to him. He felt as that he lost his opportunity. He could not believe Sarah betrayed him. How could she be with the Hebrews? The commander felt betrayed by Satan and all those around him.

Day 36

The commander woke up not knowing what to do. He was upset and believed that certain forces were working against him.

[*Satan decided to send a simple suggestion to the commander. His actions were well within the parameters of the agreement between him and God. He sent the following thought to Elrian, "It's not too late, go after them."*]

Commander Elrian decided to take matters in his own hands. He called in his executive officer into his office and explained that he would take two weeks off to undertake a secret mission. He would be leaving in an hour. He ordered the stable to get their best camel and place it at the southern gate. Elrian believed that the group was traveling south; he would follow them and allow them to lead him to the deliverer. He packed his gear and placed his sickle sword in his pack. Elrian changed into the clothes of local nomads, looking like a merchant along the trade route. He left the garrison and picked up the camel at the southern gate. He road the camel out of the city traveling toward Arad. He would kill the accursed deliverer if it was the last thing he did. It was slow going but he preferred to take a camel since he would have to go through the Negev and the wilderness of Zin. The camel would navigate the desert better than a horse and give him better cover since mostly only soldiers used horses.

The group of 12 spies left Hormah and headed toward the Negev. They were moving as fast as they could, the group did not speak with each other much and mostly stayed in their same groups. The group was able to get within 30 miles of Kadesh-Barnea. They made camp that evening and the same team watched over the camp at night; Joshua, Caleb and Fatia, and Salman took turns during the evening. Sarah wanted to know everything about the religion of her fathers and joined Joshua during his shift. None of the guard shifts saw anything coming against them that night.

Commander Elrian made it to Hormah that evening. He went into the town and got a room for the evening. He asked around to see if they had come through the town. A local merchant told them that 15 people came through the town earlier that day. Elrian thanked the man and gave him a few shekels. He did not want to catch them but instead follow their trail to Moses.

Day 37

The 12 spies, Salman, Fatia and Sarah woke up and made their way to the area where Amalek was located. The route was slow with the 15 people trying to move together. The group was getting tired which slowed their journey quite a bit. They went another 12 miles that day. The

12 spies had moved so rapidly from Lebo-hamath that their strength was sapped. They made camp that evening in the wilderness of Zin.

Caleb and Fatia watched the stars that night it was like a dark veil in the sky. The brightness of the stars, quasars and other celestial features made the sky come to life.

"It's so beautiful," Sarah said.

"Not as beautiful as you," Caleb replied and they kissed under the stars.

Palti and Shammua continued to have an attitude towards Sarah and Fatia. Gaddiel and his group just wanted to get back to their people before the commander caught them.

Nahbi and Geuel stayed mostly to themselves during this return journey. They put their bedding near each other and Nahbi asked Geuel what he was thinking about. "I really don't like Gaddiel but I have to admit that he is right about conquering Canaan," Geuel explained.

"I understand what you mean. Gaddiel is arrogant but he is right," Nahbi replied.

"You are right but that does not mean that I have to talk to him," Geuel said.

Nahbi laughed and they went to sleep.

Commander Elrian's camel went lame and he was forced to walk. There were no settlements around him so he placed his sack on his shoulder and walked south. He made camp that evening about 10 miles south of Hormah.

[*The Archangel Raphael slide the rock under the hoof of his camel which caused it to go lame. Raphael thought the commander would be better off walking.*]

Day 38

The group woke up and moved through the wilderness of Zin. They made it to the outskirts of Kadesh-Barnea but the city had already closed its gates for the day. They hunkered down outside the city with several other groups who also did not make it in time to enter the city.

Commander Elrian had begun the long walk towards the city. It was slow going on foot as he was not used to walking long distances. He was used to traveling with a horse or a camel although he was in shape. He was able to travel to about 15 miles to the outskirts of Kadesh-Barnea. He unpacked his gear and camped outside for the night. He kept warm by focusing on the burning desire in his chest to make Moses pay for what he did to Pharaoh and his country. The thought of capturing Sarah and making her atone for her betrayal stoked the fire inside of him.

Day 39

The group of spies entered Kadesh-Barnea tired, needing rest. They were going to meet Moses and Aaron on the other side of Kadesh near the wilderness of Paran. They decided to stay in that city for the next day resting before moving to meet the people who were now camped in the Wilderness of Paran. They knew that since Kadesh-Barnea was a large city; they would not be found by the commander's people. They each got rooms for two days scattered throughout the city. The group stayed mostly in their rooms resting during that time.

Fatia and Caleb stayed in separate rooms but spent many hours discussing God, the law, faith and their life. Joshua spoke to Salman about Moses and the people they would be meeting. Gaddiel spent his time meeting with Ammiel, Shaphat, Sethur, Gaddi, Igal, Palti and Shammua making plans about what they would each say to the people. Gaddiel was able to learn through Nahbi that Geuel supported his position but he did not want to meet with him. Nahbi supported Gaddiel's views about not being able to take the land from the Canaanites.

Salman, Joshua, and Caleb all welcomed Sarah into their group. Sarah was able to develop a good friendship with both Salman and Joshua along with Caleb. Joshua was able to explain details about their tribe of Ephraim. Joshua was impressed with Sarah and her determination to change her life. She asked Joshua lots of questions about scripture and Moses. Redemption was Sarah's goal and she showed her commitment to that path by providing all the information she knew about Commander Elrian.

The day went by very quickly. Palti and Shammua each became bitter not only towards Sarah but also Joshua, Salman and Fatia as well. The 12 spies planned to meet together again in a day outside the southern gates of the city in the wilderness of Paran. On that night, Caleb and Fatia went outside to look at the stars together.

Sarah stood by the building watching Caleb and Fatia hold hands looking at the stars. Joshua came out and stood beside Sarah.

"Do you think that I will even find someone who will love me like Caleb loves Fatia, after all that I have done?" Sarah asked Joshua.

"Cousin," Joshua said and noticed the expression on Sarah's face. "We are cousins, and it not my place to judge your sins. Only God can know your heart. You seem sincere in changing your life. God has someone for you and I know that he will love the person you are becoming. Just remember to keep God first and all else will fall into place," Joshua said.

"Thank you, cousin, for everything," she said before returning to her room.

Commander Elrian arrived in Kadesh-Barnea on day 39. He was tired after walking the rest of the way. He took a room in the city and immediately started inquiring about any Hebrews who entered the city recently. He had heard that there were some Hebrews who may have entered the city but he was not able to locate anyone. He was told that there was a whole community of Hebrews just south of Kadesh in the wilderness of Paran.

Day 40

The 12 spies, Salman, Sarah and Fatia met all the Israelites in the Wilderness of Paran. Joshua and Caleb were carrying two large vines of grapes over their shoulders as they walked into the camp. They were met by members of each tribe. The entire group felt relief once they were among their people because they were finally able to escape Commander Elrian. After all of the trials and tribulations during the 40 days, Joshua and Caleb felt pleased that they were among their people, safe and sound.

Chapter 53

The spies' official report from the Bible:

At the end of forty days, they came back from their reconnaissance of the land. They sought out Moses, Aaron and the whole community of Israel, in the wilderness of Paran, at Kadesh. They made their report to them, and to the whole community, and showing them the produce of the country.

They told them the story, 'We went into the land to which you sent us. It does indeed flow with milk and honey; this is its produce. At the same time, its inhabitants are a powerful people; the towns are fortified and very big; yes and we saw the descendants of Anak there. The Amalekite holds the Negev area, the Hittite, Amorite and Jebusite the highlands, and the Canaanite the sea coast and the banks of the Jordan.

Caleb harangued the people gathered about Moses: "We must march in, he said, 'and conquer this land: we are well able to do it."

But the men who had gone up with him answered (the ten other spies), "We are not able to march against the people; they are stronger than we are." And they began to disparage the country they had reconnoitered to the sons of Israel, "The country we went to reconnoiter is a country that devours its inhabitants, every man we saw there was of enormous size. Yes, and we saw giants there (the sons of Anak, descendents of Giants). We felt like grasshoppers, and we seemed to them (1)."

At this, the whole community raised their voices and cried aloud, and the people wailed all the night. Then all the sons of Israel grumbled against Moses, Aaron, and the whole community said, "Would that we had died in the land of Egypt, or at least that we died in this wilderness! Why does Yahweh bring us to this land, only to have us fall by the sword, and our wives and children seized as booty? Should we not do better to go back to Egypt?" And they said to one another, "Let us appoint a leader and go back to Egypt (2)."

"Father of my father, I know the history but tell me what is not in the sacred record," Ibnuh asked Joshua.

"I will tell you," Joshua said.

Joshua's recollections

Gaddiel thought that this was his time. He would be the leader who would lead them back to Egypt but under negotiated terms with Pharaoh.

"Listen, oh sons of Israel, you know me as one of yours. I took this mission in order to find a way to possess this land as God ordered but there is no way. I believe and trust in God but sometimes we must believe our eyes. Our eyes told us that we must seek another way. There are only two options I can think of. Either we move to Midian where Moses lived for almost 40 years but I do not believe that the land is not large or fertile enough for our people. We have another option which is to return to Pharaoh but under a negotiated settlement. We can send someone to Pharaoh to tell him that we will return but not under the same conditions as before. We will return not as slaves but as workers earning a decent daily wage who share in the profits and who can own property. We will live as free men," Gaddiel said to shouting chants of the people.

The Israelites seemed to agree with Gaddiel's plan. They had been worked up into a frenzy by various members from other tribes. Gaddiel had sent his supporters from the spy mission: Shaphat, Sethur, Ammeil, Palti, Shammua, Gaddi and Igal to go around to the tribes gaining support for his cause. Not only did Gaddiel not trust God, he went around actively seeking to turn the people against God's promises.

Eight of the tribes loudly supported Gaddiel while the tribes of Nahbi and Geuel also supported him but not as actively. The people complained about wandering in the desert for the almost 12 months. A loud cry went up in support of having Gaddiel being appointed the envoy to go to Pharaoh.

The spies' official report from the Bible:

Before the whole assembled community of the sons of Israel, Moses and Aaron fell down, face to the ground. Joshua son of Nun and Caleb son of Jephunneh, two of those who had reconnoitered the country, tore their garments; and they said to the entire community of the sons of Israel, "The land we went to reconnoiter is a good land, an excellent land. If Yahweh is pleased with us, he will lead us into the land and give it to us. It is a land where milk and honey flow. Do not rebel against Yahweh. And do not be afraid of the people of this land; we shall gobble them up. Their tutelary shadow had gone from them so long as Yahweh is with us. Do not be afraid of them (3)."

Joshua's recollections

Gaddiel heard the crowd discuss the possibility of stoning Moses, Aaron, Joshua and Caleb. Gaddiel had his agents scattered throughout the crowd yelling, "Stone them, they want us to die in the wilderness. Were there not graves in Pharaoh's land that we could not die then?"

The crowd grew loud and had clearly been persuaded by Gaddiel's speech. The ten tribes were of one mind, return to Pharaoh. Gaddiel told the crowd to hold Moses in seclusion so that he could not lead them astray anymore.

Members of Gaddiel's tribe took Moses away, tied him up and led him to the other side of the hill. Gaddiel continued to discuss the particulars of the mission to Pharaoh with the elders of the tribes.

Separately, Moses was tied to the tree on the other side of a tel (a mound). He did not worry or otherwise lose faith. He sat meditating. While Moses was in quiet contemplation, Commander Elrian came out into the open. Moses did not look up.

"Deliverer, I see you have fallen a long way from when I knew you," Elrian spoke in the specific dialect of Pharaoh.

"I see Pharaoh's dogs have a long leash," Moses replied without any worry in his voice.

Elrian took out his sickle sword.

"Deliverer, who will deliver you from my judgment, which is death?" Elrian said while making his way closer to Moses.

"I will stand for Moses. I am his strong right arm," Joshua said appearing at Moses feet.

Elrian was on guard when he saw Joshua.

"I know you; you are Pharaoh's commander from Hebron. Why are you here?"

"I came to kill Moses. I will do what Pharaoh could not do," Elrian stated.

Joshua drew his sword to engage Elrian in combat. Elrian can feel the power flowing through him as he moved closer to Joshua.

[*Satan decided to throw caution to the wind; he gave Elrian the strength and power of more than 10 men. Satan was breaking God's rules but felt it was worth it if he could kill Moses, the Prophet of God.*]

Elrian slashed at Joshua. Joshua moved and feigned with an expertise that came from being an experienced fighter but the strength of Elrian was unimaginable. Elrian swung his sword with all his power with a potential death blow but Joshua brought up his sword just in time to protect himself but Elrian's strike broke through his defenses and partially struck his shoulder.

"Agh," Joshua yelled and fell to his knee.

Elrian gloated over him, "So you are the deliverer's champion? Ha? You Hebrews are nothing and your God is a joke."

Joshua stood up and told Elrian, "God is not to be mocked." He swung his sword in a high arch at Elrian head.

Elrian easily dodged the blow and kicked at Joshua face. The kick connected and Joshua fell back bleeding. "Help me, Lord," Joshua asked.

Elrian took his sword and rammed it straight into Joshua's chest.

[*The Archangel Raphael took his God-spell power and touched Joshua's heart at that moment. If Satan was going to get involved directly then he would too.*]

A breastplate of God's righteousness appeared and stopped the blade, breaking it on contact. "How is this possible?" Elrian asked.

[*The Archangel Michael touched Joshua's shoulder.*]

Joshua felt empowered and stood up. He charged Elrian slashing and striking him with his sword. He had Elrian off balance and kicked him in the face, returning the favor. Blood trickled from his nose; Elrian looked up from the ground with surprise.

"Aggh," he yelled and then leaped up at Joshua.

Joshua easily avoided Elrian and brought his sword across Elrian's throat severing his head from his body cleanly and completely in one move too quick to be seen with the human eye. Joshua was out of breath and looked down at Elrian's body while saying, "My God is an awesome God; He reigns from heaven above, with wisdom, power and love!"

Joshua held his shoulder where it bled from Elrian's blow walking over to Moses. "Are you alright?" Joshua asked.

"I am well," Moses said.

Joshua released the Prophet of God and helped him up.

Moses spoke, "We need to walk back to where the people are gathered."

Moses and Joshua returned to the Tent of Meeting where the people were still gathered discussing what to do with Moses, Aaron, Joshua and Caleb. Moses called on God.

The spies' official report from the Bible

The entire community was talking to stoning them, when the glory of Yahweh appeared at the Tent of Meeting to all sons of Israel. And Yahweh said to Moses:

"How long will this people insult me? How long will they refuse to believe in me despite the signs I have worked among them? I will strike them with pestilence and disown them. And of you I shall make anew nation, greater and mightier than they are."

Moses Answered Yahweh:

"But the Egyptians already know that you, by your own power, have brought this people out from their midst. They have said as much to the inhabitants of this country. They already know that you, Yahweh, are in the midst of this people, and that you show yourself to them face to face; that it is you, Yahweh, whose cloud stands over them, that you go before them in a pillar of cloud by day and a pillar of fire by night. If you destroy this people now as if it were one man, then the nations who have heard about you will say, 'Yahweh was not able to bring this people into the land He swore to give them, and so He has slaughtered them in the wilderness.' No, my Lord! It is now you display your power, according to those words you spoke, 'Yahweh is slow to anger and rich in graciousness, forgiving faults and transgression, and yet letting nothing go unchecked, punishing the father's fault in the sons to the third and fourth generation.' In the abundance, then, of Your graciousness, forgive the sin of the people, as you have done from Egypt until now."

Yahweh said, 'I forgive them as you ask. But as I live, and as the glory of Yahweh fills the earth. Of all the men who have seen my glory and the signs that I worked in Egypt and in the wilderness, who have put me to the test ten times already and not obeyed my voice, not one shall see it. But my servant Caleb is of another spirit. Because he has obeyed me perfectly, I will bring him into the land he has entered, and his race shall possess it. (The Amalekite and the Canaanite dwell in the plain.) Tomorrow you will turn about and go back into the wilderness, in the direction of the Sea of Suph.'

Yahweh spoke to Moses and Aaron. He said: 'How long does this perverse community, which complains against me...? I have heard the complaints which the sons of Israel make against me. Say to them, 'As I live, it is Yahweh who speaks, I will deal with you according to the very words you have used in my hearing. In this wilderness your dead bodies shall fall, all you men of the census, all you who were numbered from the age of twenty years and over, you who complained against me. I swear that you shall not enter the land where I swore most solemnly, to settle you. It is Caleb son of Jephunneh, and Joshua son of Nun, and your young children that you said would be seized as booty, it is these I shall bring in to know the land you have disdained. As for you, your dead bodies will fall in this wilderness, and your sons will be nomads in the wilderness for forty years, bearing the weight for your unfaithfulness, until the last of you lies dead in the desert. For forty days you reconnoitered the land. Each day shall count for one year: for forty years you shall bear the burden of your sins, and you shall learned what it means to reject me." I, Yahweh, have spoken: this is how I will deal with this perverse community that has conspired against me. Here in this wilderness, to the last man, they shall die.'

The men whom Moses had sent to reconnoiter the land, who on their return had incited the whole community of Israel to grumble against Yahweh by disparaging it, these men who had disparaged the land were all struck dead before Yahweh (by plague). Of the men who had gone to reconnoiter the land, only Joshua son of Nun and Caleb son of Jephunneh remained alive (4).

Circa 1200 BC

Ibnuh listened intently as Joshua finished the story. Ibnuh thought of how God was with Joshua when he conquered Canaan 40 years later and wanted to hear more. Ibnuh had always respected his grandfather but after hearing the story; he had more love, respect, admiration then ever before.

Chapter 54

"I am glad that you asked me about this history because there are many life lessons in my story."

"Tell me, father of my father," Ibnuh asked.

Joshua looked at his grandson with love in his eyes. "First and foremost, there was no need for spies because God had already promised us the land. The people wanted to check out the land and God allowed us to reconnoiter it, but God knew the land was good. Moses, Aaron, Caleb and me all believed but the others did not. That experience was necessary for me to become the person I needed to become because God was preparing me to takeover after Moses passed away. That mission helped to season me, take off those rough edges. I did not know that I would eventually lead the people but God knew. That 40 day operation helped me so that 40 years later I could lead effectively. Sometimes, we don't know why things happen but God always has a plan. We just have to do our job and all will work itself out."

"Second, each of the spies with me had so much potential and promise. Gaddi and Igal, their sin was lust, pride and unbelief but Gaddi means 'my good fortune' and Igal names meant 'he redeems'. Nahbi and Geuel were basically decent men without any faith, they believed in what they saw instead of having faith in God. Nahbi means 'hidden' or 'timid' and Geuel means 'pride of God'. Gaddiel, Shaphat, Sethur and Ammiel were all guilty of many sins; pride, lust, sexual unchastity, licentious, lasciviousness, greed, and lack of faith. Gaddiel means 'God is my good fortune'; Shaphat means 'he has established justice'; Sethur means 'hidden'; and Ammiel means 'people of God' or 'God is of my people'. Palti and Shammua were guilty of the sin of lust, pride and unbelief. Palti means 'my deliverance' and Shammua means 'one who is heard. All of these men had the same promise as all of God's children, they had potential but they chose to follow the darkness instead of the light. The 10 men along with the people preferred to complain. A complaining spirit is evidence of an ungrateful heart and an unsurrendered will. When we grumble, we suggest to God that we know what's better for us than God does.

"My grandson, there is a price to pay for unbelief and for doing what is not pleasing to God. The price for disobedience can be costly for us. It is dangerous to trifle with the will of God. The survey of the land may have been a good idea from a conventional military point of view, but not from a spiritual point of view. God had already given us the land and commanded us to go in and take it. God had promised victory for us so all we had to do was to "trust and obey." The Lord would have come with us to help us scatter our enemies (1), but the people had to follow God by having faith. The people failed because they doubted God would keep His promise and give them the land. The ten spies who went with me were walking by sight and did not really believe God's promises. You know without faith, its impossible to please God. Defying God's will has consequences," Joshua explained.

"But father of my father, why did God want the Israelites to take that specific land from the Canaanites?" Ibnuh asked.

"God wanted Israel to drive out and dispose the inhabitants, destroy the alters, images, pagan temples, and then divide the land among the tribes. The people of Canaan were wicked and deserved to be punished for their terrible sins. Israel was a vehicle for this punishment. God wanted to move out the idolaters to make room for his holy people. The Canaanites needed to be moved because it would remove temptation from the people of Israel who were prone to worship idols. God's people could not live among such an evil and idolatrous people. To do so would invite sin into their lives. The only way to prevent Israel from being infected by evil religions was to drive out those who practiced them. In life, sometimes we have to claim our inheritance. Canaan was our inheritance and we had to take it in order to achieve the rest that was promised to us."

Joshua continued, "We must trust the word of God and enter into our inheritance by faith. We don't need to worry about the giants, the enemy, the walled cities, or our weaknesses. Caleb and I told them that the Lord was with us and that we should not fear them not (2). For we who believe do enter the rest (3). Before we arrived at Kadesh-Barnea, God put us through various trials because a certain amount of wilderness experience is good for people who want to grow and mature. But the Lord does not want us to stay in the wilderness forever. God is always willing to teach those who are willing to learn. God wants us to develop character and many times it can only be developed by going through the hard times. When Caleb and I returned, we had a choice. In life, everyone has a choice. People can go with the unbelieving majority and miss God's very best, complaining our way through life, or we can stand with the minority and dare to believe God and follow his commands. Life is about choices, we can choose to wander in the wilderness of unbelief, selfishness and disobedience, or we can choose to enter the Promised Land with its battles and trials, trusting God to give us the victory."

"In this journey of life, I have learned that the Lord is the God of second chances and new beginnings. Sarah was given a new opportunity, she took it and thrived. She entered the Promise Land with Caleb, Fatia and me. Sarah met a man of faith and got married. They had many children, had a long and prosperous life where she was able to lead others to follow God sincerely. Sarah was redeemed by God and because a mighty woman of faith. It's never too late to become the people God intended us to be. Sarah allowed God to change her heart and her life changed immensely whereby she has much joy. God can use anyone and many times it is those who led the most corrupt life who become the most effective witnesses for God," explained Joshua.

"Son of my son, these things I tell you so that you do not fall victim to a wilderness mentality. Just as God wants, I hope that no one should perish. I want you to thrive and to live a life pleasing to God, a life of abundance. I am so pleased that you asked me about this story. I had wanted to tell you but did not know when it was the right time. Now that you know it, you have a responsibility to pass this history down to your grandson, and so on. Promise me, because these lessons are important for all who follow the Lord," said Joshua.

"I promise, father of my father. You know what my favorite quote from you is? It is what you told Moses in the sacred text about serving God. Tell me again," Ibnuh asked excitedly.

Joshua thought for a moment and then remembered what quote Ibnuh was referring to. "As for me and my house, we shall serve the Lord," Joshua said.

"I love that quote. I tell you today, as for me and my house, I too shall serve the Lord, father of my father," Ibnuh said.

Joshua looked at him with such love in his heart. He rose and hugged his grandson. "Always keep the Lord first and you will always reap the bounty of the Lord," Joshua said.

[*Even after these many years later, the Archangels Raphael and Michael were still on high and looking upon Joshua and his family.*]

[*Satan was still angry and displeased over what had happened those many years ago. He sat in utter darkness, for a former creature of light, it was torture. He had heard God's words over and over in his head. He could not stand those words, "How you are fallen from heaven, O Lucifer, son of the morning star. (Isaiah 14:12)." How he hated that phrase. He had heard it repeatedly in his mind millions of times, his punishment for breaking the agreement to interfere in humanity's affairs. All Satan could do was to wait; hoping that humanity would chose to use his tools: pride, lust, anger, greed, sloth, gluttony and envy thus showing God that they choose him freely. He would try to keep his agreement with God to only influence humanity, but who really knew; after all he was the prince of lies.*]

Chapter 55

Present Day

Salman finished the story after 12 hours of non-stop speaking, just when the sun was about to come up. He had been telling his tale since 5pm the previous day. We decided to walk on the roof where the sun was just rising. It was a beautiful sunset and I could not believe that the night had gone so quickly, I had been entranced with the story. I asked him how he could remember a story in such detail over the years. He explained that it was his job to relay the story to the oldest grandson who would then relay the story exactly as it was told to him. He said that his son had died but he was fortunate to tell his grandson just last week. He explained how his oldest son had married very late in life. Salman said that he felt I needed to hear the story. He told me that he sensed sadness in me that at the time I did not see this in myself but now I see it clearly. Sometimes God speaks to us through other people but we must be in a position to hear God's voice. I could not hear God's voice at that time while working on the dark side recruiting spies and stealing secrets. I had finished my time with him but the story he told me stuck with me.

Salman told me that the story had been transmitted for longer than I could imagine. I was intrigued by his statement and asked him about the origin of the story. He told me that the story had been passed from grandfather to grandson from before the time of Jesus Christ.

I asked, "wait, are you telling me that it was someone in your family line who first heard the story first hand?"

He looked me in my eyes saying, "You probably do not know my true family name since I was not recruited by you. I know how your agency loves to compartmentalize information. You just know me as Salman but my last name is Bin Ephraim."

I just stared at him because I had the ability to recall facts and details. "That is the same tribe that Joshua came from," I said.

He smiled at me and it was like a light bulb coming on. "We used to be Jews before the Son of Man, Jesus, came in this world to save us. My family embraced the Good News and the message of the Messiah. I told you that it was a story about faith. Faith can move mountains and can heal any type of heartbreak but so many people are addicted to their pain, they can not let go. Faith will get you through those hard times and make it seem as if it's some of the best times of your life. In your life, Jack, you will have some difficult times ahead but remember that God loves you deeply and will always be waiting for you to realize that His love is the only love that matters in life. I sometimes see things; some call it visions, perhaps it's from the blessings in my family line. You must not give into the darkness when it comes to you. Let me quote a section of the Bible that Joshua learned and made God's people learn," Salman said.

Salman closed his eyes and repeated, "See, today I set before you life and prosperity, death and disaster. If you obey the commandments of Yahweh your God that I enjoin on you today, if you love Yahweh your God and follow His ways, if you keep His commandments, His laws, His customs, you will live and increase, and Yahweh your God will bless you in the land which you are entering to make your own. But if your heart strays, if you refuse to listen, if you let yourselves be drawn into worshipping other gods and serving them, I tell you today, you will most certainly perish; you will not live in the land you are crossing the Jordan to enter and possess. I call heaven and earth to witness against you today: I set before you life or death, blessing or curse. Choose life, then, so that you and your descendents may live, in the love of Yahweh your God, obeying His voice, clinging to Him; for in this your life consists, and on this depends your long stay in the land which Yahweh swore to your fathers Abraham, Isaac and Jacob he would give them (1)." Salman opened his eyes up after finished the passage.

Salman told me, "Life is about making choices, hopefully good choices. You always have a choice no matter what you think. You can view the world through a God-conscious lens therefore making your life happier and more fulfilling, or you can view it through a worldly lens. These are my thoughts for you." Jack was in thought for a few moments while Salman seemed to collect his thoughts.

"Jack, secondly I do not know if you are aware numbers are important. The name of the chapter in the Bible is called Numbers because the title focuses on the censuses taken to account for the number of fighting men in each tribe. The original name of this chapter in the bible is 'Bemidbar' which means "In the wilderness" in the original Hebrew text. This is the initial word in the text, and it characterizes much of the ensuring history recorded in the book. Being in the wilderness is not only the actual location but it's also about having a "wilderness mental state." Having a 'wilderness state of mind' will not allow you to inherit abundance from God. The ten spies who were killed by God, it was because of their lack of faith or their own personal wilderness of their minds. Many people already have everything they need but are still living in this wilderness mental state, trying to fill the void with things other than God. That unique shaped space inside of us; can only be filled with God. So, the first thing I leave with you; is to connect with God so that you will not continue to stay in a wilderness mentality."

I was about to protest and Salman held up his hand indicating that he wanted me to withhold my comments so I stopped.

"The second major point I want to leave you with is that numbers are important. There were 12 spies, one man from each tribe went into the Canaan. 12 is an important number in the bible. The Sumerians used 12 as one base for their numbering system. Both the calendar and the signs of the Zodiac reflect this 12-base number system. The tribes of Israel numbered 12 as well as the number of Jesus' disciples. When Judas Iscariot betrayed Jesus and then committed suicide, it was important for the disciples to maintain this number 12 so they quickly brought in another disciple to keep their number 12. Twelve seems to be particularly significant in the book of

Revelation. New Jerusalem had 12 gates; its walls had 12 foundations (2). The tree of life yielded 12 kinds of fruit (3). Separately, the spies operated for 40 days in the Canaan and then the Israelites were punished for 40 years for their disobedience; one year for each day that the spies were gone. If you remember, rain flooded the earth for 40 days (4). For 40 days Jesus withstood Satan's temptations (5). In the Bible, 40 years represented a generation. Thus all the adults who rebelled against God at Sinai died during those forty years in wilderness wandering around. By the age 40, a person has reached the age of maturity (6). I say all of this to you before I relay the last part of this story." Salman said.

Salman went back to telling the story of Joshua talking with his his grandson, Ibnuh.

At the end of the story, Ibnuh sat beside his grandfather, Joshua son of Nun, who had told the tale from start to finish without taking a break.

"Is that the whole story of what happened?" Ibnuh asked.

"That is just about all of it," said Joshua.

"I want to know the whole story father of my father," Ibnuh insisted.

"The last part I do not know what it means," Joshua said.

"Please tell me," Ibnuh pleaded.

"Okay," Joshua said before starting. "You know that after wandering for 40 years in the wilderness, a new generation was ready to enter Canaan and God prepared me to lead the people. I am going to start in a section of the story that you do know because I have wrote this in my sacred writings (7)."

"Now it came about after the death of Moses the servant of the Lord, that the Lord spoke to Joshua the son of Nun, Moses' servant saying:

'Moses my servant is dead; now therefore arise, cross this Jordan, you and all this people, to the land which I am giving to them, to the sons of Israel. Every place on which the sole of your foot treads, I have given to you, just as I spoke to Moses. 'From the wilderness and this Lebanon, even as far as the great river, the river Euphrates, all the lands of the Hittites, and as far as the Great Sea towards the setting of the sun will be your territory. No man will be able to stand before you all the days of your life. Just as I have been with Moses, I will be with you; I will not fail you or forsake you. Be strong and courageous, for you shall give this people possession of the land which I swore to their fathers to give them. Only be strong and very courageous; be careful to do according to all the laws which Moses My servant commanded you; do not turn from it to the right or to the left, so that you may have success wherever you go. This book of the law shall not depart from your mouth, but you shall meditate on it day and night, so that you may be careful to do according to all that is written in it; for then you will make your way prosperous, and then you will have success. Have I not commanded you? Be strong and courageous! Do not tremble or be dismayed, for the Lord your God is with you wherever you go.'

Joshua continued, "Son of my son, God told me that everything that I had been through was preparing me, all the trials and tribulations, were for my development in order for me to become the person God wanted me to become. God explained that some things I would not understand at that time but it would matter very much to others in the future. He told me that the number of spies and the number of years would be the single most important matter for future generations but it would be a mystery for me. I did not understand. 12 spies and 40 years, what did God mean by telling these numbers. 12 spies were sent into the Wilderness and the people were forced to wander in the wilderness for 40 years because they were disobedient. 1240 means nothing to me. This is why I did not mention it to you in the beginning," Joshua said.

Ibnuh had listened intently to his grandfather.

Present Day

Salman brought the story back to the present, "Jack, from that time when God spoke to Joshua and until the birth of Jesus Christ our Lord, it was 1240 years. God was connecting the dots by letting Joshua know that there was a plan for our salvation already in the works. All Joshua had to do; was his job and accept the promises of God. There are things which happen to us that we will never fully know why it happens but we must trust God with all our heart trusting Him. It's about faith. God has plans for us and through the trials and tragedies, if we listen with a willing and obedient heart, we will become the people God intends us to be. God does not want any of His beloved creations to fall or lose their way. Are you living with a wilderness mentality?"

"I think I have a sense of who you are Jack. You told me that you were having a crisis of faith. I think that you are living in a way which is preventing you from enjoying God's promises. God told Joshua that He would give him success but we must follow God's law and trust in Him. In life, we all have a menu of choices, but many people do not believe that. The devil is not bothered that we profess our belief in God as long as we don't live a life which proves we are truly a servant of God."

"People have a choice; they can choose to enter the Promised Land, the land flowing with milk and honey or they can rebel by disobeying God thus reaping what they sow. God gave us a choice and we can freely live a life of abundance. Rebellion has a price and many people are paying that price today. I know that everything I am saying now may not make complete sense but keep connecting the dots. The process of connecting the dots will move you closer to God. Respect the process and understand that the process can not be avoided if you desire to eat the best from the land. Do not live in the wilderness when God has much more in store in for you. Do not have a wilderness mentality like the stiff-necked Israelites in the book of Numbers? Accept God's love and have faith in God and the process of life. Commit to life and life will meet you in return to give you what you not only need but what you want," Salman said.

Salman continued, "The promise land is here now. It's a possible destination for all of us who listens to and obeys God. The story I told you is about great miracles during those times but great miracles still occur to this day. With great miracles, God led the Israelites out of slavery, through the desolate wilderness, and to the edge of the promise land, but the people refused to enter, to receive the blessings of God's promises."

Chapter 56

Salman told me much that day. Over the years, I have used the lessons from that story to live an abundant life.

"The Israelites were afraid to enter and often we do the same thing. We trust God to handle the small things but doubt God to handle the big things. Many people stop trusting God just before their breakthrough is about to happen, they lose faith. Many people are still in the wilderness in their own mind. There are many lessons in this story which is why it has been passed down through my family history. I have already told you about some of the important life lessons but here are ten more points of illumination."

"First, when ten of the spies gave a negative report about the land, it caused a great rebellion among the people. Two of the spies, Joshua and Caleb, gave a positive report about how to conquer the land while the other 10 focused on why they could not possess the land. Overall, the 12 spies all agreed that the Promised Land was rich and fertile, and full of abundance but the ten spies focused on their fear. They underestimated God. The discussion of giants and fortified cities made it easy for the ten spies as well as the people to forget about God's promises. When facing a tough decision, too many people focus on the negatives and their fears instead of infinite positive possibilities. The world is one of infinite possibilities when one trusts God. Further, while it may be human nature to accept opinion as fact, we must be careful when we voice negative opinions because people trust us to give sound advice."

"Next, when the 10 spies gave their negative report, the people started to despair. Their greatest fears were being realized. The people got caught up with their emotions and feeling instead of trusting in God. What if the people had not wasted time debating about whether to enter or not; and instead spent the time planning to move forward. They would have been enjoying the land instead of receiving God's judgment. During the one year in the wilderness before the spy mission, the people frequently continued to complain always focusing on the negative. Complaining only clouds our judgment and displeases God. Believing in God by staying positive regardless of life's circumstances; shows God that we have faith."

"Third, the Israelites had seen all the miracles that God had performed on their behalf but they choose to stop trusting God because of their actions. The people of Israel had a clearer view of God than anyone else. Their refusal to believe and follow God word had its own ramifications. The spies spent 40 days in Canaan, and because of their disobedience; God's judgment came in the form of what the people feared most. The people were afraid of dying in the wilderness, so God punished them by making them wander in the wilderness until they died, 40 years (a year for each day the spies were in Canaan). Failing to trust God often brings greater problems than those we originally faced. When we run from God, we will always run into problems."

"Fourth, the two wise spies, Joshua and Caleb urged the people to act on God's promise and move ahead into the land. The people rejected the advice and even talked of killing them. Sometimes following God's path and doing what is pleasing to God can be unpopular. The Bible tells us that we should be in the world, but not of the world. Living a life for God is difficult at times but ultimately we will prosper because of it. Of the Israelites who were there, only Joshua and Caleb lived to see the Israelites move into the promise land 40 years later. Living the Christian life means that we must be set apart. We must always seek to please God, not men. A follower of Christ becomes sanctified or 'set apart for sacred use' through believing and obeying the Word of God (1).

"Fifth, God is merciful and will forgive mistakes but willful defiance and deliberate sin will always lead to a harsher punishment. God killed the ten spies with a plague but the rest of the people were still taken care of by God during the 40 years. No one escapes God's judgment because we reap what we sow. God could have killed them but He did not. God punished them by making them wander for 40 years but otherwise He provided for their needs for the rest of their lives."

"Sixth, I hope that you understand the details about Satan being intimately involved in our affairs is not an analogy, it's real. The ruler of this fallen world is Satan, the angel who rebelled against God who gave in to pride. He resisted the will of God and thought that he did not need to serve God but instead tried to take God's place. Satan is real, not symbolic, and he is constantly working against God and those who obey Him. Satan tempted Eve in the garden and persuaded her to sin. Satan tempted Jesus in the wilderness but could not persuade Him to fall. Satan has great power but people can get delivered from his reign of spiritual darkness because of Christ's victory on the cross. Satan is powerful but Jesus is much more powerful. Jesus' resurrection shattered Satan's deathly power. Satan's power only exists because God allows him to act but because Jesus is sinless, Satan has no power over Him. And if we obey Jesus and align ourselves closely with God's purpose for our lives, Satan can have no power over us too. So it's easy to overcome Satan, we just need faithful allegiance to God's word, determination to stay away from sin and support from other believers. Many people try to be good, honest people who do what is right but Jesus says that the only way you can live a truly good life is to stay close to him. We cannot do it alone. In John 16:33, Jesus said, 'These things I have spoken to you, so that in Me you may have peace. In the world you will have tribulation, but take courage; I have overcome the word.'"

"Seventh, having a wilderness mentality will lead to ignorance and death. God did not kill the people but only allowed them to wander for 40 years without ever entering the promise land. God was faithful to Joshua and Caleb, living up to his promise. God's love is one promise we can always count on and God forgives over and over again. We must never give into to our fears because that shows we do not believe. Focusing on our fears will only bring then to fruition. We must focus on God's promises by putting our faith into day action. Despite all the things that Joshua and Caleb saw, they stayed faithful and were rewarded. People have to learn to stop wandering in the wilderness; the wilderness of past mistakes, past traumas and past regrets. There are people wandering around in the wilderness of their defective thinking or their dysfunctional lifestyles. The wilderness is the darkness. People must choose to not wander in the dark but must make a conscious decision to live in the light. And it's not a fixed location, just because one figured out today that one is living in the darkness, this does not ensure that tomorrow will be any easier. It takes effort on a daily basis. We must stay focused on maintaining whole, healthy and positive daily rituals."

"Eight, the Hebrews did not understand the purpose of the wilderness. They had to go through the wilderness because that was part of their process of growth. We must respect and embrace the process. The wilderness is an analogy for life. The word 'wilderness' in the Old Testament comes close to mean desert because it usually meant a rocky, dry wasteland which is inhospitable to life. Geographically the wilderness lay south, east and southwest of the inhabited land of Israel in the Negev, Jordan and the Sinai. A particular wilderness, closer to home, lay on the eastern slopes of the Judean mountains in the rain shadow leading down to the Dead Sea. This particular wilderness became a refuge for David when he fled from Saul and was the location for the temptation of Jesus. The wilderness was so harsh for the Israelites that God had to provide manna, quail, and water from the rock. It's safe to say that the wilderness is harsh and unforgiving place."

"Ninth, the Lord had freed the Hebrews from bondage in Egypt but they had to go through this difficult terrain to get to the land flowing with milk and honey. The wilderness is that difficult time that we all must go through which strengthens us so that we can ultimately serve God and live an abundant life. We must all go through a wilderness, Jesus promised that life would be difficult but it will help us to be the person God wants us to eventually be. Traveling through the wilderness is part of the process while wandering aimlessly is not. The process is a crucial part of growing and maturing into whole, healthy and productive people. We can not skip the process. It's not necessary that we wander aimlessly because we have a guidebook for life, the Bible. We just have to possess the land God has sworn to give us like the Hebrews. We can possess our promised land by living by God's word and making sure our actions are aligned with what is pleasing to God. We must be committed to the process and understand that traversing the wilderness is for our own good. God is polishing off those rough edges in us in the wilderness. God is getting us ready to be used when we are traveling in our own personal wilderness. If the Israelites had obeyed God, they would have traveled for 11 days on the Sinai and then went into Canaan to take the land God promised them (2). Instead, the Hebrews rebelled and God punished them by making them wander for 40 years. After 40 years and all those adults who disobeyed God died. God finally allowed Joshua and Caleb to enter and possess the promised land of Canaan. We must respect the process and have a good attitude along the way because it can get perilous on the straight path. And if we stay focused on God, He will make the curve roads bearable until we are ready to move to the road of our own personal promise land."

"Finally, I wanted to show you the connection between the Old and New Testaments. God wanted to give the people rest in the Promised Land and they chose not to take that rest. A millennium later, God sent His son Jesus Christ who said, "Take my yoke upon you and learn from Me, for I am gentle and lowly in heart, and you will find rest for your souls (3)."

"God wanted to give the Israelites rest but they were disobedient and did not accept God's gift. Over 1200 years later, God then sent his Son as a bridge so that we can know God. Jesus acts as a bridge so that we can inherit another promised land later. Listen to this scripture,

'Therefore as the Holy Spirit says' Today, if you will hear His voice, Do not harden your hearts as in the rebellion, In the day of trial in the wilderness, Where your fathers tested Me, tried Me, And saw My works forty years. Therefore I was angry with that generation, And said, 'They always go astray in their heart, And they have not known My ways.' So I swore in my wrath, They shall not enter my rest. Beware brethren, lest there be in any of you an evil heart of unbelief in departing from the living God; but exhort one another daily, while it is called "Today," lest any of you be hardened through the deceitfulness of sin. For we have become partakers of Christ if we hold the beginning of our confident steadfast to the end (4)."

That is another example of the connection between the two testaments. Do you know what Joshua's name means?" Salman asked. I did not know and told him so.

"Joshua means "Yahweh delivered". Jesus' name is the New Testament is equivalent to the Old Testament name of Joshua. It is another example of the dots being connected for us. Joshua led the people into the promised land of Canaan forty years later, no Moses. Joshua's story is a great testament to faith. God told Joshua that, "Just as I have been with Moses, I will be with you. I will not fail or forsake you. Joshua was anointed and blessed because of his faith. He spoke with God. Can you imagine being able to speak with God? This story about Joshua and the Israelites in the wilderness is so important that it's mentioned in at least five separate sections in the Old and New Testaments. It's told in Numbers 13-14, then again in Deuteronomy 5 and 9, then it's mentioned several times in Joshua, it's referenced again in Psalm 106 (which describes how God patiently delivers us, in spite of our forgetfulness and self-willed rebellion), and lastly, it's mentioned again in Hebrews 3-4. There are clearly important lessons for us in this story.

When we stubbornly refuse to trust or believe God and turn our hearts away by persisting in our unbelief, eventually God will leave us alone in sin. Just remember that we always have a choice. God offers us an opportunity to enter his ultimate place of rest, in the arms of Christ Jesus. As God says, "Choose life."

Chapter 57

Final Comments from Jack Romez

The last thing that Salman told me was the following, "Like these spies of promise, we all have the potential to receive the promises from God but the ten spies took their eyes off of God and their lack of faith condemned them. Don't let the promises that God has already guaranteed you, go to waste. God is looking for people to bless but you have to seek to know Him each day. There is more of God to be had but too many people put God in a box. Strive to give God more each day by learning His word and putting it deeply into your heart, in order to get to know the mind of God. I hope you will remember these things, they may save your life one day. I will leave you with the words that Jesus spoke in the Gospel of Luke 24:36, Peace be unto you."

Salman and I parted that day. Years later, I entered into the darkest period of my life and his words gave me comfort, but God saved my life. I never saw that old man again. He was right in that I did not fully understand all he said to me that day until I went from the darkness I was living in, to the pits of a living hell. I was broken and fell so far I thought I would never come back. That time of depression, desperation, and several near death experiences; I remembered Salman's story and the lessons he explained to me from that simple chapter in the Bible. I recalled the history of Joshua and found a way out of the pit. I was delivered and found that life could be beautiful even under the darkest, most challenging circumstances. I reread the Old Testament and realized how the old man's story fit perfectly into that sacred canon. I did not know whether it was real or not, but it seemed to be God focused and inspired. Thus, I decided to write it down on the off chance it could help others.

I connected the dots of where God was trying to lead me. I became free and joy entered my heart. True inner joy is a state of delight and well being that results in knowing and serving God. Joy is the fruit of a right relationship with God and is not something people can create by their own efforts. We can not fill that inner void with things other than God. The Bible distinguishes joy from pleasure. The Bible warns that self-indulgent pleasure seeking does not lead to happiness and fulfillment. God wants His people to know joy. Joy in the Christian life is in direct proportion as believers walk with the Lord. I lost all malice towards anyone who ever did wrong towards me. Life became sweet for me because my joy was because of my relationship with the Lord. I always believed in God, but I was not living a life that showed that was the case. It was Jesus Christ that taught me how to make my spiritual life real. I met the true living God through finding Jesus Christ. I no longer live in the wilderness now. Until people stop wandering in the wilderness of their own minds, they will never have deep meaning and purpose in their lives. This is what I really learned from Salman.

I send you light, love and abundance positive energy. Jack Romez

Author's Afterword

My goal was to set your imagination on fire; on fire for God. The Bible tells us that God is an all-consuming fire. If we allow God to be an all-consuming fire in our lives; perhaps it will burn off all those impurities out of our hearts which can help us to be the people God wishes us to be. Diamonds are beautiful and valuable gemstones but they start out as simple carbon which is black, dirty and combustible but through years of intense heat and high pressure, they become pure and the strongest substance on earth. This is a great metaphor for the spiritual life, God uses intense outside forces to rid us of those impurities which binds us to a life of sin.

I had a dis-ease in my heart and soul, but God healed me. My dis-ease came from worldly living and believing that the illusions of the world were real. The illusions of life come from Satan but Jesus came so that we would have life, and have it more abundantly. Jesus is a fire and He wants to burn those un-godly things out of us, so we can live a life of abundance and inner joy.

I hope that this work of fiction have helped you gain more perspective. Anyone can benefit from examining themselves deeply to see if they are in their own personal wilderness of the mind. God wants us all to prosper which can only happen if we break out of the wilderness mentality. Breaking out of the wilderness mindset is a one of the ways to come out of the darkness and live a whole and healthy life. As Christians, we are called, "out of darkness into His marvelous light (1 Peter 2:9)." As long as people still have defective and dysfunctional parts in their lives, it will continue to pollute the rest of their lives and limit their blessings. Wilderness mentally prevention can only be achieved by viewing life through a God conscious lens. I hope this work leads others to the Lord so they can have a life of abundance.

Philip Allan Turner

Reference End Notes

Chapter 1

1 (Deuteronomy 6:23)
2 (Genesis 12:7; Genesis 13:15; Genesis 17:8; Genesis 28:13; Genesis 35:12)
3 (Exodus 3:8; Exodus 3:17; Exodus 6:4; Exodus 6:8; Exodus 13:5; Exodus 33:3)
4 (Deuteronomy 1:6-8)
5 (Deuteronomy 1:22-21)
6 (Deuteronomy 1:22; James 1:5-8)
7 (Deuteronomy 1:23)
8 (Deuteronomy 4:24)

Chapter 2
9 (Exodus 22:16-17, Exodus 22:19)

Chapter 11
1 (Genesis 23:2; Genesis 23:19; Genesis 49:29-3; Genesis 50:13; and Numbers 13:22)

Chapter 14

1 (Exodus 14:15)
2 (Exodus 14:21)

Chapter 18

1 (Exodus 14:11-12)
2 (Exodus 15:24)
3 (Exodus 16:3)
4 (Exodus 16:20)
5 (Exodus 16:27-29)
6 (Exodus 17:2-3)
7 (Exodus 32:7-10)
8 (Numbers 11:1-2)
9 (Numbers 11:4)
10 (Numbers 14:1-4)

Chapter 23

1 (Deuteronomy 8:7-10)
2 (Deuteronomy 9:2-3)

Chapter 29

1 (Psalm 99:1)
2 (Ezekiel 28:13)
3 (Revelation 12:3-4)
4 (John 8:44)
5 (Leviticus 19:1)
6 (Leviticus 19:16)
7 (Leviticus 26:3-4)
8 (Leviticus 26:9)
9 (Leviticus 26:12-14)
10 (Leviticus 26:19)
11 (Leviticus 26:21)

Chapter 31

1 (Genesis 12:8)
2 (Genesis 28:10-22)

Chapter 43
1 (Leviticus 20:6, 27)

Chapter 46
1 (Exodus 34:7)
2 (1 Corinthians 13:8)

Chapter 48
1 (Genesis 50:20)

Chapter 53
1 (Numbers 13:25-33)
2 (Numbers 14:1-14)
3 (Numbers 14:5-9)
4 (Numbers 14:1-39 Jerusalem Bible 1966)

Chapter 54

1 (Numbers 10:33-36)
2 (Numbers 14:9)
3 (Hebrews 4:3)

Chapter 55

1 (Deuteronomy 30:15-23)
2 (Revelation 21:12-14)
3 (Revelation 22:2)
4 (Genesis 7:12)
5 (Mark 1:13)
6 (Exodus 2:11 and Act 7:23)
7 (Joshua 1:1-9)

Chapter 56

1 (Hebrews 4:12)
2 (Deuteronomy 1:2)
3 (Mathew 11:28-29)
4 (Luke 24:36)
5 (Hebrews 3:7-14)

www.ingramcontent.com/pod-product-compliance
Lightning Source LLC
Chambersburg PA
CBHW081149170626
46813CB00009B/3125